# Aloysius the Great

*John Maxwell O'Brien*

For Christine, Bill and Lillian,

who light up every day of my life

"We walk through ourselves, meeting robbers, ghosts, giants, old men, young men, wives, widows, brothers-in-love. But always meeting ourselves."

—James Joyce, *Ulysses*

# 1

---

That posturing hippopotamus couldn't possibly know about Marthe, could he? No. Not Dean Irwin. He's oblivious to anything beyond his own résumé.

Marthe wouldn't breathe a word of it. Or shouldn't. She's the one who did the seducing. Okay—lacing my coffee with gin while still at the college was an error of judgment, but who expects students to be knocking at your office door at ten o'clock at night?

Stop playing the victim, Aloysius. It's unbecoming. If you hadn't been drinking, you would have persuaded her to back off, or at least made a break for it. If she *has* pointed a finger at you, no one will believe your version of the story. Screwed—that's what you are.

I glance back down at the letter on top of the pile.

*Aloysius Tabeel Gogarty*
*Assistant Professor*
*Department of History*
*URGENT*

I start to unpeel the envelope but stop and turn it back around. No, it's not my absurd name that's troubling me. It's the return address in the upper left-hand corner: Office of the Dean of Faculty. Footsteps approach from the hallway. Beware of prying eyes in the faculty mailroom. Retreat to the sanctuary of your office.

*September 11, 1967*

*Dear Professor Gogarty,*

*A situation has presented itself that demands immediate attention. It is of utmost importance that we meet concerning this matter. Contact Mrs. Delagracia at my office (ext. 1922) to arrange a meeting with me and do so promptly upon receipt of this letter.*

*Francis Irwin*
*Dean of Faculty*
*Municipal College of the City of New York*
*FI/ed*

There's no please, not even a sincerely yours. Maybe civilities are superfluous when it comes to notices of execution. One vulnerable moment and—*poof*—everything you've worked for goes up in smoke.

Go ahead. Do it. Pick up the phone. Climb onto the funeral pyre.

"Hello, it's Aloysius Gogarty from the History Department. I understand the dean has been looking for me... that is . . . uh . . . wishes to see me. Yes, I'm here in my office and can stop by now if that's all right. Good. See you soon."

I walk across campus at a brisk pace but stop dead in my tracks in front of the dean's office, immobilized, gaping at the doorknob.

Take a deep breath. Open the door. Don't slam it behind you.

Elena Delagracia looks up from behind her nameplate and catches me unaware. I take a step back to process what I see. Her red hair moves upward in an irregular curl at the apex of her forehead, just as Alexander the Great's did. Her eyes are avocado green, but when the light catches her right eye, it turns chestnut brown. Alexander's eyes were said to be like that.

"Might you be Professor Gogarty?" she asks in a high-pitched voice, breaking the spell.

Off on the wrong foot again. Color me hapless when it comes to women.

"I beg your pardon you remind me of someone. Yes, I might be... I mean, *I am,*" I shake my head theatrically, "Aloysius Gogarty."

Her winsome smile puts me at ease for the moment. Elena Delagracia isn't what I expected to see; her hair and ivory skin hint at a Celtic or Germanic influence. She seems amused. Make the most of it.

"May I ask—are you from Spain?"

"Actually, Professor Gogarty, I was born in Cuba, but my parents come from Andalusia which, as you know, is in Spain."

The German tribe of Vandals left their name in Andalusia; maybe they're the guilty party. But the Greeks and the Jews and the Arabs and the devil knows who else from all the ends of Europe traipsed over that region. So, it's anyone's guess.

Didn't the dean's letter say *Mrs.* Delagracia? There's no ring on her finger?

"Simply for reasons of protocol, should I address you as Miss Delagracia or Mrs. Delagracia?"

"Either way," she says, with oracular ambiguity. "You can take a seat if you'd like. Dean Irwin will be with you in just a few minutes."

"Thank you."

I find myself stealing another glance at her. They say my mother's eyes were a different color too. She gave me life, but I killed her in the process. Now it looks like I've killed my career. I must have the Midas touch in reverse. Everything I lay my hands on seems to turn to
—

Dean Irwin emerges from a corridor behind Elena's desk and signals for me to follow him. There's no handshake, a sure sign my fate is sealed.

Irwin can't be more than five feet five but must weigh close to two hundred and fifty pounds. I can't resist mimicking his waddle as I follow in his footsteps, but this risky routine comes to an abrupt halt when my shoes sink into a thick crimson carpet.

His office is a large horseshoe-shaped room with intricately carved mahogany bookcases lining its walls. The bookshelves are filled with leather-bound classics arranged chronologically, except for one area, French literature. There, foot-high marble busts of Montaigne and Racine face out into the room, drawing a visitor's attention to the three volumes they frame—Irwin's celebrated tome on the use of the accent circumflex in France during the seventeenth century. In the next life he'll probably focus on the accent aigu.

An antique chandelier hangs over a mahogany chair directly in front of Irwin's larger-than-life desk. He points to the chair and we sit. Irwin's head is silhouetted by the sunlight streaming through a semicircular window behind him, making his round face barely visible against a postcard profile of the Manhattan skyline. A pungent wave of his cologne wafts in my direction, but I restrain myself from retching.

I wonder how he sees me. I'm twenty-seven, five feet nine and a half inches tall, overweight, and undistinguished, except for my auburn hair and small, round black sunglasses. Come to think of it, almost all of my clothes are either black or gray. I'm always seen in my undersized black beret, tilted slightly to the right. It's my Latin Quarter hat, my Hamlet hat.

"Is there a clinical explanation for those opaque glasses of yours? You always seem to be wearing them," Irwin says while reaching for a pencil.

He's been collecting evidence.

"BEB."

"BEB?"

"Yes, benign essential blepharospasm. I contracted it as a child during the war, and it left me photophobic."

"You wear them at night as well?"

"They mitigate the impact of artificial light on the pupils of my eyes."

"Really?" he asks, rolling the pencil back and forth across his desk with the palm of his hand. "Oh yes, of course . . . BEB."

He hasn't the slightest notion of what I'm talking about.

"Professor Gogarty," he lifts the pencil and stares at it, "what were your plans for this year?"

I feel the blood coursing through my neck.

The hammer descends.

"Well, I *had planned* to continue teaching here."

Irwin starts tapping the pencil on his desk. After a glacial pause, he speaks. "Well, if it were up to me, you would *not* be teaching here this year." He squints and sits there squeezing the pencil until its tip breaks from the pressure he's applying.

I flinch, and beads of sweat gather on my forehead. I reach for my handkerchief, fold it in half, and make a wide sweep of my brow. What should I do? Confess and throw myself on the mercy of the court?

"Oh?" is all that escapes from my mouth.

Irwin shifts the phlegm around in his throat and looks at me from behind the pointless pencil he's holding upright in front of his nose. "How would you like to lecture at a foreign university this year?"

"What the...? Excuse me?"

"Yes." He smiles.

He *smiled*.

"As you may know, we're in the process of transforming our study-abroad program into the largest—or I should say— the best example of international education in the world. We now have six centers in Europe and three in Latin America. This year we're moving into England and Japan, and there's an opening for you at one of our international centers."

Sweet Jesus. Recalled to life. What did he say? Japan?

"I don't speak Japanese."

"No, no, no. The UK. England. How would you like to be resident director of the New York Municipal College's Study-Abroad Program in Great Britain?"

I've already learned that the longer an academic title, the less important the position, but it's a far cry from leaving in disgrace, so I raise my eyebrows to show I'm impressed.

"You'll be teaching several courses at a host university and serving as a shepherd of sorts for our students. You'd be what the English call their moral tutor."

"Their *moral* tutor?"

"Why not? There's nothing that would disqualify you from such a post. Is there?"

"I should hope not," I say, as convincingly as I can.

He nods in satisfaction. "You may be wondering why all this has arisen at the eleventh hour. The fact of the matter is that, poised as we are to set the UK program in motion, we've experienced an unanticipated setback. A Berkeley professor agreed to lead the group, but he's taken ill—atrial fibrillation, and the poor man is only in his early fifties. His personal physician has advised him to remain in California. We need a younger man, someone who is physically fit and popular with his students.

"I've been led to believe you may fit the bill. Now I'm well aware that you are coming up for tenure this year, but there's no reason that can't be accomplished *in absentia*. If you provide exemplary leadership abroad it would be of inestimable value to the college and, of course, taken into consideration when you're evaluated for tenure. Does the position seem attractive to you?"

If I'm denied tenure I'll lose my job anyway, so it's out of the frying pan, into the inferno. Is there a choice here? I might as well probe.

"What about my classes?"

"We're already in the process of making arrangements for adjuncts to cover all of your sections. From what I've heard it'll be difficult for anyone to match your performance in the classroom, but we'll do the best we can. Don't worry about us though; we'll manage. No one is irreplaceable."

Isn't *that* comforting? By all means, go right ahead and usurp my life. Uproot and transplant me as it suits you.

"What about my research? I've almost finished the final draft of my book and planned on polishing it during the next few months."

"They polish books in England, don't they? In fact, the English are forever polishing their books. Your manuscript—it's about Charlemagne, isn't it?—should improve by leaps and bounds in such a civilized environment. Besides, the tenure materials are not due at the departmental level until April. There's no reason whatsoever you cannot accomplish all of your objectives abroad. I finished *my magnum opus* in Paris, despite all the seductive distractions there."

Irwin smiles suggestively but declines to elaborate on which seductive distractions in Paris could possibly have come between him and the circumflex.

"And that work, by the way, earned me recognition as a *Chevalier* of the *Ordre des Palmes Académiques*." His pudgy finger points to a medallion attached to a purple ribbon encased on the wall in a gilded baroque frame.

I purse my lips and nod, as if I've been made privy to an earth-shattering revelation. The truth of the matter is Irwin reminds the entire faculty of this distinction with numbing regularity and is said to wake people up on park benches to let *them* know as well. The consensus is that it was his wife's access to the corridors of power in French society, rather than his immortal broodings over the circumflex that earned him his *Chevalier* medallion. Her family traces its lineage all the way back to Charlemagne.

*Wait a minute.* He thinks I'm writing a book about Charlemagne and is probably concerned I'll say something unsavory about his wife's ancestor.

"It's Alexander, by the way. Not Charlemagne. I'm writing a biography of Alexander the Great."

"*Alexandre le Grand*, eh? Well, I'm glad to hear that. I thought it was Charlemagne. So, Alexander's the one you're making a drunk out of?"

"I prefer to think he did that to himself. I'm simply disclosing what I've discovered in the sources," I say piously. "I'm sorry if you find that disconcerting."

"Not in the least. In fact, I find it quite promising now that I know it's Alexander. Properly executed, it could draw favorable attention to the college. Still, it's a trifle old fashioned with the drinking, no? What about drugs? Didn't he use them? That might make your book more engaging and be more in keeping with our times."

"Thanks for the suggestion, but no he didn't use drugs, just wine."

"No beer, either?"

"The ancient Greeks thought of beer as a swinish potation, better left to the barbarian."

He smiles again. "How French. This isn't going to be a temperance tract inveighing against the fruit of the vine, is it? I occasionally indulge in the grape myself, and you, I've been told, are no teetotaler, correct?"

"God forbid," I blurt out. Then, realizing Irwin's just made a jarring reference to my drinking, quickly add, "I tend to follow Aristotle in seeking balance in all things." Jesus. I sound just as pretentious as *el hipopótamo*. Better change the subject.

"Won't these students require a great deal of attention in England?"

"Minimal. They're young adults, not children. Furthermore, the Berkeley man scrutinized all applications and interviewed each and every candidate. I, of course, had the final say as to whether an applicant was acceptable. Few difficulties should arise.

"Naturally, during the first couple of weeks you'll have to make yourself available to them, but after that they'll be largely on their own. Only our best and brightest students, thirteen in all, have been approved for the program. These young people are looking to absorb a foreign culture, not make a surrogate father of you."

He has an answer for everything.

"They'll be leaving by boat on the weekend. The English term begins at the end of this month, and our students will spend a few days in London to get acclimated. You will leave early next week by air, in order to establish yourself and coordinate their orientation. First, you'll go from London to Yorkshire University to introduce yourself, then back to London to greet our students. After a week or so there, you'll arrange for three of them—all girls I believe—to be transported to Berkshire University. You'll accompany a mixed group of ten students to Yorkshire University. That's where you'll teach. You'll have a liaison at Yorkshire, but that's not the case at Berkshire. Here's the name of the Yorkshire man and how he can be reached." He leans across the desk as far as his bulbous stomach will permit and hands me a sheet of paper.

It says: "Yorkshire University: Richard Tarleton Mountjoy" above a phone number and a university address. Talk about names. He's probably one of those portentous prigs the English lionize.

"It will be of utmost importance for you to make a good impression on this man and form an amicable working relationship with him."

*That* will be a challenge. We'll have next to nothing in common. Irwin still hasn't answered the most important question:

"You don't think then that this commitment could adversely affect my chances of getting tenure?"

"In my opinion—and I do not, of course, speak for members of the Promotion and Tenure Committee—if your book gets published by a scholarly press, and *if* you enjoy a successful year abroad, it would be very difficult to deny your tenure."

So, there's no hammer, but a Damoclean sword will dangle over my head until the mission is accomplished to *his* satisfaction. I raise a skeptical eyebrow. "How many students applied for the program?"

He hesitates. "Thirteen. But you can rest assured all of them are well qualified. So then, what do you say to all this? Can we count on you?"

Thirteen apply, thirteen are accepted. There's selectivity for you. Well, I've exhausted every evasive tactic I can imagine. No little woman at home who has to be consulted before any important decision can be made. No elderly father or mother who needs to be tended to. I won't have to worry about Marthe—she'll be three thousand miles away.

Don't hesitate.

"What an extraordinary opportunity. I'm most grateful for it and delighted to be able to accept!"

"I hoped you'd feel that way. Here are your students." Irwin nudges a piece of paper in my direction.

They're in alphabetical order. Only one name is familiar to me.

*Fleischmann, Marthe.*

## 2

---

As I'm about to leave campus, a car's incessant cranking lures me to an adjacent parking lot. There sits a flustered Elena Delagracia behind the wheel of a hearse-like Cadillac. Is this providential? My blood pressure rises. *Be tactful, Aloysius, or you'll scare the lady off.*

With an engaging smile, I approach her car and tap gently on the glass. Elena looks up, half smiles, and rolls down her window.

"Are you okay?"

"I'm having a little difficulty, Professor Gogarty."

"So, I've noticed. Do you mind if I take a look?"

"*Gracias.* I beg your pardon—thank you." She fidgets to extricate herself from the driver's seat, exposing black nylon stockings reaching up to a metallic clasp on the thigh. *Mary, star of the sea, pray for us sinners.* I wonder if Elena's aware of her resemblance to Brueghel's *Calypso*?

I slide behind the wheel and notice an unopened letter on the passenger seat addressed to Sra. Elena Delagracia. It's written in the bold hand of a bold man. Someone thinks she's married. Señor Delagracia.

I turn the key and hear a crisp succession of clicks and a barely audible whine. "It sounds like it's your battery or your starter."

"Oh, my."

"I don't have any cables, but if we contact campus security, they'll give you a jump-start."

"Thank you. Will it take long?"

She's more anxious than irritated.

*Carpe diem.*

"Who knows? I'd be happy to drive you home, if you'd like. Just leave your keys here in the car for the security people so they can work on it. It's probably your battery."

"Yes, I'm afraid I'm in a bit of a rush. My son's off from school today and my father's been with him all day. *Papá's* getting on in age now and he tires easily. If you can take me out to Wantagh, my father can drive me to work early tomorrow morning. We live close to the parkway there."

She has a son, but no mention of *Señor Delagracia.*

"Elena, why don't you meet me over in parking lot three? Look for a red Volkswagen convertible. I'll stop by the chemistry office next to the parking lot and call security."

She gathers her things and appears to be unconcerned that I've used her first name. I'd better take care of business promptly, and get back before she changes her mind.

That took no time. Ahh! There she is, leaning against the car.

"I like your Volkswagen, Professor Gogarty."

"Why, thank you. I call her *Pequeña pelirroja*, my little redhead." A bald-faced lie invented on the spot, but she's smiling.

*Be careful. Don't get too cute. It could backfire on you.*

"Look at the nerve of me, translating Spanish for you. By the way, you speak English beautifully. Did you study it at school?"

Elena settles into the passenger seat. "Yes, I majored in English at the University of Havana."

Her perfume is as subtle and unimposing as her looks are striking and hypnotic. How do I find out more about this exotic creature without being intrusive? What would Alexander do?

*Take an oblique approach.*

"I'll bet your father is quite an interesting man."

"Yes, there's no question about that."

"Is he the one who encouraged you in your schoolwork, or was it your mother?"

"Both did, but especially my father." She pauses momentarily. "He's very well educated."

"Really?"

"He has a bachelor's degree, a law degree, and a PhD."

"My oh my—he is well educated. So, did your father wind up being a lawyer in Cuba?"

"Yes and no. He was a lawyer, that's true, but he did other things."

"Oh?"

Elena pauses again, and then decides to continue. "Under *Batista*, Papá had some governmental responsibilities, and he was also a successful businessman, especially with his marlin and shark factories."

"So, he was a big shot, huh?" I cringe at my trite expression.

"If that means an important person, I guess you could say so. But when Fidel Castro took over, Papá had to leave everything behind and take a boat to Florida in a big hurry. With all his education, the only degree he was able to—is it *salvage*?—was his bachelor's degree from Salamanca. Now he's a substitute teacher of Spanish in a Catholic school out on Long Island."

Count no man happy until he's decidedly dead.

"How about your mother? You said she, too, was from Andalusia, as I recall."

"Actually, my mother's family originally came from Gibraltar. *Mamá* was born there, and then her family moved to Andalusia. She didn't go to college. *Mamá* passed away several years ago."

"Oh. What a shame," I say, while thinking: *At least you had a mother.* "Were you able to take your degree with you?"

"No, I'm afraid not. When I flew to Spain in 1965, Castro's Dirección General de Inteligencia kept it to make sure I'd return."

"The DGI—that's Castro's KGB, isn't it? So, you and your husband were able to escape. Well, thank God."

"Not my husband, he's still in Cuba, where he's a physician—a gastroenterologist. He was supposed to meet us in Spain, but... " Elena stops short.

He never appeared. Did he desert her? How could anyone abandon a woman like Elena? What am I saying? Men abandon goddesses. We're afflicted with the disease of never being satisfied with what we have – especially when it comes to women.

One man's Penelope is another man's Calypso.

"Professor Gogarty, are you quite sure you know where you're going? I've never been this way before."

"Please, call me Aloysius, unless you find the name peculiar. Many people do."

"Aloysius, the patron saint of young Catholics? I'm fond of that name. There's a Spanish—how do you say?—connection there."

Here's a chance to impress her. "Wasn't his mother the Lady of Honor for the wife of King Philip II?"

"Yes, that's true. Queen Isabel. Very good, Profess—oh, sorry—Aloysius," she says with a sheepish but full smile. Elena shows renewed concern for our whereabouts by rotating her head back and forth as we pass rows of pink and blue and yellow houses looking very much alike.

She seems alarmed. Put her at ease.

"Don't worry, I'm taking a shortcut. I know where we're going. Back when I was a college student, I often played basketball around here with my friends and went swimming at Jones Beach. We should be close now. When you see something you recognize, just tell me where to turn."

She points. "There! If you turn right *there*, and follow *that* street to the end, our house is the yellow one on the left. You were right. Your way's much faster at this time of day, but I'll never remember all those turns."

Tell me, Muse, about the man of many turns.

"Aloysius, would you like to stop in and say hello to my family?"

This is promising. I nod and follow her up a cement walkway to the door of her ranch-style house. She leads me into her sparsely furnished lodgings while announcing, "We have a guest."

Her father, who's wearing a handmade silk shirt, rises from a threadbare couch with frayed arms and faded stains. He's a short, stocky man with black glossy hair combed back, bright brown eyes, and a slight hunch to his back. The intensity of his stare and his wrinkled brow make me feel like a reluctant matador facing a bull who's sizing him up.

"Professor Gogarty, this is my father, Dr. Miguel de la Flora. *Papá*, this is Professor Gogarty from the college. I had some trouble with my car, and he was kind enough to drive me home."

We shake hands and he keeps a firm grip while we're being introduced.

"Professor Gogarty has just become the resident director for our study-abroad program in England. He'll be leaving soon to set things up there and get the program underway."

De la Flora's grip relaxes and his brow unwrinkles. He gestures for me to follow him into his study, which has a small desk with a folding chair behind it. A compact bookcase containing several dozen volumes in English and a Spanish-English dictionary serves as a partition from the living room.

Elena follows behind us, with a kitchen chair for me. She squeezes it into the space available and then leaves. I'm on my own in the lion's den. If you're ever going to get close to Elena, it will have to meet this man's approval.

*Be careful where you tread, Aloysius.*

De la Flora positions himself behind his desk as if it were a judge's bench, and in short order determines my height, weight, age, degrees, marital status, and the fact that I'm untenured at the college. I'm beginning to feel as if I'm courting Torquemada's daughter, and have been summoned before the Inquisition. A low point is reached when the inevitable question about my glasses is raised, and my patented rejoinder fails to evoke even a nod. Why is he so fiercely protective of her? Why not? She may have already been betrayed by one man—Señor Delagracia. De la Flora has quite a few books by Hemingway. I'll try to draw him out on that.

"Sir, what do you think of Ernest Hemingway?"

"He writes a clear English sentence."

"Yes, he certainly does," I say. Not much to go on, but enough to launch me into an impromptu lecture on Hemingway's writings, moving sequentially from his early to his later work. I stop to see how I'm faring, only to discover that de la Flora's beginning to doze off.

"Dr. de la Flora," I say, raising my voice slightly. His left eyebrow twitches. When I increase the volume, he stirs.

*Ask another question before you lose him.*

"I've been going on and on about Hemingway, and you've scarcely said a word. I suspect you might be the true *aficionado* here." I point in the direction of his Hemingway collection. "What do you think? Am I making any sense at all?"

"Of course, you are, Professor Gogarty," he says, "I basically agree with what you've been saying. He meant well. Unfortunately, he drank too much, and I told him so on several occasions."

I gulp. "You knew him?"

"Ernesto and I used to have lunch together at the Floridita in Havana, and I sometimes agreed to go to the Tropicana with him, although that was not—how do you say it?—my cup of tea."

Here I am lecturing her father on Hemingway, when he knew the man. Hopefully, he's too groggy to remember what I've said.

"I have been a bad host," de la Flora says in an apologetic tone. "Would you like something to drink?"

*Watch your step.*

"Oh no," I say, lifting both hands in protest. "Not for me, sir, but thank you."

"Professor Gogarty, you mentioned *The Old Man and the Sea*, no?" Now fully awake, he points at the book, and I raise my eyebrows and nod.

"Well, you see, Ernesto needed to know more about marlin fishing to write that book. He asked me if he could borrow Felipe, my best marlin fisherman, to teach him the particulars. He was grateful. He should've been. No Felipe, no book. And that's the one that landed him the big fish—the Nobel Prize, eh?" He chuckles. "Maybe Felipe should've been awarded that prize. I'll tell you one thing. If he had been, Felipe would've mentioned Ernesto in his acceptance speech, but Ernesto never said a word about Felipe."

Her father leans forward and stuns me when he whispers, "My daughter's husband passed away a few years ago."

"Oh, I'm sorry to hear that." He's dead? That's not what Elena said. Is this wishful thinking on Torquemada's part or an item on his agenda?

He glances over my shoulder toward the door. I turn to see Elena's son standing at the entrance to the makeshift study. "*Abuelo*," he calls.

De la Flora gets up and escorts us all into the living room proper. There he introduces me to Miguelito. The boy is about seven years old. His hair is red with a black border at the base of his neck, and both his eyes are avocado green. Miguelito's complexion is much darker than Elena's. He's a sturdy young lad who moves with athletic fluidity.

Miguelito's the same age my son would've been if Deborah had had him. I urged her to do something about the pregnancy because I was afraid that she might die in childbirth, like my mother. I shouldn't have interfered. The choice was hers. Where is she now? Where is he now?

The boy's skeptical of me at first, but I soon have him giggling at my comical faces. De la Flora observes me benignly, but he's fading fast. It's time to go.

In the midst of cordial farewells at the doorway, Elena sends a chill up my spine by lightly stroking my brow and gazing at me affectionately.

"Ahh," is all she says. It's enough.

This is encouraging, but I'll be on my way in a week. How can I court Elena with an ocean separating us? Will Torquemada allow it? How about Señor Delagracia? What if he shows up?

One man's Calypso is another man's Penelope.

# 3

It's only been a week since Elena stroked my forehead, but it feels like it happened in a different lifetime. I've had to call Irwin's office several times, but when Elena answers the phone, she sounds distant and businesslike. I ran into her in the faculty dining room, but she excused herself, saying she had to rush back to the office. Well, there's no way she can avoid me now.

"Good morning, Elena. May I collect those student applications for the English program? I'm leaving for England *tonight*, and I know next to nothing about our students."

Why is Irwin holding on to them? Maybe he's afraid of scaring me off. What am I getting myself into here? Worse yet, it looks like I'll never get to know Elena.

"They're right here, Professor Gogarty. All set to go. Dean Irwin apologizes for the delay. Have a safe flight and a wonderful year abroad."

The routine politeness of her voice sends a chill up my spine. My face gets hot and I reach for the corner of her desk to steady myself. I can't leave like this.

"Are you all right, Professor Gogarty?"

"Well no, not really. I'm upset, and I hate going overseas in this state of mind. You've been avoiding me, and I need to know something before I leave."

Elena pulls her head back, tilts it to the side, and looks puzzled.

I breathe deeply, hoping to inhale enough courage to be able to say what's been on my mind since we first met: "Are you interested in me?"

She leans forward, "How can you ask such a question? Of course, I am. Who wouldn't be? You're a very impressive man."

"Not in a general sense, in a . . . uh . . . well, personal sense."

"Personal? Professor Gogarty. We're *colleagues*!"

"Look Elena, I'm supposed to leave in a few hours, but I can't do that until I know exactly how you feel about me. In fact," I take an even deeper breath, "I'm not leaving here until I get a straight answer from you. The dean can scrape up somebody else for the job, or hire a cardiologist to accompany that Berkeley man, or, for that matter, go himself."

My voice is rising, and Elena looks over her shoulder toward the dean's chambers. She raises a finger to her mouth, and her lower lip begins to quiver. "Are you *loco*?" she whispers. "Don't you realize you're jeopardizing both our jobs by behaving like this?"

"I'm sorry, but I refuse to go in such a state. If you want to get rid of me, I need an answer, an honest answer."

She looks back toward the dean's office again. "If I am as honest as I can be, will you take these folders and leave this office immediately?"

That doesn't sound good.

*Brace yourself for rejection.*

It takes a moment or two, but I'm finally able to say, "Yes."

Elena looks down, then, slowly, raises her head and begins to speak, but so quietly I need to lean over to hear her. This draws me into the ambit of her delicate perfume.

"I do find myself in some way attracted to you. Still, there's no point in even thinking about it now. Time will tell. We may both be in a totally different set of circumstances when you return from England."

My heart stutters. I slip out of my jacket, adopt the stance of a toreador, execute a perfect veronica, and issue an "*Olé*" while prostrating myself at her desk. Unfortunately, my performance raises such a clamor that Irwin comes waddling out of his inner sanctum. I scramble to my feet and quickly drape the jacket over my arm. Elena, visibly shaken, drops the folders on her desk.

Irwin surveys the scene like the lord of the manor. "Is something *amiss* here?"

I smile widely, replying, "Dear sir, what could be amiss when 'the lark's on the wing; the snail's on the thorn; God's in his heaven; and all's right with the world'?"

"Oh," says Irwin appreciatively, "brushing up on our Tennyson, are we?"

It's Browning, you ignor*anus*.

"Yes indeed, sir, I'm preparing for England."

"Well," he says, "that's a good sign. I wish all my resident directors would embark with such unbridled enthusiasm. I take it you're pleased with your new assignment?"

"Pleased? At the moment sir, I'm ecstatic."

Elena busies herself scooping up the folders and passing them on to me.

"Remember at all times," Irwin cautions me, "who and what you represent."

Juggling the dossiers as I grasp the doorknob, I let one of them slip but retrieve it before any damage is done.

"No need to concern yourself, sir. I'm fully aware of who and what I represent."

# 4

---

Stately, slim Amalia Popper, head secretary of the School of History at Yorkshire University, appears in a smart navy-blue pinstriped suit, her oversized jacket failing to completely obscure an ample bosom.

"Hello, I'm Dr. Aloysius Gogarty from Municipal College. Is Professor Mountjoy available?"

"Dr. Gogarty, I'm afraid *Mr.* Mountjoy is presently in conference with the chairman of the department." There's a lilt to her voice. That's a good sign.

I wonder what Mountjoy's like? Maybe I can get a hint of that from Miss Popper. Try Alexander's oblique approach. It worked with Elena.

"What does he teach?"

"Mr. Mountjoy lectures on English and American history in the eighteenth and nineteenth centuries. He's suggested you might be more comfortable waiting in his office than in the foyer," she says. What a peculiar but charming Yorkshire accent.

Miss Popper leads me down the corridor of the top floor in Hammersmith Tower and opens his office door. I survey the room and my attention is drawn to a corkwood map of England covering the entire wall behind Mountjoy's desk. It's something you'd expect to see in a war room scene from a 1940s British film. The lower portion of the map is swarming in colored pins with heads an eighth of an inch or so in diameter. Whatever war is being waged southern England is getting the worst of it.

On Mountjoy's desk stand three Waterford crystal glasses and a large bottle of González Byass sherry. Stationed in close proximity is a framed black and white photograph of a gaunt female, reminiscent of Virginia Woolf. Wife or mother?

"Mr. Mountjoy will be with you shortly. Approximately half ten, I should think. I'm afraid you'll be unattended for a quarter of an hour or so. Will you be able to manage?"

"By all means, thank you."

Miss Popper notices my fascination with the map and starts to offer an explanation. "Dickie"—she gasps, and a roselike blush blossoms on her neck—"that is, *Mr. Mountjoy*, is our admissions tutor. *Mr. Mountjoy* recruits some of the department's best students from the south of England. He makes presentations on behalf of the university to sixth-formers in that region. Those pins represent his various visitations. I'm afraid he's obliged to visit the south rather frequently."

She slowly raises her left hand to explore the receding bloom. Her recitation seems to have restored equanimity.

"I'm sorry, but I must return to my desk. If I can be of any further assistance, please don't hesitate to lift Mr. Mountjoy's telephone and press the first button there at the top. You might like to glance at our brochure describing the department." Miss Popper removes a ruler covering a neat stack of pamphlets on the desk and hands one to me before carefully restoring the ruler to its original setting. She excuses herself.

I try to focus on the brochure but can only work my way through a thumbnail sketch of the instructional staff. It's the map that intrigues me. The reading material describes him as a senior lecturer, someone not at the top of the ladder, but not at the bottom either. Why is a senior lecturer engaged in the lowly task of recruitment?

Why am I so obsessed with this map? It's the pins. There's something going on here. There's his appointment book. Maybe between that and the pins I can work out a pattern of some sort. No. No. *Wait a minute.* I spring to my feet, snatch the ruler from his desk, and tiptoe behind his chair to attack the map. Measuring, measuring. That's it. *I've got it*!

The door flies open behind me, ushering in a gust of wind that rustles the papers on Mountjoy's desk.

"Ehhhhhh. *You* must be the American."

It's Mountjoy. He's about ten years older than me and slightly over six feet tall. Mountjoy's a slim man with a closely cropped head of black wooly hair highlighted by premature streaks of gray above his temples. He's wearing a double-breasted charcoal-gray suit with a pale-blue shirt and a black tie with white stripes. It must be a college tie. I place the ruler back on his desk. "I beg your pardon. I'm Aloysius Gogarty from New York."

"Yehhhhhs," Mountjoy elongates, while looking in disapproval at my suit. "Somehow I've been able to surmise that. Ordinarily, I'd suggest you make yourself at home, but courtesies of that sort are gratuitous when it comes to Americans, aren't they, old boy?"

I can't decide whether to laugh or apologize, so I say nothing, still frozen in place.

He extends his hand and startles me by using an ironclad grasp to dance me out from behind the desk and deposit me into his visitor's chair. Pleased at his maneuver, Mountjoy flashes a broad smile, exposing a mouthful of glistening teeth. He proceeds to pour two glasses of sherry and reaches across the desk to deliver mine. It's barely eleven o'clock in the morning, so I adopt my "I don't ordinarily drink at this hour" look. It's ignored, and I meekly accept the glass.

"You could use this, old boy. Culture shock or I should say the inevitable trauma engendered when someone from your hemisphere finds himself in the midst of a *bona fide* culture. It's similar to a time-warp experience, I should think."

"I get it. In this case going *back* in time."

"I'm told," Mountjoy says, ignoring my riposte, "you're working on one of the greats. Frederick, isn't it? You're undoubtedly aware of Frederick's frugality, but did you know he was frightfully defensive about the costs incurred by his sizable stable of courtiers? He justified it by reassuring all those concerned that 'dancers, prostitutes and professors come cheap'."

I nearly choke on a trickle of sherry still halfway down my gullet and spray a fine mist over Mountjoy's desk.

He beams with glee at my response while wiping the desk clean with his handkerchief. "Well, well, well, Dr. Gogarty. Here we are awaiting you with great expectations, and you shower us with great expectorations."

I laugh and regain my composure. "By the way, it's *Alexander* the Great. I'm putting the final touches on a biography of Alexander."

"Alexander the Great?" He grimaces. "Aren't there 3,197 biographies of Alexander already?"

"Well, not that many. Perhaps a hundred or so."

"Stop right there. Is your pilgrimage to our sceptered isle going to be a learning experience, or are you on holiday?"

"Septic isle?" I ask, as if I've misunderstood the phrase.

He roars in appreciation of my intentional misunderstanding and swears by his *wife's* picture—which is pointed toward the visitor rather than himself—that he'll appropriate the term and flaunt it as if it were his own.

"I'll assume you choose learning experience. Let the lessons begin. One never lies in even numbers, for if you do, the lie will fail to achieve its objective, which is, after all, to deceive, is it not? If you say, 'I've done that a thousand times,' no one will take your claim seriously. On the other hand, if you say with conviction, 'I've done that thirty-seven times,' it renders the assertion infinitely more credible, regardless of its validity."

"Your point is well taken. In defense of writing *yet another* biography of Alexander, I do have a different take on the man. My emphasis is on his excessive drinking."

"Excessive? Surely"—he screws up his face in *faux* distress —"you don't mean to suggest he drank *too much*? We're talking about a chap who conquered over two million square miles, did he not?"

Before I can answer, Mountjoy continues.

"Wasn't it your Lincoln who, when someone suggested Ulysses S. Grant drank too much, said, 'Tell me what brand of whiskey Grant drinks. I'd like to send a barrel of it to my other generals.' In him, old boy, you had a president."

"Yes, that's true. But, for some, getting sozzled lubricates genius, while for others it proves to be debilitating."

Mountjoy nods. "I choose to believe I fall into the former category. And you?"

"Me too." This is going to be quite a year.

"Come to think of it, Gogarty, your scribbling on Alexander's tippling could be of value. Every time you lift a jar you are, in a manner of speaking, at work in the laboratory, are you not?"

"I never thought of it that way, but you're right, you know."

"Ehh, yehhs. I do know. Well, let's assume the world is your laboratory and drink to Britannia, you, and your wards."

He raises his glass and I raise mine.

"Down to business. I've been designated by Professor Bisgood— that is, Professor Bertram Endicott Bisgood, our chairman, referred to henceforth by the initials BEB, as the link between you, your program, and the university. You'll occasionally hear me refer to him as Bertie. Refrain from doing so yourself unless he asks you to."

We place our empty glasses down at the same time and a mellow glow steals over me.

"What do you think of the sherry?" He refills our glasses.

"It's the best I've ever had." If the truth be known, I've never tasted sherry before. It does kindle the veins though, like the mild fire of wine.

"Not the *very* best, but 'twill do." We reach for our glasses simultaneously.

Mountjoy lifts the bottle with his left hand and studies the label. "The great-great-grandson of *the* González and I roomed together at Magdalen."

"You roomed together at *maudlin*? Did others room at melancholia and moribundity?"

He stops, drains his glass, and settles his chin into cupped hands.

"Magdalen College... Oxford? M-A-G"—he wags his head with each letter—"D-A-L-E-N?"

"Ohhhh, so it's Mary Maudlin now, is it?"

"Yehhhs. And it's been that way for seven hundred and thirteen years. You'd better stick with me, old boy, or your music-hall act will make you comic relief in this domain."

"Isn't Maudlin," I say casually, as if I've always pronounced it that way, "Oscar Wilde's college?"

"It *was*. He's been dead for some time now."

"True. But his spirit lingers on. I can see it in you." I laugh freely, this time drawn toward the moose-like features of Mountjoy's wife.

He notices. "That's Priscilla—a woman as purebred as one's likely to find among the upper class in times like these. In fact, one might even say her beauty lies in her genealogy. Nevertheless, approved by M'mah, whose standards are, shall we say, imposing." He looks back at me. "I say, before we go any further, why, may I ask, do you wear those hideous glasses?"

"I have to. They're necessary because of an eye disease which happens to bear the same initials as your chairman, BEB. Extreme light sensitivity, *old boy*."

Mountjoy clears his throat. "Nothing, my dear boy, *nothing* is more vulgar than an American attempting to speak like an Englishman. Now, whatever this *illness* requiring such obscene spectacles may be, let me advise you to alter its name."

"But BEB is the acronym for its name. Benign essential blepharospasm. Do you want me to choke on that each time I describe it?"

"Yehhhs, precisely. Either that or simply refer to it as DMZ or LTD or DOA, any variant of your choice, *but not—I repeat, not—BEB*. There are those in our department who look upon our chairman rather unfavorably. Bertie is well aware of this, and it fuels his paranoia. We can't have BEB living in fear that some malcontent will make a malicious analogy between your affliction and Bertie's stewardship of the department.

"Furthermore, I'm numbered among his favorites, which yields advantages, none of which I'm prepared to relinquish. And, I daresay, I suspect you don't really need to wear those preposterous eyeglasses at all... do you?"

I fidget and Mountjoy takes notice of my distress.

"I withdraw the question," he says with a rueful grin. "Furthermore, and upon due reflection, under no circumstances should you discard the glasses; just your explanation for them."

"Huh?"

"They"—he points to my glasses—"are, in any event, of use to you and hence to us."

"I think you're supposed to brief me on procedures and protocol," I say, attempting to redirect the conversation.

"Procedures yes, protocol no. Learning our *modus operandi* will allow you to conduct your business in a more proficient and less taxing manner. I can be of help there. Genteel behavior is a byproduct of breeding. Unfortunately, *no one* can help you in that respect. I can say this, however: your year here will be a painful ordeal if you intend to say and do *the right thing*. Simply put, you will *never* succeed in acquiring social graces.

"Just bear in mind at all times that you're *only an American*. Therefore, aside from certain extremities—for example, sodomizing one of your male students *while class is still in session*—the more barbarically you behave, the more likely you'll find yourself well received here."

"I get it. The more asinine I act, the more it reassures all parties concerned I'm exactly what I claim to be, an American, and therefore nothing to concern themselves with."

"Precisely. And you need not, for the most part, act. Just... ehhh... be yourself. You might, of course, occasionally speak a bit more like Humphrey Bogart or Edward G. Robinson. And... oh yes, do smoke a cheap cigar now and then.

"The purpose in all this is for you to embody the image of the American we British have come to hold dear to our hearts and loathe at the same time. And, in a similar vein," he gestures toward my clothes, "let's not ignore the advantage of being oafishly shabby. Thus, for the most part, almost anything unwonted you do will be welcome."

"What, may I ask, prompted you to speak to me so candidly? Don't get me wrong, I'm anything but offended. I just never expected to feel this comfortable with anyone over here, particularly in a university setting."

"Breeding and instinct, my dear boy, breeding and instinct. And, I might add, the manner in which you inhale the fruit of Andalusian labor, even though sherry is clearly not your customary beverage. I knew by instinct that you were a man"—he contorts his jowls to speak out of the side of his mouth—"wid cobbler's awls, who spends a night or two at the rub-a-dub."

Is this local dialect, or is he reciting a fairy tale?

"That's Cockney, old boy. It means you've got balls and obviously have lifted a jar or two hither and thither."

"I knew that," I lie.

"Really? Then you must have noticed an exhibition of Bristol Cities when BEB's secretary, Miss Popper, greeted you."

"Duck soup," I say, eager to level the playing field. "Titties. We call them titties."

The door flies open once again, and a short plump gray-bearded man projects his head into the room. Still grasping the doorknob, he stares down at the floor and says absently, "I beg your pardon, gentlemen. I had no idea you were having breakfast." He enters the room and closes the door behind him.

Mountjoy, unruffled, says, "Oh, Bertie, this is Dr. Gogarty, our American visitor. Dr. Gogarty, this is Professor Bisgood, Professor *Bertram Endicott Bisgood.*"

"Well, I'm honored, sir. I've heard a great deal about you and, of course, your work on wool combing and worsted spinning in West Yorkshire." I'd just read the title of his book in the departmental brochure, and noticed it came out in 1937 with no other publications being mentioned except "numerous book reviews in scholarly journals."

BEB blushes but seems pleased by my reference to his book. He clears his throat, guffaws, and looks down as he rocks slightly back and forth on the balls of his feet. "I'm delighted to make your acquaintance. Mountjoy here should be of considerable help when it comes to policies and procedures and things of that sort, but I may be useful in other matters. Please don't hesitate to call upon me."

He looks with curiosity at my glasses. "Is our lighting a trifle too harsh for you, Dr. Gogarty? We can do something about that, I should think."

"Oh, Bertie," Mountjoy interjects, "Dr. Gogarty here has a nasty ophthalmic condition making it necessary to wear those beastly spectacles of his. They reduce the impact of light on his retinal equipment."

"How unfortunate for you, Dr. Gogarty. What affliction is that?"

Mountjoy's eyes rotate anxiously in my direction.

A moment's hesitation.

"OPO," I say, tapping on my lens.

"Really?" the chairman responds. "Be a good chap and remind me what OPO signifies."

"*Obscurum per obscurius.*"

"Oh, yes, indeed. OPO." He nods and waves an open hand as he leaves.

"Hell's teeth," Mountjoy gasps. "Where did *that* come from?"

"I have no idea. Maybe from hell's teeth, whatever they are."

"*Obscurum per obscurius*, eh? If I can still trust my Latin, that phrase means clarifying an obscurity by referring to something even more obscure. How good *is* your Latin, Gogarty?"

"Fairly good."

"Fairly good, eh? Well, aren't you one lucky chap. You see, poor Bertie's a redbrick product. Any Latin he may've learned in grammar school is far too rusty to be of use to him in working out whole phrases. If you want to see BEB nod convulsively, cast an entire sentence at him. But I must warn you, there are those here who are able not only to decipher your feeble subterfuge but will gleefully torment you with Ciceronian queries. Any display of esoteric terminology should be kept to a bare minimum, or you'll find yourself hanging alongside it."

"Well, I'll have to stick to OPO now, won't I?"

"Better than BEB, my dear fellow, better than BEB. If they ask, tell them you don't remember the Latin. They'll find that plausible and amusing. In fact, it'll help confirm their suspicions of your vacuity. Incidentally, I see you've gotten yourself a mackintosh. That's a wise move in this corner of the world."

"I see you have one too," I say agreeably, pointing toward his coat rack.

He smirks. "*That*, my dear boy, is a *Burberry.* Do get yourself settled in. I'm off to the south later today on university business, but let's see each other soon."

I think I'll keep my revelation about his recruiting trips to myself for now. It should be deployed at just the right time for maximum impact.

"Oh, before you go, Bertie suggested I ask you for facsimiles of the students' applications to your program. We're curious as to who these young people are you're inflicting upon us. Make no mistake, we're well aware of what's going on in that Garden of Eden of yours —race riots, assassinations, druggery, hippies, etcetera, etcetera. And these students are, after all, products of your"—*cough, cough*—"*'culture'*."

I smile at him savoring his own sarcasm. "Please keep this to yourself, but I know next to nothing about our students. The dean of faculty, who's also the Grand Wizard of the program, asked me to be resident director at the last minute and delayed passing their applications on to me until just before I left for the airport."

"Hmm. I'm sorry to tell you this, old boy, but that sounds rather tactical on your dean's part. So, you know nothing of substance about any of them?"

"I do know one of them, a student of mine. The others? From their applications, two of them may be a problem, but that remains to be seen. They arrive on Monday and I'm meeting them in London. Any suggestions as to where I can have them stay for a few days?"

"Not to worry. I'll book them at Passfield Hall. It's part of the London School of Economics and I'll have an old schoolboy chum there take care of your students. I'll arrange for you to be at the Hotel Russell. It has tolerable accommodations and is within walking distance of the hall."

"Shouldn't I be staying at Passfield Hall with the students?"

"My dear boy, either you adjust to British life or you wallow in the trammels of misguided egalitarianism. Which is it?"

Where does he get these phrases from? "Somehow the former sounds more attractive. I'll adjust."

"Splendid. Rather than lowering yourself by living in the fulsome squalor of student barracks, you reside like a gentleman at the Hotel Russell and thereby demonstrate that success breeds privilege and comfort."

"Any suggestions as to what I should say to them? This *is* supposed to be an orientation meeting of some sort, and I don't know a damn thing about England."

"First of all, keep it just that way. Most of what you think you've learned here will be something you've misunderstood. Second of all, tell them the best way to experience England is without resorting to some specious tour book as a guide."

I smile and nod.

He leans over and replenishes our drinks. "What can you tell me about the student whom you know? Perhaps he can offer a clue as to what we're taking on here."

I hesitate. "It's a she. Marthe Fleischmann. Brilliant young woman. She has a 3.97 GPA—that's a student's grade-point average, based on a scale of four."

"Marthe Fleischmann? Hmm, sounds like a New York student. I'm more interested in weaknesses than strengths. Are there any potential problems with her? What does she intend to read?"

"Medieval paleography, *Beowulf*, Old English, Old Norse, and Medieval Latin, as I recall."

"So, a glutton for the arcane, eh? Well, *her* plate's full. We won't have to concern ourselves with Miss Fleischmann, will we?"

"I hope not."

# 5

---

Better steady your nerves and look confident, it's the first meeting with your students.

No. You're not stopping for a matitudinal bracer.

If you've learned anything, Gogarty, it's that alcohol and students don't mix. Besides, the dormitory's only a block away; there's no time for a detour.

A tall, wiry man in his early forties emerges from the front door of Passfield Hall and extends his hand. "Good morning, Professor Gogarty. I don't think I've had the pleasure. I'm Horace Taylor, one of the assistant deans attached to the study-abroad program, and it's my job to deliver your charges to you."

He leads me down the hallway to the conference room on the left. "Unfortunately, I'll have to leave it at that. They want me back in New York straightaway. So, here's your brood."

He's anxious to unload them.

"No real trouble aboard ship, although," Taylor says, lowering his voice, "you might want to keep an eye on Mr. Stein. Bye now." He starts to leave, but then pauses and places the palm of his left hand against his mouth, whispering, "Uh, that O'Brien boy as well. He tends to wander to the outer limits of the tether."

I open the door to take a quick head count. Something's wrong.

"Mr. Taylor," I shout down the hallway. He scurries back.

"By my count, we're one short."

"Really? They were all here a minute ago. Someone's probably off to the bathroom. Could be Stein." He opens the door and surveys the group. "Yup. That's who it is all right. Don't worry, he's around somewhere. You'll notice him. I *guarantee* that."

All eyes are fixed on me as I enter the room. Speak loudly. It inspires your confidence, if not theirs.

"Hello, one and all. I'm Dr. Gogarty, your resident director. Let's start with a roll call. Raise your hand when I call your name. Bunyan, Robert. Caldwell, Mary. Fleischmann, Marthe."

There she is. No lipstick. No makeup. No jewelry. No smile. Her buttoned-up black sweater covers her blouse and her skirt drapes to the floor. She might as well be wearing a nun's habit. How ironic. How paradoxical.

"Goldberg, Florence. Gould, Gerald. Klepper, Alicia. Martí, José. José, you bear an illustrious name—any relation?"

"No sir, but I'm familiar with his work."

"You're Cuban?"

"Cuban American."

"Marx, Leo. Tell me Leo, is Karl or Groucho in your family tree?"

"Both."

"Wait a minute. I'm in charge of the jokes around here." A faint chuckle comes from a few students.

"O'Brien, James. Mr. O'Brien are you aware that with a name like yours you may be related to an eleventh-century Irish king?" O'Brien is short, chunky, redheaded, and freckle-faced. He winces at the question.

"*May be*? I'm a direct descendant of Brian Boru, king of Munster and high king of Ireland."

All Irishmen have a king lurking somewhere in the family tree. Mine's O'Fogarty, king of Ely. What is it they say? "Ireland is a paradise of pretenders."

"Excellent, James. But do remind me never, ever, to inquire about your lineage again." A ripple of laughter.

"Rosenshine, Barbara. Sokol, Lillian. Sparer, Ellen. Stein, Frank... Stein? The rest of you *have* seen him around here, haven't you?"

"More or less," O'Brien mutters.

I hear footsteps outside, the door to the room creaks open, and a lanky, unwieldy young man, no more than one hundred and forty pounds, but well over six feet tall, glides around the oval table and slumps into his seat. So, this is our mysterious thirteenth guest.

I use my index finger to count heads once again and then turn my attention back to our new arrival.

"Let me guess. You're Frank."

"And let *me* guess. You're a professor of multivariable calculus." He's mocking my head counting.

"It's history, Mr. Stein."

"*You* are history," he says, eyes alight with mirth.

Ignore him for now. "Well, most of you are English majors, aren't you? Raise your hands. Uh-huh. About two-thirds. Let's see how good you are at what you do. What was James Joyce's definition of history? Anyone?"

O'Brien looks up at the ceiling pensively but fails to find the answer there.

"No takers?"

Marthe raises her hand.

"Yes, Marthe?"

"Well, the truth of the matter is Joyce himself never, as far as I know, defined history. However, in *Ulysses*, James Joyce's Stephen Dedalus refers to history as 'a nightmare from which I am trying to awake'."

Stein applauds robustly. Now there's a couple for you.

"Impressive, Marthe—"

Before I can continue, Stein interrupts and says, "*Life* is a nightmare from which we are trying to awake."

"Frank, please, it's too early in the day for such deep thoughts—at least as far as us lesser creatures are concerned. What's your major, Mr. Stein?"

"Philosophy."

"That explains a lot." This elicits general laughter. Stein smirks.

"Well now, I've set up appointments with each of you for later this afternoon. Do be careful when you're crossing streets here, or your stay in this nation of shopkeepers will be all too brief. By the way, who described England as such?"

"Napoleon," O'Brien shouts without raising his hand. He adds, "Pity he lost the war with them."

"James, my boy, the truth of the matter is Napoleon lifted it out of Adam Smith's *Wealth of Nations. You* expropriated the term to disparage the English. Whatever happened to playing the humble guest? And who said that, by the way?"

O'Brien shrugs.

Marthe's right hand shoots up. "As far as I know no one except you—a moment ago. Shakespeare's Macbeth however, in act three, scene four, says, 'Ourself will mingle with society, and play the humble *host'*."

"Just testing," I say in a supercilious way, caricaturing a professor whose error has been exposed by one of his students. Everyone laughs, including Marthe and Stein.

"Now, a few of you will be off to Berkshire. Raise your hands, please. Ellen, Alicia, Marthe." Thank God. She's going to Berkshire. "You three will be picked up, let's see... next Saturday at noon here outside Passfield Hall. You'll be taken directly to the university. If you need to contact me, for now call Mr. Mountjoy. His name and number are printed on the front of the material I'm distributing to you.

"Yorkshire people will head north with me on the same day. A word to the wise. London pubs are great for a quick snack, but don't loiter there. I don't fancy collecting you from the local constabulary or mopping you up from the floor of some sleazy establishment. Temperance is the watchword. Got that, O'Brien?"

He avoids my gaze.

"Any questions? Yes, Ellen."

"Professor Gogarty, when will we Berkshire girls see you?"

"I'll be there every few weeks or so to check in with you. No more questions? I'll see you individually in this room later on. Check the bulletin board at the information desk to see what time you're scheduled for. I'll post the times in a few minutes."

I'll camp out here and await the parade. Individual sessions should give me a better idea of what I'm up against.

An hour later there's a knock at the door and James O'Brien struts in like an heir to the Irish throne.

"O'Brien. Who said, 'Give crowns and pounds and guineas, but not your heart away'?"

"Crowns and pounds and Italians?"

"No, *wise guy*. By guineas he did not mean Italians. It's A. E. Housman. What do the *A* and *E* stand for?"

"Alfred Edward, another English poofter."

"Is that type of word really *necessary*, O'Brien? Why study English literature when you despise the English? Know thine enemy?"

He smiles broadly without answering.

"Uh-huh. I trust they ransacked your luggage in Southampton, as they did mine at Heathrow."

He nods.

"Don't give them any reason to take a special interest in you. That's all for now."

O'Brien unfurls a leprechaun's smile and marches out the door thundering, "What makes you think I'd ever do something like that?"

O"Brien's crusty, but is he mean-spirited?

Frank Stein lurches in without knocking at the door.

"And here, on time for his appointment, we have the cryptic Mr. Stein. Frank, I'm glad to see you and grateful I didn't have to traipse after you. Is this an omen indicating you intend to cooperate with me this year?"

"I wouldn't count on it."

"Well, nevertheless, this is the second thing you've done today that leads me to believe this could be a good year for you."

His grin turns into a frown. "What was the first?"

"When you applauded Marthe Fleischmann for her response to my question about Joyce."

"I wasn't applauding her. I was ridiculing the process. One more automaton rolling off the academic assembly line."

"How disagreeable."

"Which word—*automaton* or *academic*?"

Let's give oblique another shot. Attack him where he thinks his strengths lie. "Let me guess—your favorite philosopher is *not* Aristotle, correct?

"Correct."

"Uhhhhh... Kierkegaard . . . or . . . Nietzsche?"

He tilts his head inquisitively. I think I've struck a chord.

"Well, which is your poison: To suffer and stand apart against the herd or—rise above it as an *Übermensch*?"

A noncommittal smile.

"Both?"

No response. I think I've thrown him off his game.

"Well, whatever the case may be, all I need to know right now is if any of your contemplated leaps into a higher humanity could be construed to be a violation of British law. You know—the law of the herd?"

"I almost like you, Professor Gogarty. You show promise."

"I almost like you Frank, you show promise too. I read some of the poetry you attached to the application. It's good, very good, and reminds me of Dylan Thomas. Don't squander that gift, Frank. And please, please, be careful out there."

The next ten interviews are uneventful. No apparent problems. Marthe's last on the list. No accident to that. Just blot out what happened last May and pray that she does.

Marthe walks in and sits across from me with an anxious look on her face. What does that mean?

"Dr. Gogarty, I've heard the English are inordinately harsh when it comes to grading. Is that so?"

The A-minus I was about to give her last May almost brought on a nervous breakdown. All Marthe could see was the minus. That's when the assault began. Still, there's no excuse for succumbing, even though you were ginned up at the time. She got her A all right, but I'm left with inwit's aching bite, that damn Catholic conscience of mine.

Marthe's acting as if nothing ever happened. That's good. Maybe she's just not showing her hand—yet.

"Yes Marthe, I'm afraid that's true. The British are much more severe when it comes to grades, but there's no reason to fret. It's my job to translate *their* grades into what I consider to be equivalents in our own system. So, we have a built-in curve to protect our students against anything catastrophic."

She stares at me unconvinced.

"Marthe, given your record, which shows you're well on your way to a *summa cum laude* degree, rest assured there's absolutely nothing for you to worry about."

She's still brooding. If I don't do something to ease her anxiety, she'll wind up badgering me day and night—or, worse yet, resort to something more drastic. Marthe sure knows how to get what she wants, but what a troubled young woman she is. I'll bet there's a man somewhere, probably her father, burdening her with unrealistic expectations. Everyone we meet carries an invisible weight they'll never share with anyone.

"I'll tell you what, Marthe, and I say this strictly *entre nous*, do you understand?"

She nods.

"Good. I personally guarantee that as long as you put the same effort into your studies here as you did back home, you'll be awarded the highest possible grade in all your classes."

"How will you determine whether or not I'm performing up to that standard?"

"Quite frankly, Marthe, the less I hear from you or about you, the more certain I'll be you're laboring intensely over your studies. Will that work?"

"Professor Gogarty, you have my word I shall earn every single A and call upon you only if a crisis of exceptional magnitude arises. *I*, of course, will determine when that's the case."

That's what I'm afraid of.

Defile one of the oxen of the sun—and the rest will trample on you.

# 6

---

Opening his office door, I find Mountjoy standing up with his back to me rearranging the pins on his map. I'm barely seated when his right-hand darts past my head and produces two tinkling sherry glasses from behind my ear. Brimming with satisfaction at his sleight of hand, Mountjoy sits down and gingerly fills both glasses.

I say, "By the way, what would you have done last week if I accepted the glass, but didn't touch the sherry?"

"I wouldn't have touched a drop of mine, either. I do, however, have impeccable instincts when it comes to judging whether or not a man drinks, and your name, after all, *is* Gogarty."

"True. My people come from what they call 'the isle of dreadful thirst.' Their blood is in me and a parched palate comes with the territory."

"So, I'm dealing with a self-professed dipsomaniac, eh? Not to worry. I have a lorry full of this stuff. I believe I've mentioned to you that when I was at college I roomed with," he points to the González on the label, "that chap's great-great-grandson. We were inseparable back in those days, and he swore a solemn oath to the Blessed Virgin Mary—of all people—to provide me with an unlimited supply of the family's very best sherry for the rest of my—more or less—natural life. Several cases of it arrive at Batey's Importers Ltd. in Liverpool every six months, and one is routinely forwarded to my office. I'm obliged to exhaust the stock in order to keep the supply flowing. I also took a vow in that respect, but one of a more secular nature. I swore on the grave of my beloved great-great-granduncle, Sir Reginald—who, by the way, was the lord mayor of Liverpool back in the days of yore—that I would do so."

"Sir Reginald must have been quite impressive. Are you from Liverpool?"

"He was a singular man, and I shall tell you more about him if and when the opportunity presents itself. Yes indeed, I am a Liverpudlian, but *not* of the same breed as those strident Laners you may have heard of who've been clattering about lately and causing quite a commotion."

"You mean the Beatles? You don't happen to be related to any of them, do you?"

"Heaven forbid!"

"That's too bad; I'd like to meet John Lennon."

"I shall be of no service to you in that regard. However, permit me to turn to a far weightier subject. You, my dear Aloysius, have somehow managed to leave quite an impression on BEB, which is no small accomplishment. Reference to his book was a clever ploy. He's a prime example of those among us defensive about their reputations —meaning, of course, all of us. Aside from his ludicrous monograph, which made its appearance before the war, he's never published a blessed thing except reviews—scores of closely-argued reviews of books dealing with every aspect of nineteenth-century English history.

"Aspiring scholars in the field have learned that whether you're discussing Lord Palmerston at the Congress of Vienna, or the color of Disraeli's trousers, you'd damn well better refer to BEB's book. He's been cited more than Gibbon, Carlyle, and Trevelyan combined. BEB now looms among the immortals in the field—a bountiful harvest for someone conspicuously uncomfortable in the presence of an original thought."

He pauses momentarily to bask in the glow of his mordant mockery.

"Bertie has managed to blend congenital languor with initial productivity and today enjoys a Mafia-like control of his domain. As for me, I hope to modify the process by eliminating the initial productivity portion of the equation. I've always shuddered at the thought of producing anything of substance. You may occasionally hear me lamenting the endless research entailed in laboring over a definitive work. Pay no heed to my grousing. If I have anything to say about it, and I daresay I do, no such work will ever see the light of day.

"In the meantime, BEB, who's placed himself on the editorial board of every learned journal in the field, ensures that all my insufferable articles get published in respectable organs and criticized by no one."

"I should have written a book entitled *Alexander the Great in Nineteenth-Century England.*"

"You might consider doing so in the future. As long as you keep BEB well-disposed towards you, you'll have respect where it counts —which, of course, is here in England.

"In the same vein, you should prostrate yourself before *our* Alexander expert, someone I refer to in private as 'the pseudo-Somerset.' You see, he was born with the unenviable name of Jacob Schumacher. When his family arrived from Austria in 1942, he became James Aubrey Somerset, flagrantly filching two distinguished British surnames straight out of *Burke's Landed Gentry.*"

"Didn't Oscar Wilde call that book the best thing in fiction the English ever produced?"

"Ehhhh, no. He was referring to *Debrett's Peerage and Baronetage.*"

"Wait a minute. Somerset's here at Yorkshire University? Oh my God. That man's a holy terror. I've never met him, but I heard him at a conference a while back. He crucifies anyone who says something complimentary about Alexander or uncomplimentary about his own work."

"You do make a wino out of Alexander, don't you? Scarcely sounds like a panegyric to me. Depicting him as soused to the gills is a far cry from extolling his virtues. Particularly, I should think, to a Jew."

"Easy there, Dickie boy. My middle initial stands for Tabeel, an Old Testament figure. I too have a few drops of blood from the chosen people running through my veins."

"Really? How deliciously perverse. A New York Jew named Gogarty. Now that I'm more fully aware of your"—*cough, cough*—"background, let me assure you your credentials will be considered beneath reproach here. Nothing you do will surprise anyone, and the pseudo-Somerset will be delighted to learn you're characterizing Alexander as a *shyster*—is it?"

"*Shikker*. But I do point to some of Alexander's saving graces. I've tried to portray him as an ambivalent genius, the stuff of which tragic heroes are made."

"A drunk and a tragic hero at the same time, eh? Good luck in pulling that one off, old boy. However, you may need more than luck when it comes to Somerset. BEB has suggested that he's even more paranoid of late, and if Somerset discovers there's someone in our midst trespassing on Alexander without offering liege homage, he'll undoubtedly assume you've been positioned here by *them* to subvert him." He shakes his head, smiling. "Be as obsequious as possible and make a point of weaving news of *your* contaminated bloodline into the conversation. You might even consider adopting a hangdog apologetic look, with a hint of perfidy lurking just below the surface."

I shake my head. "You're beyond redemption, aren't you?"

He nods agreeably. "I'm working at it. Are you, by the way, actually of the Hebrew persuasion—that is, religiously?"

"No, I was brought up a Roman Catholic."

"Equally deplorable but do keep it to yourself when speaking to Somerset. So, what are you?"

"I am a . . . ." I pause. "Not sure I can answer that question yet."

"Well," Mountjoy says, standing and smoothing out his wrinkled suit jacket, "now's as bad a time as any to introduce you to a man of genius."

I follow Mountjoy to Somerset's office, where he knocks at the door and waits.

A voice with a thick German accent growls, "Who's there?"

"I beg your pardon, Professor Somerset," Mountjoy says meekly, opening the door, "I thought you might like to meet Dr. Gogarty. He's a visiting American lecturer who brought some of his students with him to study at the university."

"I'm at work, can't you see?"

"I beg your pardon. I'd never dream of interrupting your work. All of us know how very important it is. You see Dr. Gogarty here has written a book about that Alexander chap of yours and keeps referring to you as the *doyen* of Alexander studies. He simply wants to pay his respects."

"I can afford," Somerset, lifting a fob watch out of his watch pocket, says, "exactly nine minutes."

This is going to be a long nine minutes.

Mountjoy leaves the room and Somerset scrambles to his feet from behind an oversized desk, across which notes are haphazardly strewn. He strains to rise to his full height, and even then, is no more than five feet tall. A kinky-haired nimbus frames his temples, and a scrimpy pointed beard juts out from his chin. He looks like Trotsky.

An electric shock shoots across our handshake. Somerset keeps a grip on my hand, looks directly into my eyes, and proclaims, "It's them."

"Them?"

"Yes, them."

"Oh. *Them.*"

He frowns. "They're looking to get me."

"Well, if there's anything I can do to help stave them off, I'm at your service."

"You understand? Bring that chair over here and we'll talk." He pauses, extracts his watch, and announces, "For seven minutes."

"Yes sir."

"Dr. Gogarty, describe Professor Schachermeyr's *Alexander der Große*."

He's a talented conversationalist as well.

"Well, Professor, his best work on Alexander, *Alexander der Große: Ingenium und Macht*, was published in 1949. Schachermeyr was interested in psychology as well as politics and military considerations, in attempting to understand the man."

"You—how do we British say?—'butchered' the pronunciation of his title."

I nod apologetically.

"What does Schachermeyr say about the man?"

"Well, he basically depicts him as a titanic brute bent on world domination."

"What's your judgment of Schachermeyr's thesis?"

"Well-documented, skillfully developed, slightly slanted, but quite valuable. His thesis, of course, has been modified and made more persuasive by your own artfully-crafted argument about the nature of power and its corruptive influence."

"Good. Most of you Americans cite German works in your bibliographies, but very few of you understand the language. You come from a nation of linguistic cripples."

I wonder if he picked that phrase up from Mountjoy?

"Dr. Gogarty, your origins are Irish, are they not?"

"Yes sir, and Jewish as well. My middle name is Tabeel."

"Tabeel? Are you aware that this is one of those names in the Bible no one knows anything certain about?"

"I am, sir."

"Did you know some Hebrew scholars think it means 'good for nothing'?"

"No sir, I was unaware of that, but thank you for bringing it to my attention."

He looks at his watch. "At what stage is this manuscript of yours?"

"I have the full text, Professor Somerset. I just need to make a few changes and clean up my footnotes."

"How many footnotes are there?"

"About a thousand."

"How often do you cite *my* work?"

"Oh, about forty-seven times as I recall, but perhaps more. I'm not certain." Thank you, Your Lordship, for sharing your wisdom on numbers.

"Good. When it's readable, I may be willing to take a quick look at some sections of it."

"I'm honored, Professor. You're by far the most distinguished of Alexander scholars, and I never dreamed you'd be generous enough to share your valuable time with someone whose work lacks distinction."

"One last question."

"Professor?"

"What do you know about American universities and how to get hired by them?"

Where did that come from? I'd better sound knowledgeable about this.

"I'm sure I could be helpful in that respect."

"Well, you may be useful after all. I'll tell you just one time about something, and if I ever hear about it from anyone else, I'll know exactly where it came from. Do you understand, Dr. Grogarty?"

I nod, ignoring *his* butchering of my name.

"They think they're going to get me, but I will fool them. I'm going to escape to your country. Do you understand what I've just said?"

He's testing me. "No sir, I'm afraid I'm at a loss to recall even one syllable of our conversation."

He looks at me and nods approvingly.

"Your time is up. I'll see you soon enough in the tearoom or the Senior Common Room. Don't come over to me unless I ask you to do so."

"Certainly, Professor," I say, resisting a temptation to click my heels.

Sherry suddenly sounds like a glorious idea. I march into Mountjoy's office asking, "*Gott bewahre, mein Bruder*, vot vuz dat?"

"Something to aspire to. He's told you about *them*, I take it."

"He has. I'm crushed; I thought that he was sharing a confidence with me."

"He was. But it happens to be one he shares with everyone he speaks to for more than twenty-seven seconds."

"What form do these demons take?'

"Customarily, they're in a mortal mode, but they can transform into inanimate objects—such as, for example, carpets. They seem to have invested the bodies of several members of our department. Somerset may not be so far off his chump in that respect. There has to be an explanation for some of our staff members."

"Are you one of *them*?"

"Oh no, dear boy. It seems I've remained repugnant enough to ward off any interest on their part."

"So, in the eyes of he who counts, you are not one of *them*?"

"Absolutely not. I had enough foresight to look into Somerset's deportment before he arrived. He was a reader at Liverpool University before being awarded the chair here, and an Oxford confrère of mine briefed me on his more bizarre idiosyncrasies.

"For example, three years ago he shared with some select confidantes, by which I mean the entire staff, the tragic news that he'd been afflicted with what appeared to be a fatal brain tumor. Somerset spent several months exasperating every eminent brain surgeon on Harley Street for information about a surgical procedure which would ameliorate his condition. To Somerset's dismay and consternation, not a single physician among them found the slightest evidence to corroborate his self-diagnosis.

"Somerset, convinced that the entire medical profession was now in league with *them*, returned to Liverpool and revealed his condition to the chairman, whose skepticism provided *prima facie* evidence that he, the chairman, was one of *them.* Certain he was terminally ill, Somerset retired to his home and prepared to breathe his last breath while reading Thucydides, as if dying weren't painful enough in and of itself."

I burst out laughing. Mountjoy smiles smugly and continues.

"All of his classes were taken over by a graduate student of his. On the very first day of the following term, without informing anyone of an alteration in his condition, Somerset appeared in class, ordered his graduate student out of the classroom—in fact off the campus— and proceeded to teach as if nothing had happened. The perplexed student waited anxiously outside the classroom. When Somerset emerged, he advised the young man it would be in his best interest to work under another mentor at the university. The student had no choice but to do just that.

"When the chairman was informed of Somerset's presence on campus, he hastened to his office to enquire about his health.

"'Very *gut,*' Somerset said. 'In fact, I've never felt better'."

"'What about that nasty tumor?' asked the chairman. 'What tumor?' replied Somerset, looking at the chairman as if *he* were crazy. It had become evident to Somerset by then that the entire staff had been supplanted by *them,* and at that point he began to look for greener pastures. Eventually, I'm afraid, in our direction."

"Let me guess. They continued in their relentless pursuit of him, and today he encounters them in every square inch of Yorkshire."

"Yehhhs. The first sign that something was amiss here came when his office was about to be carpeted. You see, in our system, at every university, there's only one professor in each specific field, not scores of mediocrities sharing the same equally meaningless title, as is the case"—he stares at me intently—"elsewhere."

He continues. "And, there are perquisites for a *real* professor. One of these is a carpeted office. When the unhinged dwarf arrived, he insisted on an imperial-purple carpet. All right, Your Majesty, an imperial-purple carpet it will be. And 'twas, but not swiftly enough for our impatient psychopath.

"One day Somerset burst out of his uncarpeted office, stormed through the foyer, got into a taxi, and went downtown to make the selection himself. It was delivered and emplaced on the same day, something that rarely happens in Yorkshire and which probably occurred because local merchants would go to any lengths to rid themselves of him."

Mountjoy raises his open palms as if to ask, "Who wouldn't?"

"Somerset appeared content. That is, until he strode across the carpet like Agamemnon returning from the Trojan War, only to be jolted by an electrical shock. You see, the carpet he selected was woven out of materials notorious for their electrical conductivity."

"And so, he returned it."

"Oh no, my dear boy, you speak of normal natures. At first Somerset suspected he'd been hoodwinked by a cabal of Armenian anti-Semites. But being hoodwinked implied he'd been outsmarted, which was unthinkable.

"Therefore, he placed the responsibility squarely on the shoulders of the department. Fuming, he marched into BEB's office and demanded that the situation be dealt with in short order. BEB referred the issue to Alexander Horton, the university's fix-it man. Horton, a versatile chap, applied his practical acumen, but to no avail. Somerset continued to fume.

"Horton's own lid finally blew, and in utter frustration he composed a letter to Somerset explaining that the professor had three alternatives. He could replace the rug, wear tennis shoes to work, or water his carpet daily. Any of these would either diminish or eliminate the shocks, and the university would be more than happy to provide him with a watering can.

"That, my dear fellow, is where things stand now. Let's hope he starts searching elsewhere for a demon-free environment."

"He's already begun. It's westward ho to America."

"That's splendid indeed, on two counts. First of all, BEB has spoken to those he knows in Oxbridge circles, but fears that were he to inflict Somerset upon them, he'd never be forgiven. Second of all, that "melting pot" you call home might be just the right place for him. Half the people there will probably think he's British because of his name."

I smile at his barbed witticism. "He actually asked for my advice on this. My instincts tell me to point him toward California, probably Berkeley. He's unlikely to be interested in a position at a dinky city college like mine."

"Even *he* doesn't deserve that."

Ignoring him I say, "There may be a saving grace here. Somerset's agreed to look at parts of my book. Believe it or not, his scholarship makes a great deal of sense, and I agree with much of what he says. But for him that may not be enough.

"When I saw him at that conference, he went berserk, savaging the credentials and basic intelligence of some young scholar who had the audacity to disagree with him on a minor point. After that, I didn't have enough nerve to even introduce myself. I may be feebleminded, but I'd rather not hear it broadcast or see it in print. I'd better polish my paean to Somerset. His disapproval of my work could spell disaster."

"Well then, feed his ravenous ego. You and I both have a multitude of things to do before term begins next week, so what say we meet again next Monday?"

"I'll be here with bells on, Your Lordship."

## 7

---

Monday's come quickly, but I do have a place to stay and a means of transportation. I'll drop in on my confrère and share the news with him

"Good afternoon, Sir Reginald."

He brightens at my allusion to his ancestor.

"Good *morning*, Dr. Gogarty."

"Morning?"

"Yehhhs. I haven't taken lunch yet, and therefore it is still morning. Well, classes are underway. Are you all settled in?"

"Yes. I found a little chateau across town. It's at 77 Ecclesiastical Street. Are you familiar with the neighborhood?"

"Familiar enough to know it's far too posh for the likes of you. How on earth did you find a *little chateau* in that area? Is it a vacant gardener's cottage?"

"In fact, it's a Victorian mansion complete with seven bedrooms, three fireplaces, a charwoman, and a black cat with green eyes. It's quite a bargain, too—only seven hundred and forty-seven pounds a month!"

"Well done on the odd numbers. You're learning. But, if what you say approximates reality, they've robbed you blind, my dear boy."

"Not if it's paid for by the City of New York. Money is no object, *old sport*."

He winces and says, "That's some distance from here. How, pray tell, will you manage to get back and forth to the university?"

"Miss Popper gave me the number of a taxi driver, Frank Budgen, who's agreed to put himself at my disposal day and night and provide receipts for all trips, both real and imaginary. Budgen's six foot three. He has the physique of a prizefighter and the hands of a bricklayer. I pay him by the month."

"So, a chauffeur, bodyguard, and accomplice all rolled into one, eh? It sounds auspicious as well as practical in your case. I won't even query about the astronomical fee *he's* charging you. Nevertheless, I gather you're satisfied with your palatial lodgings?"

"Love them. Mr. Kgnao—that's my new cat—and I are quite cozy, thank you. *But*, I had quite a shock the other day. I went out for a little afternoon stroll to absorb some of that culture you've been raving about. In the process I kept an eye out for a nearby pub where I could mingle with the local gentry.

"The closest establishment turned out to be the Shoulder of Mutton, but guess what? It was closed. *Closed—at three o'clock in the afternoon*? I meandered a few more blocks to the Nag's Head and it, too, was closed. Subsequently I came across a dozen or so pubs— on what was rapidly becoming a pilgrimage to Scotland—*and every single one of them was padlocked*. You call this civilization?"

"Perhaps they saw you coming. On the other hand, you *might* have consulted with the local constabulary about licensing hours in this region. You would have learned that Yorkshire pubs close at half two and stay closed until five. Here, in this country, rule of law still prevails. And that, my dear boy, is the law."

"You're kidding."

"Not in the least."

"Since you're so smart, can you please tell me what it takes to get someone deported from this relic of a country?"

"Ask your students—they seem to know."

"What do you mean by that?"

"A confidante of mine tells me someone in your flock is using drugs and may be looking to establish himself as something of an entrepreneur, trafficking in cannabis and more lethal substances."

There it is again. That feeling of the earth opening up beneath me. "Oh no."

"Oh yehhs."

"Stein?"

"Gertrude? I don't think so. It's a he, and the only surname I recall from your litter is the Fleischmann. Stein certainly sounds like one of yours.

"I must warn you, though. There's no hesitation here when it comes to students and drugs. First-time offenders are summarily expelled from the university. Foreign students are deported. Those who indulge are treated like cancer: excise the infected area and cauterize anything polluted around it to protect the well-being of the body politic. In other words, if this information proves to be accurate, your entire program may be in jeopardy."

"Wonderful. If the program gets tossed out, my tenure and job go with it. How reliable is your source?"

"Well, we're talking about a student, and a female student at that. Nonetheless, in the past this young woman's been spot-on in much of what she's told me."

"I need help. What's the best course of action to take at this point?"

"Join me for lunch. I'm famished. We could also have a libation or two to lubricate the digestive process and hone our analytical skills."

"You can scratch the libations. It's two-thirty and pubs are closed in this wasteland you call civilization. It's the law, you know."

"My dear boy, one man's desert is another man's oasis. Yes, 'tis the law, but by no means does that mean a gentleman cannot slake his thirst. Surely, you're aware of what went on in your country during prohibition?"

"A speakeasy?"

"How quaint, but I'm afraid not. I'm thinking of something a step or two below that called the Polish Club. It's a private establishment and not subject to licensing laws."

"Are there other clubs like this?"

"There are. And speaking of abasing oneself, there's always the Irish Club. You'll find atavistic aggregations with similar names in any English city large enough to attract the vile elements among us. But please, not today. We need an ambience tranquil enough to plot a strategy to extricate you from your present dilemma."

"Well, that settles it. There's nothing like a Polish club to sharpen one's wits."

He offers a slight nod and a faint smile in vague appreciation of my quip.

"They do, by the way, put on a decent chicken paprikash."

"Chicken paprikash? I thought that was Czechoslovakian."

"Try Hungarian, Gogarty. And do remember this is a Polish establishment; the menu is therefore, shall we say, eclectic."

The club turns out to be a good twenty minutes away. It's undecorated except for a Polish flag on the wall in the restaurant area and, clustered around it, several paintings of the Polish countryside. The bar is jam-packed, but we're able to get a table in the dining room. We order, and the waitress brings us steins of beer, followed shortly by the paprikash.

"I take it back, Your Lordship. This is delicious, and the Dinkelacker beer is—"

"Yehhs, German. But don't expect to get stout here. They do observe *some* proprieties."

"Okay, Mountjoy, let's get serious. Have any of the powers that be at the university been informed of what's going on with the student in question? Is the vice-chancellor aware of any of this?"

"The vice-chancellor is a fossilized diplomat who hasn't the slightest notion of what goes on at the university. The registrar is the one who deals with any issues of consequence, and my informants in his office have reported nothing to me about any of this. All I know is that the lad in question is something of a queer duck, even by American standards."

"That must be Stein. I'd better start off with him and see what I can find out."

"The best information comes from the police. Some of them make a habit of popping in here. I'll keep an eye out. Incidentally, I'll be visiting schools again by midweek, but I should be back in Yorkshire by Saturday or Sunday."

Here's what I've been waiting for, it's time to strike.

"Heading south again, are we?"

"The burden of mundane labor."

"Yet you go about it with considerable gusto, don't you?" Set him up. "Always on the go. Isn't that sort of behavior a breach of the slacker's code, if such a code exists?"

"Certainly not. There's an illusion disguising the reality here."

"I know. I—"

"Don't waste your time speculating, my dear boy. Simply put, it works on my behalf. No one wants any part of the work I do, and it's in everyone's best interest to keep me as happy as a lark in my endeavors."

"Okay, but when you get to Oxford, do say hello for me."

"To whom? The Irish janitor at New College?"

"No. To *that* woman."

"What woman?"

I've got him.

"Who else? The object of your affection—the inspiration for your tireless peregrinations—*that woman in Oxford*!"

"What?"

He's squirming. "No use denying it; you've told me yourself."

"I've done no such thing."

"Unbeknownst to you perhaps, but you revealed it through your pin-laden map and appointment book, the one you display on your desk."

"Continue," Mountjoy says with stoic resignation.

"Through those two sources I was able to uncover a pattern in these trips and see through your 'undercover' operation. If you'd escorted me out from behind your desk five minutes sooner, your secret would've remained intact.

"The last stop you make is *always* within thirty miles of Oxford. Therefore, the only logical explanation for your 'system' of visitations is an assignation—that is, *un affaire d'amour* with a *femme fatale* in or around Oxford."

I lean back in my chair and laugh at Mountjoy trying to conceal his shock behind a raised stein of beer.

He puts the stein down and clears his throat. "You need not explain assignations to me, my dear boy. I'm quite familiar with the term and the practice. However, I must admit that you're a lot smarter *than you look*. I'll spare you an elaborate defense of the allegation since I have been, as your American detectives say, 'busted.'

"And, speaking of some such considerations, a member of the local constabulary has just entered this establishment. So perhaps we can suspend further intrusions into my private life while I redirect his attention towards our table. I trust that what's just been said will remain between us."

I nod.

A tall, slender man with a slight moustache approaches our table, directing an expansive smile at Mountjoy, who stands and extends his hand.

"Good morning, Detective. May I introduce Dr. Aloysius Gogarty, an American chap who's at the university looking after some of his students this year on his college's study-abroad program?

"Dr. Gogarty, this is Detective Sergeant Robert Ferguson."

"Hello, Dr. Gogarty. It's a pleasure to meet you."

"And for me to meet you."

"How about some lunch, Ferguson?" Mountjoy asks. He knows this man well. That could be a big help. Follow Mountjoy's lead on this.

"No, thank you. I've already eaten, but I'll join you for a pint of bitter, if it's all the same with you."

Ferguson's beer is ordered along with a round of large gin and tonics for ourselves.

Mountjoy asks for permission to share my situation with Ferguson, and I nod my approval. Ferguson listens with squinted eyes and a furrowed brow. He says, "We've heard nothing about any of this as of this morning. If I were officially informed of it, I'd be required to create a file, and it might be wise to keep this out of any paperwork for now."

Ferguson senses my anxiety.

"If you'd like, Dr. Gogarty," he says, "you can pass on the particulars about this lad to me and I can keep an unofficial eye out for him during the next few weeks. It might be wise to wait before approaching the registrar about any of this. Once informed, Dr. Ogden tends to act rather decisively on such matters. And, let's not forget, you have that program of yours to consider.

"I should advise you though that our remand centers"—he sees the confused look on my face—"that is, our *jails*, are anything but rehabilitation centers. They're cesspools, and exceptionally unhealthy for young lads. There's no such thing as probation here for violations relating to using, much less selling, drugs, and first offenders ordinarily get put away for a long stretch of time."

You're going to need this guy. Let him know about the family. That'll give us something in common.

"Sound advice. Thanks for the information. By the way, three of my brothers are on the police force in New York."

Ferguson leans forward looking interested, and says, "Really? In what capacity?"

"One's a precinct captain, another's a detective sergeant in narcotics, and the third is on the TPF—the Tactical Patrol Force."

"Tell me more about the TPF."

"It's basically the Riot Squad—helmets and all that. My brother Tommy works Manhattan North. That's the South Bronx and Harlem."

Ferguson listens attentively.

Maybe I can parlay this into a favor. "Detective Ferguson—"

"*Bob* will do nicely."

"Bob, the boy we're concerned about is Stein, Frank Stein. Forgive me for saying this, but could you possibly contact me before any official action is taken in regard to him?"

"I can and will unless the situation requires immediate intervention on my part."

I scribble my work and home phone numbers on one of my cards and pass it on to Ferguson.

"Oh, and please call me Aloysius—or, for that matter, just plain Al. Is it all right if I poke around and see what I can dig up myself? I did learn a few things from my brothers."

"I'm sure you did, but you want to be circumspect with such pursuits in England. It's wise to remember that you have no badge to hide behind. So, do be a good bloke, if you would, and let me handle the situation."

I agree. We all drain our glasses and rise to leave.

"Well, is it back to the university or off to your castle, Gogarty?" asks Mountjoy.

"To the castle, Your Lordship; it's time to retreat. There are lecture notes to flesh out and footnotes to correct. There'll be a state of siege over on Ecclesiastical Street. That's where you'll find me, kind sir, ensconced in my scriptorium and oblivious to any barbarians clamoring at the gate. So—raise the drawbridge and lower the portcullis!"

# 8

---

The ring on my house phone startles me out of a deep, boozy sleep. I grope for the phone and knock over an open bottle of gin. It's empty. That's good. This splitter of a headache isn't. Ferguson's voice instantly awakens me. "Hello, Bob. What's happening?" I listen attentively.

"Let me get this straight. Stein's been shooting heroin and peddling cannabis, but if I'm able to ship him back to the States by Monday, no charges will be brought against him.... I understand. Stein has to lay low between now and then. Don't worry. He'll be on his way back to New York by Monday.

"And, by the way, I'll be flying off to Paris for a resident directors' meeting on the same day. That's November sixth, right?... Okay. I'll leave you a telephone number where I can be reached in Paris if, God forbid, any further complications arise.... As far as I know there are no other troublemakers in my group. There's a boy named O'Brien. He's one of those Americans obsessed with being Irish, but this one's more likely to shoot his mouth off than shoot up. So . . . don't worry about O'Brien for now?... Okay. Many, many thanks, Bob."

I'll buy Stein a one-way non-refundable ticket to New York and see if I can track him down. I've got his schedule, but I might as well start at his residence hall. All things considered I doubt he's going to class.

A half-hour later I knock on Stein's door and he's there all right. Stein looks at me and half smiles, in a distant, unconnected way. Jesus. His pupils are constricted and he's looking past me, even though he's staring straight at me. That spells heroin. I let myself in and continue to stand as Stein collapses onto his disheveled bed. This is no time to mince words.

"I've got bad news for you, Frank. The local police have proof positive you've been using and selling drugs. Either you return to New York Monday on this flight"—I wave the ticket at him—"or on Tuesday you'll be arrested *wherever you are* in England. So, let me present alternate snapshots of you next week: A) casually strolling through the streets of Greenwich Village flipping the morning's bread crumbs out of your tattered and taped copy of *Fear and Trembling*, or B) getting a taste of real life fear and trembling in an English prison. That's the choice. It's up to you."

He seems unconcerned. It must be the drugs.

"If it's such an open-and-shut case, how come I'm not in jail right now?" Stein asks, smiling oddly, as if he's amused.

"You *will be* unless you cease all such activity immediately and get on board this plane." I wave the ticket at him again.

He looks at me confused, as if he can't find the words for his question.

Help him out. "How do I know? All I can say is I'm telling you the gospel truth, and it comes from an impeccable source. If you have any doubt about what I've said, or truly believe you're innocent of any and all charges, then, by all means, go ahead and roll the dice. Just remember, it's your future at stake here."

Stein pauses for a moment, displays an enigmatic grin, and says whimsically, "I choose Greenwich Village and Kierkegaard. It might be worth it just to see dear old dad's face when I show up at the door."

"Good choice. I noticed on your application you have an asthmatic condition. I'll tell all parties concerned you've had a severe asthmatic attack, had to return to New York for treatment, and will continue having it treated there. We'll both be leaving Yorkshire at the same time. I'm on my way to France for a conference.

"Remember this: over the next few days the Yorkshire police will monitor your every move. If you do what I've told you, you should make a clean getaway. But if you ignore the gravity of your situation, disaster awaits you. Now, if you're half as smart as you *think* you are, you'll look at what's happened here as a shot across the bow. End of sermon. I'll be in touch."

All I can do now is hope he has enough brain cells left to do the right thing. I turn and leave, heading toward the School of History.

I'd better make sure that letter to Paris booking my hotel reservation has been sent. When I arrive, Miss Popper is sitting at her desk, typing something. Good. I thought she might be out to lunch.

"Miss Popper, I'll be leaving for France on Monday. Could you kindly tell me if one of the girls has taken care of my French letter?"

She turns her head, and I see a familiar blush creeping up her neck. What've I done now? Better excuse myself and consult my translator. I pop in on Mountjoy, who's going over his lecture notes.

"I had a strange reaction from Miss Popper to a very simple request. Maybe there's something going on here I'm not aware of?"

"There's a great deal going on, my dear boy, of which you are totally unaware. What did you say or do?" He listens to my account and lets out a lusty laugh.

"You've asked Miss Popper if one of her assistants has taken care of your *condom*."

"You're kidding."

"Not in the least."

"Will I be forgiven, I mean, being an American and all that?"

"Probably," Mountjoy says, filling two sherry glasses, "once the shock has worn off. The brighter side is you're adapting by not adapting. Nevertheless, there's a more troublesome concern at present. What's the situation with your drug peddler?"

"Stein will be on his way back to New York on Monday. Incidentally, I'll be off to France at the same time for that resident directors' conference in Paris I sent you the note about. I'll be gone for a week or so. If anything goes awry, here's how I can be reached." I jot down the phone number of my hotel in Paris on one of my cards and pass it to Mountjoy. He studies the card and then looks up.

"I loathe conferences."

"So, do I, but I'm not going to miss this one."

"Why?"

"Before I left New York I met a woman and was, well, there's no other way of describing it—smitten by her. She's the dean's administrative assistant, and I'm sure she'll be there."

Mountjoy frowns. "Please, don't get mawkish on me."

"Agreed, but Elena is different."

"Really? Is there a combination lock on her knickers? Three breasts? Different in what respect?"

"Only two eyes and they're both green, but in a certain light one of them turns chestnut brown. And—she's a redheaded Cuban. Shall I go on?"

"You need not. Collecting specimens for a carnival menagerie, are we? I knew there was a hint of the grotesque in you, old boy, but hoped for something better than infatuation with the preternatural. Besides, there are bound to be complications with a creature of this sort, are there not?"

"Well, she does have a son. And she may still be married to someone in Cuba. Her husband was supposed to meet Elena and their son in Spain, at which point they'd continue on to America, but he apparently abandoned them and threw his lot in with Castro. He's a gastroenterologist. By now, when he's not treating Che Guevara's flatulence, he's probably living on a confiscated estate, consorting with some zealous *Fidelista*."

"A real charmer, eh? Speaking of conferences, let me tell you about my experience at a meeting of headmasters in East Anglia last year. It was one of those tedious academic gatherings that go on interminably. Worse yet, it was presided over by a man who salivates at the prospect of unleashing stale platitudes on a captive audience. To come to the point, I had a more appealing alternative waiting for me in Oxford, and this boorish chairman continued to prattle on. The situation clearly called for a *coup de maître*."

"A master bait?"

"Yehhhs, or in a similar vein, a master stroke. Well, as it happened, I was seated next to the podium and began peering at the chairman's crotch with a look of dismay on my face. I then turned away with upraised eyebrows and caught the attention of some chap in the first row. I looked back at the chairman's crotch and shook my head disapprovingly. Before long, that fellow in the first row was pointing towards the headmaster's groin and asking the man sitting next to him if he saw something inapt. In no time, the entire assemblage was staring intently at this fellow's fly.

"The speaker reacted by gazing in the same direction himself. A ripple of laughter spread throughout the hall, and the victim himself began to chuckle defensively. This brought on a wave of unruly chortling which, in turn, gave way to chaos. I shook my head in disgust at the impropriety, scooped up my papers, marched out of the hall, and sped away towards Oxford."

I applaud. "Bravo. There's a lesson to be learned from that."

"Yehhhhhs. There's a penalty to be paid for strutting around like the cock of the barnyard. Speaking of such things, you might want to be cautious with the lady frogs of Paris. They—"

I interrupt. "Well, Mr. Know-It-All, were you aware medieval prostitutes in Paris had their own guild and a patroness saint as well?"

"And who might that be, old boy?"

He walked right into it.

"Who else? Mary Maudlin, of course."

Mountjoy cringes.

"Yes, Your Lordship, they also wore distinct garb, so you didn't tap some *ingénue* on the shoulder and inadvertently ask, 'How about it, Toots?' The guild established a *prix fixe* for various services rendered and were regularly inspected by physicians to protect themselves—and their clients—from disease. Their quarter in Paris was known as *le clapier*, from which we get the clap. Or, I should say, the word *clap*."

"Well, those students in your lectures on France in the thirteenth century are certainly getting their money's worth, aren't they? Still, you'd better exercise prudence while in Paris, old boy. Personal hygiene has never been a priority among French women from any walk of life."

"Don't worry. I'm saving myself for the face that launched a thousand ships."

"So, within the space of a few days, you hope to leave her as spellbound as you are."

"Dante said Adam and Eve had only six hours together in paradise."

"True, but that was enough time for her to get them both evicted —wasn't it, old boy?"

# 9

Golden-bordered glass doors open automatically to *Le Pachyderme d'Or* with its army of bellboys, receptionists and plush carpet. Irwin's spared no expense for this extravaganza, and the hotel's name couldn't be more appropriate. There must be a concierge. Here we are.

"*Monsieur*, could you kindly tell me which room Elena Delagracia is in?"

He looks through the guest list, raises his hands, and shakes his head.

"No? Well, she probably hasn't checked in yet. Which room is reserved for her?" I slide a fifty-franc note in his direction. He slides it back to me.

"I'm terribly sorry, *monsieur*, but I have no such name listed. And, even if I did, I couldn't disclose her room number without permission being granted."

She must've booked elsewhere. "What other hotels are people from the Municipal College Resident Directors Conference staying at?"

"As far as I know, *monsieur*, all participants are staying here."

"How about de la Flora? Could you try that name?"

He inspects the guest list again and shakes his head.

I lean over the desk while asking, "May I take a quick glance to see if the lady might have registered by another name?"

He clutches the register to his chest and draws back. "*Monsieur,* I sense your concern, and should any woman of, shall we say, *interest* enquire about you, I will most certainly inform you. If you are pleased with our services here, it is customary to leave gratuities at the end of your stay. For now, if you can tell me *your* name, I will retrieve your key and have one of our staff, escort you to your room."

I enter the room and see a note's been slipped under the door. Damn it. It's not from her.

> *There will be an organizational meeting in the grand ballroom at four p.m. today; the conference convenes there at eight o'clock sharp tomorrow morning.*

I return to the lobby looking for someone who might know Elena's whereabouts. A staff member directs me toward a table where our badges are laid out in alphabetical order. Here it is: DR. ALOYSIUS GOGARTY. GREAT BRITAIN. Ouch! I stab myself putting it on. Some of these names ring a bell. DR. MARTHA CLIFFORD. DR. HENRY FLOWER. DR. ALFRED HUNTER.

Here's a perky little groundling with a study-abroad badge: MLLE. RENÉE DUJARDIN. NEW YORK. Mademoiselle's smartly dressed in a long, tight black skirt. Petite, but what did the master say? Fine goods come in small parcels.

"Mademoiselle Dujardin, *pardonnez-moi . . .*" I pause to think of the appropriate term in French.

She answers in a sultry voice, "You can speak in either English or French, whatever you wish *monsieur.*"

"I'm Aloysius Gogarty." I point to my badge. "My penance is to visit the bones of Thomas à Becket at Canterbury. What's yours?"

She laughs. "I just started working for the study-abroad program in New York a month ago, and I'm surprised to find myself here. However, it's anything but penitential in my case. Dean Irwin asked me to help coordinate the conference, since French is my native tongue."

And an attractive tongue it is at that. Wet red lips. Bronzed hair. Mlle. Douce incarnate. "Where are you from?" I ask.

"Montreal. I was the director of a bilingual school there, and the dean hired me as an administrative assistant to help out as a liaison with the French program."

"Well, it's a pleasure to meet you. By the way, I haven't seen Mrs. Delagracia about. Is she here yet?"

"No, and I'm afraid you'd be looking for her in vain this trip. She'll be coming next year when the conference is in Madrid."

My jaw drops noticeably. I won't even get a glimpse of her. My left hand begins to shake, and I feel lightheaded.

"Are you all right, Dr. Gogarty? You don't look well."

"Uh... yes... just a lack of sleep. But I'm surprised we won't be seeing Mrs. Delagracia. I had a few questions for her."

"The dean thought it best that she stays in New York to handle problems that might arise. All the directors are here, and you never know what's going to happen when it comes to students, do you?"

"Quite true I'm afraid." So, it's Irwin who's come between us.

"Elena's remarkably efficient; she'll handle any situation as well as it can be handled."

You can't afford to disintegrate in front of this woman. It'll get back to Irwin.

"Of course. Well, you're here, and that's what counts, isn't it?"

"That's a good way of looking at it. I've heard you're an historian, Dr. Gogarty. What's your specialty? I've always been intrigued by history."

"Ancient and medieval. I'm just finishing off a biography of Alexander."

"Alexander the Great? Fascinating. I love the story of Alexander and Roxane. It has all the ingredients of a medieval romance."

"I'm afraid it's not quite as romantic as you've been led to believe. The truth of the matter is Alexander found himself stuck in the hinterlands of the Persian Empire, and Roxane was his ticket out.

Her father was a powerful local warlord. The marriage enabled Alexander to forge ahead eastward."

"Why, Dr. Gogarty, you're destroying my illusions. But that's what historians do, isn't it?" She momentarily rests her hand on my forearm and says with enthusiasm, "Did you bring your manuscript with you? I'd love to read it."

*Watch your step with this one.* "I'll tell you what. What if I give you one of the chapters I've just finished revising? What aspect of his life interests you?"

"All of it, but since you've spoiled his romance with Roxane for me, I'd like to see what you have to say about *young* Alexander. I've always been curious about the early development of men of genius."

She licks her upper and lower lips in anticipation.

Uh-oh, there's a stirring in the nether regions.

*Suppress it, Aloysius.*

"Sure. I'll bring it with me to the meeting this afternoon."

"Wonderful. And, if the truth be known, I'd like to find out more about *you*, Dr. Aloysius Gogarty. There's something mysterious there," she says pointing to my heart. "Your book would be a good start though, since men reveal themselves through their writing."

"Really? I must ask you to guard it vigilantly, though. It's the only copy I have right now."

She straightens my tie and pats me on the chest. "I do hereby solemnly swear I shall return your manuscript to you intact this evening, or, at the latest, tomorrow morning."

"Fair enough. See you at the meeting."

Is this a siren singing her song? Odysseus never tormented himself with such questions. On the other hand, he wasn't a very good Catholic.

Irwin's at the podium droning on and on. "And our program has been acclaimed as the *most* . . ." Mountjoy should get the *Croix de Guerre* for all those conferences he goes to. I'd stare at the dean's crotch if his paunch didn't cover it. This shouldn't take too long.

Tomorrow's the gala opening when Irwin's glorious plans for our ever-expanding program are revealed. He'll have us landing on the moon before NASA and planting the Municipal College flag there while he's at it. I wonder if Irwin will black tie it? I wouldn't put it past him. He's winding up. Hallelujah.

I search the crowd for Renée and spot her heading in my direction.

"Well, I'm a man of my word, here's the relevant chapter. I've also included the prologue, which hints at a hidden agenda to the book."

"More mystery, huh? Wonderful. I'll get right to it after dinner. Ring me up in my room around nine. I'm a fast reader." She glances at her key. "Room 327."

"Room 327? That, Mademoiselle Dujardin, is the year in which Alexander met Roxane. Her name means 'little star,' by the way."

"Oh?" she says, looking up at me wide-eyed, like a star-struck undergraduate.

At nine p.m. sharp I show up at Renée's room unannounced. The door opens and she's holding the manuscript and smiling.

I apologize. "I probably should've called first."

"*Pas du tout*, I love surprises," she says. "Why don't you sit in the armchair? I'll make myself comfortable, too." Renée props herself up on the bed with two pillows set against the headboard, glances down, and notices she's revealing more of herself than she intended to. Smiling, she gives a playful snap to her garter before tucking her skirt between her legs.

Renée holds the manuscript up, waves it a few times, and says earnestly, "Let me tell you something, Dr. Gogarty. You write beautifully, and that's a rare quality among historians these days. The prologue has the sweep of Michelet and the poetic elegance of Sophocles. There's a quality unique to your book that I can't quite put my finger on. It's as if something is going on subliminally while Alexander's story's unfolding. Are my suspicions groundless?"

74

She rolls the manuscript into a scroll, grasps it in her left hand, and begins to glide her right hand slowly up and down over it as she waits for an answer.

*Stirring again.*

Distract yourself.

"You're right on target, and that's reassuring to me. I'll be candid, if you promise to keep what I say between us."

She smiles and nods.

"After anguishing over what approach to take, I came to the conclusion that the only way to do Alexander justice was to write his story as a Greek tragedy in the guise of a conventional biography. Thus, for example, the prologue is written in elevated language to do justice to the magnitude of the subject. The quotes you've seen interspersed throughout the chapter serve as a Greek chorus. That's the underlying rhythm you sense. In fact, the entire book was written with Aristotle's criteria for tragedy in mind. But it all takes place unannounced."

"Why?"

"First of all, publishers are unlikely to be interested in a biography written as a Greek tragedy. Second of all, why take all the fun out of seeing who'll be clever enough to realize what I've done?"

"So, you're pragmatic on one hand, and diabolically furtive on the other."

"*Exactement.*"

"Well, it's perverse but brilliant."

"You're at least half right. The brilliant part I'm not quite so sure of."

"Well, I am." Renée gestures for me to stand and slowly approaches me with an intense stare. She's stroking my lips. Taking my glasses off and... is . . . getting... on her knees? All noble intentions are cast astray. But, no child can come of this. Forgive me, Elena. What a shallow man I am. How can I redeem myself? Vow with conviction never to let this happen again.

Renée returns to the bed with a smile on her face, and I slump into the armchair. We talk about meaningless subjects for what seems an eternity. All I can think of is how to escape gracefully and get myself a drink. My left hand starts quivering again, this time intentionally.

"Professor Gogarty, you don't look well."

I ask, "Do you remember me being dizzy this morning?"

She looks concerned and says she does.

"It seems to be the same sort of thing. Maybe I'd better get back to my room and catch up on my sleep."

"I think you'd better," she says.

I kiss Renée on the cheek and leave.

What've you done? She works with Elena. You *need* a drink. I walk into the elevator mumbling a prayer that the bar will still be open. My prayer is answered. I hold up two fingers, signaling for a double, and then point toward the G'Vine Nouaison Gin.

"Oh, and a glass of that Pelforth Blonde, *s'il vous plaît. Parfait.*" I down the gin, take a gulp of the beer, and hold my right thumb up in approval. He refills the large shot glass. I carry my drinks over to a table which can't be seen from the main lobby and sit with my back to the door, so no passerby will notice me. How nice it is to relax alone. The bartender replenishes my drinks, and while he's making his way back to the bar, I hear someone approaching from behind. Dear Lord, please, not some nitwit from the program.

Jesus. It's the chief nitwit!

"Dean Irwin. What a pleasant surprise!"

His face is flushed and he's swaying a bit. *L'hippopotame* must have had more than a few. That means *he's* vulnerable. Maybe I can steal a page from Mountjoy's book.

"Professor Glogarty?" Irwin takes a deep breath as if he is about to hold forth, stands still, and starts swaying again. He regains his balance and announces, "I'll have you know I've just returned from a reception at the mayor's home, where I was honored by a duke, a marquis, and a fellow *chevalier* in the *Ordre des Palmes Académiques.*"

"Two *chevaliers* under the same roof? How impressive."

"Yes, that's what the mayor said."

"Sir, would you like a nightcap to toast your amazing achievements, and those, no doubt, awaiting you in the near future?"

"No, thank you . . . but wait . . . since you put it that way, I'll have a touch of scotch in some soda water."

I go to the bar and slip the bartender two hundred-franc notes along with a request to mix some stiff drinks and inconspicuously continue to replenish them. He pockets the money and smiles knowingly.

Irwin smarts at his first gulp but says nothing about the strength of the drink.

"Dean Irwin, may I ask you something about the program?"

"By all means."

"It's so well-conceived and implemented that I couldn't help but wonder what your vision of its future is. Is there a master plan of some sort?"

"Well, Professor Gilhooley... "

He's on his way.

"Do you have any new centers in mind?"

He launches forth.

The bartender intermittently comes to our table under the pretense of tidying up and continues to stealthily splash whiskey over Irwin's ice.

I'd better keep the target engaged. "Are there any other foreigners who've become *chevaliers*?"

He nods, and I ask who they are. That's all he needs to hear.

"Well, there's a—" He swallows a hiccup and continues.

Then, somewhere in the middle of a sentence, Irwin's head lands in the palm of his hand and he mumbles, "I'd better, um, retire." He's trying to get up. Uh-oh, he's wobbling. I spring into action and miraculously manage to keep him upright.

The bartender shouts to me, "Monsieur is in room *sept cents*."

I'm having a devil of a time navigating Irwin to his room. It's a good thing the bartender mentioned the room number; Irwin keeps heading in the wrong direction.

There's a bronze plaque on his door that reads "*La Suite du Président.*"

"I'll b-b-be shush fine," he blurts out and careens his way into the suite. You've done your part, Aloysius. Head back to your room. You need some sleep.

My portable alarm clock goes off. Eight o'clock? Jumping Jesus! I must've set it wrong. I should be down there by now. This calls for lightning-fast dressing and an Irish shower. First task accomplished! Two squirts of Guerlain's Vetiver in all vital areas and it's all systems go!

I race down the staircase to the grand ballroom where everyone's seated and the room's buzzing. Where have they put me? Here we are, Great Britain, in between Germany and Holland. It looks like everyone's here except the impresario.

I glance at the badge to my left: DR. GEORG GOYERT. GERMANY. "Dr. Goyert, is the dean being photographed elsewhere right now?"

"I don't know. He's yet to be seen. Perhaps he took breakfast in his room. He's staying in the presidential suite, you know."

"So, I've heard," I reply, as a murmur ripples through the crowd accompanied by a flurry of flashbulbs. It's Irwin, making his grand entrance, dressed in a black tuxedo with a white shirt and a white bow tie. He's smiling, but in an awkward way, and he looks pale, very pale.

Irwin raises his hands and calls for silence. "*Bienvenue.* Welcome to a plenary assembly of the most extensive and, may I say, the *best* study-abroad program in the world." We applaud ourselves.

On cue the Argentinean director stands up and says, "*Bienvenida.*" As he sits, the Brazilian director rises to say, "*Bem-vindos.*" In rapid succession comes, "*Willkommen,*" me with "Welcome," "*Welkom,*" and a litany of further greetings, climaxing in another round of self-congratulatory applause. A farce, but a well-orchestrated one.

Irwin quiets the crowd.

"Yes, welcome. We have a great deal to accomplish today."

He pauses.

"A schedule for the week's activities has been left at your place setting. Take particular note of the time and place for each resident director's meeting with me. That's when I expect you to submit a report on the developments at your center."

We're supposed to have a written report?

Irwin pauses again, but this time his face begins to change color. He clears his throat and forces himself to continue. "This morning I want to inform you of a significant expansion of our program."

Irwin turns ashen white and grabs the tablecloth. Suddenly, vomit spews forth from his mouth, drenching the front of his tuxedo. He attempts to regain control of himself, but a second eruption jerks his head to the side, and he splatters the mayor and a fellow *chevalier.* Irwin tries to speak, but totters and collapses in a heap, causing the walls to shake and the chandeliers to rattle.

I jump up to get a better view of what's happening, but I've inadvertently tucked part of the tablecloth under my belt with the napkin, causing dishes and silverware to fly in every direction. Startled heads swivel between the high table and mine. Some people leap up, panic-stricken, as if under attack by an unseen force. The waiters remain frozen in mid-step, and the guests on the dais display that glazed look the French wear every time a German invasion occurs.

Pandemonium erupts and a number of people rush to the exit. I elbow my way up front to see how Irwin is doing. The maître d's waving his hands and shouting directions in French, but he speaks too rapidly for me to understand him. Irwin's eyes open, and somebody with a little black bag reaches him and takes out a stethoscope. After cleaning off Irwin's mouth and shirt, he takes his pulse and listens to his heartbeat. Irwin responds to a question he's asked.

The concierge appears and shouts, "*Attention, attention, s'il vous plaît.* Everyone, please leave the ballroom—*lentement*—through the main entrance."

Renée comes up to me and asks, "What's just happened?'

"I have no idea. What *will* happen? That's the question. We can't have the conference without Irwin; I'll bet no one else knows what the hell's going on around here. He's not the type to delegate authority, is he?"

"Not that I've seen. By the way"—she stops and looks around before speaking—"I trust that our little 'conversation' last night will be kept *strictly between us*, right?"

"Absolutely," I respond, breathing a sigh of relief.

"Wait," Renée says anxiously. "Here's someone with news."

It's Horace Taylor, the man I met in London. He acknowledges me with a nod, then announces in a loud voice, "Please return to your rooms. In due course we'll be informed of the situation and any change in plans. When Dean Irwin feels well enough, he'll summon directors to his suite individually to discuss your respective centers."

Renée says, "Professor Gogarty, would you care to join me in my room for some morning coffee?"

How can I say no diplomatically? "Thanks. But I'd better get back to my own room just in case he wants to see me for one reason or another."

"True. We'd better follow directions to the letter. If not, we may be subject to the wrath of God once he's recovered." We both head back to our rooms.

I've been working away at the book for several hours when an ear-piercing clang comes from the antique bronze telephone in my room. I recognize the voice. "Hello, Taylor, yes, it's me. Two-thirty for my conference? *Today*? I'll be there. Thank you."

There's a surprise. Either Irwin's made a miraculous recovery or he's toughing it out in fear of losing control of the proceedings. I can fiddle with the book in the meanwhile.

*Rrrriiinnnnng.* These French phones are grating. It's Renée.

"Oh, hi. . . . Yup, I got my call. I have to meet with Irwin at two-thirty today, which is ten minutes from now. How about you?... Tomorrow morning? Well, I'd better get going. Talk to you later. Bye."

President's quarters? They look more like Louis XIV's private chambers. Taylor said to walk right in without knocking. I stand still in shock. Irwin appears motionless and looks like he's lying in state. *Don't tell me.* He moves and opens his eyes. Thank God!

"Dr. Gogarty," Irwin says in a frail voice, lifting the index finger of his right hand, which drapes down the side of the bed, "come sit in this chair and let me listen to your report about England."

I should pay more attention to those study-abroad memos. Think fast.

He reaches beneath a rococo embroidered purple bedspread for a lace handkerchief and daubs his mouth several times, giving me enough time to come up with an excuse.

"Dean Irwin, I thought it would be best in my case to wait on the written report. You see, some unanticipated events occurred as I was leaving for France, and I didn't have enough time to incorporate them into my report. I'll take care of it as soon as I return to England."

"What sort of events? Nothing deleterious to the program, I trust."

"No, no, nothing like that. It concerns a student of mine with a severe asthmatic condition who had to return to New York."

"How unfortunate. Which student is this?"

"Stein. Frank Stein."

He sits up, noticeably more attentive.

"Asthma? That's all?"

"Yes sir."

"Oh." He collapses back onto his pillow, retrieves his handkerchief, and applies it to the corner of his mouth.

"Well, these things happen. Where is he now?"

"He should be safe and sound in New York. Stein left from Heathrow at the same time I left there to come here."

The phone clangs away. Irwin answers it. "*Allo. Oui.* What?" Irwin listens, and his face goes pale again. Instinctively, I slide my chair back and nudge the bedside canister toward him with my foot—just in case.

"Dr. Gogarty is here with me. Yes, I'll turn the phone over to him." He reaches out with the phone, and I edge my chair closer to grasp it. Before he lets go, Irwin whispers, "It's an emergency. He's an English detective of some sort. I gave the front desk a list of my appointments, and they've transferred your call here."

This can't be good.

"Yes. Hello, Bob, what's wrong?... What for? Can you give me some details?... Okay. Where is he now? I'll do what I can.... Yes. I'll be in touch with you as soon as I get back. Thanks."

"Is there trouble?" Irwin asks.

"It's Mr. Stein. He's been arrested."

Irwin closes his eyes and says, "For what?"

There's no way to sugarcoat this. "The detective said for possession of LSD."

"Oh my God. Was he at the university at the time?—*well, was he?*"

"No. He was at Heathrow Airport, about to get on a plane for his flight back home."

"He'd hidden it in his luggage?"

"No. It was in the vest pocket of his jacket while he was boarding the plane, and it fell out when he leaned over."

"He intended to take it on the airplane?"

"Apparently so."

He props himself up again. "This could be a disaster. Was Stein scheduled to return to Yorkshire after getting treated in New York?"

"No. He was going to continue his studies back at Municipal."

"Good. Did you separate the boy from the program *before* he left Yorkshire?"

"Well . . . uh . . . yes . . . I suppose you could say that."

"Well then, we really have nothing to do with this, correct?"

"What do you mean?"

"Just what I said. There's no reason to bring the program's name into any of this, since he was not a part of it when the arrest was made."

He raises his head and stiffens his neck to reinforce his statement.

I frown and ask, "What about *the boy*?"

"He's no longer *our* concern, is he?"

"Are you suggesting, sir, that we leave Stein to his own devices—*under these circumstances*—in a foreign country?" I raise *my* head and stiffen *my* neck.

He says, "I'm not *suggesting* it. That's precisely what I'm telling you. Why should we put the future of all our other students at risk because of one student's irresponsible behavior?"

"I'm sorry, sir, but I beg to differ with you on this."

He glowers at me. "What, then, do *you* propose to do, Dr. Gogarty?"

I stand up and look down at him.

"Get the first flight I can back to London and at least let Stein know I'm there. He's at a remand center near Uxbridge."

"A remand center? A prison?"

"The equivalent."

Now he's really upset.

"Well, I can't stop you from doing that, but let me make it clear that anything you do must be undertaken in a private capacity. You'll do *nothing* in the name of the program. Do you understand?"

"Yes," I say, through gritted teeth.

"You should leave your resident director's report with me now. It does include Stein's separation from the program, does it not?"

He's deaf too. "I'm afraid not. Remember? That's why the report's not ready for your examination." I shake a folder at him with some random papers I've tossed into it to serve as a prop.

He looks at me blankly and pauses before he speaks.

"In that case you should hang on to the report for now, but as soon as you get back to England, update it, predate it, and send it directly to me in New York. Just make sure you include a full description of Stein's health status and a sentence explicitly stating that Mr. Stein was separated from our operation *before* he left Yorkshire.

"If the program is brought into disrepute here, someone will pay for it." He winces and stares at me. "Also, make sure you send me a letter explaining exactly how the Stein situation was resolved, once it is. That letter should be marked personal and confidential and shown to no one but me. Is all this clear to you, Dr. Gogarty?"

"Clear as a bell, sir; clear as a bell."

# 10

---

A thick pane of glass separates me from Stein, the bank teller-like hole in the center skewing his face. His mouth twists into a smirk. His complexion is good, which makes it easier to be irritated with him.

"LSD on an airplane? What the hell were you thinking, Frank?"

"What it would be like to take a trip within a trip," he says in a singsong voice.

I swallow my smile. Don't let his naiveté disarm you. "So, this is an example of genius at work, huh? Conceive a thought and implement it without ever considering what its implications might be."

"Professor Gogarty, you remind me of my father. Haven't you learned that 'the secret of reaping the greatest fruitfulness and enjoyment from life is to live dangerously'?"

Christ. He's lucky this glass is between us. "Sounds to me like a Nietzschean prescription for being locked up or *covered up*. Take a good look around, Frank." I wave at the premises. "How is this razor's-edge approach working out for you? Or, maybe I'm wrong, and you're having a grand old time behind bars. Is that so?"

"Far from it. But you know the plight of *Übermenschen*—to be persecuted by those unable to understand them."

I sigh and roll my eyes in exasperation, finally realizing that he's not yet back from the land of the lotus-eaters. The drugs are still in his system. "Good luck explaining that to your fellow inmates."

"What's your advice?" he asks, this time in a serious tone.

Take a deep breath. "Okay. Here's some counsel minus the bullshit. Your hearing is later this morning. Don't be a moron. Keep your mouth shut, and, hopefully, the judge will view you as a noxious weed that needs to be transplanted. Make one condescending remark to that man and you'll pay for it, *dearly*."

"I'm not that big a fool, Professor Gogarty," he says reassuringly.

"Admit you've been irresponsible and are genuinely sorry for the problems you've caused all parties concerned. That's it!"

I arrive at the courtroom shortly before eleven. Stein's face is hard to read and I don't know what to expect. The court clerk announces: "Regina versus Mr. Frank N. Stein," and the hearing proceeds.

He seems to be following instructions and acting respectfully. Ferguson said if he pleads guilty, they'll probably pack him up and send him home. Let's hope so.

Finally, the judge reads his name and says robotically, "You are hereby ordered to leave the country forthwith."

Praise be to God. Everyone rises and we all begin filing out of the courtroom. A court official intercepts the judge on his way out and whispers something to him. What's that all about? Who cares? It's not about Stein; he's on his way home. I'd better get that confirmed. Whom can I ask? Wait. That looks like the information desk.

The clerk's phone rings just as I arrive in front of him, and he holds up his index finger, signaling me to wait. When he finishes his conversation, he looks up and asks me to identify myself.

"Here's my passport and my card. Frank Stein, whose deportation was just ordered by the judge, is part of the program I represent. May I ask—will he be escorted to the airport?"

"Mr. Stein is not being escorted to the airport."

"All right then. I'd like to arrange to take him there myself. Where can I pick him up?"

"He's not on his way to any airport."

"You're turning him loose?"

"No. We're not. I've just been informed that Mr. Stein has been rearrested."

"*What*? Did he do something wrong at the remand center?"

"No. We received notice from the Yorkshire constabulary that before leaving their area, Mr. Stein purchased various items—jackets, sweaters, records, and books—from a total of seven establishments, amounting to two hundred and sixty pounds."

"So…what's wrong with that?"

"Nothing, except he wrote checks for these items without having any money in his bank account. He's being transported back to the Yorkshire authorities."

"Jesus Christ Almighty!" I put my hand to my temple, shake my head, and mutter obscenities under my breath.

The clerk smiles empathetically and lets me use his phone to call Ferguson. I'm so upset I misdial. The clerk encourages me to try again.

I finally manage to dial the right number, and Ferguson answers. "Bob, it's Aloysius. I'm at Uxbridge, and they were on the brink of deporting Stein, when he was rearrested. Do you know anything about it?... So it's all true, then?... You're handling the case? What a relief! I'll be back later in the day and give you a call as soon as I arrive."

I decide to press my luck and ask the clerk for a second phone call. He consents without hesitation. Where has this guy been my whole life? I dial Mountjoy's number, slowly and carefully.

"Hello Richard, I'm afraid the plot has thickened. I'm grabbing the next train from King's Cross Station, and as soon as I get back I'll stop by your office. Okay, thanks. See you soon."


Mountjoy inspects and blows on the sherry glasses, fills them, sits back, and waits for me to speak. I gulp the sherry down and he refills the glass. This one disappears as well and is instantly replenished.

I exhale. "Okay. I'm ready. Shoot."

"Well, there's been an avalanche of phone calls for you. It's still a muddled state of affairs, but don't get frenzied, at least not yet. The registrar knows about the nasty check issue but won't do anything until he has more information. If it's bad, rotten bad, it could prove to be awkward for the university. In that case, I'm afraid you and your three-ring circus might be crossing back over the pond sooner than anticipated. Happily, the registrar, Dr. Ogden, isn't one to jump to conclusions, so there's still some hope here. He'll undoubtedly wait to see how seedy this all turns out to be.

"I spoke to Ferguson a few minutes ago, and he was obliged to inform the registrar about the checks, but he soft-pedaled their significance and the police have not yet released any information to the local newspapers. Ferguson said he'll use whatever influence he has to persuade the courts to deal with this quickly. Even with that, however, Stein will probably be stewing in the nick for a while." Mountjoy looks toward me for a response.

"I'd say my first job is to get a list of the places where he wrote those checks, determine the exact amounts, and compensate the aggrieved parties. If nothing else surfaces, maybe I can persuade them to drop the charges against him."

"You'll have to ask Ferguson about that. There's supposed to be two hundred and sixty quid involved. Are you prepared to ante up that sum?"

"Municipal gave me an emergency fund, but when I spoke to the dean in France, he insisted Stein was separated from the program the minute I handed him a ticket to go home."

Mountjoy shakes his head. "Darling fellow. Are you going to absorb the loss?"

"Nope. I'm going to call Stein's father and ask him to wire the money to my account."

Mountjoy slides his telephone to my side of the desk.

"Thanks." Miss Popper makes the connection for me. After a few rings, a male voice says hello and introduces himself as Leo Stein.

"Yes, Mr. Stein. This is Professor Gogarty. I'm resident director of Municipal College's study-abroad program here in England. I'm afraid your son has gotten himself into quite a mess. He wrote checks to the tune of six hundred and fifty dollars, for which there were insufficient funds available in his account.... Yes. He bounced six hundred and fifty dollars' worth of checks. . . . No, I'm afraid we can't keep him here even if you send the money for the checks. He's already been dissociated from the program for reasons Frank will disclose to you, and he was on his way back to the States when all this took place."

Mountjoy shakes his head sympathetically.

"In fact, he is currently being detained by the Yorkshire police because of the checks and is awaiting a hearing.... Yes, he's in jail, and it might be advisable, if possible, for you or Mrs. Stein to be here to support him when his case is heard.... No? All right. But unless this financial situation is dealt with immediately, your boy is certain to get a jail sentence. It's in everyone's best interest that you forward the money to me as quickly as possible.

"Yes, Mr. Stein. My account number at Barclay's Bank is 221882. It's in my name: Dr. Aloysius T. Gogarty. Thank you. Goodbye."

I hang up and turn to Mountjoy. "Well, Papa Stein is coughing up the money, but he'd prefer to see your coppers hang on to his boy for a while."

Mountjoy smiles. "Now there's a smart chap. He probably needs time to change the locks in his house. If young Stein were English, they'd put him away, but since he's an American, if there's no other mischief he's been caught at, they may just ship him back home."

This calls for full disclosure.

I take a deep breath. "This is much worse than you think. Stein was arrested at Heathrow for attempting to board an airplane with LSD."

Mountjoy's eyebrows rise and he shakes his head incredulously. "I take it Ferguson has been informed of this?"

"He's the one who called me in Paris to tell me what happened. I spoke to him from Uxbridge and again just now at the train station here. He advised me not to say anything about Heathrow to anyone, except you."

Mountjoy holds up his index finger momentarily, and then speaks.

"Do what he says and tell him you've decided *not to tell me*. That way he'll be more comfortable doing whatever he's got in mind. I'll speak to my contacts in the registrar's office and make sure Ogden knows the boy was disengaged from the program when all this occurred. He doesn't take kindly to tomfoolery of this sort, and if the papers or the local telly connect Stein with the university, the boy's technical separation from your group will become irrelevant—as may your program."

"And my tenure... and my career. You don't happen to have any contacts at Australian universities, do you?" I ask offhandedly.

He surprises me. "In fact, I do. But what, pray tell, is your motivation for such a drastic relocation?"

"I may have no choice. In fact, I'm not eager to go anywhere except New York unless I can convince a certain party to accompany me."

"That Fleischmann girl?"

"Bite your tongue. Why would you say such a thing?"

"A tightening of those hideous lines on your forehead whenever her name is mentioned."

"I'm sorry I asked. I'll have you know Alexander the Great had deeply incised furrows on his brow, as do most deep thinkers. But no, *not* Marthe Fleischmann. God forbid. I mean my Cuban—the exquisite creature with anomalous eyes who happens to have an unlined forehead and a hairline identical to that of Alexander the Great."

"Still tilting at windmills, are we?" he asks.

"When I'm not tilting at gin mills."

He smiles. "I've given some thought to that *Cubana* of yours. When you wake up on one side of the bed, you're with a green-eyed woman; on the other side, you're with a brown-eyed woman. Two, as it were, for the price of one. However, I must say, you do have a proclivity for getting yourself onto sticky wickets, don't you?"

"They seem to seek me out."

His phone rings. "Mountjoy here.... Oh yes, I'll hold on." He places his palm over the transmitter on the phone and mouths, "It's the office of the American vice-consul in Liverpool."

My eyes widen.

"Yes sir, it's Richard Tarleton Mountjoy here, the liaison with the American study-abroad people at Yorkshire University. I'm aware of the situation, and, in fact, the resident director of the program happens to be with me at the moment. Do you wish to speak to him?" He hands me the phone.

"Mr. Stein called your office and wants you to be at his hearing? Yes sir. I know how difficult it is for someone in your position to take time out for something of this sort. I think I can persuade him he'd be just as well off if I were there, since neither of us is an English barrister. May I suggest you leave it in my hands for now?... I don't mind at all. In fact, I'm glad to be of service." I hang up the phone and look toward Mountjoy.

He nods his head and says, "Well done, luv," laying on a thick Yorkshire brogue. "That chap may be of use to you in the future."

"The thought crossed my mind. But that's if all goes well, which looks like a long shot right now."

"Oh. Dr. MacCumhaill, the principal at Edinburgh University— the equivalent of our registrar here—rang as well."

"That's Francis Irwin and his insatiable appetite for glory. He wrote me a note saying I have to go up there and sell our study-abroad program to the Scots, implying I'd damn well better do a good job of it. When in doubt, expand."

"How boringly American. Would you like to ring up MacCumhaill and make an appointment now?"

"Might as well." After a brief conversation with the principal's secretary, I turn to Mountjoy. "I meet with MacCumhaill on January second. That's if I'm still here."

Mountjoy says, "I'm afraid there were one or two other calls for you I was unable to deal with personally. Both parties insisted on speaking with you and you alone. Not to worry though—they were

American students. And, after all, what kind of trouble could they possibly have gotten themselves into?"

"Uh-oh. Let me guess. O'Brien and uhhh... I give up... tell me."

"Ehhhh, try Fleischmann. Marthe Fleischmann?"

"O'Brien and Fleischmann, huh? Nice."

Mountjoy replies, "O'Brien, I can understand. The name itself spells trouble. But Fleischmann? Isn't she your Sylvia Plath or something of the sort?"

"Not quite. No head in the oven for this one. She's more likely to shove mine or yours in there."

"Is the situation in that quarter similar to mine at Oxford?"

"Nothing of the sort, so stop fishing," I say, loosening my tie.

"Well, she was the more persistent of the two. The O'Brien boy was insolent but spoke with less urgency. And, by the way, Miss Popper has some post for you."

"Ever feel like the sky is falling, Mountjoy?"

"Daily. I do, however, have a remedy for such an affliction." Mountjoy reaches into his lower left drawer and produces a half liter of Glenfiddich malt whiskey. He fills two sherry glasses to the brim and carefully inches one toward me.

"This will cushion the collision."

"Cheers."

"*Sláinte.*"

There's a knock at the door. It's Miss Popper, who delivers the mail and leaves. Let's see, a letter from the Oxford University Press, something from Marthe, and a study-abroad envelope with the initials ED in the upper left-hand corner. Good God, it's from Elena. I feel my face heating up again.

"My, my, old darling, you look you've just seen Banquo's ghost or, worse yet, Lady Macbeth."

"Neither. There's something here from the OUP. I sent them some chapters and an outline of my Alexander biography. If you don't mind, I'll take a look at what they have to say now and bring the rest of this stuff over to my office."

"I fail to see how anything coming from the Oxford University Press could be urgent, but, by all means, indulge yourself."

I read through it quickly.

"Well, they're 'seriously' interested in my book. That's followed by some extravagant compliments. They'd love to offer a contract but are procedurally unable to do so until the entire manuscript is in their possession. Therefore, they urge me to pass it on to them at my earliest convenience." I turn the letter over to Mountjoy, who races through it.

He raises his index finger to caution me. "Beware of the blandishments heaped upon you by those chaps. They've taken to the American style of doing business. What that means is you can expect an unctuous flow of drivel often amounting to naught. They now keep as many authors as possible in tow until they've made up their own sweet minds about which manuscripts they intend to publish. I suppose the most important question is whether an Oxford contract will secure this *tenure* you seem so preoccupied with?"

"I think so. My book on Alexander should be the key, but who knows? What happens around here could very well sabotage my standing at Municipal, regardless of any scholarly accomplishments. However, even if Municipal lets me go, an Oxford publication means I'm sure to get picked up by another college somewhere. With my luck, it'll probably be in Idaho or South Dakota."

He pours two more drinks and says, "Let's stay in a positive frame of mind and assume this"—he reaches over, snatches and shakes the letter—"is simply evidence to support my contention that the Oxford University Press has abandoned its august standards and will allow even your scribblings to see the light of day."

I raise my glass and proclaim, "*L'Chaim.*"

"Yehhhs. I suppose so. Why, my dear boy, are you clutching one of those envelopes so tenaciously?"

"This, I'll have you know, is an epistle from the fair lady Elena. With my luck it's probably the minutes of the program's last meeting or another pointless memo. There are, however, a few things here"—I point to the correspondence—"I must pay attention to. I'd better watch out, or I'm going to find myself overwhelmed."

Mountjoy gives me a stern look. "Would you be willing to take some advice?"

Without pausing for an answer, he cups his head in his hands and says, slowly and deliberately, "One whelm at a time, my dear boy, one whelm at a time. By the way—how was that conference, or at least what you saw of it?"

"Oh Jesus! It was too good to be true, at least until I got that phone call from Ferguson. I hate to tell you this, but I made your speaker's fly routine look like a schoolboy prank. I'll give you the sordid details as soon as I can. For now, I'd better retreat to my office. I'm going to let Stein 'stew in the nick' for a while so he can ponder his fate. Thanks for the help."

Back in the privacy of my office I open Marthe's letter first and skim through it. She needs to meet me in Berkshire within the next two weeks. It doesn't sound like an emergency, but she makes it clear that I damn well better be there. God is she exasperating.

Where's Elena's letter? Hmm. Marked confidential. I open the envelope in haste and tear off the top portion of the letter in the process. I have to hold the two pieces together to read it.

*October 27, 1967*

*Dear Aloysius,*

*I have a personal problem I'm reluctant to share with you, but the truth of the matter is I have no one else to turn to, and I need some advice. My father told me last night he plans to take a trip to England. I'm very concerned about this. Papá has never said anything about going to England before, and it doesn't make sense. He has hardly any money, and I should think if he traveled anywhere, it would be to Spain. He says he's doing it for his job, teaching Spanish, but I find that difficult to believe. He's been exchanging letters with some people in Miami, and these letters were nowhere to be found when I cleaned his room. I know he plans on leaving during the second week of spring break, which is in early April next year, because that's when I planned to take a few days off from the college, so I can spend time with Miguelito during Easter week.*

*But something else is going on. With your permission, I'm going to remind him you are in England and tell him I'd be more comfortable with the trip if I knew he was contacting you there. Of course, I wouldn't say anything to him until I knew you were willing to look in on him. I know this is imposing on you, and I deeply regret putting you on the spot, but I simply don't know who else to turn to.*

*I will certainly understand it if you prefer not to involve yourself in this matter. However, would you be kind enough to respond to this letter one way or another? Thank you.*

*Yours sincerely,*

*Elena*


A golden opportunity.

*Pounce on it but don't overreact.*

Call Miss Popper and ask her to send Elena a telegram. Make it short and sweet. Let's see. DELIGHTED TO BE OF SERVICE ELENA STOP I AM AT YOUR DISPOSAL STOP SIGNED ALOYSIUS STOP. Done.

I'd better call Marthe and get *that* over with. "A special problem? Marthe, I'm afraid I'll have to stay put in Yorkshire for now because —just between us—the police are involved in a situation relating to one of our students here.... Yes, I promise I'll call as soon as I get my head above water.... No, I'm sorry, but I can't disclose who it is and what the situation is, either. I hope you understand. I would do the same for you. Thanks, bye." Don't ignore *her* request or you'll pay for it.

Well, they're coming at me from every direction. Which one will deliver the coup de grâce?

Lest we forget—one whelm at a time.

## 11

---

November 13, 1967. Judgment Day for young Stein and Aloysius T. Gogarty.

Let's see what a Yorkshire jail looks like. Good Lord, it's an old Victorian prison. Cold and austere.

All these English prisons seem to have the same gray, dank ambience and musty smell. At least they let inmates wear their own clothes here. There's Stein now. He's thinner and pallid, and his eyelid is twitching.

"Well, Frank, you look a little worse for wear. How are you holding up?"

"This place is a nightmare. Yesterday there was a guy with his knuckles this close to my face"—he clenches his fist and jerks it up to his right eye—"but a guard intervened. Every night I hear them chanting, 'gypsy,' 'queer' and other terms of endearment. One creep keeps staring at me like I'm a liverwurst sandwich." He tries to laugh at his joke but has to stop to wipe a tear from beneath his left eye. He's quivering. The drugs have worn off and the bitter sting of reality is taking its toll. Stein takes a deep breath, so he can continue. I'd better be the rock of Gibraltar for this boy.

Stein says, "I made a phone call to the office of the American vice-consul and left a message when I got here, but never heard back from them."

I nod to confirm I'm listening. "Don't worry about that. I've spoken to the vice-consul. He was willing to come, but there's nothing he can do here that'll be of any use to you. Maybe, just maybe, I can do something, as long as you follow directions. I'll be there to support you today, okay?"

"Yes, thanks."

"They've only given me a couple of minutes to see you, so let's get right to what could be a critical stage in the proceedings. If they ask you a general question about your activities in England, don't say a damn thing about what happened at Heathrow."

"You want me to lie about it under oath?'

"No. I didn't say that. I said I don't want you to voluntarily refer to it. And, if you're asked if you've done anything to break the law here, you might consider saying 'Never knowingly.'"

"*Never knowingly?*"

"Yes. Let me ask you a question. Did you think—at any time—that what you did at Heathrow was wrong or a violation of any law you respect?"

"Well, no. But, what if—"

"No ifs, ands or buts. For now, just follow instructions."

"Okay."

"The court knows I'm here. They may call on me to be a character witness for you."

"You're not going to tell them what you *really* think—are you?" he asks, like the frightened child he is.

"Hell no, but I won't blatantly lie either. All I want out of this is the pleasure of seeing you on an airplane heading back to New York. Oh, and something else that's important: your father forwarded the money for the checks. I have bank checks with me to cover all your rubberized ones. What you tell the judge about the checks and the money will be up to you. Just be smart in what you say and how you say it."

"Thanks. I think I know what to say. How come you know so much about how they do things around here?"

"All I can tell you is I've been getting useful information from a few friends. Frank, if you survive this, it can make you sturdier without completely leveling you. Joyce's Stephen Dedalus said, 'A man of genius makes no mistakes. His errors are volitional and are the portals of discovery'."

Here comes the guard. My time is up. "I have to go. See you in court, Frank. Good luck." I leave Stein chewing on his index finger. He looks more like a wounded sparrow than a mighty hawk.

I'll go straight to court and wait there for the case to be heard. I hope Mountjoy's contacts in Australia are solid. I'm going to need all the help I can get.

This courtroom's smaller than the one down south and more cramped. Here comes the star of the show, another gray-wigged judge on leave from the eighteenth century. He looks like someone equipped with an arsenal of medieval tortures he's eager to apply. What will it be today? The rack? White-hot coals? How about the strappado? That's it! Hang the bastard twenty feet high with a rope, drop him, and dislocate his vital organs with a jerking halt before he hits the ground. Repeat as necessary until *mea culpa* can be heard up in the rafters of heaven.

"The court will come to order. All rise."

The clerk announces, "Regina versus Mr. Frank N. Stein."

The judge peers over his spectacles as he thumbs through pages of documents. He clears the phlegm in his throat and asks, "What are the charges against Mr. Stein?"

The clerk reads, "Mr. Stein purchased two hundred and sixty pounds' worth of goods with draughts for which there were no funds available in his bank account."

The judge turns to Stein with a laser-like stare. God help us.

"Mr. Stein. How do you plead?"

"Guilty, Your Honor, with explanation."

"What is that explanation, Mr. Stein?" the judge asks sharply.

"I thought, Your Honor, that my father had already transferred the money to my account when the purchases were made."

"Is your father here to attest to this assertion?"

"No sir, my father's in New York. Apparently, he thought he had followed the proper procedure in transferring the money, but it never went through. I do know it's arrived and funds are now available to settle all outstanding accounts."

He *was* listening to me.

"What is your status in this country, Mr. Stein?"

"Until recently, I was a student participating in my college's study-abroad program, and I was taking classes at Yorkshire University."

"Until recently?"

"Yes, Your Honor. I'm afraid my asthma reacted so severely to the climate I was advised to return home."

Good boy, lying so convincingly.

"Is there anyone present who can attest to that?'

"Yes sir. My professor, Dr. Gogarty, is here in the courtroom."

"Mr. Stein be seated for now."

They swear me in.

The judge says to me, "Dr. Gogarty, what is the nature of your relationship to Mr. Stein?"

"I, sir, in my capacity as resident director of the program already referred to, have been directly responsible for Mr. Stein, while also serving as his moral tutor."

The judge raises a theatrical eyebrow and quips, "Moral tutor, eh? Not doing such a good job of it, are you, Dr. Gogarty?"

I smile at his wry comment. "No. I'm afraid not. But, Your Honor, in regard to Mr. Stein, may I suggest there are extenuating circumstances here."

"What are those circumstances?"

"Well, sir, first of all, let me say that he's a fine young man. And, I emphasize, *young*. Mr. Stein is barely nineteen years of age. He's an outstanding student, very bright, but I'm afraid rather naïve and inexperienced when it comes to the real world. This is his first trip abroad, and it has been a debilitating one for him physically. From the moment he set foot in England, Mr. Stein has been suffering from severe allergic reactions and an asthmatic condition so aggravated the poor lad has had considerable trouble simply breathing."

"What's caused these reactions, Dr. Gogarty?"

"Undetermined, Your Honor. The climate? The food? No one seems to know. My only alternative, as his mentor, was to arrange for him to return home."

"How do you explain his criminal negligence in writing checks for a substantial amount of money... let's see, some... two hundred and sixty pounds without having the requisite monies available in his account?"

"In his case, Your Honor, it was sheer ignorance. As Mr. Stein stated, he assumed the money necessary to cash the aforementioned checks was already available to him."

"Didn't Mr. Stein inspect his account to confirm that it was so?"

"He did not, Your Honor, and there's no question the fault lies with the boy in that respect. However, very clearly, there was no malice or fraud intended here, and Mr. Stein was, if anything, a victim of his own carelessness and irresponsibility. Perhaps Your Honor will take this into consideration, as well as the fact that his departure from this country was imminent when these unfortunate events took place. Would it be presumptuous of me, Your Honor, to request that the court consider the alternative of simply deporting rather than incarcerating this young man?"

He grimaces and says in a deeper voice, "Yes, it would be and *is* presumptuous of you. What, Dr. Gogarty, will be done to redress the grievances and losses of the aforementioned merchants victimized by Mr. Stein?"

"Your Honor, I am in possession of bank checks for each and every one of the offended parties."

"Where did this money come from?"

"Mr. Leo Stein, Frank's father, who was able to get the proper advice in regard to a transfer of funds and has wired the money directly to my account."

"Let the court clerk examine these checks and determine if they are in proper order."

The court clerk carefully matches the checks against his own list. "Yes, Your Honor, they are as the witness describes them, and duly made out to each of the parties concerned."

"Dr. Gogarty, what do you intend to do with these checks?"

*Go on a binge and run amok through the English countryside. What else?*

"Hand-deliver them to each and every offended party, Your Honor, immediately after these proceedings conclude."

"Hmm." The judge looks at the dossier and mumbles audibly. "Mmmm. Let me see. Mmm huh mm huh. Will the accused please rise?

"Well"—a crackling cough—"there seem to be no other charges laid against the boy."

Sweet Jesus, he's totally unaware of what happened at Heathrow. That's why Ferguson said to tell Stein not to mention it. Ferguson, how on earth did you manage to pull that off? I turn my head, and there's Bob in the third row. He's staring past me at the judge. I love you, Sergeant Constable Robert Ferguson. Truly love you.

The judge looks at his watch, and I reflexively glance at mine. Eleven forty-five. It's practically lunchtime. That could be to our advantage. The judge looks like he's getting bored with the case. That could help, too.

"It is the decision of this court that Mr."—he pauses to refer to the indictment—"Mr. Frank N. Stein be deported from this country as soon as it can be ascertained that the said monies are in the possession of all the offended parties in this case. Dr. Gogarty is hereby designated by this court to oversee the compensatory process. After this has been properly executed, Mr. Stein will be taken by an officer of the law to Heathrow Airport, where he will board an airplane and return to his native country. Mr. Stein's right, which is really a privilege, to visit the United Kingdom, is hereby revoked in perpetuity.

"Do you understand the sentence, Mr. Stein?"

"I do, Your Honor."

"Mr. Stein, you will remain in custody until full restitution has been confirmed. Then, your deportation will be effected immediately."

I jump up out of my seat and almost shout, but the judge's sobering stare sits me back down. Stein is crying as they escort him out of the courtroom. He turns to me and mouths a thank you through his tears.

Everyone else files out and I thread my way through the crowd searching for Ferguson, hoping to plant a big wet smacker on his cheek. Alas, he's nowhere to be found. I'd better do what they said and get back to the university later.

The merchants are dealt with one by one. By the time I get back to the department, it's after four. I'm surprised to find Mountjoy still there.

"Hey. I thought you'd be heading south by now."

"Something arose requiring my attention. But first, what's come of your dope peddler's encounter with English justice? I thought you'd be back sooner."

"I spent the afternoon groveling to disgruntled entrepreneurs and paying them off. But, guess what? Justice of sorts did prevail, meaning of course the outcome was to our benefit. As soon as the court gets confirmation that the merchants have received the money, Mary Shelley's abomination is on his way home."

"I'm relieved to hear that but must tell you there appears to be a new chapter unfolding in this melodrama."

I feel a shooting pain in my left arm. "Don't tell me Stein's escaped and is on the prowl. I can't stomach any more of him."

"Worse yet," Mountjoy says, nibbling away at his lower lip. "It involves another one of your disciples."

"O'Brien?

No?"

"A certain Gerald Gould. Rumor has it he was smoking cannabis in his room at Walcott Hall. Several students reportedly smelled marijuana in the corridor and concluded that he was the guilty party."

I let out an exasperated sigh.

"How did you find out about it?"

"Another confidante of mine, this one quite reliable, regaled me with the particulars just a few minutes ago."

"Who is this confidante?"

"Let's leave it at a close associate of mine? Another Oxford man. This chap happens to be one of the few university administrators who enjoys the confidence of the registrar. Ogden just learned of the latest situation within the last hour. He's well aware of the Stein check saga, but, thank God, not the drugs and what happened at Heathrow.

"Ogden also knows Stein was technically detached from your program before all of this unfolded. It seems he does not intend to pursue the matter if the boy is deported and there's no adverse publicity for the university. However, if these new allegations pertaining to Mr. Gould prove to be valid, I doubt that we shall be suffering your presence for very much longer."

There it is once again—the bittersweet odor of failure.

"So, this is it, huh? Australia, here I come! Where did you say you had contacts there?" I ask in all seriousness.

"I didn't, but of course I shall. At Macquarie University in New South Wales. Another Magdalen roisterer has been appointed, of all things, registrar there. Australia is a haven for outcasts and ne'er-do-wells. You should fit right in," Mountjoy says mirthfully.

I can't even smile. "What else do we know about Gould?"

"Everything revolves around whether there's enough evidence to charge him. The registrar's office is obliged to inform the constabulary of any possible criminal violations taking place on university grounds. I daresay Ferguson found out about the latest calamity when he returned from court."

"Poor Bob. He's stuck his neck out enough for me. I can't ask anything more of him."

"Don't underestimate Ferguson. He's a stout fellow and has taken a liking to you. Knowing Ferguson, he's probably addressing the matter as we speak."

"I hope so. It would be merciful to have this gloom-and-doom scenario played out as soon as possible, regardless of the outcome."

"Well, I can understand lending thought to the style of tombstone you prefer, but I wouldn't start chipping away at your epitaph yet. Here." He pours two glassfuls of Glenfiddich, slides his telephone across to me, and says, "If Ferguson's on it, he may not answer his direct line. Why not try police headquarters and see if he's available? That number is taped to the phone, underneath Ferguson's direct number."

Mountjoy points to the phone, and I reach for it and dial. A constable named D'Arcy, whose voice sounds like a recording, answers the phone.

"Detective Sergeant Robert Ferguson, please. Dr. Aloysius Gogarty here, I'm from the university. A-L-O-Y-S-I-U-S.... He's not? Could you kindly tell him that I called? Thank you very much."

No sooner have I put the receiver down than the phone rings. I reach to answer, but Mountjoy stays my hand.

"Mountjoy here.... Oh yes. Hello. Any further developments?... I understand. Yehhs. Kindly let me know the outcome.... No. I'm putting my trip on hold until this works itself out. Cheers."

He looks over at me.

"That was my confederate. Ferguson has been contacted by the registrar and the investigation is already underway. There's nothing we can do now but wait. Was there a directive from your dean about any of this?"

"You mean about Stein? Irwin's washed his hands of the matter. As you'll recall, he insisted that Stein was no longer part of the program at the time of the infraction. I don't think he wants to hear from me until everything's been dealt with."

"Leading from the rear, eh? He sounds like Sir Reginald, my great-great-granduncle."

"Oh, I meant to tell you. In Paris, Irwin made the mistake of drinking with me on the eve of the conference's official opening. We were in the hotel bar until the wee hours of the morning. Irwin was so sick the next day at the grand opening that he started it off, and finished it off, by heaving all over the honored guests on the dais." I stand up and reenact Irwin's gyrations and cataclysmic eruptions. "By the time I left, the whole damn conference was in disarray."

Mountjoy lets out another lusty laugh. "Superb! You're right: my fly gazing doesn't belong in the same conversation." The phone rings and Mountjoy answers, "Hello, Bob.... Yes. He's here. Just a moment, please." He hands over the phone.

"Hi, Bob. Give it to me straight.... Really? Are you certain? Absolutely certain?... Could you possibly hold off passing this information on to the registrar's office until, let's say, noon tomorrow? If that's too much to ask, just say so.... Great! Thank you. Thank you.

"Mountjoy, listen to this! The corridor in question at Walcott Hall has been checked out; Gould and several other students have been interrogated. There isn't one shred of credible evidence pointing in Gould's direction. In fact, there's no sign of any pot having been smoked anywhere in the residence hall, by anyone. Gould will not be brought to police headquarters and no charges will be filed against him."

"Well, my dear boy, this *is* welcome news. You must realize, however, that Ogden may, nonetheless come to the conclusion that your flock has become more a blight than a blessing, and still jettison the lot of you. My contact implied as much."

"That's why I asked Bob to buy me some time. I have an oblique stratagem in mind."

"Oblique? Hmm. That smacks of your Alexander. What do you intend to do?"

"Write a letter to Ogden, which I will hand-deliver this afternoon. About what time does he leave his office?"

"He leaves at *exactly* four forty-seven p.m., with Kantian precision."

"Well, it's about three-fifteen. I'm running over to my office to write it up now. I've got to run."

An hour later, I crumple up a fourth piece of paper and toss it into the wastepaper basket. This isn't working. I've got to go.

I poke my head into Mountjoy's office. "I'm going to tell his secretary I need to see Ogden *now*, about a matter of grave importance."

"Her name is Butterworth, Miss Butterworth. She's as cranky as a poisonous spider. Address her as if you know who she is. She'll be gratified by that, even if she doesn't show it. Butterworth may be the most important woman at the university."

"So, it would be worth my while to…uh…*butter* her up?"

He shakes his head in contempt as I scurry off to the registrar's office.

Miss Butterworth lives up to Mountjoy's description. I bow to her, as if she were an Oriental potentate. "I beg your pardon, Miss Butterworth. I'm Dr. Gogarty from the American study-abroad program. A matter of grievous importance has arisen, and it's one I thought Dr. Ogden should be informed of immediately."

Ogden's secretary stares at me and says nothing. She gets up, knocks on Ogden's door, and disappears. When Butterworth returns, she resumes her icy stare and says, "Dr. Ogden will see you when he sees you. Be seated."

"Miss Butterworth, may I ask you a question?" She frowns sternly but doesn't voice an objection. "That cameo you're wearing. It's a stunning piece of jewelry and looks as if it were handcrafted especially for you, even though it's clearly a product of the last century—the Victorian era?"

She pulls back momentarily, and then smiles while fondling the cameo.

"This? You think so? You're quite right, you know; it is Victorian. Isn't it odd that you should say such a thing about me, especially in relation to this particular piece of jewelry? You see, it's a family heirloom, and, although perhaps it's vain of me, I've always felt that it suited me best. Of course, there was little hope of ever inheriting it. I'm the youngest of four girls in the family, and it was coveted by all of my older sisters.

"To their regret, when my mother"—she pauses to collect herself—"passed away, she left a note saying I was the daughter to whom she was bequeathing the cameo." She unconsciously strokes it. "Since *I*, she said, 'was the only one who truly did it justice.' I'm afraid this caused considerable consternation within the family. But none of my sisters dared to go against *Mama's* wishes, even when she was no longer with us."

"What a fascinating story—"

The phone rings. Miss Butterworth amicably escorts me into Ogden's office and returns to her desk.

C. K. Ogden is in his early sixties and looks like an older version of Gary Cooper. He has a sturdy frame and a head of raven-black hair without the slightest trace of gray. Ogden towers over me, has an angular face, a high forehead, and an exceedingly long, thin, straight nose. He's wearing a school tie—another one unfamiliar to me.

"Dr. Ogden, I'm Aloysius Gogarty, coordinator of the American study-abroad program?"

"Yes. I know."

Another laconic Englishman. "I apologize for the intrusion. I've come to speak to you in regard to something relating to our American students here."

Ogden gestures for me to sit at a chair to the side of him. He folds his arms like a school principal about to lecture a delinquent pupil but says nothing.

"I'll come right to the point. As you may know, one of our students, who, in fact, had already left our program and been separated from the university, managed to get himself into a bit of trouble. That situation has been resolved, the grievances against him have been redressed, and the student in question will be on his way back to the States shortly. The whole affair developed rather quickly, which is why I'm only reporting it to you now. I beg your pardon for being remiss in that respect."

He stares at me, blinks once, but still, says nothing.

"However, another problem has arisen, and I'm here to apprise you, promptly this time, of the situation." No response. "To my surprise and dismay, another one of our students may have gotten himself into trouble. The boy's name is Gerald Gould. It seems rumors are circulating at Walcott Hall, where Gould resides, that some marijuana smoking has been going on. It's also been suggested Mr. Gould may have something to do with it. I must emphasize however, sir, no clear picture has yet emerged of what actually transpired. That being the case, Gould's involvement in any of this remains a moot question at present. Nevertheless, I have come here to inform you, sir, of what I intend to do should Gerald Gould prove to be guilty of any infraction, large or small."

He leans forward and winces inquisitively.

Do I have the guts to say this?

"If that should prove to be the case, I give you my word I shall pack up the entire program and take our students back to New York." I gulp in amazement at my own words.

Ogden's left eyebrow elevates a fraction, but he still says nothing. This calls for elaboration.

"From the outset I've considered myself and our students to be guests, honored guests, at your university. Stein's irresponsibility was one thing; this is quite another. Together, in my opinion, they'd constitute a breach of the hospitality you've so graciously extended to us and provide grounds for an abrogation of the agreement our two universities entered into with the best of intentions. I would, let me be clear, bear full responsibility for this course of action and duly inform my superiors of the reasons why I've done what I've done. All of this, of course, is contingent upon Gerald Gould's culpability." Steel yourself for his response.

Ogden looks at me squarely and finally speaks, "I must say, first of all, that I fully understand and generally agree with your line of argument and intended plan of action. I must also say that I am personally indebted to you for the decisive stand you've taken. Let us, however, hold it all in abeyance until we're better informed about the current state of affairs." He nods his head once, a signal for me to leave.

I make a beeline to Mountjoy's office and barge in. Out of breath, I struggle to speak. "I just informed Ogden I'll take the whole kit and kaboodle home if Gould's guilty." I slump into the chair, stick out my shaking right hand for a drink, and slap myself against the side of my head.

He pours and delivers a sherry glass filled with malt whiskey. "Well, aren't you the bold chancer? Are you comfortable with such a ballsy gambit?"

"Not at all. Ogden may go right ahead and throw us out, even when he discovers Gould is off the hook. I'll call Ferguson and see if he can get to the registrar's office *early* tomorrow morning. That'll give Ogden less time to think this through."

Mountjoy sits back with a contemplative look on his face, pauses momentarily, and then says with a smile, "There's nothing else we can do at this juncture, so what say we resort to some good old-fashioned pub-crawling?"

"Finally, a constructive suggestion," I say brightly. "What about your trip?"

"I'm putting it off, at least until this situation works itself out. Miss Popper will dream up some emergency to absolve me of any pressing obligations."

"Will she cover your base at Oxford as well?"

"Heavens, no. The lady in question was Amalia's predecessor as BEB's secretary. They are well aware of one another. Letters that my *inamorata* sends from Oxford are clearly marked 'personal and confidential,' without a return address on them. If this envelope is inadvertently opened by someone here, there's a second envelope actually containing the letter, which is also labeled 'personal and confidential.' Opening up two consecutive envelopes of this sort would require a great deal of explanation."

I ask, "What's this Oxford woman's name?"

"Georgina, you snoop. And, I might add, she has two eyes, both of which are gloriously blue. Of course, to the likes of you, that might seem rather parochial, but let me express this with unfettered clarity: I refuse to go beyond what I've just said when it comes to any physical description of her, at least with a bounder like you on the loose."

"Getting defensive, are we? Too insecure to even give me a last name? She does have a last name, doesn't she? Can I be that much of a threat?" I bat my eyes coyly.

"You, my dear boy, are a threat even when you're sleeping. Her name is Georgina Goodfellow."

"Georgina Good*fellow*?" My body begins to shake with laughter. "No wonder all this James Bond stuff. *Georgie* Good*fellow* is the *girl*? Ha!" I leap to my feet, glass in hand, and announce, "O'Brien claims you're all feminine. Hmm."

"What rubbish! And what a bumptious little man you're proving yourself to be. I'd match Georgina up against that Cuban *lusus naturae* of yours any day."

I sit down wallowing in my own smugness and brush off a few drops of malt liquor running down my jacket.

Mountjoy shakes his head derisively and leans over to refill my glass. "Has your spasm run its course?"

"For now. Oh, before I forget, can I have the name and address of your contact in Australia? I'd better start exploring other options and I'd better nail down that book contract from Oxford if I'm going to have *any* options next year."

Mountjoy checks his card file and jots down the information.

"I hope something comes of this. Australia deserves you. For now, you look like you could use a drink. What say we pay our respects at the Polish Club and then, the pubs?"

I drain my malt liquor and announce, "*Żubròwka!*"

Mountjoy takes a sip from his glass, and murmurs, "*Wyborowa.*" Then, standing erect, he raises his glass, looks up and down, and shouts, "*Ad captandum Vulgus.*"

"Did you just make that up?"

"*Please.* I'll have you know this has been my family's motto since the War of the Roses. Sir Reginald had it inscribed on his stationery. To him it meant 'throw the rabble a bone or two.' I trust that your band of aborigines wasn't impudent enough to adopt a motto of its own?"

"Underestimating us once again, eh, *old boy*? Of course, we have a motto: *Quidvis Agendum. Nimis Agendum.*"

"Hmm. If it's worth doing, it's worth *over*doing. Sounds like Blake. I'll tell you one thing: if excess is the yardstick for measuring worth in your family, you're certainly living up to their expectations. But enough of this ludic banter, Gogarty. Shall we storm the palace?"

"Take no hostages!"

## 12

I wake up with a merciless hangover and a Housman poem on my mind.

> *Oh, I have been to Ludlow Fair*
> *And left my necktie God knows where...*
> *Then the world seemed none so bad,*
> *And I myself a sterling lad...*
> *Then I saw the morning sky:*
> *Heigh-ho, the tale was all a lie;*
> *The world it was the old world yet,*
> *I was I, my things were wet...*

Mine too, but not from falling in any stream. Didn't I pick up some headache tablets along with that smelly lemon soap at the pharmacy? Here we are. Take two every four hours. Three should do it. I'll apply a cold, wet compress to my forehead and close my eyes. Think euphoric. Relief already? I scrutinize the label. Aha! There's codeine in them. And they're over-the-counter? Stock up on these magic tablets, Gogarty. I pick up the phone and dial Budgen's number.

"Yes, Frank, off to the groves of academe.... Frank, Frank, Frank. The beacon of *lux et veritas* . . . the citadel of virtue . . . the Elysian Fields . . . the university, goddamn it! . . . No, Budgen, I haven't been drinking—at least not *yet*. But a friend and I did lift a jar or two last night.... No, I haven't forsaken you. My colleague, Mr. Mountjoy, chauffeured and chaperoned me. Do you mind if we get back to the now? It's ten after nine. Can you get me to the university by ten?... Good." Shower, and change every stitch of clothing.

It takes me longer than I expect to resurrect myself. When I get downstairs, Budgen is impatiently tapping his fingers on the side of the cab.

"Sorry, Frank. School of History, please. Our eyes meet in the mirror and Budgen's squinting at me, so I squint back at him. His thick eyebrows soften, and he offers his usual half smile. "No problem, luv." He sets the car in motion and we're at the university in short order.

I knock softly and open Mountjoy's door, determined to take the offensive. "And how are you this morning, Your Lordship?"

"Rather chipper. You, on the contrary, look like something excreted from a rancid bog."

There goes my offense. "Death's second self. That was me when I woke up. I'm all right now, though, thanks to those high-test headache tablets of yours. Remind me to bring a duffle bag of them back to the States. Chipper? You drank at the same rate I did last night, didn't you?"

"You mean as if the electric chair awaited me at midnight? No. You were so preoccupied with your own guzzling that you never noticed." He clears his throat and recites:

> "*Oh, many a peer in England brews*
> *Livelier liquor than the muse—*"

To his dismay, I join in with

> "*And malt does more than Milton can*
> *To justify God's ways to man—*"

He glares me down.

> "*Ale, man, ale's the stuff to drink*

*For those fellows whom it hurts to think—"*

I intrude once again.

*"Look into the pewter pot—"*

He won't let me finish.

*"To see the world as the world's not."*

"A veritable Gilbert and Sullivan," I proclaim.

"More like Leopold and Loeb," Mountjoy intones grimly.

I ask, "Did I say or do anything outrageous last night?"

"Neither to me nor the barmaids, and respectable patrons would have nothing to do with you."

"Good. Any word yet?"

"Nothing, except Ferguson was at Ogden's office at the crack of dawn and conferred with him for a quarter of an hour. The registrar may still be deliberating with himself as to what to do, but it shouldn't be long before we hear something. Incidentally, that Fleischmann girl called my office again. You might want to attend to that."

"I apologize. They do have my number now, but back in London I made the mistake of telling them to call you directly if they had an urgent problem. A misplaced bobby pin can spark a crisis. I've decided to have a meeting with all my students here tomorrow. I'll either be telling them to pack their bags or warning them they'll be doing just that if any more transgressions occur."

His phone rings.

"Mountjoy here. Yehhs? In fact, he's here in my office." He covers the mouthpiece on the receiver while transferring it to me and whispering, "Ogden's office."

"Hello? Yes, this is Dr. Gogarty. Half eleven? I'll be there. Thank you, Miss Butterworth."

Mountjoy retrieves his phone and I explain, "I have to scoot over to my office to pick up a few things, I'll call Fleischmann from there.

Then I'll go directly to Ogden's office and wait to see him. I may be strapped into that electric chair after all."

Mountjoy grunts from the side of his mouth. "See ya. Take it easy, buddy. Remembuh who's wit ya."

"Where on earth did you pick that accent up?"

"Films and the telly, of course."

"You should stick to them as your sources for your lectures on American culture. Don't sully yourself with William James, Santayana, or T. S. Eliot."

"James had something to say; no wonder he's such an enigma to his fellow countrymen. Santayana was a fool who couldn't tell the difference between philosophy and aphorisms. Eliot was a man who wrote crossword puzzles masquerading as poems and spent most of his life anguishing over the fact that he wasn't born an English noble*woman*."

"Thanks for putting them in proper perspective for me."

"A tot of whiskey?" Mountjoy asks while pouring some into my sherry glass and then his.

I hesitate, reach, quaff it down and hurry off, arriving at my office in a halo of hurried breath. I reach for the phone.

"Hello, Marthe. I'm terribly sorry. I should've been down to see you girls already, but when I tell you what's been going on up here, I think you'll understand. What type of special problem do you have?... You need *an entire day with me?* Marthe. I'm not only taking care of nine students up here—" She interrupts to ask about the missing student. "Oh, it's Frank Stein. He became ill and had to return home." She persists about my visit to Berkshire. "Okay. I'll work it out. But I must see the other girls as well. Fair enough? No, I'm not angry. Bye."

*Don't disappoint her.*

I arrive at the registrar's office short of breath again, but am able to say, "Good morning, Miss Butterworth."

"Good morning, Dr. Gogarty," Miss Butterworth says with concern. She waves both hands up and down, telling me to slow down. With a reassuring smile, she says, "Dr. Ogden is expecting you. He requested that you be brought to him as soon as you arrive. But— *not yet!*" She makes me wait until I'm fully composed before she escorts me in to see the registrar. There's a great deal more to Miss Butterworth than I would have guessed. Treat a woman with respect and concern and watch your preconceptions disappear. That Betty Friedan was on to something in *The Feminine Mystique*.

Ogden looks at me with his customary blankness. "Oh, Dr. Gogarty, do sit down." Without changing his expression, Ogden says, "I'm most pleased to be able to convey some good news for a change."

"I love good news, sir."

"Well, the allegations concerning Mr. Gerald Gould have proven to be baseless. We were all relieved to learn that. I had a representative of the local constabulary confirm this to me in person this morning."

I put on my very best look of surprise. "Dr. Ogden, I must say how impressed I am by the fact that you were right on top of this, and able to get to the heart of the matter within such a brief compass of time."

"That, Gogarty, is what I do. And, I must say in turn, how impressed I am by the way in which you handled your role in this. I certainly did not anticipate someone in your position exhibiting such steadfast adherence to principles which might prove to be severely damaging to his own career. That's something we admire around here, Gogarty, and, I'm afraid to say, rarely witness nowadays."

"All I did, sir, was what I thought necessary under the circumstances."

"Precisely, but you did so regardless of the consequences. That, my dear fellow, deserves recognition."

"Well, sir, it's an honor and a privilege to work under your aegis."

"Yes, yes. Well, it's been a pleasure to have you here." He stands and holds out his hand. That's my cue to leave.

It's *been* a pleasure to have you here? Did Ogden just pat me on the back and bid me farewell? He must be calling my bluff. That means we're on our way home. Well, so much for ballsy maneuvers. There'll be nothing but angst and recriminations from here on in. *You're not just a failure, Aloysius. You're a colossal failure!*

Miss Butterworth stops me on the way out.

"Dr. Gogarty, don't dash off so quickly." She glances at Ogden's door to make sure it's closed. "I simply had to tell you I mentioned what you said to my sisters about the cameo being made for me. They were infuriated by it!" She giggles.

The sky's falling, but Butterworth's world couldn't be brighter. God bless her. There's always a silver lining somewhere for someone.

She carries on. "There was stunned silence on their part for several seconds, and then they started cackling among themselves about what this world had come to. Shame on me for saying this, but I can't tell you how happy I am about their reaction. Now; lean over here, please." She gives me a kiss on the cheek, blushes, and hands me an envelope marked "*Sub Rosa.*"

Still blushing, Miss Butterworth shoos me out of the office.

If this is a love letter, I'm in deeper doo-doo than I thought. I'd rather face a battalion of Frankensteins. Huh? It's a carbon copy of a letter on official stationery—Yorkshire University stationery.

*November 14, 1967*

*The University of Yorkshire*
*Yorkshire 3*
*Telephone 31711*

*From the Registrar to Dean Irwin:*
*You will undoubtedly be aware of the problems Dr. Gogarty has had with some of your students who are with us during this session. May I say at once that we entirely approve of the line of action he has taken, and indeed have been most*

*grateful for the trouble he put himself to in connection with your students.*

*The point I should particularly like to make you aware of is how successfully Dr. Gogarty has dealt with cases needing his immediate attention, and how effectively he has established and maintained contact with your students and, when necessary, various authorities inside the university who were concerned.*

*Permit me to tell you that the vice-chancellor and I are glad to have your students here and, as you should by now be aware, particularly glad to see that Dr. Gogarty has been able to come and help us. As long as men of his calibre and forthrightness are at the helm of your programme, we shall continue to welcome your students to our university.*

*My best wishes.*

*Yours sincerely,*

*Dr. C. K. Ogden*

*Registrar, University of Yorkshire*


Benjamin's balls. I'm a hero!

I barrel into Mountjoy's office. "Well, old sport, you *must* read this," I say, handing him the letter.

Without blinking he asks, "You've written your own obituary?"

"Not yet."

He reads to himself, shaking his head. "Yet another symptom of Britain's imminent demise. When Englishmen like C. K. Ogden— who was there at Dunkirk by the way—are unable to see through charlatans like you, what's still left of the empire is unlikely to survive for a thousand days, let alone a thousand years."

"I think you're congratulating me."

"You could say that. What I would like to know is how in heaven you managed to get a copy of this. You're already familiar with

Ogden's opacity, and he's not the sort to gratuitously make others privy to what he's doing."

"Let's just say I have my ways."

"Pleeasse. Don't tell me you've stooped to courting old Butterworth."

"You could say that."

Mountjoy's jaw drops. "My dear boy, you're obviously unaware of the magnitude of such an undertaking. It puts Dunkirk to shame. They may put you up for a VC."

"Huh?"

"The Victoria Cross. Who knows? Given current standards, even knighthood might not be out of the question. 'You're a better man than I, Gunga Din.' I hesitate to ask, but what depravity is next on that perverse agenda of yours?"

"I have to call Ferguson. He's the hero. I won't thank you because I noticed you were already congratulating yourself while reading Ogden's letter." I look toward him for confirmation.

Mountjoy snarls, "How uncommonly percipient of you."

I reach for the phone and dial Ferguson's number. He answers. "Bob. It's Aloysius. Where do I begin? Thank you. Thank you. Thank you. . . . Oh. Okay. I understand. Get to it. We'll be in touch soon."

I hang up and turn to Mountjoy. "He was abrupt, but that's a policeman for you. They act as if nothing's ever happened. Hear all evil, see all evil, but speak no evil." I shrug and put up my hands.

"You're spot-on. I've seen that before. He doesn't want to be reminded of anything he's done for you. If he hadn't wanted to help you, he simply wouldn't have. So, once again, what's next on your agenda?"

"Well, I still have to meet with my students. Should I ask Miss Popper about getting a room, or would you prefer to handle it?"

"I'll do it for now, but you can deal with her directly soon. She's still intimidated by you and perhaps a tad concerned about our camaraderie, but that seems to be wearing off."

"Really? She knows you well enough to call you Dickie and is naïve enough to think *I* might be a bad influence on *you*? Now I'm worried about *her*."

Mountjoy's poised for a counterattack. "Think what you wish, but do remember anyone who has taken to wooing Miss Butterworth is scarcely in a position to judge others—is he?"

"Granted, but you'll have to forgive me. I think I've fallen in love with her."

He rolls his eyes, tilts his head to the left, and announces, "You deserve one another."

"Well, the sooner the better with my charges. Let's set it up for Thursday afternoon at four. Everyone else around here is in the tearoom then so there should be a classroom available."

"What do you intend to say?"

"That the program has been placed in jeopardy by some of their fellow students, and everyone will suffer if there are *any* further violations of protocol around here. I can't be more specific, or they'll be telling mommy and daddy they're in danger of losing an entire year here. I think I can deliver a fire-and-brimstone homily without throwing them into a panic. All I'll say is we have to look out for the welfare of our brethren, and they'd better let me know if anyone's getting out of hand."

"Turn the horde upon one another under the pretext of being their brother's keeper, eh?"

"Yup. It's time to get totalitarian. Next, I have to go down south myself to see those three girls at Berkshire. I've been neglecting them."

"Is that what the Fleischmann conundrum is all about?"

"I hope so."

"Are you at liberty to embellish on that?"

"No. Because honestly, I have no idea what she has in mind."

"Why are you so concerned about whatever predicament this particular student happens to find herself in?"

"Well, with her, the odds are that this is not a run-of-the-mill student problem."

"Forgive the question"—his eyebrows rise—"but have you had any dealings with her otherwise?"

"On one occasion, but not exactly what you might imagine."

"Whatever that may have been, Aloysius, it was momentous enough to leave you solicitous in your responses to her."

"Well, Miss Popper is obviously infatuated with you. How did you handle *that* situation?"

"By telling Amalia that my wife was likely to commit suicide if she ever suspected that anything at all was taking place between us. Thus, I said—tearfully, by the way—that I had no choice but to act like any gentleman would under the circumstances and detach myself. Amalia agreed and reassured me she couldn't live with the thought of having another woman's blood on her hands."

"Would your wife really have killed herself?"

"Heavens, no. She would have killed *me*. So, is this Fleischmann similarly disposed towards you?"

"Thank God, no. It appears I was just a means to an end."

The phone rings and Mountjoy answers.

"Mountjoy here.... Yes, Miss Fleischmann. In fact, he's sitting here in my office at the present moment.... Of course; hang on please; here we are." He sticks out his tongue and clutches his throat as if he's gagging. Then he starts gagging for real.

I put my hand over the receiver until Mountjoy regains control of himself. "Hello, Marthe, good to hear from you.... Yes, in fact I'm coming down to see all three of you in a couple of weeks. Make that December first and second, for certain. You'll make sure the other girls are available, Okay?... Thank you. Bye."

Mountjoy studies me. "That didn't sound so bad."

"Fleischmann wants a whole day from me. She didn't spell it out, but implied '*or else!*'"

"Well. That casts a rather different light on things, doesn't it? Why on earth would she insist on a whole day with you?" He looks up, raises his index finger, and smiles lasciviously.

A knock at the door rescues me from the impending assault. Miss Popper has a telegram in hand, which she delivers to me and then leaves.

As I tear open the envelope, Mountjoy blurts out, "Well?"

"Here it is: 'NEW YORK NOVEMBER 14 1967 STOP RECEIVED A TELEPHONE CALL FROM THE AMERICAN VICE-CONSUL IN LIVERPOOL STOP INFORMED ME YOU WERE DEALING WITH SOME STUDENT PROBLEM STOP DOESN'T CONCERN ANYONE PRESENTLY IN THE PROGRAM DOES IT STOP CLARIFY AT YOUR EARLIEST CONVENIENCE STOP DEAN FRANCIS IRWIN STOP.'"

Mountjoy comments, "He obviously doesn't know and doesn't want to know the gruesome details."

"Well, Ogden's letter will supply all the answers he's going to get from me. In the meantime, I have to wire a response of some sort. I think I'll give that tub of guts something to anguish over until he hears from Ogden. Is it Okay if I ask Amalia to send him an answer?"

Mountjoy telephones Miss Popper, gets approval, and passes the phone back to me.

I say, "Here's the way I'd like it to read: 'DEAR DEAN IRWIN STOP SITUATION RESOLVED THROUGH MASTERFUL DIPLOMACY STOP SIGNED ALOYSIUS T GOGARTY STOP'... Yes, that's it. Really, that's it.... Thank you so much. Bye."

Mountjoy looks surprised at my brazen phraseology. "So now it's Manolete working close to the horns, eh?"

"I couldn't resist it. He's such a—"

"Pillock? Well, I'll have you know, old boy, I witnessed Manolete perform the Manoletina in Spain when I was sixteen years old. A year or so later, which would make it 1947, Islero gored him in the upper leg and they were never able to stop the bleeding. Every man, woman, and child in Spain mourned the great matador for three days. How many will weep for you?"

"No one in Spain, that's for sure. Come to think of it, as far as I know only one."

"Don't look at me," Mountjoy protests.

"No. No. Not you! Budgen. That is, if I still owe him for the month."

Mountjoy smiles in acknowledgment.

# 13

---

The rain batters away at the window during my train trip to Berkshire. Every minute of it is spent imagining what Marthe has in store for me. Nothing I can think of sounds appealing. It's a good thing I brought my umbrella and raincoat. This is torrential. I step out onto the platform and see a young woman underneath a large crimson umbrella waving at me. She looks familiar.

"Marthe? Is that you?" It's her all right, but she's wearing purple lipstick and there's a sheen to her hair. A single braid dangles down from the right side of her head—Bohemian style. Look at those nails. They're talon-like and the same shade of purple as her lipstick. I hope this has nothing to do with me.

"Yes indeed, Dr. Gogarty. It's Fleischmann here."

"You took me by surprise."

"You did specify December first and second as the days of your visit, and I surmised you might arrive today on an early afternoon train, so I've been waiting for you. I've taken the liberty of *sheduling* a meeting with the other girls back at our residence hall tomorrow morning at half nine. I do hope that proves to be convenient for you."

Listen to that accent. "You've really gone native, haven't you? What's the old adage? 'Speak British and think Yiddish.'"

"I believe it's 'Dress British and think Yiddish.' In regard to pronunciation, in my case it's simply a matter of reclaiming a portion of my lineage. My family spent a great deal of time here in England before leaving for America."

"Oh, I see. I was hoping I could collect all three of you girls today and head back to Yorkshire later on, or early tomorrow. Do you think that's possible?"

She scowls. "Absolutely not. Surely you recall I claimed an entire day for myself out of the two days you were *supposed* to set aside for us."

"Oh, yes. Sorry I forgot about that. So much has been happening up at Yorkshire that it slipped my mind."

"Well, my mind's not so slippery. Let's go and get some tea and scones at Finn's Hotel, shall we? It's not far from here."

"Uh... all right. Marthe, I see you have a traveling bag. Where are you off to?"

"Utopia."

"Utopia?"

"The Greek meaning of the word."

"Oh, you mean nowhere? You're off to nowhere? Then, why the luggage?"

Marthe ignores the questions and leads me into the hotel. We sit down at a table in the bar area. She gestures to the woman behind the bar to get her attention and asks her to bring our order.

"How did she know what our order would be?"

"I was here earlier. I told Nora to have it ready for us."

This is strange. But then again, so is she. We take off our raincoats. Look at Marthe. Nausicaä comes of age. Her skirt is slightly above her knees, and her sweater is tight and revealing.

*Disengage.*

On the other hand, I can't afford to alienate her.

"My, don't you look nice. You've made some alterations to your appearance."

"Your first name is Aloysius, isn't it?" Marthe asks. "I put you down as Albert. I hope it doesn't offend you, but I'm going to refer to you in that fashion under the present circumstances."

"Huh? Uh... Okay, but it might be wise to observe some formalities when we're with Ellen and Alicia. Agreed?"

126

"Certainly. But right now, it's different. Let me explain."

"Please do."

"Well, first of all, the good news. You see the lecturer in my Beowulf and Old Norse classes, who happens to be my advisor here, has taken a personal interest in me, as I hoped he would. I trust that doesn't alarm you?"

"Well, no, I guess not. These things happen. Let's just hope it doesn't create any major problems for either of you. Some degree of prudence is called for in the academic world."

She snickers at my hypocrisy but responds in conciliatory fashion. "I understand."

This calls for clarification. "I'm merely suggesting that complications could conceivably put either or both of you at risk. You wouldn't want to imperil anyone's academic career."

"I wouldn't dream of doing that to *him*. I love the man and plan to marry him."

You wouldn't dream of doing it to yourself either. What about me? Oh, that's a different story.

"Why are you telling me this? I should think the less I know, the better for you and the gentleman in question."

"There are certain things you ought to be aware of. First of all, his name is Lionel Blum, and he comes from a distinguished Jewish family that fled Vienna to get away from the Nazis. Lionel attended King's College, Cambridge, where he earned a triple first in medieval Germanic languages."

She's looking for a reaction, so I oblige her. "I'm impressed. He's quite the match for you."

"Yes and no. Lionel was born here and has become so secularized that he's on the brink of abandoning his Jewish heritage altogether."

"Well, you seem to be changing too."

"This"—she indicates the length of her body with both hands—"is a facade and nothing more than ephemeral. You see, Lionel's so hostile towards traditional religion I doubt he would've shown the slightest interest in me had I retained my customary mien."

"So, you're setting a trap for him?"

"You could say that, but it's with a noble objective. I intend to marry the man and bring him back to the religion of his ancestors."

"How do you hope to accomplish that?"

"Initially, through some temporary external changes and the acquisition of skills that he, being the type of man, he is at present, is drawn to."

"Look, Marthe, the less you tell me about this the better."

The tea and scones arrive, and Nora leaves.

"You must be informed. You're the silent partner in my plan."

"Me? Now you're making me nervous. I—"

"I'm afraid there's no choice here."

I spring to my feet. "Look, let me scoot out to the university and see the other two. That'll give you enough time to think this over and, hopefully, make a more considered decision."

She stares intensely at me for a moment, and then says, "Sit down!"

After I'm seated, Marthe continues. "I've already thought this through, and I'm certain this is the best way to go about it. If you disagree, I'm afraid I'll have to resort to an alternative I'm not at all eager to pursue."

"Oh?"

"Yes. If necessary, I'm prepared to send a letter to Dean Irwin informing him of our brief interlude at the end of last term."

I let out a sigh of resignation and raise both hands in surrender. "Okay, Marthe. You're in charge."

"I thought you might see it that way. I don't like adopting Machiavellian tactics, but the stakes are too high for me not to. It's unlikely I shall ever cross paths with someone like Lionel Blum again, and I have no intention of missing out on the opportunity. I'll elaborate on this upstairs."

"Upstairs?"

"Yes. Upstairs. I'll ask Nora to take our tea and scones up to our room."

"*Our* room?"

"Yes. Our room. I've told her you're my fiancé and confided in her that we're having a little tête à tête here. You see, you're in on a very brief visit from America."

"Oh, lovely. What other surprises do you have planned for me?"

"A few. But trust me, nothing to be fearful about. Would you mind carrying my bag?"

"Uh, sure." God, it's heavy. There's probably a flail and a mace in here to teach me a lesson. I dutifully walk in Marthe's footsteps, and Nora trails after us with her tray. She carefully places the tea and scones on a small round table near the window and inspects a bottle of champagne on the nightstand next to the bed. No ice. Nora pockets the pound note I place in her hand, glances back at us with a salacious grin, and closes the door.

Marthe says, "Sit down, Albert. No! There on the bed. I'll sit in this chair in the meantime, so I can explain what this is all about. But first, let me give you a drink." She pours a large tumble glass of champagne for me and a thimbleful for herself. "The rest of this"—she points to the bottle—"is yours. What I have here will suffice for me."

"The fatted calf? Abraham's Isaac?" I say meekly.

"Nothing of the sort. Surely you remember Eve in the Garden of Eden; Delilah with Samson; Bathsheba and David."

"I know one thing. I'm neither Adam nor Samson nor David, and a far cry from Solomon."

"Let's get something straight. None of this is for you. It's for Lionel."

"Lionel?" I jump up and look under the bed, and she laughs in an almost human way. I'm hoping my antics help alter her mood and intentions. They don't.

"No, no, no. Sit down. You see," she explains, "I've only had quasi-sexual experiences consisting of that brief dalliance with you and one unfortunate comedy of errors in the back seat of Avi Goldberg's Buick. There, Avi awkwardly, and for the most part unsuccessfully, attempted to poke away at me. Thus, I am anything but a *virtuosa* in this area. That simply won't do for someone as sophisticated as Lionel.

"I'm well aware that women in the Bible are often depicted as seductive instruments through which otherwise good men are undone. However, my intention is to reverse the process by employing my sexual attributes to slowly but surely reel him back into the fold. To achieve that objective, I've decided to master the art of love in its erotic manifestation. And you, Albert, are the vehicle through which I intend to accomplish that."

"You mean—?"

"Men have suffered worse fates." Marthe lifts her valise up onto the bed, unzips it, and takes out a movie projector and a roll of film. No wonder it's so heavy! She reaches in and removes a book whose pages are marked off at various intervals with numbered index cards.

"Here, I want you to study this."

Marthe hands me the book and a whiff of her perfume assails me. It's saccharine-sweet and even more repulsive than Irwin's cologne.

"The *Kama Sutra*?" I ask in utter astonishment.

She ignores my concern and says, "I have seven sections marked off. Before we finish here, I want to have mastered each and every one of them. I'm going across the street to the pub to get you a few sandwiches. You may need additional nourishment. I'll be back presently."

How in God's name do I get out of this—alive?

Marthe points to my glass as she leaves, and I dutifully sip at it. The champagne is flat and tepid. You'd better read the damn book. She's likely to give you a pop quiz when she gets back. Let's see. Penetrating the Eye, The Gazelle and the Stallion, The Pivot. Driving the Nail Home, The Door Ajar... what makes her think that I'm the right man for this? I haven't been comfortable with a woman since Deborah. Renée took me by surprise and there was no need for any focus on my part. One thing's certain: I'm anything but a stud, and she's no Circe.

*Make a break for it and face the consequences later.* Which way is the staircase? There it is. Holding onto the banister, I hop down the staircase at breakneck speed, only to come to a screeching halt when I see Marthe glaring up at me from the ground floor. She puts down the package she's holding, opens up her pocketbook, and takes out a stamped envelope. Waving it at me, Marthe declares, *"This* is addressed to Dean Irwin."

I turn around and trudge upstairs like a zombie. Back in the room, Marthe acts as if nothing's just happened.

"Here's some sandwiches and beer." She points to the book and asks, "How does it seem to you?"

"Challenging."

"I'll turn around. *You* will undress yourself and climb into bed." She glances at the wall across from the bed and sets up the film projector. After a few mishaps, she has the film all set to go. "I'm going to prepare myself in the loo, and I've got something for you to look at in the meanwhile."

Marthe lifts black mesh stockings and purple lingerie out of her valise. She flips the switch on the projector and heads for the bathroom. It's an adult film. She's thought of everything.

This is supposed to arouse me, but it's not working. I was half loaded when she came to my office and much easier prey then. Not now. This is wrong, and you're bound to make a fool of yourself. You can't go through with this. What were those words? *Vow with conviction never to let this happen again.* What can be done? *Use your brain. It's the only useful organ you have right now.* Where's the hotel stationery? There it is. Scribble a note.

*December 1, 1967*
*Dear Marthe,*
*I have no choice but to tell you something I've haven't told a*
*living soul. A medical problem arose over the summer as a*
*result of which my equipment (that part of the anatomy crucial*
*to your plan) has been rendered temporarily dysfunctional. As*

*you can well imagine, this is a most distressing situation for me. I can only hope and pray that you'll understand how upset I am over this and forgive me for lacking the courage to explain it to you face-to-face. I am genuinely sorry for disappointing you in this respect.*
*Albert*

I wonder if she'll believe me. No matter. Throw your clothes back on and bolt. The toilet flushes. *Hurry.* She's about to emerge. Quickly, but quietly, I slide the window open, climb out onto the fire escape, and hastily close the window. Descending stealthily, I soon find myself wandering down a myriad of alleyways trying to get my bearings. Finally, I stumble onto the main thoroughfare and a passerby points me toward the train station.

Good. There's a public phone here. I let the huffing and puffing subside before calling Ellen and Alicia. They say they're doing very well and have no need for a personal conference. God bless uncomplicated people.

I need to shake myself loose from this travesty. There's a choice here, isn't there? I can fret and sulk and head back to Yorkshire, or, like Alexander, turn a calamity into an opportunity. But how can *I* do it? First, steady your nerves and then bring your head back to where your feet are. Now think. Nothing . . . wait . . . there's an idea! Let's see what they say at the ticket office.

"I beg your pardon sir, does the train on the opposite side go to Oxford?" He nods. I thought so. "Thank you. A one-way ticket to Oxford, please." He repeats my request as a question. I answer, "Yes, *one way.*" It's a short distance and too tempting to resist.

There's a pay phone with a local directory at the Oxford station. Let's see. Nope, there's no one with her name in the phone book. Give Mountjoy's alma mater a shot. "Hello, Magdalen College? School of History, please. Yes, may I speak with Miss Georgina Goodfellow? Dr. Gogarty from Yorkshire University.... Yes, thank you, I'll hold on."

"Miss Goodfellow?" Jumping Jesus, it worked! "It's Aloysius Gogarty, I'm a friend of . . . you know about me? I'm sort of in and out of Oxford and I was wondering if it's possible for me to say hello to you in person, perhaps over a drink or a late lunch? . . . Marvelous. I'm a stranger to Oxford, can you suggest a restaurant? . . . Got it. The Mitre on High Street. I'll be outside wearing a mackintosh, a black beret and small round sunglasses. I'm very much looking forward to meeting you. Bye."

Hailing a taxi proves an easy task and I'm at the Mitre in just a few minutes. Probably best to wait by the door. Before long I focus on a young woman who's looking in my direction. She greets me with a warm, engaging smile. Georgina's tall, but not imposingly tall, and has the legs of a thoroughbred. There's a blond tint to her hair, and both eyes are blue all right. Well done, Mountjoy.

"Hi. I'm Aloysius Gogarty. What a pleasure to meet you."

She continues to smile as we enter the restaurant. The receptionist greets us, and we're directed to a table.

"You look a little frazzled, Aloysius Gogarty."

"Well, I've just spent time with some American students at Berkshire, and I'm sure you know how trying students can be."

"I most certainly do. Yours, however, are more taxing than most— or so I've heard. Having a trying time of it, are we?"

"American students are brilliant at manufacturing mayhem."

"Don't underestimate the English in that respect. I could curl your hair with a few tales about our Magdalen 'men'."

"Well, if Richard's any example, you need not elaborate. He must have been quite a rip in his college days."

"I suppose so. Mercifully, I was a little girl when he was bounding about at Oxford. I'm grateful that by the time we met he'd acquired a semblance of maturity. When I hear of students like your Frankenstein, most of what I encounter at Magdalen seems rather vapid."

"Stein's been quite the challenge. Without Richard's advice and counsel, I may have wound up in the hoosegow myself."

With a smile on her face she asks, "Hoosegow?"

"Jail. It doesn't surprise me that—" Our waiter appears and stands there poised to take our order.

Georgina says, "Yes; I'd like to try your beef Wellington and Yorkshire pudding. I'll have a Babycham to go with it."

"I'll have the same," I say, "except for the Babycham. I'll have a tall gin and tonic instead.... Oh yes, with ice, please. Three or four cubes of ice in a large glass, if you would, and don't skimp on the gin. Thanks."

He retreats, and Georgina picks up on the conversation. "Well, it's actually a surprise to me Richard has taken a liking to you; it's rare for him. He may seem gregarious, but he's actually quite the loner."

"I can identify with that."

"I'll tell you what he likes about you. It's your candor and quicksilver wit. Knowing Richard, your humor must be of the sarcastic variety."

"I'm afraid so."

"An alumnus of the college where I work once said sarcasm is the lowest form of wit."

"Oscar Wilde. Yes, but he also said it's 'the highest form of intelligence'."

"See that. Richard always has to have the last word, too. Anyway, you two are kindred spirits, and that makes you the type of chap the rest of us, particularly ladies, have to be wary of. Richard has entertained me with some particulars of your saga at Yorkshire, and, I must say, it's something of a classic."

She pauses and says apologetically, "Forgive me if I appear to be too familiar in my conversation. It's unlike me, but through Richard's letters I feel I know you rather well."

"I'm not offended in the least. In fact, I'm gratified by it. He speaks so highly of you I feel like I know you as well." Untrue; but I can see why he's hesitant to supply details about this woman.

"Really, what does he say?"

"Well, he's described you to a T. He's said you're exceptionally attractive, sophisticated, well spoken, that you cut an impressive figure in tastefully-chosen outfits, and you're one of those rare women who enjoys a story well told."

The beef Wellington arrives and rescues me from further embellishment.

"Once again," Georgina says, "you're just like Richard. Sitting there spouting outright lies with a straight face. You two are clearly birds of a feather."

I put my hands up and say, "Busted!"

The word takes Georgina by surprise, and she unleashes a salvo of Yorkshire pudding in my direction that winds up decorating my tie. Both of us laugh fitfully, drawing the attention of everyone around us. Georgina blushes and covers her mouth with her napkin to regain her composure. We both settle down and eat heartily without speaking.

After chatting about Oxford and the weather, Georgina searches for her handbag and finds it. "Well, this has been lovely. I'm afraid I must be off. Long day ahead today."

I offer to escort her in a taxi.

"No, thank you. I enjoy walking." She stops for a minute, and then puts her things back down.

"Oh, before I forget. Let me finish this." Georgina settles back down in her chair, takes out two sheets of stationery on which she's already written, and scribbles a few more lines. She carefully places the letter in an addressed envelope and prints "personal and confidential" in large block letters on the front of the envelope. Then she takes out a slightly larger envelope, also addressed, and labels it "personal and confidential." The smaller envelope is carefully deposited inside the larger one and she hands me the finished product.

"But," I remind her, "there's no postage on it."

"I was hoping you would hand-deliver this to Richard."

When I've processed what she's said I respond eagerly, "Nothing would please me more."

Georgina kisses me on the cheek and scurries off.

I think I'll go back to London, do a little work at the British Museum, and spend a few days there without even thinking about students. I'll head for the Russell, see some sites, have a few drinks, and recharge the batteries.

But when I get back to Yorkshire, *have I got a surprise for you, Your Lordship!*

# 14

"Sooooooh," Mountjoy bellows, "were you able to service those young ladies to their satisfaction?"

"Which ones?"

"Your students, my dear boy. Why, were you servicing others as well?"

"I'll give you a proper report shortly. As far as my students are concerned, let's just say I escaped. For now, and I hesitate to ask, what's been happening here?"

"Well, first of all, Amalia has delivered another telegram for you from New York which arrived while you were away." He shuffles the telegram across his desk.

"You could have opened it up. If I've been fired, it would be nice to know."

"I felt no sense of urgency"—he points toward the envelope—"at least from what you've told me thus far. Besides, we happen to respect privacy in this country, unless directed to do otherwise by the party in question. Open the blasted thing."

I glance at it and turn it back over to Mountjoy without comment.

He reads out loud. "'NEW YORK STOP DECEMBER 6 1967 STOP WILL COME TO ENGLAND IF YOU NEED ASSISTANCE STOP PLEASE ADVISE STOP.' Signed by your feckless leader. How frightfully considerate of him. May I offer some *explication de texte*?"

"Do I have a choice?"

"No. It seems your dean has been informed by the vice-consul that all concerns here have been adroitly attended to by you, and, as of now, nothing remains to be done. Of course, he's willing to *visit* England since no perilous predicaments await him here. I'd be inclined to discourage him. He strikes me as a buffoon capable of undoing the goodwill you've created."

"That makes sense, but why do you assume his information came from the vice-consul? Did he call Irwin *again*?"

"It could be Ogden's letter. That's true. However, I never assume anything. I was told so by the vice-consul himself. His name, by the way, is John Woolsey."

"Why does that name sound familiar to me?"

"I have no idea. Nevertheless, he rang yesterday, hurling superlatives at you with embarrassing monotony, while enquiring if you were available to share a meal with him in Liverpool. He also mentioned that he called your dean and informed him of how impressed he's been with you. So yes, he did call Irwin again—this time to sing your praises."

"He told you all this?"

"He may have thought he knew me or should know me. In Liverpool my name is displayed on street signs, historic buildings, and, for all I know, public toilets as well. Not even an American vice-consul could remain unmindful of its ubiquity. It's probably because of this he exhibited a trace of diplomatic sensibility by extending an invitation to me as well."

Mountjoy opens the palm of his hand in my direction, awaiting my reaction.

"I don't know about you, but this would be a good time for me to travel. Apparently, everything around here shuts down a week or so before Christmas, and my students will be scattering in all directions for the next month or so. Besides, in person, I might be able to wangle a letter out of the vice-consul that could give me a boost as far as the tenure situation is concerned. Well, are you interested in going?"

"I suppose I could. I owe M'mah a visit, and you'd be an alibi for not being able to spend a great deal of time with her."

"That bad, huh?"

"Worse. Case in point: one day an evangelical missionary had the temerity to venture onto the estate. He knocked on the front door. 'Yehhhhs?' M'mah said, in tones that would freeze Mount Vesuvius in the midst of an eruption. 'Christ has sent me,' this fellow announced. Without hesitation, M'mah replied, 'I doubt that very much.' Perplexed, the poor chap asked, 'Why do you say that?' M'mah responded, 'Because he would have mentioned it to me.' The missionary promptly turned and left, muttering to himself about how the Good Lord makes witnesses out of the most unlikely of his children.

"Tell me, Aloysius, is your beloved mater of the same ilk?"

"I'll never know. She died giving birth to me."

"Well, that spared her a great deal of grief, didn't it? And... your father?"

"Dead too, but on a voluntary basis."

Mountjoy looks concerned. "By his own hand?"

"In a way. He was a captain in the New York City Fire Department and always insisted on being the lead man on the hose when they charged into a burning building. He did it once too often. An apartment roof collapsed on him. All of the other firemen survived unscathed."

Mountjoy raises his eyebrows and says, "So, he too was a hero. In fact, he sounds a bit like your Alexander."

"I suppose you could say that, but I was in my early teens at the time and would have preferred a cowardly father who was still there for me. I think of his death as a glorified suicide. It may be just as well, though. If he didn't die a hero, he probably would've drunk himself to death. They say I have his voice. People are always telling me I'm my father's son."

"Is that why you wear so much black?"

"It could be. I never thought about it. What about... ?" I point toward his wife's picture.

"Her Ladyship and our trip? She wouldn't be caught dead in Liverpool; especially since M'mah resides in the area. You see, those two are of the same stripe, self-absorbed and contentious. I must be back here for Boxing Day, however."

"Boxing Day? So that's how you keep your marriage fresh and exciting, huh? An annual fistfight with Her Ladyship. I'll bet the smart money is on... " I point in the direction of his wife's photograph.

Mountjoy nods in agreement and says, "As well it should be. But that's not the situation you fatuitous featherbrain. It's the day after Christmas, when we English exchange unwanted and inappropriate gifts. I must be there to heap lavish praise on Priscilla for her tasteless duck and hideous presents while tiptoeing around our vacuous conversation. I'm obliged to play the same ludicrous game on New Year's Eve. You see, we host an annual dinner party on that occasion attended by several influential members of the department, including BEB and Somerset. You might consider coming yourself."

"Somerset—I forgot all about him. I'd better stop by his office. And your mention of Christmas reminds me—I have to send Elena a Christmas card. I want her to keep me in mind."

"While you're at it, Edinburgh called again to remind you of your appointment in January with the registrar. Those Scots are odious little creatures with the tenacity of a pit bull."

"After all the abuse you English heaped on them, I should think they're entitled to their own brand of quirkiness."

"Touché. Which reminds me; that vile O'Brien boy called again. I said you've been trying to reach him at his residence hall, but no one ever seems to know where he is. And, believe it or not, that feculent facsimile of a human being had the audacity to laugh at *me*. Can you imagine? An *O'Brien* acting snippy with an English gentleman?"

"Unimaginable; unless you take into consideration that this particular boy is, after all, a direct descendant of Brian Boru, King of Ireland. Even *I* know royal blood trumps the minor gentry."

"Yehhhs. Royal blood in this case, tracing its origins back to some barbaric chieftain sporting a bone through his nose. Didn't that Boru chap wind up being hacked to death?"

"Yup, by Vikings. He was killed at Clontarf, where the Irish beat the bejesus out of them *and* their inept British accomplices."

Mountjoy counters: "Did you know Jonathan Swift claimed Ireland was the most disagreeable place in Europe?"

"Did *you* know Jonathan Swift was the most disagreeable *man* in Europe?"

"History bores me. What's happening with that Fleischmann girl? Did you manage to sort it out?"

"Not really. It turns out that Marthe is quite taken with some lecturer at Berkshire. All I can do is hope and pray it doesn't amount to a scandal. She's an insistent young lady."

"What's the victim's name?'

"Blum, Lionel Blum. Familiar to you?"

"No, but he certainly sounds like someone who deserves her. I do have some contacts at Berkshire and can look into this if you'd like."

"I don't think so. I'm afraid the more involved I am, the worse the situation will get."

"You could've assumed the conventional posture and advised her against such action on moral grounds."

"You think I'm capable of such unconscionable mendacity?"

"Without question."

"It's time to strike.

"By the way, I picked up some mail for you."

"Really? I thought I'd collected everything. What have you got there?"

"A letter." *Let it sink in.*

"Let's see... hang on. This resembles Georgina's handwriting. Something's off the mark here. There's no postage on this envelope.

How... ? *You bastard!* What sort of perfidy have you resorted to now?"

"Nothing malicious. In fact, I spent most of my time singing your praises. I think she tacked on an explanatory note at the end."

"Bastard."

"You said that already."

Mountjoy's finger guides him as he reads further.

He grimaces and says, "Georgina states you are *simply charming* and tells me not to worry because the two of you did *nothing wrong.* Nothing wrong? What did you do right?"

"I spread goodwill. That's what goodwill ambassadors do. And there's a simple and honest explanation." He glowers at me.

"I had a very unsatisfactory visit to Berkshire, thanks to Miss Marthe Fleischmann, and when I realized how close I was to Oxford, I said to myself, what a nice gesture it would be for me to pay my respects."

"How quaint. Let me put you on notice, dear boy. I'm prepared to reciprocate by paying my personal and, I daresay, accomplished respects to your cross-eyed Madonna."

"Go right ahead. In the meantime—"

"Quiet. Let me read the rest of this. Hmm. You don't seem to have broken the spell I've cast over her." He smiles broadly in my direction.

I ask, "Should we call the vice-consul?"

He hands me the phone. "No; *you* should. Mid-December is suitable for me."

I dial, and a secretary with an American accent answers the phone.

"Hello. Dr. Gogarty here from Yorkshire University. I understand the vice-consul would like to see me.... I'll hang on.... December sixteenth for lunch at twelve? That's perfect. Mr. Woolsey also expressed interest in meeting my colleague at Yorkshire University, Mr. Richard Tarleton Mountjoy.... Excellent. He'll be there, too. Thank you. Bye."

I turn to Mountjoy as I hang up the phone, "All set, Your Lordship."

"Yehhhs. That should work out well. If we stay for just a day or so, it'll afford me the opportunity to make a trip to Oxford before Christmas. I'll do the driving to Liverpool, and on the way, I can fill you in on some members of the department. A few of them may be of use to you at one time or another. For now, lest you forget, your dearly beloved führer queried you in his wire. Shouldn't you respond?"

I nod. He calls Miss Popper and hands the phone back to me.

"Hello, Amalia. Would you be willing to send another telegram to New York? Yes, to Dean Irwin. Just say, 'NO STOP'." I pause, as if I'm finished.

Mountjoy furrows his brow in objection.

I continue. "BUT THANK YOU FOR YOUR CONSIDERATION AND GENEROUS SUPPORT STOP SIGNED ALOYSIUS T GOGARTY STOP."

"Thanks again, Miss Popper. Bye."

Mountjoy sighs. "That's a relief. I was concerned for a moment how you might address him."

"How about, '*Dear Posterior Rectal Orifice*'?"

"That should get his attention."

"I'd better get going. Two more stops, Somerset and O'Brien. Sounds like a law firm."

"Not here, my dear boy. Not here."

# 15

---

I knock on Somerset's door and, without even knowing who's knocking, he grumbles, "What do you want?" When I identify myself, he says, "Oh, it's *you.*" He opens the door, takes out his watch, and announces, "I have *drei minuten.*"

"Sorry to disturb you. I just wanted to say hello and see how you were."

"Well, I'm surviving, which is a miracle in and of itself around here. What have you found out about American universities for me?"

"Well, I teach at Municipal College, which is part of the New York city university system."

"Never heard of it. Where else?"

"I have a master's degree from Columbia and know some people there, and a PhD from the University of Southern California."

"I've heard of Columbia. I might consider going there."

"I also have contacts at Harvard."

"Harvard? That's good. I want that or Columbia."

I say, "You would fit in comfortably at both places," while I'm thinking: *even more so at Creedmoor*. "I'll pursue this and see vat... uh... what I can do. Have you, by any chance, taken a look at my manuscript yet?"

"I have. It's good, except for those *shtupid* quotations of yours. Take them out and you've got something worthwhile."

Did he say *worthwhile*? That's huge from him.

Somerset adds, "I had a phone call from some Oxford editor. He wanted to know if you were reliable with your *Alexander der Große*. I told him I was reading your book, and I'd call him back when I finish it."

"Oh, okay."

"What did you say you were doing about Columbia *und* Harvard?"

Tell him what he wants to hear. "I've already contacted Harvard, and I'll write to the Columbia people today."

"Then I'll call Oxford when you leave, which"—he looks at his watch—"is now."

"Must you say something to them about the quotations in my book?"

"How do the possibilities look for me at Harvard?"

"I'd say excellent. What I've heard is very encouraging."

"Then I don't know what you mean about quotations. I will talk only about the history in your book, which is *sehr gut*."

He suddenly stands, and I mechanically follow suit. The next thing I know, he's ushering me out of his office and slamming the door behind me.

I turn around facing the closed door and say, "Thank you, Professor. Goodbye for now." He'd fit right in at Harvard. They say there's a wrench to fit every nut there.

I think I'll stroll over to O'Brien's dorm and see if I can surprise him. He's on the second floor. What's his room number? I walk down the corridor looking for a clue. Aha! Here's one's with an Irish flag on it. I knock, and O'Brien opens the door.

"What are *you* doing here?" he asks through squinting eyes.

O'Brien's got books on the floor, books on the bed, books on the table, books on the windowsill, books everywhere.

"Well, James, it's a pleasure to see you as well. Maybe I was misinformed, but I was told *you* were seeking *me* out."

"True. I tried to contact you without any luck. I assumed you were too busy ingratiating yourself with our hypocritical hosts to spare time for one of your own."

"Not so. Some of those 'hypocrites' have given me advice that's kept our ship afloat. You heard what I said at the meeting."

"It's a smoke screen. They're disarming you with their genteel manners. Have you noticed what's happening with the other kids in our group? They're all starting to talk like fags."

I'll throw a dose of Mountjoy at him. "Ehhh, I say, my dear boy, you mean er, ah, er, ah, like cigarettes?"

He guffaws. "You got it. Well, maybe there is some hope for you. There *ought* to be with a name like Gogarty."

"Not necessarily. What's happening? Are your classes going all right?"

"They're stressful. Whenever they mention the Irish, they do so in a condescending way. It's all I can do to stop myself from taking their lecture notes and shoving them up their 'arses.' The trouble is they'd probably enjoy it."

"How can I be of help?"

"I'm going to Ireland for about a month and may be back after classes start up. Could you speak to my instructors about this?"

"Why don't you tell them yourself?"

"I'm afraid if they give me one of those snotty down-the-nose looks, I'll uncork one and deck the sonofabitch."

"What are you up to in Ireland?"

"Up to? You sound like one of *them*."

"Easy does it, Jamesy boy. Don't get rambunctious with *me*."

"Sorry, Doc—just kidding."

"You'd better be. So, what's your itinerary like?"

"Family in Cork. Kiss the stone. See some folks on the West Coast. Dublin for a week."

"A whole week in Dublin?"

"I'll be up and down the Liffey and in and out of every Joycean nook and cranny from the Martello tower to Glasnevin Cemetery. I'll track down as many references from *Ulysses* as I can."

"You're serious, aren't you?"

"Dead serious."

"Well, we do have something in common. I happen to be an admirer of Joyce as well. He seems like an odd favorite for you, though. Didn't he call Ireland 'the old sow that eats her farrow'?"

"He was going through an identity crisis. At heart he was a patriot and despised the Brits."

"You think so?"

Before he can respond, there's a short knock on the door, and, without waiting for an answer, two burly young men in paint-splattered overalls jostle their way into the room. I spring to my feet and instinctively clench my fists.

O'Brien intercedes. "*Easy*, Dr. Gogarty. These are friends." When they hear my name, they smile.

"Dr. Gogarty, this is James Carey and James Fitzharris."

"Well, hello there," says Carey amiably. He's got the map of Ireland all over his face.

Fitzharris, the taller and huskier of the two, apologizes. "Jimmy, we're sorry to interrupt you, and you as well, Dr. Gogarty. We've come by to leave some telephone numbers and addresses for your trip. Put them away in a safe place. Well, we have to get back to our painting. Nice meeting you, Dr. Gogarty." He hands an envelope to O'Brien, and they both leave.

I turn to O'Brien, "What was that all about?"

"Those guys? They're house painters. I ran into them at a pub in the Irish section of town. There's no law against that, is there?"

"No. But it's a little strange seeing you making friends with local laborers and getting contacts from them in Ireland."

"No law against that either. Are you becoming an elitist, like *them*?"

"Far from it."

"You *are* Irish, aren't you? What does that *T* in your name stand for—Timothy?"

"No; in fact, it's Tabeel, and that's a Jewish name." I brace myself for his reaction.

He surprises me. "Good. In a way, very good. We've always had a special bond with them, haven't we? In *Ulysses,* Joyce has some ignorant headmaster claiming there was never any anti-Semitism in Ireland because 'she never let them in'."

I attempt to comment on the quote, but he tramples on my words.

"There must have been close to four thousand Jews in Ireland by 1900. Do you know when the first Jews got there?" He has no intention of letting me answer. "Well, according to *The Annals of Innisfallen*, five Jews arrived in 1062, bringing gifts to my ancestor Turlow O'Brien, a grandson of Brian Boru and the king of Munster. We're talking about the 'Stone of Destiny'—the one used for the coronation of Irish kings, the one that's now on The Hill of Tara in County Meath. It's the same stone that Jacob used to climb to heaven."

"Beware of conflating myth with history."

"Maybe it's myth to the unbeliever, but not to me. The Tuath Dé Danaan. Are you familiar with them?"

"No, but I expect I soon will be."

"They were the prototypes for the *shee*, the wee people, and they were said to come from the Tribe of Dan."

I manage to slip in a question. "In the book of Judges? Those who 'stayed on the ships'?"

"Yes. That's right. Not bad, Gogarty. But please don't interrupt me. When will I ever get another chance to lecture a professor?"

I nod in acquiescence.

"It's an historical fact there was a synagogue built in Ireland in the seventeenth century, and Hebrew was taught at Trinity College in the eighteenth century. Another synagogue was built north of the Liffey by Saint Mary's Abbey, and around then a few Jews brought their goldsmithing talents to Waterford and Cork. Gerald Goldberg became the lord mayor of Cork, and, as everyone knows, so did Robert Briscoe in Dublin. I'm going to check out the name Lawlor Briscoe and the place where they had a furniture shop on Lower Ormond Quay, when I'm in Dublin."

He stops to compose his thoughts, and I cash in on the pause. "Fascinating. You should think about teaching interdisciplinary courses in Irish culture someday. Your knowledge of the Jews *and* the Irish would go over big in New York. Didn't Joyce himself speak of the 'facile pens of the O'Brienite scribes'? If you write well, you might have quite a career ahead of you."

"I may, but I've had to listen to professors for so long now I'm not sure I can stomach it for the rest of my life. I'll tell you how I got into all of this, though. First of all, finding out that the Chief, Charles Stewart Parnell—"

He's forced to stop when I chip in, "Was Joyce's father's hero."

He quickly adds, "Yes. I think he was the son's hero, too, but James was reluctant to admit it. Parnell's mother was Jewish, and I think I've discovered something else that may have drawn Jews to Ireland. There's this group called the Loyal League of Yiddish Sons of Erin."

"You'd better check your facts on Parnell's mother. That was rumored but never proven. 'The Loyal League of the Yiddish Sons of Erin'?" I suppress a laugh.

"If you want to hear more, I'll be happy to tell you."

"That's enough for now. Just be careful. Don't start consorting with hooligans."

"There's nothing for you to worry about."

"Let me spell this out clearly for you. If you get involved with anybody who attracts the attention of the local constabulary, I won't hesitate for a split second to pack you up and ship you back home. Do we understand each other?"

"We do"

What on earth is he *really* up to in Ireland? Here's hoping I never find out.

Well, my trip to Liverpool may provide some rest and relaxation. I could sure use it.

# 16

"*You drive like a maniac!*" I scream as we narrowly miss an approaching sports car.

Mountjoy glances sideways at me. "What do you mean, *like*? I'm beginning to realize you're paranoid, Aloysius. Not to worry though —there's nothing wrong with paranoia."

"What's right with it? *Jesus! Look out for that truck!*"

"First of all, although I can understand the confusion, I am not Jesus. Had I, for example, been at the wedding at Cana, *I* would have turned water into single malt whiskey." He reaches across me into the glove compartment and extracts a small bottle of Glenfiddich. "This," he says with confidence, "will calm your nerves.

"Where was I? Oh yes. In most cases paranoia is a survival tactic. A paranoid is someone who knows all the facts and elects to avoid the undesirable fate others have planned for him. If Jesus had been paranoid, he could have avoided what your people had in store for him."

"My people? You mean the Jews? First of all, they weren't responsible for his death. It was the Romans who crucified him."

"Do you really think the Romans wanted any part of that ghastly business? Reread the Gospels. There's no question there as to who was to blame. And who authored the Gospels?"

"Matthew, Mark, Luke, and John, who, by the way, bless the bed that I lie on."

He growls, "They were merely amanuenses. It was God himself you, spiritual cretin."

"Father forgive me, for I know not what I do."

"There's a more serviceable reply than that, you know."

"What is it?"

"*Nescio sed Invenire Possim.*"

"Uh . . . I don't know, but I... I can... look it up?"

"Yehhs. Now, either go ahead and drain that vessel, or pass it back to me."

"Sorry." If it weren't for Mountjoy's spine-tingling driving, I'd be enjoying this trip. Those Pennine Hills are the jewel in the crown of the Yorkshire Dales. The weather is brisk and invigorating, the countryside is postcard perfect, and this Daimler's holding the road like a train holds the rails. Thank God.

Mountjoy reassures me about the liquor supply. "There's more in the boot; in fact, enough for an entire regiment. Confused? A boot is what you people inexplicably call a trunk. Even elephants know their trunk is in front. And, by the way, it was a lorry and not a truck testing my prowess and your paranoia. But teaching you English is as wearisome as teaching history. You may recall me suggesting that I might give you a thumbnail sketch of some of my colleagues."

He steals a glance at me and says, "Easy on the staff of life, my dear boy. Remember, you're the passenger and bear some responsibility on this odyssey. Yours is to remain sufficiently alert to remember into which particular ditch we've careened *en route* and precisely where, between Yorkshire and Liverpool, that ditch is."

I add, "That is, if either of us survives the trip."

"Yehhs. Before I carry on about other *cognoscenti* in our department, permit me to share a vignette with you relating to Somerset and British snobbery at its finest. Jacob Schumacher, which you'll recall is the real name of our Somerset imposter, fled the Nazi persecution with his father and brother and arrived in this country as a teenager. The family settled near Cambridge, where our Schumacher was taken on as a vice-assistant under-gardener at King's College. His chief responsibility was to tease the grass out of the flagstone cracks in the quad with a sharpened teaspoon.

"Being of an ambitious nature—*you* know what *they're* like—Schumacher decided to study for matriculation exams and get himself placed at a British university. He also asked the bursar if he might use the college library for said purpose. The bursar referred this unprecedented request to the entire college council. Intrigued by the notion of a vice-assistant under-gardener being able to read, let alone wishing to use the library, they granted the request, not least to demonstrate how unsnobbish they were.

"In due course, young Jacob passed his exams and secured a place at London University. Thereupon, he went to the bursar and announced his intention to resign his humble post at the college. To which the astonished bursar replied, 'You know, Somerset, we're sorry to see you go; indeed, I do not think I exaggerate when I say we had very high hopes for you and thought that one day you might even become head gardener here.'

"When in a good mood, which is as frequent as a solar eclipse, Somerset tells this very story, concluding his rendition by saying, 'And I vonder vot dhey dhink ov me now? Pruhvessor uf Ancient History at Yorkshire University.' To which I always reply to myself, 'I'll tell you exactly what they think of you now, and in fact what they say, old chap: "Do you know who they've got now as their professor of Ancient History at Yorkshire? One of our bloody gardeners! Ha!"

I applaud enthusiastically. "More, more."

Mountjoy pulls to the side of the road on and goes to the trunk. He returns with a large bottle of Macallan malt whiskey, gargles a small amount of its contents, and spits it out on the grass. He hands the bottle to me, explaining, "I had better keep an eye on my intake, at least until we get to Liverpool." He changes his mind and snatches the bottle from my hands, explaining, "Perhaps a touch of the grand elixir will fuel a few more profiles. Or am I already wearying you with all this."

"On the contrary, I'm fascinated by it. In fact, some day when I'm old and gray and full of sleep, I'd like to write a novel about this year in England. Would you mind if I included some of what you've said in it?"

"Not in the least. I'll be dead by then. What would you call your novel?"

"*The Lestrygonians*," I say, sarcastically.

"Snappy title. As I recall, those chaps spent most of their time cannibalizing one another. Sounds like our profession, and brings to mind several colleagues, notably A. R. G. Graham-Gram, and Peter and Pippa Urquhart-Piper. Would you like to hear about them?"

"I've already figured out what the *G* stands for in Graham-Gram's name, and you're probably going to describe how Peter Piper pecked at Pippa's private parts. So, can I make a request?"

"Yehhhhhs?"

"Well, we *are* heading for Liverpool, and the only relative you've ever referred to without snarling is Sir Reginald. That's who I'd like to hear more about."

"My dear boy, you managed to awaken me with that request, which portends well for both of us." He takes a deep swig and hands the bottle back to me.

"I believe I've already mentioned that my venerable great-great-granduncle was the mayor of Liverpool. I must warn you, however, that some members of the family shudder at the very mention of his name."

"Why?"

"Because they consider his career to be, shall we say, tainted. On the other hand, there are those among us," he unfurls a panoramic smile, "whose judgment is decidedly different. Who could fail to admire, for example, his handling of official responsibilities? Throughout his tenure, Sir Reginald expressed a conspicuous disdain for concrete accomplishment and exhibited uncanny elasticity in avoiding it. All those earnestly seeking change were invariably stymied by his uncompromising torpor.

154

"Now, there are always misguided souls willing to sacrifice their careers and even their persons to achieve reform; and, if the truth be known, there was an epidemic of that sort at the time. The more assertive of misguided souls were dealt with directly by Sir Reginald. One disagreeable chap, seeking the liberation of oppressed minorities, particularly Orientals, woke up one morning on a ship to Singapore being buggered from stem to stern by Chinese sailors. You see, Old Reginald was blessed with a quality rare nowadays: a devil-may-care, damn-my-soul outlook. His favorite saying was 'There's no substitute for prevarication,' and he practiced what he preached."

"He must've been one hell of a mayor."

"The city, of course, collapsed into shambles while he wielded the scepter for two full terms. Rubbish remained uncollected, sewers backed up, and bridges were left in dire need of repair. Two actually collapsed. The entire constabulary went on strike because he reduced their salary, etcetera, etcetera.

"On the other hand, criminal types, for the most part Irish—as one might suspect—worshipped the ground he walked on and turned out in besotted battalions to vote for him. I daresay he scored the political coup of the century by singlehandedly politicizing the entire criminal element in Liverpool. He lost reelection for a third term by a hair, a single vote. Something of course which would not have happened had he cast *his* vote. Alas, the poor man died more of *ennui* than anything else."

"Because he failed to vote for himself?"

"Heavens, no. That required exertion. Reginald's dismay came when it dawned on him, later in life, that had he granted full pardons to every inmate in the local prison and guaranteed free-flowing Guinness, he would have enjoyed a glorious victory."

"What a role model. You must feel daunted having such an imposing ancestor. Sort of like Alexander growing up in the shadow of Philip II."

"It was quite similar in some ways. Nevertheless, attempting to rival Reginald's indocility would have left me a broken man with a perennial sense of failure. His journals make it clear that in the end this was how Reginald felt about the path he had taken. You see, no matter what he did—or, I should say, didn't do—there was always someone inventing a way to intrude on his privacy and bedevil him with righteous solicitations.

"As a young man, I took note of this disappointment and determined not to make the same mistake. I sought out a profession in which Reginald's priorities could flourish, but one that could nevertheless command respect. By listening attentively to and closely observing my dons at Oxford, I began to realize what I was looking for was by no means a utopian fantasy. It not only existed it was staring me right in the face—the university!"

"But there *is* a price to pay. Advanced degrees, publications."

"Advanced degrees? Oxbridge men purchase their master's degrees. Is there another way?"

"Well, you could earn it. But what about the PhD?"

"Happily, we continue to resist 'doctoritis' here, although, I must admit, alarming symptoms of it have recently begun to surface. It must be the infectious tentacles of America spreading out and slowly but surely defiling the entire planet. You'll find most of our heralded historians simply bear the initials MA after their names and have no need for further credentials. American universities, on the other hand, disgorge doctorates like boxes of cornflakes, rendering the degree virtually meaningless. Isn't that so, *Doctor* Gogarty?"

"Ha! The insolence of the unqualified. So, you do nothing to contribute to the profession?"

"Steady, old boy. I'm pliant enough to relax *some* of Reginald's principles. I won't deny it's necessary to pay our dues, or at least appear to have done so. In fact, I'm currently in the process of writing a definitive tome entitled *Family and Politics in Nineteenth-Century Liverpool*. By my reckoning, to which you and you alone are privy, I should at this rate see it to fruition by the year 2073, at which time I shall, I can assure you, be permanently retired to an even less demanding environment. For the time being I occasionally exhibit

156

illusory signs of intellectual life by publishing articles hither or thither from my 'work in progress'."

"What kind of articles?"

"Those pretentious and stultifying enough to discourage all, save someone beyond redemption, from actually reading, much less criticizing. One article alone warrants attention." He coughs and clears his throat. "'Liverpool's Reginald Tarleton Mountjoy: *Redux*.' In it I reduce every scandal attached to my dearly departed forebear to the status of a misbegotten legend, akin to Saint Patrick ridding Ireland of snakes. The latter, of course, being disproved by simply engaging any of its present-day inhabitants in conversation. In my piece on Sir Reginald, I proceed to call attention to hitherto undiscovered documents revealing several formidable achievements on his part, which, ultimately, made possible the prosperity enjoyed by the city today. This prosperity, I assert, provides incontrovertible evidence that the disparaging accusations attached to Reginald were ill-conceived and baseless."

"So, you contend the evidence for Liverpool's deterioration during Sir Reginald's era is unconvincing."

"Let's say insufficient, shall we? I simply argue that the paucity of sources available is such that only a political partisan or a damned fool would lend credence to the theory that Reginald's era was a retrogressive one. As you know, academicians, on the whole, would rather be flayed alive than be labeled a fool."

"What contributions of his led to prosperity?"

"In reality? None." He raises a single finger. "But there's not one shred of evidence available to contradict my thesis. You see, the family kept all incriminating documentation safe under lock and key. It was stored in the barn on Sir Reginald's country estate. At the beginning of the present century, when malicious rumors began to circulate about corruption burgeoning during his heyday, vultures from our discipline began circling the family for permission to sift through his papers. They had the intention, naturally, of feasting on his carcass and scattering the bones. That was just before the Great War."

I gasp as an approaching car swerves to avoid us. The other driver continues to blow his horn; Mountjoy smiles in retaliation.

"Never one to tolerate hectoring from anyone, my grandfather personally put a torch to the barn, having, of course, first removed Reginald's papers. He lodged these papers, along with other of Reginald's items, securely in his attic. All inquiries in the future were met with regrets that, alas, all of Reginald's materials were consumed in the conflagration.

"As fate would have it, my branch of the family inherited the estate. In rummaging through his papers, which were abundant because of Reginald's inability to discard anything not emitting a foul odor, I discovered a treasure trove of archival material. More to the point, there was an ample supply of his unique stationery and seven large inkwells (five of which still contained dry ink), as well as three gray-goose quills."

He looks up toward the sky, places an open palm on his heart, and begins to recite.

> *"Oh! Nature's noblest gift—my gray-goose quill!*
> *Slave of my thoughts, obedient to my will,*
> *Torn from thy parent-bird to form a pen*
> *That mighty instrument of little men!"*

"Byron."

"Good heavens, how did you know that?"

"I'm really a professor of English literature *manqué*."

"I see. That explains a great deal. Well, I was speaking of Sir Reginald and the mountain of documentation surviving him. And, oh, of all things, he also left behind seventeen-pint jars of securely corked water. Well, I knew beyond the shadow of a doubt which documents were from his own hand because my prized possession since the age of five has been a framed letter of Reginald's to my great granduncle. To summarize its contents, in it he advises his son to do everything he

158

did, but less of it. I was so impressed by this memento that I modeled my own penmanship on that of Reginald's and did such a splendid job of it that it became impossible for even the most talented of forensic examiners to distinguish one from the other.

"You are, I trust, familiar with the more celebrated intuitive leaps of mankind: Saint Augustine in the garden; Newton under the tree; etcetera, etcetera. Well, one day, while rummaging through Reginald's memorabilia, it dawned on me that if I were to add a few drops of *this* water to *that* ink and write on *that* paper, I could make my mark on history by the stroke of a quill, as it were."

"Oh my God, this is priceless. Go on. Go on. What did you do next?"

He pauses, digests what he's just said, throws up his hands, and announces, "Enough of that. We're now on the outskirts of Liverpool." He turns to grin at me with his hands still upraised and waits until the last second to grab the wheel, somehow managing to keep the car on the road.

"Don't stop now."

"One clarification. Sir Reginald's title was actually 'chief magistrate' back in his day, and 'lord mayor' did not officially come into fashion until the 1890s. Nevertheless, old Reginald called himself lord mayor, and those seeking to approach him had damn well better address him in that manner. His intransigence in this respect may be why they decided to change the title."

"More. More. I want to hear more!"

"You do, eh? Well, I'll tell you what. When you regale me with an unbowdlerized version of your dealings with Miss Marthe Fleischmann, I shall continue with my tale of historical decep... uh... redemption."

"Let me think about it."

"Yehhhs. I thought you might say that. There'll be enough time after lunch to see some of the city. I have a few places in mind, but you may as well. The Walker Art Gallery? The Hornby Library? Speke Hall? Sefton Park? Saint James Mount? The Botanic Garden?"

"How about the Cavern Club?"

"What, pray tell, is that?"

"Oh, just a modest tavern that someday will attract millions of pilgrims from all over the world. People who couldn't care less about Beowulf, Becket, or Brontë will change their itineraries in order to genuflect there. By the end of the century, if tourists still come to this museum of a country, the Cavern Club will be one of their main destinations."

"Forgive my ignorance when it comes to Liverpool, but what in blazes are you talking about?"

"The bare ruin'd choirs, where late the sweet birds sang—"

"Enough. Come to the point!"

"The Beatles, you ignor*anus*. That's where they met Brian Epstein, and where their meteoric rise to stardom began."

Mountjoy sighs. "How stolid of me to be unaware of that. If you insist, I'll find out where this shrine of yours is located and we'll pause there later, for a fleeting moment. For now, it's almost noon, so we might as well go straight to the Shaftesbury Hotel to meet your vice-consul."

"Well then," I guffaw. "Tally ho, Jeeves. It's time to muddy the waters of international diplomacy!"

Mountjoy groans.

# 17

---

The Right Honorable John Woolsey turns out to be six foot-two, with a square jaw, a ruddy complexion, and thinning silver hair. He sticks his hand out like the greeter at a county fair looking to yank someone into a sideshow. Mountjoy will love this guy. He's everything His Lordship expects to see in an American diplomat.

Woolsey begins, "Well, this really is a pleasure. You, Dr. Gogarty, have saved me considerable time, which is precious at the moment because of what's going on at home and off in Asia. And you, sir"— he turns to Mountjoy—"bear names I encounter frequently in these parts." He looks back at me.

"Dr. Gogarty, I must underline my indebtedness to you for handling the Stein situation in such impressive fashion. I remain ignorant of exactly how you went about resolving this dilemma, but I am certain of one thing: whatever you did saved us from a regrettable, if not calamitous, situation."

"Why, thank you, sir. I'm pleased to have been of service."

We sit, and the waiter asks if we'd like something to drink before lunch. The vice-consul insists we do the ordering. Mountjoy defers to me.

"Well, I'm tempted to order a bottle of wine, but my ignorance in this area would probably leave both of you disappointed." I turn to Mountjoy.

"Yehhs. Why don't we start with a nice Riesling? What's the best you have?"

"We have a Noble Rot, sir, and there's been an excellent response to it."

I snicker at the name.

Mountjoy, unperturbed, says, "That should do quite nicely. Agreed, gentlemen?" Woolsey and I look at each other and nod.

The vice-consul turns to me and says, "Dr. Gogarty, I'm particularly intrigued with one aspect of the case. That is, how you were able to engineer Stein's deportation. If the reports I received are reliable, the boy was charged with and convicted of two offenses, something they treat with the utmost severity here. The first involving drugs—LSD, no less—and the second, outright fraud with checks he wrote. Other Americans have been put away for one, much less two, of those charges. How on earth did you manage to achieve such a marvelous outcome to such a complex problem?"

"Well, I had a great deal of help. Mr. Mountjoy here was with me every step of the way and saved me from making grievous errors which would have spelled disaster."

Mountjoy waves a hand, dismissing my comment. "Dr. Gogarty gives me far too much credit. It was due to his perseverance, ingenuity, and rapport with the powers that be that we sit here celebrating a brilliant resolution to a nettlesome chain of events."

Woolsey notices we've drained our glasses and follows suit. I gesture for the waiter to continue filling our glasses when empty.

"Forgive my density, Dr. Gogarty," the vice-consul says apologetically, "but I don't quite get a sense of your strategy, or the tactics you employed."

"In all honesty, sir, I wish I could explain it myself, but I can't. I was informed of the details of the procedure involved and thought the best tack for the boy to take was to be prepared to reimburse the victims of his check-writing binge."

"But didn't the monkey business at Heathrow come into play?"

He knows more than I thought. I'd better be cautious here. What did my brothers say? When you lie, stick as close to the truth as possible.

"As the fates would have it, the presiding judge seemed unaware of what transpired at Heathrow."

"Well, that was an extraordinary piece of luck, wasn't it? One can understand something like this happening in France, where their suffocating bureaucracy is a recurring nightmare, but here in England these matters are customarily handled rather efficiently. Well, nonetheless, you've provided a solid service to the boy and the diplomatic contingent here. An American exchange student imprisoned in England would have been a major headache for us."

Woolsey raises his glass. "Let's drink a toast to Dr. Gogarty." He glances down, sees we've both finished, and hastens to catch up.

The waiter waves the bottle behind Woolsey, indicating it's been drained. Well, I'm enjoying diplomatic immunity for the moment, why not capitalize on it?

"Gentlemen, may I be so bold as to suggest that on this auspicious occasion we join together in drinking a good old-fashioned American libation?"

Woolsey smiles agreeably, and Mountjoy adds, "By all means."

"We'd like a dry martini," I tell the waiter.

"Ahem," Mountjoy interrupts. "My dear fellow, in England, with such a request, we shall in all likelihood be served a glass of Martini & Rossi dry vermouth and nothing else. Is that what you want, or is it the lethal American variety you're seeking?"

"My savior." I turn to the waiter. "The American type, please. May I suggest the way in which they should be prepared?" The waiter nods. "Thank you. For mine, three muscular jiggers of gin blended gently with a whiff of dry vermouth in a cocktail shaker with at least a half dozen ice cubes in it. Pour the mixture slowly through a strainer into a martini glass." I outline the shape of the glass. "Oh, and over an olive, please." I raise my index finger to stay the waiter's departure and ask my companions, "Is that all right with you gentlemen?"

Mountjoy says, "It sounds challenging, but these are trying times. I think I'll have the same."

The vice-consul shrugs his shoulders, which the waiter takes as a sign he wants to be included in the order. As the waiter leaves, Woolsey tilts his head and asks, "Would it be imposing of me to inquire as to how close the program was, or is, to getting scuttled? Having learned a little about the English while being here"—he nods apologetically toward Mountjoy—"I was concerned that this situation might jeopardize the arrangement between Yorkshire University and your own institution.

"Dr. Gogarty. I realize that this is perhaps none of my business, but there's a larger question here. You see, with everything that's going on around us, and in particular the troubles back home, should your program be undone for a reason of this sort, it would not bode well for other American universities with the same intentions. Here and elsewhere, I'm afraid."

I reach into a folder I've brought with me and take out my copy of Ogden's letter to Irwin. I pass it on to the vice-consul and warn him, "This, Mr. Woolsey, is *strictly confidential.*"

After reading the letter, he exhales a long, deep breath and says, "Thank you. This certainly puts things in a different light and is a huge relief to me personally. To be quite candid, gentlemen—and you two deserve nothing less—had the worst possible scenario eventuated, I would have been in a very difficult position. Not just because of repercussions in academic circles, but because my presence had been requested by an American citizen, and I delegated that responsibility to an ambassador without portfolio, as it were." He gestures in my direction.

We all drain our glasses, and I call for a refill.

Woolsey looks at Mountjoy and says, "Tell me, sir, with Tarleton among your names, you wouldn't happen to be a descendant of Banastre Tarleton, would you?"

"Indeed I am. You probably remember him from his exploits during the Revolutionary War."

"Exactly. With all due respect, wasn't he referred to as 'Bloody Ban,' and isn't he the British officer who ordered his troops to fire upon American soldiers even though they'd raised a white flag?"

Mountjoy elevates one eyebrow and says, "Mr. Woolsey, surely you're familiar with the old adage that the English and the Americans are two peoples divided by a common language?"

The vice-consul chuckles and nods in confirmation.

"Well, the same is true as far as historical events are concerned, particularly when our paths have crossed. You see, what actually happened at what you Americans call 'The Waxhaw Massacre' was quite different from the way it's described in American history books. In fact, after the white flag was raised by the colonists, old Banny's horse somehow came out from beneath him, and his troops mistakenly assumed their beloved leader had been a victim of the enemy's duplicity. In response, they charged of their own volition without orders from any officer, and indiscriminately slaughtered everyone in sight.

"I might add the American version of the event served a very useful purpose for your side in the rebellion. News of the 'massacre' spread, and many of those undecided, about where their sentiments lay, elected to cast their lot in with the rebels. Throughout the course of the war, the story was also an effective deterrent to colonists inclined to surrender to us. In fact, just a few months after the original incident, your soldiers, believing they were turning the tables on the British, engaged in their own orgy of butchery, and did so with considerable zeal."

"Sure, we did," I say. "Give the English a taste of their own medicine. 'Tarleton's Quarter,' they called it."

"So," says a hesitant Woolsey, who now, thanks to a waiter I've been silently colluding with, is fighting his way through a third martini and losing focus, "Dr. Mountjoy, uh, I mean Dr. Gogle, uh... sorry, I mean Dr. Gogarty, would you like to know what's happening in our country right now?"

"From what I've been reading in the *International Herald-Tribune,* things seem to be going from bad to worse."

"Well, we're talking about monumental problems," Woolsey says, "what with racial unrest and the president getting besieged by war protesters."

"How is Lyndon bearing up under all of this?" I ask. "Can a good old Texan with a Southern drawl handle racial inequities effectively?"

Woolsey struggles to remember the question, but nevertheless says, "I think you'll find Kennedy far more progressive than anyone ever expected him to be on racial questions."

"You mean Johnson, don't you?" Mountjoy signals for me to back off, but now that Woolsey's unable to concentrate, I can't resist a taunt.

"Maybe its Jack Kennedy's ghost still haunting poor Lyndon."

"I don't know about that," Woolsey says. "They seem to see eye to thigh on many issues."

Mountjoy's eyes grow large and I pretend Woolsey's making sense by nodding. "Well," I say, "I must admit to being mesmerized by President Kennedy. I wouldn't have traded one of his press conferences for a weekend with Marilyn Monroe." I pause for a moment, place my index finger on my mouth pensively, and retract what I've said, "I lie. Yes, I would. In fact, I'd trade all of his press conferences for a weekend with Marilyn!"

Mountjoy smirks and Woolsey lets loose a gutsy locker-room laugh.

I can't resist probing for some inside information while the vice-consul is defenseless. "Sir, this war is getting serious. Are we staying in Vietnam or getting out?"

"That, Dr. Gogarty"—he pauses for a moment to make sure he has the right name—"is the sixty-four-dollar question. Right now, it looks like we're... " He's lost his train of thought. I chip in.

"A lost cause?"

He rebounds. "No, no. In September, the president signed a seventeen-billion-dollar defense bill, the largest single expropriation, I mean, appropriation, in history."

I say, "I think that was *seventy* billion, at least as reported in the *Herald-Tribune*."

"That's what I said—seven billion. Has the climate here affected your damned hearing?" He roars with laughter at his remark, and Mountjoy and I pretend to join in the merriment.

"So," I say, "we're in for the duration. Well, I hope we're there to win the war and not just sacrifice American lives in a noble gesture."

In between all this we manage to get our food ordered. The soup arrives just as Woolsey starts to swoon. He stares at the vichyssoise as if struggling to identify what it is. Then, ever so slowly, he falls, face-first, into the soup. The waiters charge from all four corners, but Mountjoy and I get there first and rescue him.

Woolsey shakes his head in disbelief while being wiped down. "Oh my God. Very strange. I'm not... I don't... usually get dizzy. I'd better have myself looked at, don't you think?"

Mountjoy and I look at each other and simultaneously say, "Taxi." We walk Woolsey outside and angle him into a cab before instructing the driver to deliver him to the American vice-consulate, and then return to the restaurant.

"This is turning into a symposium, isn't it, Dickie boy?"

"If you're referring to an academic symposium, let's hope not. Drinking is a serious enterprise."

Our entrées arrive, and we pick at the food as we talk.

"Okay, Sir Reginald, who do you think is likely to prevail at the end of this symposium, you or me?"

"With gluttony pitted against restraint, there's no doubt in my mind as to the outcome."

"Words, words, words. I'll be looking down at you before the night is over."

"Really? Let's see if your durability matches your optimism."

"Let's. And don't forget, we have to get to the Cavern Club."

"Heaven forbid. Rest assured, the time will come for atavistic recreation. For now, however, I thought that you might profit most from a visit to"—he pauses for emphasis—"Batey's Wine Importers. They boast a private collection of vintage miniatures unrivaled by any other in the world. Our itinerary, then, will include . . . let's see . . . Batey's . . . then"—*cough, cough*—"the Cavern Club . . . and finally, a part of town you might find quite interesting."

"The ritzy part, huh?"

"Not exactly. I think it's what you'd call the red-light district. Nonetheless, no man can claim he's been to Liverpool without witnessing the painted tarts on parade there. This city's been the capital of harlotry in Great Britain since the days Maggie May strolled up and down Lime Street. Sir Reginald, rightfully, thought their trade would provide a stimulus to the economy and centralized activity on Blandford Street, which happened to be within walking distance of his town house."

"The more I hear about that guy, the more I like him. So, we polish off the evening with a visit to Nighttown, eh?"

"Is that what you call it?"

"That's what somebody called it. Mind you, I'm not one to pay for it. It's a matter of principle."

"I'm rather impressed. I had no idea standards of any sort intruded upon your thought process."

"Not many. But there's one anyway. They do have pubs there, don't they?"

"Not to worry. Drinks are available at all establishments."

I ask for the bill, and the waiter informs us that everything, including the gratuity, has been taken care of by the American vice-consul. I stuff a large roll of ten-pound notes back into my pocket and as we leave salute the staff, regimental style, with a quivering right hand.

## 18

---

"Aloysius. Aloysius. *Aloysius!*"

"What the—?" My God, I'm in the back seat of Mountjoy's car. "Your Lordship, what's going on here?"

"You, my dear boy, have been having a nightmare."

"Where are we?"

"On our way back to Yorkshire."

"Did I sleep back here all night?"

"This morning you did. Last night I helped the hotel clerk pour you into our suite at the hotel. You were still in a trance when I managed to wrestle you into my machine two hours ago."

I search in vain for my money. "Well, I blew over thirty ten-pound notes last night. I hope I had a good time. What did I do?"

"Among other peccadilloes, you showered one *cocotte* in 'Nighttown' with your bankroll, but I salvaged the lion's share of it." The back of Mountjoy's hand appears, and he drops a sizable roll of bills on my chest.

"I didn't pay for it, did I?"

"No. Your virtue remains intact. Of course, you were in no shape to frolic with a woman by then. You did entertain *them* though."

"How?"

"By singing a little ditty nauseating enough to be indelibly inscribed on my psyche."

"What is it?"

"If I must:

*'Italy's maids are fair to see*
*And France's maids are willing*
*But less expensive 'tis to me:*
*Becky's for a shilling.'"*

"Jesus. That's from Ellmann."

"Ellmann? Isn't that the American mayonnaise king?"

"James Joyce's biographer. The other one is Hellmann."

"I gather Joyce is up there with the Beatles in your beggar's pantheon of cultural *illuminati*."

"The words from *Ulysses* never stop dancing through this crazy—and right now throbbing—brain of mine. I brought my copy of the accursed thing to England and spend most of my spare time rereading and annotating it. Joyce is *il miglior fabbro,* the best of all wordsmiths."

"That's Dante referring to a medieval troubadour. Does your literary icon have a Mountjoy in his life? Shakespeare did."

"Well, his father, John Joyce, ran into a Jesuit at Mountjoy Square in Dublin, and with that chance encounter young James was able to go Belvedere College, free of charge. That's probably why Joyce refers to the Jesuit and the square in *Ulysses.* The only other reference is to a prison by that name."

"Why such abiding interest in *Ulysses*? I read the first few pages when I was at college and concluded it was rubbish. Why torture yourself with meaningless esoterica?"

"It's penitential. Infidels like you wouldn't understand. Besides, I have an ulterior motive. Joyce's brilliance was in layering modern particulars on a Greek mythological matrix. I'd take it a step further and have later circumstances layered onto *his* structure.

"For now, can we stop somewhere so I can take a leak? I also need to grab some headache tablets out of my bag. It's in the trunk, isn't it?" He nods. I free myself from the back seat with difficulty, letting loose a deep, rich, noisy fart in the process.

Mountjoy glares in disdain, points and says, "Yehhhs. Try the bogs in that direction. I recommend a full flush of your system, considering the fact that you are—how does one put this delicately?— ehhh... flatulent. If the truth be known, you've been unleashing volleys of toxic emissions in my direction to the point of asphyxiation."

"Sorry, boss. I'll oblige."

When I return, I see the trunk's been left open and reach under a large plant covering my bag to grab a handful of pills, finally resettling myself into the back seat of the car.

"I noticed you bought a plant for your wife."

"I did no such thing. The fact of the matter is you purchased that plant for an obscene amount of money last night."

"Me?"

"Yes, you. We did visit the Cavern Club, which, by the way, was the equivalent of paying homage to the cave from which Cro-Magnon himself first emerged, and that's where the purchase occurred."

"Why did I want it?'

"You were adamant about acquiring a relic of the Beatles, and it had to be something with which one of their singers, John Lemon I think, had actually had physical contact. When the proprietor mentioned that whenever the individual in question had too much to drink, he relieved himself on this particular plant, you had to have it at all costs."

"How much was *at all costs*?"

"A hundred and twenty quid. You were convinced you had struck quite the bargain."

"It sounds like I did. Is there any water in here? I could use it to wash my hands and swallow these headache tablets."

"Frightfully remiss of me not providing toiletries for you, my dear boy, but we all have shortcomings, don't we?" The car starts moving again, and Mountjoy reaches back, extending a large bottle of Glenfiddich. "This will accomplish two purposes. First of all, it is *l'eau . . . de vie*, and second of all, what you need is a little 'hair of the dog' to restore equilibrium after last night's *débauche*."

"Was I *that* bad?"

"No—unless you consider riding on the back of a porcine trollop while snorting a tune entitled 'Who goes with Ferguson?' *bad*."

"You're kidding."

"Not in the slightest. It was fairly comical until you became convinced that the abominable plant, to which you ascribed talismanic qualities, had been pilfered. It was then you caused the affray."

I put my hand to my head. "That sounds bad. What did I do?"

"Let's just say at one point the local police took a special interest in your allegations and were on the brink of introducing you to the rest of the Liverpudlian constabulary down at the station house."

"*Jesus.* What happened?"

"I intervened, identified myself, and explained you were a long-lost American relative from a disreputable branch of the family who would return to his little hog sty in America the following day."

"Did they let me go?"

"No. They still have you at their headquarters. Of course, they let you go. And, as you've seen, your precious plant is safely secured in the boot."

"So—you were sober enough to straighten things out?"

"Someone had to be. You were so intent upon achieving saturation you remained blissfully unaware I was merely sipping drinks at Batey's, and thereafter ingested nothing to speak of. You see, I prefer to avoid scandal in Liverpool. Especially while M'mah is still among us."

"So, you never saw her?"

"I most certainly did. Early this morning. She's always up at the crack of dawn."

"Too bad. I would have liked to have met her."

"Perhaps in the next life. I don't want her railing against me about those with whom I associate, and one whiff of you would have provoked a tirade."

"Well, I can understand that. I'm surprised you're letting me meet your wife New Year's Eve."

He hesitates for a moment. "Priscilla has been raising questions as to why I've been so inattentive lately and is getting peeved about the amount of time I spend 'at work.' Eventually, she may draw a connection between my recent deportment and our companionship."

"So, she already suspects I might be a bad influence on you?"

"I don't think her curiosity has quite taken that turn yet, but she is probing for an explanation of my protracted absences."

"We'd probably both be better off if I weren't there. Besides, I have to get back to my book. That should keep me busy day and night until I go up to Edinburgh and peddle our program there."

"Splendid. That will be right before the new term begins. Do you want me to look into the situation at Edinburgh and see if I can be of any assistance?"

"No thanks. I'm not sure I want to saddle anyone else with our students, and I'm only going because there's no choice. I have to mollify the Grand Wizard.

"About my antics last night . . . do you... I mean... could I... do you think I should be concerned about my drinking?"

"That, my dear boy, is something you'll have to determine for yourself. And it's not a consideration I'd be able to judge with any objectivity. However, if it concerns you, then perhaps there's something there."

"Well, right now some dwarf has gotten inside my head and is hammering away at my frontal lobe. Is it okay if I go back to sleep for a while?"

"Rest peacefully. Not a thing to worry about, old boy. You're in good hands."

He stomps on the gas pedal, the wheels squeal, and I fall asleep, smiling.

# 19

And on the second day in the year of our Lord nineteen hundred and sixty-eight, Aloysius T. Gogarty, BA, MA, PhD, BEB, OPO, SOS, RIP, SOB, ETC, travels north on the express train to Edinburgh. What perils await you this year, Aloysius?

Well, I've prettied up Alexander and packed him off to Oxford, but I did go a bit overboard in my celebrations last night. Four tablets should rectify the problem. Epic dreams lately, and they come in the most unlikely guises. Drifting off...

> *THE VIETCONG SURRENDER*
> *In a stunning reversal of personal ideology and public policy, Ho Chi Minh announced Friday morning at 6:16 a.m., EST, he was calling upon North Vietnamese troops and sundry supporters to lay down their arms and surrender to the nearest South Vietnamese or American soldier. Condemning Communism as a virulent infection and claiming temporary insanity for his addiction to it, Minh explained that he had a revelatory experience and has become a devout eclectic. Citing the Blessed Virgin's exodus from Hanoi to Saigon and his own spiritual awakening at the Tay Ninh Temple, where the word surrender was mysteriously spelled out to him, Ho Chi Minh assured his followers this directive emanated from a higher power and superseded previous orders. Vietcong soldiers were authorized to shoot on sight any miscreant*

*refusing to obey the order. American soldiers in the combat zone greeted the news by smoking what they describe as "peace pipes" and appeared oblivious to the historic events unfolding around them.*

## BOBBY KENNEDY WINS THE ELECTION

*Robert F. Kennedy has become the thirty-seventh president of the United States of America. A victor in all fifty states, President-elect Kennedy thereby became a successor to his ill-fated and much-beloved brother, John F. Kennedy, our thirty-fifth president. Attired in full plate steel armor complete with sabatons, greaves, a skirt of tasses, breastplate, gauntlets, roundels, gorget, helm, and visor, Mr. Kennedy announced from his bunker (at an undisclosed location in the Mojave Desert), "I have complete trust in my fellow Americans and their willingness to help carry the torch of my late brother in his attempt to spread freedom throughout the world and make this world safe not only for democracy, but for... (continued on p. 13)*

## NOBEL PRIZE IN LITERATURE AWARDED TO A. T. GOGARTY

*To the astonishment of Nobel Prize observers and the president of the American Historical Association, Aloysius T. Gogarty has been awarded the 1968 Nobel Prize in Literature. Informed of the decision, the Municipal College professor, vacationing at his summer retreat in the Queensbridge section of Long Island City, was asked what he would do with the 50,000 dollars that comes with the award. Professor Gogarty declared he would be in Tiffany's that afternoon looking at engagement rings. Asked who the lucky woman was, Gogarty replied, "Oh, just the girl-next-door type, a redheaded Cuban with one green eye and one brown eye, whose hair resembles Alexander the Great's." Asked how long he had been keeping*

*company with this young lady, Professor Gogarty responded,
"Altogether? Three hours, twenty-seven minutes, and thirteen
seconds."*

In other news:

*FRANK N. STEIN RENOUNCES DRUGS AND WRITES A
VILLANELLE*

*JAMES O'BRIEN CONTRACTS ANGLOPHILIA*

*LORD MOUNTJOY READS THE KREUTZER SONATA AND
TAKES VOWS OF POVERTY AND OBEDIENCE BUT
BALKS AT CELIBACY*

*DEAN IRWIN CHOKES TO DEATH ON A PENGUIN'S
WING BONE WHILE NEGOTIATING FOR A NEW STUDY-
ABROAD CENTER IN ANTARCTICA*

"Edinburgh... Edinburgh... Edinburgh . . . *last stop.* Collect all
your baggage before departure, please." Passengers shuffle out past
me. Pleasant dreams for a change. Where did they come from? Hell's
teeth? Of course, that's where all good things come from. Off to the
university to witness the death of another salesman . . . unless hell's
teeth rescue me.

"Hello, I'm Dr. Gogarty, and I have an appointment with Dr.
MacCumhaill."

The secretary leads me into MacCumhaill's office, which is
spacious but Spartan, and reminiscent of Ogden's. The only striking
feature is a raised relief globe on a tripod stand by the window. It
must be forty inches high. MacCumhaill stands up from behind a
large walnut desk and offers a firm handshake while appraising me
from head to toe. He looks like Ogden, except for his gray hair and
broad nose. I'd better make a good impression here, or there'll be hell
to pay.

176

MacCumhaill speaks first. "I understand your college has expressed interest in bringing some of your American students here. Is that correct?"

"Yes sir. Our study-abroad director, Dean Francis Irwin, has asked me to explore the possibility with you. We believe if such an arrangement could be made, it would prove beneficial to both institutions."

"I must be straightforward with you, Dr. Gogarty. I have serious reservations about an arrangement of this sort."

Who can blame you? "Sir, perhaps you could tell me what these reservations are, and we can discuss them. I, too, promise to be forthright in what I say."

"Well, we've been approached by a number of American universities, but have denied their requests because we saw nothing in their proposals that would benefit *our* students and staff."

"I understand, Dr. MacCumhaill. But you may find what we have in mind could be just as profitable to you as it would be to us."

Why did you say that? Now you have to come up with something. Irwin would prostitute his mother to make a connection here. Just remember. If you fail here, *you fail.*

MacCumhaill stares at me and says nothing.

"First of all, sir, are you aware that our students pay handsome fees at all host universities?"

"Noted. However, we have more than our share of qualified students in the British Isles, why should we sacrifice their places for your students?"

Damn good question. "Of course, we're aware of that, sir, but as you well know, reciprocal agreements between universities speak to the future of international education."

Did I just say that? What arrant nonsense. I shake my head in self-reproach and apologize. "Sir permit me to reclaim those vacuous words."

He smiles in appreciation of my remark and nods for me to carry on.

"The real question is what, can we do for you, correct?"

"Indeed, it is. I need to show my staff and students there's something advantageous for us in the arrangement. Let's talk particulars."

I'm not authorized to make a specific offer. What should I do? Roll the dice. Go down in flames. Propose *something* that makes sense.

"We're not quite set up yet to accommodate your students and staff throughout the academic year, but I think we could start off by offering—let's say—a dozen, of your students' places in our summer school program, while providing several of your instructors with summer teaching positions. Our fees for summer students are nominal, and we pay visiting professors quite handsomely. It would also mean a summer in New York and, as you know, we have impressive museums, Broadway, the Metropolitan Opera, and a multitude of other cultural attractions." I sound like P. T. Barnum.

"That may be, but their interest in some such prospect remains to be seen, does it not?"

"Of course, Dr. MacCumhaill."

"Dr. Gogarty. There's another consideration of equal concern."

"Yes?"

"Please don't be offended by this, but it has to do with the character and quality of your students."

This guy doesn't pull any punches.

"Could you be more specific sir?

"Yes. I'm afraid it's mostly American students who've been instrumental in some of the disruption afflicting our campuses recently. For example, last spring at the London School of Economics, an American student named Bloom—Leopold or something of the sort—managed to become president of the student union there and organized a number of disquieting events. That sort of *espièglerie* is something we frown upon here. Mind you, we have our own troublemakers, but they've not gotten out of hand, at least thus far. Honoring that candor, we agreed upon at the outset, I must admit I'm reluctant to approve any agreement which might result in our university being encumbered by agitators posing as students."

"Sir, if I may, the Bloom you refer to at LSE is a certain Marshall Bloom. He's a graduate student from Amherst, who, I believe, applied to LSE on his own and was not a participant in any particular study-abroad program. My point being he was not subject to a screening process in the States, which, if worth its salt, would have weeded him out along with any other potential troublemakers." That took balls.

"I thank you for that information, Dr. Gogarty. However, there's a related matter I hesitate to broach."

"Please do so sir."

"Well, rumor has it there were difficulties at Yorkshire University this year involving students from *your* program."

My cue.

"Sir, speaking frankly, you're both correct and, if I may say so, not quite correct. You see, the difficulty there involved *one* of our students, no others, and that one student presents a unique case in no way similar to that of Marshall Bloom, for example. Our student was anything but a radical organizer of strikes and protests. If the truth be known, he was incapable of organizing himself, much less anyone else."

MacCumhaill chuckles. "Well said, Dr. Gogarty. Some of our own students, I'm sorry to say, suffer from the same ineptitude. However, I've learned through my counterparts at other British universities that the success or failure of any arrangement of this sort depends to a great extent on the quality of students sent and the type of resident director who accompanies them.

"In that context, I have another question for you, Dr. Gogarty. I've heard about you from Dr. Ogden at Yorkshire, who's been quite favorably impressed with what you've done there. Would *you* be willing to become your college's resident director here?"

Where did that come from? He's put me on the spot. What do I do?

"Thank you, sir, for thinking of me in that way. However, I must confess anything I do of value at Yorkshire is accomplished because of the steadying hand of Dr. Ogden and the advice and counsel of Mr. Richard Tarleton Mountjoy, my liaison there. And I must tell you it's most unlikely I'll continue in the same capacity next year, either at Yorkshire or anywhere else. My plan as of now is to return to my research and teaching in New York. I am certain, however, the dean would send someone more than capable of dealing with whatever situation might arise here."

MacCumhaill looks down reflectively and then back up at me.

"Dr. Gogarty, your answers are keenly appreciated. I intend to have further discussions concerning this matter with our vice-chancellor and other officers at the university. Regardless of what comes of this, it's been a pleasure to meet with you and discuss the matter."

"Thank you, sir." I stand and offer my hand. "Goodbye."

What's the name of that pub Mountjoy recommended up here? The Ensign Hughes? A cold lager or two is certainly called for on such an occasion. You just can't get carried away. There's nothing to worry about; Liverpool was a fluke. All you have to do is keep a cautious eye on your intake.

# 20

---

"So, it's Ensign Ewart, not Hughes, huh? Who was this Ewart?"

My chubby, flush-faced taxi driver responds with a spirited soliloquy. "He was a lad from Kilmarnock who enlisted in the Scots Greys around the time of Napoleon and became a sergeant. At Waterloo, the Greys and the Gordon Highlanders faced the French Forty-Fifth, the 'Invincibles,' as the frogs called them. The Scottish lads were champing at the bit to get at them, and when the officers finally let them loose, they rode at the French line screaming, 'Scotland Fore ere,' scaring the French out of their *fookin* lace skivvies. Ewart went straight for the French standard bearer, cut his way through a half dozen of the bastards, snatched their eagle and carried it up on high back to the regiment. They gave him the Waterloo medal, and after that it wasn't just the *fookin* officers who got medals, but men from the ranks—the ones who did all the dirty work."

"You should teach history. You're better than the ones who get paid to do it. Is Ewart's grave around here? I enjoy rummaging through old cemeteries and looking at epitaphs."

"Well, it used to be at the castle, which is only a stone's throw from the pub. But it's in Midlothian now until they fix it up and bring him back. His spirit's in the pub, though, and they've got mementos of what I've been telling you about. In fact, here we are now. Hoist one in his honor while you're there."

"I shall. And I'll hoist one in your honor, as well." I tip him with a couple of pound notes for his recital, and he shouts at my back, "You're *fookin* officer material, you are, laddie."

Mountjoy said this pub is on one of the highest hills in Edinburgh. Get a load on and roll all the way home. Not this time, old boy. Controlled drinking is the order of the day.

Ensign Ewart's pub is brimming with memorabilia. It looks like a cross between a museum and a ritzy pub. The barkeep seems affable enough. I'll ask for advice.

"What would you recommend, to wet the whistle, my good man?"

"Well, if you're one for ales, have a lick at our Deuchars IPA."

"Why not?"

I drain the schooner. "Yes sir. That does the trick all right, and it's not as stale as some of the lagers down south."

"Our beer is hand-pumped up from the cellar. There's a difference, you know."

"Now I do. It looks like you've got three more kinds there. Let's have a taste of each in turn if you don't mind."

"Here's some wee glasses, if you want a sampling."

I drink them in rapid succession. "Well, they're good except for the last one. It doesn't have much life in it."

He agrees. "It tastes like dishwater. That's the one you Americans usually rave about. But I can see you're a man who knows his way around a tap."

"I've drained a jar or two in my time, but I'm trying to keep an eye on myself. I've been known to get carried away on occasion."

"It's many a good man's fault. Who hasn't had a night or two he'd rather forget?"

"Nobody I'm comfortable with. I'm only passing through Scotland, though, so I should get a sip of your malt whiskey. You do have it, don't you?"

"Aye. Speyside, Lowland, forty varieties. Is that enough for ya?"

"I should think so. I only want to partake of a few, though, and I'd like to remember which ones they are."

"I tell you what, laddie. I'll write them down on this here coaster. You can tuck it away and keep it as a souvenir. Now, let me tell you something about whiskey. It's like a woman: it's all a matter of taste. I can give you something smooth with a long, round finish; something spicy with a peaty aftertaste; or something soft with a heathery, honey flavor. What suits your mood today?"

"Do you have any with red hair and one green and one brown eye?"

He laughs. "That won't be in until next week. What would you settle for now?"

"Surprise me. Let me have a couple of fingers of something you'd drink yourself and a refill on the Deuchars to wash it down."

The bartender places an empty larger-than-conventional shot glass on the bar alongside a schooner of ale.

"What's this?" I ask.

He points to each in turn. "This is the Deuchars, and this is what I drink."

"But that's empty."

"I know. You asked me to give you what I drink. When it comes to booze, this is it for me. Even Bucky Barabas hasn't made it past these lips for the last seven years."

"Nothing *at all?*"

"Me dear departed father once told me, he said, 'Billy boy, every man has his own God-given quota when it comes to drink, and you'll know when yours has been reached. That'll be the crossroads. Either you'll keep sucking it up like a sponge or you'll step back and watch the other laddies blow themselves up with it.' I reached my limit seven years and thirteen days ago."

"How did you know your time was up?'

"When it dawned on me I was allergic to the stuff."

"*Allergic?* How did you know you were allergic to alcohol?"

"Because when I overdid it, I kept breaking out in handcuffs!"

I choke on a mouthful of Deuchars, spitting some of it on the bar. He wipes up the mess cheerfully, pleased with my reaction.

"Did you just stop? It must be difficult. The good juice is everywhere, and you, with your job, are surrounded by it."

"I got, and still get, help. Other lads who're in the same boat meet twice a week, and we remind ourselves it's not for us anymore."

"Is that Alcoholics Unanimous?"

He laughs. "Anonymous. It's Alcoholics Anonymous."

"I know. I was pulling your leg. My brother Tommy back in New York is a member of your club, and he hasn't had a drink in three years."

"Well then, good for him. If the thought ever passes your own mind, have a chat with him. He'll tell ya what it's all about. Better yet, get to a meeting with him and see if it's for you."

"I'll remember that. Well, where were we? Oh, yeah. If you were back in your prime and decided you wanted nothing but the best, what would you ask for?"

"This." He lifts a bottle from behind the bar, pours it in a shot glass, and says, "Macallan, ten-year old."

I down the shot. "Oh my, that's smooth. I tell you what. I'd like one more, a large one, and I was wondering if you could point me toward a more local type of pub. This has been great, and you're a fountain of information, but"—I lean over to him and whisper—"your joint is a little too touristy for me. It's crawling with Americans."

He chuckles. "I know what you mean. You're looking for a pub with some local color, a knockabout type of a place that sells cheap beer and rotten whiskey. Edinburgh's bursting at the seams with them. There's one over on Little Britain Street where the university students and some locals hang out. But I have to warn you, you're just as likely to see a brawl between those two groups as not. Is that more in line with what you're thinking?"

"Exactly." I slip him a five-pound note under my palm and ask him to call a cab. He looks around, pockets the fiver, and pours a shot of whiskey from a bottle previously hidden from view in a cabinet behind the bar.

It burns as it goes down. "Whoa! This stuff is volcanic. What is it?"

"Cask-strength Macallan. On the house." He starts pouring another shot. I put up my right hand to stop him, but it's too late. Well, can't waste it. "What's the name of that pub?"

"Barney Kiernan's."

"That's an Irish name."

"It sure is. We've got quite a few Irishmen around here. Nothing to brag about, mind you, but we've got them. Keep to yourself and curb your tongue there, though, laddie. If the students and the Irish ruffians aren't beating the shit out of one another, they're just as likely to pick on a stranger. I'll have a taxi take you right to the front door. You'll be there in two shakes of a stick. Oh, here's something you can enjoy even if you're not crazy about the crowd there."

He takes a small box from underneath the counter and opens it.

"A cigar? You're talking to the right man. I enjoy a good cigar every once in a while."

"This isn't a good cigar; it's a *great* cigar. This, my friend, is a genuine Cuban cigar. It was given to me by one of my sailor friends. Cubans are the best."

"I know. I know."

He leans over so no one else can hear what he has to say. "Did you know laddie, that those *chiquitas* in Havana roll the tobacco slowly back and forth over their inner thighs, dangerously close to their private parts, just to give each and every authentic cigar the faint scent of Spanish pussy?"

He has a way with words.

"No, I can't say I knew that. But I'm sure it'll enhance my appreciation of it."

"Here's your taxi. It's right there at the curb."

"Thanks. The best of luck to you."

"You too. Don't forget to talk to your brother about the club."

I raise and wave my right hand as I walk toward the taxi.

"Barney Kiernan's please." The cabdriver hears my accent, turns around, and gives me a strange look.

"Are you sure about that?"

"Yup."

"Okay. Kiernan's it is."

Jesus. It smells like stale beer in here, and there's a hint of urine coming from somewhere. Who cares, as long as it's not mine? The bartender fits right in. He's got a scar on his left cheek and a black patch over his right eye. Sure enough, students on one side, Irishmen on the other. I'll station myself in neutral territory in between the warring parties.

"Hello, may I have a beer please?"

"I'm not a mind reader," the bartender snaps. "What kind do you want?"

Charming. "Half a pint of ale, please."

"So, you're on the wagon, huh?" He roars at his own comment, momentarily drawing attention from both factions. I'd better establish my credentials.

"You're right. I've been on the wagon long enough. I'll have a pint of bitter, and a double shot of Macallan."

"Now you're talking. We're not a high tea operation around here, if you know what I mean, but we do have Macallan."

He turns his head, so he can see me with his good eye and barks, "What's your name?"

Throw him a curve ball. "Cashel Boyle O'Connor Fitzmaurice Tisdale Farrell, but my friends call me Nemo."

He glowers. "All right, Mr. *Nemo*. My name is Mickey Cusack. I'm just an ordinary citizen, but *you* can call me *Mr*. Cusack." He smiles mockingly and walks toward one of the students whose calling out, "Mickey."

Everyone's smoking here. It's time to light up my prized possession. God, that's smooth. No whiff of female genitalia yet, but you probably have to be well into it to get all the benefits. The Irish

186

have the dartboard. I'm surprised they're not competing against the students. That would guarantee a donnybrook.

"*Mr*. Cusack."

He turns his head in my direction. "What do *you* want?"

Cusack's barely my height but has massive shoulders and arms. He must've been a boxer or a shot-putter. He's also got the hound of the Baskervilles stationed close by. This dog is enormous, and his ears and muzzle look like they belong to a wolf.

"I'll have another double and another bitter please. Great-looking dog you've got there."

He gets my drinks.

"I'm glad you like him. Owen, come over here and say hello to the gentleman."

Owen gallops over to me, plants his front paws up on the bar, flashes his incisors, and snarls ferociously. I jump back, drawing belly laughs from both contingents.

Cusack grunts. "Down, Owen. Back over there." The beast's paws drop to the floor, and he mopes back to his spot and collapses.

Reclaim your post at the bar.

Cusack's mouth curls back in a vulpine snarl. "You still like him?"

"Sure. He's an exquisite animal. You're a lucky man." I get it. Owen's the bouncer and Cusack's in charge of public relations here.

He puts the drinks down, points to his patch, and says, "Lucky, huh?" He lifts his patch up so I can see his vacant socket. I turn to get a better look, and the tip of my cigar narrowly misses his good eye.

"What the fuh—are you looking to finish the job?"

"I'm sorry, Mr. Cusack. It's my damn reflexes." I need to change the subject. "What's that the students are drinking?"

"Buckfast." He brings the bottle over and lets me examine the label.

"My, oh my. Thirty proof and loaded with caffeine. You can get drunk and stay wide awake at the same time. Tailor made for students. I wonder what it tastes like."

He pours me a touch.

My God is that sweet! Look at the students. They're going to town on this stuff. I glance left at the Irish, and sure enough, most of them are drinking Guinness. Cusack awaits my verdict on Buckfast.

"Okay, I guess, but not for me. Too cough syrupy. Another double of Macallan please."

"Now there's a man after me own heart. I'm with you," he says, leaning over to speak confidentially. "These students get polluted fast and cheap on this panther piss and wind up looking for trouble."

"That's what they're like," I say agreeably.

One student in a drinking circle close to me shouts over in my direction, "So we have an American here, huh?" He announces in a loud voice, "There's a stranger in our house causing trouble, like they do everywhere they go."

That's all I need—a brawl. I look over at him. "Yes. I'm visiting from New York. What are you studying at the university?"

He puts a scowl on his face and belches. "Syphilisation. But what would you know about that?" he asks, looking to bait me.

"Civilization? Western European? Asiatic? African?"

"American. You know why? It's the easiest way to get a degree because there's so little to study. Instead, we hang around here waiting for people like you to enlighten us about your contributions to the world, like slavery and imperialism. Since you're here, why don't you explain to us what the fook you're doing in Vietnam, and when you plan to get the fook out of there?" The other students grumble in agreement.

"I'm sorry, my dear boy, but I'm not privy to information of that sort. But, from what I do know, we're trying to help the South Vietnamese stay independent by stopping Ho Chi Minh and his thugs from steamrolling over them."

I gesture for another drink and offer my adversary one, but he waves me off scornfully. He's enjoying his tirade too much. The Irishmen to the left of me are becoming interested in our exchange. If it comes to it, maybe I can get some support from them. This student is smaller than I am and not particularly husky, but he's going at it like a bulldog.

"When *are* you Americans going to get the *fook* out of Vietnam?"

I roll the cigar back and forth across my mouth several times, drawing deeply from it, and sending a string of circular smoke rings in the boy's direction.

"I'll tell you what, *laddie.* When I get back to the States, I'll give Lyndon a call and let him know how you feel. In the meantime, don't you think you're being a bit too modest about your own role in slavery and imperialism?"

"I and we"—he sweeps his right hand across his group—"have nothing to do with any of that. And we certainly have nothing to do with war. We're pacifists."

How do you like that—truculent pacifists. "Really? What about the British Empire, or has that slipped your mind? Okay. Let's pretend you're the prime minister of Great Britain and I'm the president of the United States. I've just received your ultimatum to evacuate Vietnam, and I agree, with one proviso."

"What's that?" he growls.

"*That you withdraw all your troops from Ireland.* Just a little *quid pro quo* between imperialists."

"Ireland has nothing to do with this. That's an entirely different question. You're making false comparisons. The Irish needed us then, and they need us now. They're like Americans. They don't have what it takes to govern themselves."

Shouts come from my left. "Like fookin hell we don't. You little shit."

My God. Cusack's urging the Irishmen to ratchet it up. I turn back to the students. "Aren't *any* of you reading history at the university? If you were, you'd know that Henry II's lads invaded Ireland in 1171, and the British have been exploiting the Irish ever since. Eight hundred years of oppression is long enough, wouldn't you say?"

The Irish begin stomping their feet, clapping their hands, and shouting, "Out of Ireland. Out of Ireland." Cusack starts chanting along with them, and now he's waving a bat in the direction of the students. He slams it down so hard on the bar we all stop dead in our tracks and turn to him.

Cusack hollers, "Let's hear once more from each of the parties concerned, and that's that. If anyone disagrees, they can continue discussing it with my partner here." He taps the top of his head. In one leaping bound Owen lands on the bar, scattering drinks in all directions and sending a bone-chilling howl across the room. I retrieve my drink in time. Cusack snaps his finger, and the hound retreats. Then he turns to the student and orders him to make his final statement.

I signal for another double.

"We want you," the student thunders, pointing both of his index fingers at me, "to get the fook out of Vietnam, and we want it *now*!"

"My dear boy, I hereby solemnly swear that the very moment the last British soldier departs from Irish soil, our evacuation from Vietnam begins."

Glasses are breaking, and punches are flying in every direction. Oh Jesus, I'm right in the middle of it. I've been hit in the face. I'm down. My God, they're kicking me. Christ, I'm bleeding. I feel the wind get knocked out of me and begin gasping for breath.

The hound—he's getting the students off me. Whistles. What are those whistles? It's the police. They're picking me up.

"Yeah, yeah, I'm Okay," I tell a constable. "I just have to get washed up.... No. I don't need to go to the hospital. No. No doctor. I'll be all right. I need a taxi.... No. I don't want to file any charges. I'll be fine. Don't worry.... Yeah, thanks. I'm going to my hotel."

They steer me toward a taxi, and I collapse into the back seat. "The Royal Scot Hotel on Glasgow Road.... Sure, I'm Okay. No problem."

I finally get a glimpse of myself in the hotel bathroom mirror. Jesus Christ! I look like Rocky Graziano after a Tony Zale fight. I'd better get home and go into hiding. I can't let anyone I know see me like this. There's still a couple of a weeks to go before we're due back at the university. Hopefully, I'll look more human by then. What's next? Breaking out in handcuffs?

# 21

Well, it's been more than a week since my pummeling. I sneak a peek in the mirror to reassure myself. "I think you're presentable now."

"Jesus Christ, luv!" Budgen recoils as I climb into his cab.

"The university, Budgen."

He turns around and stares at me, then grunts.

"Accident, Budgen. It was *an accident*. I tripped and fell down a flight of stairs at the hotel in Edinburgh. I'm a lot prettier than I was a week ago."

Now he's staring in his rearview mirror and shaking his head.

"Yes, Budgen, I do look a wee bit ragged. Don't worry. There's no permanent damage. I'll be looking like Steve McQueen again in a week or so."

Another grunt.

"I'll tell you what, Budgen. The next time I take a trip anywhere and have the slightest concern about the company I keep, I'll let you drive me there, Okay? In fact, I'll sit on your lap. Is that better?"

Another slight shake of the head, and he finally sets the car in motion.

When I'm dropped off at the department, I use the back-door stairway to sneak into Mountjoy's office. Take the offensive.

"All right, Your Lordship, how do I look?"

Mountjoy's eyes open wide he thinks for a moment and says, "How do you look? Like a Lazarus whose resurrection was botched by a clumsy deity." He starts to pour a glass of sherry. I try to stop him by raising my hands, but it's too late, so I accept the glass.

"Not to worry," says Mountjoy. "The way you disport yourself is of no concern to me." He shifts his lower jaw to the right and mutters, "Yah see. We're like brudders, Mack. You lie and I sweah to it. Got dat?" Before I can react, he adds, "I'm getting rather good at this, am I not?"

"I'd swear dat you wuz a nadif Noo Yawkuh. By the way, how did that New Year's Eve *soirée* of yours go?"

"It was as tedious as one could possibly imagine. Priscilla, however, was pleased. After all, you weren't there, and Somerset chose to isolate himself and pout the entire time. On cue, the assembled recited from their scripts and seemed happiest when the evening had drawn to a close. While departing, Somerset mumbled something about being ignored and treated as if he were a pariah. He *was*, of course, ignored, and he is, without question, a pariah."

"I'm glad you mentioned Somerset. My footnotes now cite everything he's written since the age of three. That should please him," I moan, "almost as much as it embarrasses me."

"Splendid. That'll make it all the more difficult for him to find fault with your work. But you'd better keep making queries about a place for him to relocate. He asked me about you when he first arrived at the party, and your absence may in part explain his pouting. Since he's sociopathic as well as paranoid, I think the main reason for his dismay was being unable to hear what you've done for, *or*—to him."

"Maybe it's the company he was keeping."

"Ehhhhhh, true. How did it go up in Scotland? Or does your appearance speak to that question?"

"I got along quite well with MacCumhaill."

"Really? I've heard he's not the genial type."

"MacCumhaill mentioned he's been in contact with Ogden."

"Quite likely. Those in their position often commiserate with one another about respective cock-ups."

"Anyway, he wanted to know whether or not I'd be willing to be resident director there should they decide to take on our students. I can usually lie with the best of them, but he seemed to be looking right through me. So, I felt I had no choice but to tell him that, in all likelihood, I could not accept. Ogden must have given me a ringing endorsement. I suspect they might take a chance with us if I were on board, but my not going could kill the deal. Being a savior is a two-edged sword, isn't it?"

"Ask Jesus of Nazareth. I can't recall him pleading for an opportunity to give it another go. By the way, did you look like this before or after your meeting with MacCumhaill?"

"After. I'll say just this in the way of explanation. I was nearly beaten to death by a gang of pacifists at a local pub there."

Mountjoy smiles and, to my relief, changes the subject.

"I see you've harvested a bushel full of posts. Anything there from Interpol?"

"I didn't see any in this batch, but there *is* something from the Oxford University Press. This could be their verdict. Let's see." I study the letter. "They love my book, yak, yak, yak, and are anxious to go to contract. That's good. *But* they want a stipulation stating they are authorized to edit my quotations if the editorial board recommends it be done. Translation? They want the right, should they so choose, to modify or eradicate every damn one of them."

"Why are they so concerned with your quotations? They're the stuff of history, the signature of our craft, the ruse through which we disguise the fact that these books are the ones we've been copying from."

"Agreed. However, you're referring to conventional quotations and footnotes. I've got over a thousand of *them*, but that's not what they're talking about. There's a dimension to my book that sets it apart. It's laced with quotations from two literary works that serve as still, small voices throughout the text—a sort of poor man's Greek chorus. Although I shouldn't say 'poor man's' when the authors I'm talking about are Homer and Euripides. The editors at Oxford apparently can't make head or tail of how I'm using them. I'm not going to compromise. I've made up my mind on this."

"Standing up to Oxford, are we? There's hope for you yet. But perhaps you need not rebuff them. Merely put them at arm's length for now, just as they do with authors. Why not tell them this is something that requires further reflection and a rereading of the manuscript on your part? In the meantime, send it off to let's say Cambridge, or Routledge, for that matter. Now there's a good scholarly press. Is this type of publisher suitable as far as that bedeviling committee of yours is concerned? If you need another copy or two of the manuscript, I'm sure Miss Popper could arrange to have one of the undersecretaries see to it."

"I get it. Keep the gold medal within reach while flirting with the silver and the bronze. Any of those three publishers will do. To tell you the truth, I didn't realize you could submit a manuscript to more than one publisher at a time. It's a great idea. They take forever to let you know where they stand. It could take longer to publish a book than it does to write one. If Miss Popper can get me a couple of copies typed, I'll follow through on it."

He nods and says, "What else have you got there? Heard anything from your wandering and wayward scholars requiring attention?"

"They're wandering and wayward all right, but scholars? Aside from one, possibly two, I doubt it. They should be back by now or here soon. Classes start next week, don't they?"

"Yehhhs. We say lectures, old boy."

"Let me thumb through these. Well, there's a full deck of postcards from my urchins, no doubt boasting about where they've been. Look." I hold them up in clusters and announce, "Three Eiffel Towers, two Davids, two Sistine Chapels, one Parthenon, one Prado, one Munich Glockenspiel, and a partridge in a pear tree.

"You know something strange? At times like this I almost miss Stein. He would have sent me a Bosch, or a Brueghel, or a snapshot of Kafka's death mask. There's nothing of that caliber here. Uh-oh. Wrong again. Here it is. A letter that looks like it's written in

Carolingian minuscule. This has to be Fleischmann." I lift my sherry glass, look skyward, and say, "Here's hoping Marthe is closeted with Lionel and they're exchanging Beowulf puns to the point of orgasm."

"Shades of Barrett and Browning, if not von Flotow's *Martha*. Whatever happened must be of consequence, judging by your insouciant reaction to the letter. In bygone days, a fleeting reference to Fleischmann was met with a furrowing of your brow, but I see none of that now. Perhaps you'd like me to take a stab at reading *that one*." He reaches over, but I instinctively clutch it to my chest.

His grin blossoms into a full smile.

Regroup. "Looks can be deceptive. One always has to be concerned about the likes of her. I'd better see what's going on down there." I open the envelope and pull out the single page. *Brace yourself*. Hmm. Nothing about the hotel débâcle. No mention of any communiqué to Irwin. No threats. How strange. Maybe posing as a eunuch has advantages. "She says everything is going *splendidly*."

"That's a shock," says Mountjoy.

"It sure is. It looks like her relationship with that lecturer has taken a serious turn. They're talking about getting married, and soon. That could be a problem, no?"

"It all depends on when it happens and who's involved. If the wedding takes place after the academic year, I doubt anyone would hold you responsible for nature taking its course. However, if it occurs during the academic year, then there could be a problem, at least with *your* people. We generally turn a blind eye towards such nonsense. Americans, on the other hand, tend to be puerile when it comes to such matters."

"I get it. Here's my advice to the young lady: 'My dear Miss Fleischmann, may I, as your moral tutor, offer some counsel in regard to your matrimonial intentions? I say, with all due respect, go right ahead and fuck the right honorable Mr. Lionel Blum's brains out for now, but do put off marriage until the academic year has drawn to a close. I think you will, upon reflection, agree this course of action is in the best interests of all parties concerned. Yours sincerely, Dr. Aloysius T. Gogarty.'"

Mountjoy comments, "Pithy, circumspect, and to the point. What else would a responsible mentor say under such circumstances?"

"Oops." Two more postcards fall from the stack. "Well, speaking of wayward students, guess whom these are from?" I hold them up in my right hand. "The one on the left is a picture of the boulder of granite covering Charles Stewart Parnell's grave, and all the unsigned card says, in larger-than-life print, is 'Kitty O'Shea put the Chief here.' The other is the Martello tower in Dublin, where Joyce stayed before he left for Europe. What's this scribbling say on the back? Oh yeah—'*Non serviam*,' I will not serve."

Mountjoy adds, "The Chief? Parnell? He was a Cambridge man who had no love for England. In the same vein, you, I presume, are referring to the obstreperous one whose name I'm always forgetting. O'Flaherty, O'Toole, or something equally disagreeable."

"O'Brien. The heir apparent to the Stein legacy. But the question is, who or what does O'Brien refuse to serve? Me? The study-abroad program? The IRA? The church? The queen? I hate fragments."

"I wouldn't be unduly concerned about your Fenian unless he's caught blowing up Parliament; which may not be a bad idea, considering what the Labour Party has been up to lately."

"Bite your tongue. No, not about the Labour Party. About blowing up Parliament. That's all we need—another Guy Fawkes Day."

"I shouldn't have alarmed you with that. Perhaps you'll find some solace in the fact that O'Brien strikes me as a twattler rather than a man of action. He thinks too much and continues to get in his own way. He'll probably wind up being a professor in America."

"Wait. Here's a letter from Elena. Sorry, Your Grace—I have to retreat to my sanctuary for this one."

"Abandoning a glass of sherry? Bewitched, are we?"

"Bewitched, bothered, and bewildered." I gulp down the sherry and rush off to my office.

As I open the letter I breathe in a muted, but evocative, scent. It's Elena's perfume.

*December 26, 1967*

*Dear Aloysius,*

*Thank you very much for your lovely Christmas card. It was very thoughtful of you.*

*You may recall I said in a previous letter I would contact you once again. This is what I'm doing presently, and I hope I'm not making a nuisance of myself. I'm afraid the situation with my father has not improved. If anything, it's more troubling than ever. Recent developments lead me to believe my worst fears are well-founded.*

*Those fears have me doing things that I'm not at all comfortable with, but I see as necessary under the circumstances. I've been prying into my father's personal business by asking him many questions about his trip to England. His answers have been unsatisfactory, or, I should say, unconvincing. I'll give you an example. He told me that he was going to a conference in London for Spanish teachers working with students whose native language is English. That would make sense. However, I went to some people I know from the Romance Languages and Education departments here at Municipal, and none of them could find any reference to a conference of that description in London at that time of the year. I fear this is an invention on my father's part, designed to prevent me from becoming suspicious of what he's actually up to.*

*I know, shame on me. I've even gone so far as to look through my father's notes in his study while he was sleeping. That's what I'm writing to you about. It seems he's been in contact with someone named Rodriguez, which is a common name among us, but I suspect a pseudoname (is that the right word?). Anyway, this man has been passing information on to him about something that's going on in Cuba and a Cuban who's going to be in England at the same time as my father. I'm very concerned about what Papá's getting into. You see, he's had trouble with his blood pressure and has already suffered a heart attack. At his age, and in his condition, this trip could prove fatal to him.*

*I told my father I could arrange to go with him, but he got terribly angry with me for even mentioning it and said my place was here with Miguelito. I suggested he contact you there, but he dismissed the idea. I don't even know what I am asking of you, so I would fully understand it if you simply tore up this letter or ignored it. All I know is something has been telling me to seek your help on this.*

*Here's the rest of what I've discovered in a letter he'd hidden under his bed. Whoever it is that my father needs to see is going to be in London to meet with someone else on April third. On that day the person in question from Cuba is supposed to make contact with whomever else it is at ten-thirty p.m. in a London subway station. It gets even more confusing here. This meeting will take place either at a train station called Waterloo or another one called Cockfosters. My father himself won't know which station it is until he gets a phone call at his hotel in London. I don't even know what hotel he's staying at, or if I'll be able to find that out. Papá must have hidden the information somewhere else or destroyed it.*

*This is a real mess, isn't it? Don't get me wrong. I don't expect you to do anything in particular about this. The whole thing is scary, and I don't want to put you in a dangerous situation. All I really needed was to tell someone else about all of this. To be honest, I don't feel comfortable enough with anyone else. Of course, if there's anything you can suggest that I can do to protect my father, or there's anything you can do at your end to help, it would be immensely appreciated.*

*Yours,*
*Elena*

I'd better get back to Mountjoy's office and have him take a look at this.

He reads the letter and looks up at me.

I say, "Yup; that's the whole background. From the beginning I had a feeling that someday Torquemada—his real name is Miguel de la Flora—might be looking for a way to make Elena's husband pay for the way she was treated. My suspicion is he may have contacted someone in Cuba and is arranging for an encounter of some sort with his son-in-law."

"What does he have against him?"

Mountjoy's forgotten.

"Apparently the husband was supposed to meet Elena and their son in Spain and then all of them would go to the United States and be granted political asylum. I think I mentioned already that he never left Cuba."

"Oh yes. So, *is* your Torquemada capable of killing his son-in-law?"

"I wouldn't put it past him."

"Well then, it could be a cloak-and-dagger operation, but it may just as well not be. Let's step back for a moment. First and foremost, what do you expect to gain from playing a role in this *telenovela*?"

"I'm not sure. At the very least, I suppose, Elena's gratitude for being supportive of her."

"Is that enough? Will that do?"

"Not really. What I'd like to do is get her father back to New York in one piece. My best guess is Elena's husband's coming to England for whatever reason, and the old man wants to wreak havoc on the good doctor for abandoning his daughter and grandson."

"How old is de la Flora?"

"Late sixties or so. It's hard to tell. As you've read, he's already had a heart attack, but he appears to be healthy otherwise. I would guess he's determined to confront the husband."

"So, you're convinced something untoward will occur?"

"Not necessarily. But his trip here doesn't make much sense otherwise."

"I have two suggestions. First, let me ascertain whether there's a conference of any sort suitable for a man of his background taking place in England in March or April."

"Good idea. And?"

"Should there be nothing of the sort, and I will know soon enough, I'd urge you to consult Sergeant MacChesney on this matter."

"From *Gunga Din*? Oh, you mean Ferguson. I really don't think I should get him involved. I've got a bad feeling about all this, and I don't want to have to ask him to stick his neck out again. He's already made himself vulnerable by," looking behind me to make sure the door is closed, "I can't say it any other way—suppressing evidence. I have no right to jeopardize him further."

"Granted. And a jolly good fellow he is for that. But if you can explain to him what you do know, perhaps he can unofficially advise you about what course of action to take."

"Yes, but even then, if something goes haywire, he could be guilty of being an accessory before the fact, or whatever they call that. My inclination is to not let him know a damn thing about it."

"Understood. However, if this de la Flora chap won't know which Tube station is in play here, simple logic dictates someone else needs to be posted at the other locale."

"I've thought of that, but no, I don't want to involve *anyone* else."

"Don't despair, Gogarty, there's always someone"—he points to himself—"who's damn fool enough to take the bait out of curiosity, if nothing else."

"No. No. Not you."

"Who then? Somerset? Fleischmann? *O'Brien*? Not many options here, are there? Not to worry. I have a strong feeling this is going to resolve itself and nothing will come of it. However, if something unpleasant does occur, I'm your man. I've always had a talent for rising to the occasion and introducing unanticipated tactics that confound the opposition."

"You sound like Alexander."

"Precisely. What was it he did at the Punjab when his horses refused to cross the river against that rajah's elephants?"

"He had a soldier who was his double dress in royal attire and parade in and out of the king's tent accompanied by his usual advisors, while the real Alexander was up north crossing the river unopposed.. It was a brilliant *coup de théâtre*. So, you think you could match the great one?"

"Well, I doubt that I have a double, and it seems unlikely I'll encounter elephants in London. However, I can assure you that, should I be the chosen one, I shall come up with something unique in conception and bold and brazen in execution. Bring on the skullduggery!"

# 22

---

"Goodbye, O'Brien." I sigh and place my office phone back on the receiver. Well, there goes the other shoe. It's a good thing I told his lecturers he might be back late from Ireland. I'd better see Ferguson on this.

Budgen drives me to police headquarters and I ask the desk sergeant if Ferguson is in. He does a double take when he sees my face, scrutinizes my passport, and points me toward Ferguson's office. Inside, Ferguson is studying a file at his desk.

"Bob, I hate to take you away from what you're doing, but I need advice."

Ferguson looks up and doesn't even blink at my battered appearance. He points to a chair and gestures for me to sit down.

"It's that O'Brien boy I mentioned to you—James O'Brien. The one I said had an attitude toward the English?" He nods. "Well, he just called from Dublin and claims he's lost his passport. I could've told you that over the phone, but there may, just may, be something more to it. A little while back when I tracked him down at his residence hall, there were two Irish workmen there. They described themselves as housepainters but were clearly there for reasons other than painting. O'Brien says he met them in a pub in the Irish part of town. They're rough-edge sorts and not the type university students ordinarily associate with. O'Brien is one of those Irish Americans who tries to out-Irish the Irish, if you know what I mean."

"I do."

"I don't *think* O'Brien's the criminal type, but you never know. Anyway, for whatever reason, I remember the names of those fellows. One calls himself James Carey, and the other James Fitzharris. Now, I may be off base here, but I couldn't help but wonder if maybe one, or even both, had ties to one of those Irish groups you and your colleagues keep tabs on. Anyway, they're all named James, and they're all Irish."

"The James Boys, eh? We keep track of everyone here with last names like theirs, including professors, by the way."

"How do you like that? The customs officials at Heathrow wound up probing every orifice in my body, and I thought it was because I was cuter than most guys."

Ferguson laughs. It's the first time I've seen him laugh.

"That's standard operating procedure for Irishmen of any sort today. Rest assured, I'll make this a priority and run those names through our special unit. They monitor potential troublemakers—especially those who might have a political agenda. I don't want to alarm you unduly, but if either one of the two turns out to be on any of their lists, we've got a much bigger mess on our hands than Stein's escapades. I hope you appreciate the fact there are certain issues I simply cannot involve myself with, and this, I'm afraid, could be one of them. Anything related to terrorism or having international implications has to be referred to the appropriate authorities in London."

I feel the blood drain from my face.

Ferguson puts his hand on my shoulder and says in a soothing tone, "Easy there, Aloysius. Let's not assume a doomsday scenario—at least not yet. And nothing at this stage prevents me from determining where the jurisdiction lies. Until then, it's perfectly legitimate for me to make inquiries."

"Bob, under no circumstances do I want you, in any way, to stick your neck out any further for me. You must promise me the minute it becomes clear to you this case belongs in somebody else's bailiwick, please, *please*, drop it immediately. I should let you know something else that came to mind, though. There's always the possibility that O'Brien might be pulling a fast one by supplying his painter friends, or somebody else, with his passport. They could replace his picture on it, couldn't they?"

"Yes, and change the name, and alter the accompanying data as well. They're very good at it these days. But let's see what we can find out before we begin fretting. Write down everything you know about the O'Brien boy, including his address here. In addition, jot down the names of those painters and anyone else he's been seen with. I also need to know exactly where he's been in Ireland. Can you do that now?" He hands me a notepad and a pen.

As I'm writing I tell him, "I'm fairly certain he went to Cork and stopped at the Blarney Stone, and he was supposed to visit the West Coast, but apparently he's been spending most of his time in Dublin."

After I hand the list to Ferguson he says, "Why don't you go back to the university, at least for now? Just leave numbers where you can be reached today."

I take the list back and scratch down my office number and Mountjoy's, too, even though I know Bob has them. "I promised the O'Brien boy I'd call him back at exactly five fifteen tonight. I've got the phone number of his hotel in Dublin and his room number there, so I'll scribble those down, too. I advised him to sit tight until we know more."

Ferguson nods and says, "This demands immediate attention. I hope to be back in contact with you before five o'clock."

"Look, Bob. If you ever figure out how I can repay you, you've got it, whatever it is. I mean *whatever*. No strings attached."

"Just doing my job," he says blankly. His inflection stops me dead in my tracks. Look at that smile. He knows what he's saying and how he's saying it. Now he's putting on a deadpan expression, and I think I know what's coming next.

"All we want are the facts, ma'am."

"You... *you* are a *Dragnet* fan? Boy, you guys really are going down the drain, aren't you? Joe Friday? Whatever happened to good old Sherlock Holmes?"

"Who's that, ma'am?"

I shake my head and leave, smiling. Budgen drives me back to the university and I head straight to Mountjoy's office.

Mountjoy takes a glance at me and remarks, "That look of anguish on your face matches your appearance, Dr. Gogarty."

"Well, let's put it this way: you ain't seen nuthin' yet."

"Don't tell me Frankenstein's left his crypt. No? Then it most certainly has to be you, or another one of your darling students."

"Your favorite, O'Brien."

"Lovely. Tell me. What's he done? Mutilated the Whistler collection at the Tate Gallery?"

"Not yet, but he may be up to something just as mischievous. He's stuck in Ireland because he's lost his passport, or so he claims. I'm suspicious, though, and I've just gone downtown and spoken to Ferguson about it."

"A wise move. What concerns you?"

"I don't know, but there's something fishy here. A few weeks ago, when I was with O'Brien, a couple of Irish pals of his showed up— the confrontational type."

"The only type."

"Well, they may be a problem. Anyway, the boy's stuck in Dublin and can't get back here until he retrieves his passport or gets a duplicate from the American embassy there. And if he doesn't get his wallet back, he'll need a couple of hundred bucks to pay his hotel bill."

"The money for O'Brien's hotel can be transferred from your account at Barclay's. Amalia Popper can arrange it without any difficulty."

"That makes sense, and it's a relief. I've got to scoot back over to my office. There's a pile of mail from the States there, and I owe Fleischmann a phone call."

"As a Catholic, Aloysius, have you ever considered the possibility that you may be paying for some unthinkable transgression earlier in life?"

"I often have that feeling—and not just about what I did as a kid. I've got to run. Bye."

Just as I walk into my office, the phone rings and startles me. It's always a shock when this damn phone rings. The room is empty except for a desk and two chairs, and every tiny sound gets amplified.

"Dr. Gogarty here. Marthe?" Oh great; what does she want now?

"So, tell me, what's up?... Oh, sure, Marthe. I'll be there toward the end of this month or the beginning of March. Would that suit you?... Great. Goodbye." Nothing said about my absconding from the hotel. That's good. I think.

Might as well find out what Cambridge has to say. Let's see. They like the book very much and are quite impressed by the notes and the bibliography . . . they like the style... there it is, *but*. Let me guess. Yup. If they could trim the quotations down or perhaps eliminate some of them, they feel they'd have an impressive biography on their hands. They sound like Oxford, except Oxford didn't come right out and say it.

I should've asked for a hundred and forty-seven copies of the manuscript. It would improve my chances of getting published. Routledge will probably go through the same song and dance. If that's the case, I may have to be flexible. What's the point in writing a book if it never sees the light of day? What was Joyce's fear? "Who anywhere will ever read these written words?"

This note says call Routledge. I dial the number and a secretary answers the phone.

"Yes, this is Professor Gogarty, and I am returning Sydney Schiff's call.... Yes, I'll hold. Thank you.... Hello, it's Aloysius Gogarty. I have a message here to call you.... Really? Well, what do you think?... Oh, I'm glad to hear that. Do you have any reservations about my approach?... Great!"

I might as well find out about the stumbling block now and get it over with.

"What do you think of the quotations from Homer and Euripides I've interspersed throughout the book?... You *love* them? What role do you think they play in the book?... You're spot-on." Better not let Mountjoy hear me talking like that.

"I'm delighted you picked up on my intentions, and I'm sure it didn't happen by accident. What's your background?... Classics at Cambridge? I'm impressed. Any major changes anticipated?... Great. What's our timeline? I'm being evaluated for tenure back at my college in the States, and it's critical I have a contract in hand as soon as possible.... Oh? Okay. I understand, but I'm counting on you to accelerate the process. Otherwise, I'm afraid I may have to go elsewhere with it.... Okay. Goodbye for now."

That got him. I think we may be in business and *on time*. I hate to manipulate a man like Schiff, but desperate times call for desperate measures.

Here's a surprise. I pick up the envelope. What does Abe Rosenbach, my drinking buddy back at Municipal, have to say?

January 15, 1968

Dear Aloysius (what a stupid name),

Thought I'd let you know my chairman forced me to serve on the Promotion and Tenure Committee, the one deciding your fate. Keep this to yourself (we're sworn to secrecy), but at our first meeting Irwin offered a profile of each candidate. When it came to you, let's just say you'd better have a contract for that book of yours, and you'd better do what's necessary to keep the University of Edinburgh happy. Otherwise, it looks like your goose is cooked. Irwin, who isn't worth a roasted fart in hell, didn't come right out and say it, but that's what he implied. And, by the way, if he ever discovers you found out about this through me, you'd better plan on auditioning for the papal castrati. Get it?

Abe R.

Mountjoy is right. Just because you're paranoid doesn't mean they're not after you. Better pop in and get his take on this.

"Here I am again, boss, a glutton for punishment."

"And well deserved. What, pray tell, is the latest installment in your lugubrious saga?"

"Well, I just heard it confirmed from a colleague back at Municipal that Irwin isn't enamored of me, and my tenure looks, well, precarious."

"Who can blame him? I wouldn't feel beholden to anyone who damned near killed me, either. Tell me something I didn't know."

"Routledge loves my book. At least the editor whose desk it landed on does. In fact, he thinks it ought to be published basically as is, meaning without major changes."

"Well, it sounds like you've stumbled upon someone as unbalanced as yourself. What more could you ask for?"

"True, but he has to present his recommendation to their editorial board, and *they* will decide whether or not to go ahead with it."

"That's what publishers do, isn't it?"

"I guess. But as far as I'm concerned, they have to do it in time for me to pass on proof of a contract to the committee in New York."

"What else did that colleague of yours have to say about this tenure nonsense?"

"Well, just between us, he's on the committee. Top secret and all that, but he says the book and what happens with Edinburgh will be the determining factors in my case."

"You may not need to concern yourself about any of it. O'Brien might be in the process of blowing up your future as we speak."

"True."

The phone rings.

"Mountjoy here. Hello, Bob. Yes, he's here right now. Just a moment, please." He hands me the phone.

"Yes, Bob, I'm sitting down.... Really? What does that mean? What's my next step?... Okay, wait a minute. . . . Bye."

"Yehhhs?"

"You're not going to believe this."

"Everything you do strains credulity."

"O'Brien's passport was found at the entrance to the Blarney Stone. The Cork police are forwarding it with his money intact to their counterparts in Dublin. They'll pass everything on to O'Brien at his hotel. They also know what O'Brien's been up to in Dublin. He has, by and large, been retracing the footsteps of Stephen Dedalus and Leopold Bloom in Joyce's *Ulysses.* He's also interviewing Jewish people in Dublin about when their family first arrived in Ireland and asking if they know any Jews who can trace their presence on the old sod back past the nineteenth century."

"He sounds like another half-breed, similar to... uh... *you.* What about those troglodytes he's been socializing with?"

"Nothing nefarious. Just two Irishmen doing what they said they were doing: painting houses. Can you believe it?"

"Barely. So, you've been spared once again, Houdini. What's your next step?"

"First, I'll call O'Brien and tell him to sit tight at the hotel until he gets his stuff back. Then I'll instruct him to pay his bill and get his royal Irish arse back here in due haste."

"And... no reverberations from down south?"

"Who are you, Tiresias? I spoke to Fleischmann earlier today, and she needs to see me when I get down there."

"When is that?"

"Soon."

"I have an ultimatum for you."

"Oh?"

"If you dare put Oxford on your itinerary, mark my words, I shall book a flight to New York and have *una conversación intima con su monstruo de una mujer.*"

"That sounds like Elena. You win. Oxford is stricken from the battle plan, at least for now. One more thing. Didn't you say you had contacts in Australia? I'm getting a strong feeling I may be somewhere other than New York next year, and that's the only destination that interests me."

"Yehhhs. It is highly unlikely there'll be anything available for the likes of you here, but Australia is quite a different story."

"Thanks, pal. No offense, but I couldn't take another year here, anyway. Who's your rabbi down under?"

"Rabbi? If by that you mean associate, it's an old schoolmate of mine from Magdalen, who happens to be the registrar at Macquarie University. Rare for someone his age, but as I've already suggested, standards are considerably lower there. Without elaborating, let me say that I have every reason to believe that, should I press the point, he'd do everything in his power to find something for you."

"Jesus. What do you have on him? It must be a doozy for you to talk like that."

"I suppose it is a 'doozy,' whatever that might be."

"Would you be willing to write to him soon?"

"I'll get to it immediately after conferring with Bertie. I'm on my way there now to attend to some school business. It relates to our departmental retreat. And, while you're here, let me put it this way about that event: I trust you haven't the slightest interest in attending."

"I knew nothing about it until this very moment, but it sounds like something I might really enjoy. What is it? When is it? Why wouldn't I be interested in it? Or, I should ask, why don't you want me there?"

Mountjoy recites, "'The School of History's annual retreat at Otterburn is an event where both staff members and students spend three days discussing the historian's craft.' In other words, it's guaranteed to be a stupefying experience."

"You haven't answered all my questions. When is it?"

"At the beginning of March. Bertie and I are working out the dates and logistics of it today."

"Well, I might be able to juggle my calendar to include it."

"You're forcing me to tell you something I intended to keep to myself. It's not me who doesn't want you there; it's my colleague, Gerald Duckworth. Duckworth, you see, always takes charge of the retreat once we get to Otterburn, and he's already expressed concerns about the prospect of your being there."

"To BEB?"

"Of course not. To me."

"Why?"

"He fears your presence may be—how can I say this without offending you?—the equivalent of unleashing a lethal contaminant at the event."

"On whom? You?"

"I think it's fair to say the entire gathering. Before you become irretrievably despondent, let me explain. You may recall I once described Duckworth as one of those Marxists you'll find on any university campus in England. Someone as unspeakably bourgeois as can be imagined. Duckworth is a puritanical Marxist to boot, the most repulsive of all. He looks upon you as a cardinal example of moral turpitude, the reprehensible type American capitalism inevitably breeds."

"I thought the more I caricatured what Americans are thought to be, the more acceptable I'd become."

"To most of us. For someone like Duckworth, the notion of redeeming qualities in men of your ilk is unfathomable."

"The more I hear about this retreat, the more I like it. What if I said, for public consumption, that regrettably I am unable to attend? But then, let's say on the second day of the retreat, I appear from out of the heavens in a helicopter—rented of course—with a blonde floozy on my lap, smoking a gargantuan cigar, with bottles of Seagram's 7 bulging out of both of my pockets?"

"Duckworth would simply sigh and nod. It's precisely what he'd expect of you."

"Let me mull this over. I'll tell you what. If I'm for all practical purposes banned from the retreat, I may have to revise my schedule, regardless of the consequences. All things considered, especially in light of a personal affront, I might very well decide to stop in Oxford, just for old time's sake."

212

"You wouldn't dare."

"Wouldn't I?"

"Ehhhhh... I suppose you would."

"It looks like the beginning of March is going to be a busy time. If you were me, would you go to Oxford? Otterburn? Both?"

"If I were you, I'd have dispensed with myself earlier in life."

"You're dodging the question. I'll have to think this through."

Mountjoy's face takes on a grim expression. "*That*, my dear boy, is anything but comforting."

# 23

The office phone rings and it doesn't startle me. I must be getting accustomed to things around here. The voice at the other end sounds familiar.

"Sure, I remember you. You're the *New York Times* reporter who interviewed me about my articles on Alexander. You were going to wait until both of them were published to write your piece.... They're out now and so is your article? Great.... Today, February twenty-ninth? There's a place downtown that gets a couple of copies of the *Times*, but they're usually a day behind. Where is it in the paper?... Thanks for tracking me down and letting me know.... Good luck to you as well."

The phone goes off again.

"Norma? *Norma* from the History Department at Municipal College? Hi, Mrs. Mendes. What a nice surprise hearing from you.... Oh. I'm sorry you're getting bombarded with phone calls. Tell them to call the School of History here. I left that number with the chairman. I apologize for the inconvenience. Hello? Hello?" Gone.

This damn phone is ringing off the hook.

"*Five* calls already, Miss Popper? I *am* sorry.... You don't mind? Oh, good. Look, these calls must be about an article that came out in the *Times*—that is, the *New York Times*—today. I just found out about it, or I would have alerted you. I'm afraid there may be more calls, some coming from the States. I just told our secretary back in New York to give anyone who's looking for me your number. Is that all right?... Good. How do you suggest we handle this?... Okay. I'll relocate to Mountjoy's office.... The *Times*? Why would they call me? Their article is out already.... oh, the London *Times*. Mountjoy calls it *Thee Times*.... The BBC? Okay. I got it. All calls will be routed through you."

I charge into Mountjoy's office. "All hell has broken loose."

"So, they tell me, old boy. So, they tell me."

"Miss Popper suggested I camp out here to field these phone calls. Apparently, your extension is easier to connect with than mine. Are you all right with that?"

"Amalia and I already discussed this, and we agreed it makes sense."

"I have to get to these two right away—*Thee Times* and the BBC."

Mountjoy ushers me into his seat while screeching in a falsetto, "A celebrity among us. How thrilling!"

"You think so? We'll see."

The phone rings. "Hello. You're from *Thee Times*?... No, I'm afraid I haven't seen the *New York Times* article yet. In fact, I just heard of it a few minutes ago.... Yes, that's what my articles are about.... Well, there are as many definitions of alcoholism as there are researchers in the field, but if someone burns down a billion-dollar palace while he's intoxicated, and winds up killing a man who once saved his life in a drunken brawl, there may be a drinking problem of some sort, wouldn't you say?... I see. You just want to be sure what's been said in the *New York Times* article represents how I see the problem. Well, since I don't have the paper at hand right now, why don't you quote what interests you from the article, and I'll tell you if it's accurate or not." I listen as he reads.

"Yup, that's true.... Yes, more or less.... Uh-huh. It sounds like the reporter basically paraphrased what I said in my articles.... No. I haven't seen my articles in print yet, but of course I know what I said in them. . . . Okay. When will this appear in your paper?... Tomorrow? March first? I am really looking forward to reading it. Thanks." I think Miss Popper said the BBC call's up next.

"Hello, it's Professor Aloysius Gogarty.... Yes, that's right. I am up at Yorkshire University this year.... When do you want me there? Yes, I can make it. What do you need from me?... Okay. I can do that."

I look up at Mountjoy. "Guess what? I'm being interviewed by the BBC in London tomorrow afternoon. The timing is perfect. I told the girls at Berkshire I was coming down to see them this weekend and to make sure they're available."

Mountjoy looks impressed but doesn't say it. I'll put him on the spot.

"Well, what do you think of the BBC wanting to interview little old me?"

"Indisputable evidence the world we once knew is now on a death watch. How did all this come about?"

"I wrote a couple of articles on Alexander and *his* guzzling."

"A subject in which you are well versed."

"Just doing some lab work, Your Grace."

Mountjoy's face lights up, and he says, "Lesson well remembered."

"Anyway, I was wondering where I should publish them and thought of a friend of mine at Harvard. He's the editor of a journal that publishes scholarly articles on unconventional topics taken from an unconventional point of view. I told him about the two Alexander articles I was working on, and he said they were exactly what he was looking for."

"What are their titles? That would give me a sense of what they're about."

"One is called 'The Enigma of Alexander: The Alcohol Factor,' and the other is 'Alexander and Dionysus: The Invisible Enemy.'"

"What's unconventional about them?"

"Well, they were written to complement each other. The first is historical and documents Alexander's drinking. The second is sociological and deals with Greek perceptions of self-destructive drinking."

"Will your articles withstand the scrutiny of peers in the field?"

"I don't see why not."

"It doesn't surprise me so many people are making such a fuss over this. The idea of Alexander the Great being an alcoholic seems patently absurd on the face of it."

"I understand. How could anyone have a drinking problem and do what he did?"

"Precisely. The BBC interview is on the radio, not television, I trust."

"Yes. So, don't worry. I look good on radio."

Mountjoy fills a sherry glass for me. "You don't want the real stuff, do you?"

"Uh-uh. I'm going to hold off on everything. Haven't you noticed that I can take it or leave it?"

"What I *have* noticed is that you always take it."

"Well then, why disappoint you?" I swallow it in one gulp. "No more for now though. I need to remain clear up there in the committee room. Look at all these people I have to talk to," I say, holding up a paper with a list of single-spaced names reaching down to the bottom of the page.

The phone rings again.

"That's right. The Municipal College of the City of New York.... Macedonians drank wine.... No, they did not drink beer . . . except . . . under conditions of duress. Just joking.... Yes. He engaged in epic drinking bouts during the last few years of his life. No dramatic incidents involving drinking until he was twenty-six or so.... Yes. There was a progression. Drinking parties increased exponentially at the end of his life. I suppose the lesson to be learned is someone can be extraordinarily accomplished and have a drinking problem at the same time.... No, I haven't read the *New York Times* piece yet, but I hope to by tomorrow.... Yes. In fact right now I'm putting the final touches to a biography of Alexander. . . . No, I haven't selected a publisher yet, but expect that issue to be settled soon."

Mountjoy studies the list. "There are newspapers and magazines stretching from Yorkshire to Australia. You've stirred up quite a hornet's nest."

Miss Popper knocks once, enters the room, and does a double take when she sees me sitting in Mountjoy's chair. She delivers a typed sheet with more names on it and says, while looking at me, "Here we are, Mr. Mountjoy—or should I call you Dr. Mountjoy now?"

Mountjoy and I laugh. Miss Popper leaves, looking pleased with herself.

"My dear boy, we've just witnessed a momentous event."

"You mean all these journalists pandering to *me*?"

"No, no, no. Amalia. I would have bet my last tuppence she didn't have a humorous bone in her body."

"So, you're finally beginning to appreciate the positive ripple effect I'm having on those around me?"

"Yes, like the Great Plague of 1665. However, I was particularly pleased at the reference to your book a few moments ago. You should weave that into your BBC interview. The Oxford and Cambridge people and—who was that third publisher we spoke about?"

"Routledge."

"Right. They'll most likely hear about what you have to say on the BBC."

Mountjoy gathers his class notes and says, "Well, I wish I could stay here and listen to your inane jabbering, but I'm off to my two o'clock tutorial. If I were you, I would be most discreet in what I say; the newspapers can distort anything. Be particularly chary during your BBC appearance. Don't succumb to the unguarded moment and say something you'll regret. Once said, it's irretrievable. If things go right, this may serve you well."

"Thanks for letting me operate out of here."

"Not to worry. I'll have the office fumigated over the weekend."

The phone rings.

I look apologetically at Mountjoy and say, "There's Miss Popper putting a call through."

Mountjoy writes some words in capital letters, which I can't decipher because they're upside down. While I'm watching him, I check the list and answer the phone. Should be *Life Magazine*.

"Yes, this is Dr. Gogarty."

Mountjoy reverses the paper he's written on, so I can read it.

Veritas odium parit!

Uh... Truth... can... breed... animosity. In other words, beware of being *too* honest with them.

I throw a thumbs-up in Mountjoy's direction as he leaves.

They all seem to be asking the same questions. Let me look at this list. *Thee Times*. Check. The BBC. Check. *Life Magazine*. Check. The *Guardian*. Check. The *Los Angeles Times*. Check. The *Washington Post*. Check. *Der Spiegel*. Check. *Le Point*. Check. I'm not going to have any voice left for my BBC interview.

Isn't it odd? Yesterday, I would have been thrilled to be contacted by any one of these people, but I'm already getting sick of it. Fame isn't exactly what I thought it would be. How many so far? Too many.

Mountjoy returns, hears me reciting the same script, and leaves for home. Where's that list? Hmm. The *Weekend Australian*. That might come in handy. Better call Amalia.

"Miss Popper? Would you mind if I change the list around a little? Good. Could you put the *Weekend Australian* up next? Thanks. After that, I'm afraid I've had it for today. It's about time to close up shop anyway, isn't it?...

"Good. I have to be in London tomorrow for the BBC. If anyone else calls, kindly tell them I'm sorry, but I had to go out of town and won't be available until Monday afternoon. Oh, please slip in *Punch* right after the Australians; I don't want to leave them out, although God knows why they'd be interested in any of this.

"Could you also cancel my tutorial for tomorrow? Tell George Roberts he's been trumped by the BBC. I'm sure he'll understand. Miss Popper, how lucky Di... uh, Mr. Mountjoy"—God, I almost said Dickie—"is to have you."

"My pleasure," she replies.

I'll have Budgen drop me off at my local for a pint or two, then I'll pack it in for the night. Fame is not only fleeting, it's exhausting. Off to the Shoulder of Mutton for a touch of—what does His Lordship call it? That's it—the grand elixir.

# 24

Behold, Aloysius T. Gogarty on the brink of being interviewed by the BBC. My hands are sweaty, but my head isn't pounding. Praise be to God Almighty for including codeine in the creation. It cushions the burden of those who occasionally reach beyond their limits.

The red light flashes. We're about to go on the air. Focus on the host. *Speak louder than usual*—it breeds confidence. The host introduces the program and turns to me.

"And here's our first guest of the day, Dr. Aloysius T. Gogarty. Can you tell the audience a bit about yourself, Dr. Gogarty?"

I'm still sipping the water in front of me and nearly choke trying to gulp it down. The host smiles and waits patiently for me to recover.

"Certainly. I'm a visiting professor from Municipal College in New York currently lecturing at Yorkshire University and shepherding some American students on our study-abroad program."

He pats the air, telling me to lower the volume. I nod.

"How are your students adjusting to life in England and our university system?"

"They're learning a great deal and very much enjoying their experience here."

He throws a thumbs-up in my direction on the volume. "I'm delighted to hear that, Dr. Gogarty. You, however, have become the talk of the town. Or, I should say, your research has."

"I'm afraid that's true. My articles on Alexander's drinking have attracted a great deal of attention. I must confess I never expected anything of this magnitude."

"How did you become interested in Alexander the Great's drinking?"

"Well, like many others, I've always found Alexander to be a fascinating individual. Then one day during my undergraduate studies, a professor of mine remarked that Alexander's life was enigmatic. The enigma, he said, revolved around the fact that while Alexander was piling one victory on top of another, a perplexing change for the worse occurred in his personality. This change deepened during the last seven years of Alexander's life and was marked by a progressive deterioration of character. If anyone could unravel this enigma, the professor told us, he'd be making a significant contribution to history. There and then I decided that, someday, I would take up the challenge."

"Could you elaborate on this 'deterioration of character' for us?"

"Certainly. Alexander became suspicious of friends as well as enemies, unpredictable, volatile, and increasingly megalomaniacal. Toward the end of his life, Alexander was almost totally isolated, a warrior king feared by his own soldiers, an unpredictable man capable of doing just about anything."

"And you link this metamorphosis to his drinking?"

"Yes, and I do so mainly because the sources point in that direction."

"Was Alexander's drinking a problem early in life?"

"Not as far as we know. In fact, in his youth, Alexander was highly critical of his father, Philip II, in this respect. At Philip's seventh and last wedding, Alexander, about nineteen at the time, was insulted by the bride's uncle, and a quite drunk Philip thought his son was causing the disruption. Philip drew his sword and lunged toward Alexander, but the drink had gotten to him, and he wound up sprawling headfirst to the floor. At that point, Alexander peered down at his father and said contemptuously, 'And here is the man who

222

intends to cross from Europe into Asia, and he can't even make it from one couch to the other.' Clearly a reference to his father's drinking."

The host interjects, "And yet, he would wind up walking or, in your view, stumbling in his father's footsteps, no?"

I smile. "Yes. Eventually it was 'like father, like son.' Nine years after that wedding, while in outer Asia, Alexander, in the grip of a drunken rage himself, attacked a family friend named Cleitus who he thought was disrupting *his* party. Unlike his father, Alexander got to the man and skewered him on the spot. With that Alexander ironically and tragically emulated the behavior he found so reprehensible in his father."

"Why hasn't anyone else noticed this pattern?"

"Some historians have hinted at it, but up until now no one has assembled the evidence necessary to make a persuasive case. We also have to remember that Alexander is considered by most people, including many distinguished scholars, to be a hero, and who's keen on seeing their hero demythologized?"

The host nods his head in agreement and winks an appreciation of my response.

"Did any of those around Alexander drink in like fashion?"

"His dearest friend Hephaestion was a notorious tippler. They were so close Alexander likened their relationship to that of Achilles and Patroclus, and the king once referred to his friend as his *alter ego.*

"That's of special interest to us, because Hephaestion's death parallels that of the king. In 324 BC, the year *before* Alexander died, Hephaestion, after intensive boozing, came down with a high fever and remained ill for a week. Then, feeling better, and against the advice of his physician, washed his *breakfast* down with *a half-gallon of chilled wine.* That morning bracer proved to be his last drink. Hephaestion's fever soared, and he died shortly thereafter."

"And how does Alexander's demise compare with that of his friend's?"

"Alexander went out with a bang as well, binge drinking for days on end in Babylon. Like Hephaestion, he developed a high fever and, even though medical wisdom at that time dictated against patients drinking wine when they had a fever, Alexander, like Hephaestion, kept slugging away at it. One source, perhaps an eyewitness, said Alexander was seized with a raging fever, became dehydrated, insisted on wine to slake his thirst, and gulped it down. Immediately thereafter he lapsed into *delirium tremens* and died. It was a most unlikely dénouement to a life of unparalleled triumph."

The host comments, "For all of Alexander's success, it sounds like he was a very unhappy man. Tell us, Dr. Gogarty, what lessons are to be culled from his experiences?"

"I'm not a philosopher, just an historian, but I can tell you what his tutor, Aristotle, who was one, might say."

He nods, urging me to continue.

"Our job as a human being is to find out who we are and what makes us tick, then deal with our shortcomings and attempt to strike a balance in what we do. The result, according to Aristotle, will be a sense of well-being, and the byproduct of well-being is happiness, which is, of course, what we're all after.

"Alexander the Great was an insecure man who spent his entire life seeking external solutions to internal problems. As a result, he was incredibly successful on the outside but profoundly unhappy inside."

"Fascinating. Are you doing any further research on Alexander?"

"Yes. I'm in the process of putting the finishing touches to my biography of the man. The next step is to decide on a publisher."

"And Alexander's drinking and these changes in character will loom large in your biography of Alexander?'

"Biography *is* character."

"Well said. I'm sure your biography will be most engaging. And, I'm equally sure our listeners will agree with me when I say you've provided us with a fascinating and informative discussion. I doubt that any of us will think of Alexander in quite the same way again."

224

"Thank you for inviting me."

The host begins introducing his next guest, which is my signal to relinquish the chair and exit.

I think it went well. Maybe I'll head straight for Berkshire and get that ordeal over with. I use one of the BBC phones to alert the girls I'm on my way.

When I reach Berkshire Station, amid the throng of people coming and going, I spot an all too familiar face: Marthe.

"Hi, Marthe, I'm afraid I'm in bit of a rush today. Alicia and Ellen are waiting for me in the Junior Common Room. That's where I'd hoped to meet you too."

"They'll be there in the JCR waiting for you."

"Wonderful. Let's get started, shall we?"

She smirks and shakes her head.

"No? Why?"

"We're stopping elsewhere for a few moments."

Uh-oh. "Where?"

"The Ship Hotel." She clarifies, "It's close by. We're dropping in for some tea and cake." Sensing my apprehension, she adds, "There's nothing for you to trouble yourself with."

She's already bagged her quarry. What's Marthe up to now? While we're wending our way through the town's narrow streets, it begins to rain heavily. We're both armed with raincoats, and Marthe's brought an umbrella, which she shares with me. I point. "There's the Ship. You're right. It wasn't far at all." Let's get this over with.

Marthe escorts me into the dining area, which is empty except for a gentleman wearing a salt-and-pepper tweed jacket and a college tie. She steers us toward him.

"Professor Gogarty, I'd like you to meet Mr. Lionel Blum. I believe you've heard of him."

Blum gets up to shake my hand. He's in his early thirties, stately and plump, with large jowls and small brown eyes. Not exactly tall, dark and handsome, but that's not what she'd be looking for anyway.

We sit down, and Marthe comes right to the point. "Professor Gogarty, *we've* decided" —I glance over at Blum, who looks anything but resolute—"that we're going to get married. We'd very much like to have you present at our ceremony, which will take place in two weeks."

I turn to Blum. "Well, congratulations, but you must know this presents a perplexing situation for me. I mean, one of my students marrying her teacher? I realize things may be different in that respect here in England, but back home it's bound to raise eyebrows. Mr. Blum, do you anticipate any difficulties as far as the Berkshire community is concerned?"

"I'm not certain, but I tend to think since Marthe's a visitor here, it'll probably be of little, if any, concern to them."

"Oh?

Marthe, have you told your parents?"

"No. But that's not necessary. I am, after all, twenty-one years old."

"Granted, but you might want to let them know as a matter of courtesy."

Marthe mumbles, "My father would settle for nothing less than Maimonides."

Blum's eyebrows rise and he suppresses a smile.

So that *is* it. Intellectually brutalized at home. I wonder how many women have been victimized by a man's unrealistic expectations.

"I have to tell you both something. I've got to be concerned about what the reaction to this might be at the study-abroad headquarters. What about going ahead with your plans *after* the school year is over?"

Blum looks like he's considering the suggestion. Marthe glares at me as if I were the devil incarnate and says sharply, "We're talking about *our* lives and it is *our* choice to make." Blum says nothing.

"Well then, I'm sorry, but I can't afford to attend the ceremony."

"Why?" she asks.

"Because there are those back in New York who will say that by simply being there, I sanctioned the event. They may wind up asking for my head. Feigning ignorance about what's happening is hazardous enough, but I'm willing to do that."

Marthe, miffed, is about to launch an assault, but Blum intercedes. "We understand. Let me assure you as far as we're concerned, this conversation has never taken place, and anything that eventuates will do so without prior knowledge of any sort on your part. Fair enough?"

"Absolutely."

Blum then says in an affable tone, "Dr. Gogarty, I have my car with me. What if I drop you off at the JCR back at the university? You won't need Marthe present when you meet with the other American students, will you?"

"No, I won't. Thanks. I'll take you up on that."

In the car Blum and I chat about our research while Marthe sits in scornful silence.

Blum says, "Here we are. Just up those stairs."

"This will do nicely. Thanks, Lionel. Goodbye, Marthe."

She stares straight ahead and says nothing.

The Blum is on the rise—or is it on the rye?

## 25

The Ides of March are upon us and my pigeonhole overfloweth. I start sifting through the mail. Oxford, Cambridge, and Routledge. Let's see. Oxford is offering a contract including an option for them to make changes to the quotations. Cambridge is offering a contract contingent upon "minor alterations" to the quotations. Schiff at Routledge says the contract will stipulate that any and all changes in the manuscript *must meet with my approval.* He compliments me on the BBC interview and asks me to give him a call.

"Mr. Schiff?... Oh yes, it was fun. Thanks. I have to ask, is the contract drawn up yet?... How long will that take? When will it be available?... Ouch. I'm afraid that may be too late. Is there any chance of you accelerating the process? I need the letter well... now.... Thanks. Please get back to me as soon as possible."

Here's another unwelcome missive from Irwin.

*March 9, 1968*

*Dear Professor Gogarty,*

*It's rare that I contact resident directors at this time of the year, as I am immersed in the preliminary phases of the promotion and tenure process at the college. However, there are two considerations making it necessary to communicate with you.*

*First, it seems you've made a very favorable impression on Dr. MacCumhaill, the principal at Edinburgh University. We at the study-abroad program were most pleased to learn of this. In fact, the impression you made was so significant that at present they would only be agreeable to becoming a host institution if you're willing to serve as their resident director. This is a most unusual turn of events, and I must say, something I have never encountered before. As you undoubtedly realize, Edinburgh's a very desirable location for our program. Therefore, we must do everything in our power to establish a center there. That would, it seems, require our guarantee you will accompany our students to Edinburgh.*

*Therefore, I need you to express your willingness to serve in that capacity during the upcoming year. You would, I've been assured, be lecturing at Edinburgh as well and therefore be provided with an additional year of teaching experience at another distinguished European university. Your service there would count as service here at Municipal College. Thus, you would lose nothing in this endeavor and gain a great deal from it.*

*Second, something has arisen that presents a rather unique challenge. All of us here at Municipal are well aware of the uproar over several articles you've recently published concerning Alexander the Great and his drinking habits. Usually, we'd be most pleased with such extraordinary attention being directed toward one of our professors. However, in this case there have been unanticipated and unsettling repercussions in a quarter of particular interest to us. I'm speaking, of course, about Greece, and more specifically about Athens and a university there.*

*It seems that a number of Greek authorities have taken objection to what they consider an attempt on your part to denigrate their illustrious heritage. More directly, we're concerned that the university we've been negotiating with may now see that prospect in a less favorable light. The publicity surrounding this seems to have taken on a life of its own, and your cooperation with the media has done little to quell the situation. Therefore, I'm asking you in the name of the college, and with everyone's best interests at stake, to refrain from giving interviews and speaking publicly about this matter in the future.*

*I must say I have never had a resident director work for me who's generated more complications than you. On the other hand, you're certainly intelligent enough to realize when it's in your best interest to do what's right for the college.*

*There's something else. Should you, and I can't see why you would do otherwise, accept the Edinburgh position, I want you to say nothing about it to anyone. I would rather not have this information widely circulated because the Athenian university (whose officials have been enquiring about you and your connection to our study-abroad program) is unaware you'll be playing any further role in our organization in the future.*

*Dean Francis Irwin*

I make *your* life complicated? Wait. Here's something from Elena. I wonder. Yes. It is her perfume. Dante and Proust were right. I can feel her presence.

*March 8, 1968*

*Dear Aloysius,*

*I waited until now to write because I was hoping and praying my father would change his plans and cancel his trip to England. It's now clear this is not going to happen. I've felt it necessary to continue to pry into his affairs, looking for some clue as to why he would insist on making such a trip at this stage in his life.*

*I still think there's something peculiar, if not ominous, going on here. Whenever I ask any questions about it, Papá becomes rigid and talks sternly like he did when I was a child. Clearly, he wants me to know nothing about what's really going on, and that's probably to protect me, something he's always been vigilant in doing.*

*Anyway, all I've been able to establish for certain is that he's supposed to meet somebody or some people in London at ten-thirty p.m. on April third at either Waterloo or Cockfosters station. However, the time itself seems strange, as does leaving it uncertain concerning where that meeting will happen. Papá is so precise in everything he plans this is completely out of character. All I can put together from the scraps of information I have gathered is Papá will not know in advance where the meeting will take place until the afternoon of April third. Does that make any sense to you?*

*Before I finish this letter, let me tell you about something else I feel obliged to share with you. I've overheard Dean Irwin telling the dean of Social Sciences you will become the resident director at a new center that we hope to open in Edinburgh. Is that so? I ask because none of the official correspondence (which customarily goes through me) says anything like that, and I never sent a letter to you in which the dean formally asked you to take that position. Your appointment in England came under unusual circumstances, but ordinarily the dean makes an offer in writing. Anyway, I thought you ought to know about this.*

*Yours,*

*Elena*


I'd better run this by my co-conspirator.

Mountjoy takes one look at me and says, "You need a drink. And, I owe you a thank you."

"Really? Not that I need a drink; that you owe me a thank you. What for?"

"Otterburn. You graced us by your absence."

"Damn it! I forgot all about it in the midst of this media brouhaha. Another missed opportunity, the story of my life. But, you're right in one respect. I do need a drink. Nope. Not sherry. A *drink*."

"That bad, eh?" He fills both sherry glasses with Macallan malt whiskey.

"A mixed bag. I need a cooler head to prevail here, and you were the best I could do."

"Stated like a true celebrity. Speaking of which, Amalia has a list of journalists who are still hounding her for interviews with you."

"My days as a media superstar are over. It seems the more attention I attract, the worse my relationship gets with the man who holds my fate in his hands. You see, the intrepid Sir Francis Irwin now intends to open a center in Athens, and he says the Greeks are up in arms over the way in which I've besmirched the reputation of their fabled forebear."

"I thought the Greeks abhorred Alexander. Didn't Demosthenes describe his father as a barbarian?"

"He sure did. But, as usual, our protean discipline adapts to current politics. Alexander has metamorphosed into a Greek folk hero who kicked the bejesus out of the Asians while, of course, quoting inspirational passages from Aeschylus and Sophocles."

"History is an acquiescent whore at the beck and call of all suitors."

I nod. "Well, anyway, Irwin wants me to lay off on the publicity surrounding Alexander's drinking. It seems the Greeks have been checking up on me, looking to discredit what I've said, and have discovered that I'm part of Irwin's overseas empire. They know he's dying to establish a center in Athens; so, they're using this as leverage to shut me up."

"Do you have any problem with that?"

"Not really. It's out there already. I can't and won't retract what I've said, but this interviewing is getting boring anyway."

"How do you think your dean will handle this?"

"He's probably reassuring the Greeks they'll hear nothing more about me and my theory and telling them I'll be separated from the program in a few months anyway. He's using the old Frankenstein maneuver. However, the plot thickens. He needs me in Edinburgh next year, or MacCumhaill threatens not to accept the program."

"You mean we may be saddled with you for another year? I don't know if the British Isles could endure that, old boy. I certainly couldn't."

"Nor could I; and Edinburgh is the last place in the world I want to be—ever again."

"How will this affect that grating obsession of yours with tenure?"

"That's the problem. I may have to play a dangerous game here."

"Something you ordinarily relish."

"Yes, but in this case, it could be suicidal. I can't outsmart the dean, get tenure, and then refuse to go to Edinburgh. If I did, I'd never —ever—get promoted. I started off at Municipal as the youngest assistant professor they've ever had. If Irwin feels betrayed, I'll wind up being the oldest assistant professor they've ever had. All roads lead to Irwin."

"Couldn't you, after the tenure issue is resolved, invite him out for a cocktail or two and finish off the job you started in Paris?"

"Now, there's a plan! But wait, there's another pressing problem I need to talk to you about."

"Oh?"

"The Cuban version of your *Coronation Street*. The father's due in London in three weeks or so, and Elena is worried sick about what he's up to. I've been thinking about this, and I don't want you to have anything to do with it. It could turn out to be a waste of time, but it might turn out to be dangerous or even —don't laugh—fatal."

"Either way, you're saddled with me, old boy. I've been looking forward to a trip to Oxford, and the timing would be just right. If we simply waste our efforts with this, that's nothing new to either one of us. If it proves to be perilous, all it would mean is that one of us is in for a challenge. Are the basic elements the same as last discussed?

Does the Tube station at which your Cuban's *pater familias* will make his appearance remain undetermined?"

I pass the letter over to Mountjoy, and he refills our glasses. After reading it, he says, "Yes. It's *status quo*, all right. Charming. Which station appeals to you? Waterloo or—what is it? Oh, yes, Cockfosters."

"My guess is you want Waterloo; so, I'll take Cockfosters. Are they within striking distance of each other?"

"Not in the least. Cockfosters is far north of the city proper, and Waterloo is close to its center. Do you think geography is part of the equation in whatever game is being played?"

"I don't know, but it sure doesn't sound coincidental."

Mountjoy asks, "Do you have any further reflections on what might actually happen?"

"Here's pure speculation. Her father has gotten involved in a plot to provide a day of reckoning for Elena's husband. What form that might take is anyone's guess. But I do know Elena's convinced her father is putting himself in harm's way and is concerned he may not survive whatever he's exposing himself to. That, I'm afraid, is the shaky ground we stand upon."

"Therefore, you want me"—Mountjoy points to his head—"to mastermind a plan of attack, and use this"—he stands, removes his jacket, rolls up his shirtsleeve, and flexes a barely visible muscle in his right arm—"as a sledgehammer to smite the enemy." He puts his jacket back on and returns to his seat.

I raise my eyebrows in mock awe of his posturing. "But remember," I remind him, "Elena fears there may be violence—make no mistake about it."

"Aloysius, there may be a reason we've been drawn into this. It could be the crossroads where *we* are taken measure of."

"Are you serious?"

"I am. Do you ever feel we arrived on this planet just a trifle too late, missing the war and all that? Maybe that's why we're always trivializing our own undertakings."

"So, we're the 'just missed it' generation, and this is our own little war?"

"Yehhhs. Our own *little* Light Brigade."

I add, "And into the valley of death rode the two, having lost contact with the other five hundred and ninety-eight."

"Waxing poetic, are we?" asks Mountjoy.

"Are you really ready to meet your Maker, Your Lordship?"

"The question is—is He ready to meet me? Even if the worst comes of this, it'll be brief, and that is, is it not, the most desirable way to go?"

"I don't know about that, Dickie boy. Shouldn't we have a plan?"

Mountjoy responds, "If we truly had our faculties about us, we would've already contacted Ferguson and let him devise a strategy. But no, your inflexible obstinacy has closed that door, has it not?"

"He could've lost his job for what he did for me with Stein. It's a matter of principle. Enough is enough."

"My dear boy, I for one get into the most trying of situations whenever I delude myself into thinking I'm acting out of principle. Righteousness rarely corresponds with right action. In this case, you could simply ask him to bring the London authorities into this. That would relieve him of responsibility and guarantee professionals were handling the situation."

"True. But we don't know who and what's involved. You've already determined there's no appropriate teacher's conference in London at the time. What are we going to ask Ferguson to pass on to his London counterparts? That there's this American by the name of Gogarty who has a Cuban girlfriend, who's not really his girlfriend, who has a father who was exiled by the Cuban revolution and may want to do harm to his daughter's husband, and the father is meeting somebody or somebodies somewhere in London for an undisclosed purpose, and we want the London police to make sure nothing bad happens. How do you think Ferguson's going to react to that?"

"He'll probably take *us* into custody and have us committed to Broadmoor."

"Precisely. That being the case, knowing Ferguson, he'll manufacture some excuse to be in London himself to make sure nothing calamitous occurs. But something may, and if it does, Elena's father could wind up spending the rest of his life in an English jail. That's not going to endear me to Elena. And, more important, there's no way in which this can be of any benefit to Ferguson."

"Well then, it's entirely up to us. Rather heady, isn't it? All I know is that I'm going to importune whatever gods I'm still in contact with to ensure I'm the one confronting it. You, Aloysius, are a man of excess and thus limited in circumstances of this sort. On the other hand, my mercurial personality invariably enables me to rise to any occasion. I hereby prophesize that, should the mantle rest on my shoulders, I shall conjure up a Merlin-like solution to whatever problem presents itself."

"You win. Let's drink to this unholy alliance. *Sláinte!*"

Mountjoy empties his glass as I do mine.

"Okay, boss. Another stiff one, and I'll serenade you with an Irish toast or two, in English. I'm no John McCormack, but I don't have a bad voice."

"If you must." He reaches into his lower left drawer and blows the imaginary dust off two outsized schooner glasses.

"Hey. I haven't seen that type of glass in any of the pubs around here."

"Nor will you. At least not for beer. These are Australian schooners, holding three-quarters of an imperial pint."

"Just the right size. Lay on, Macduff!"

Mountjoy pours, and I carry out my threat.

> *"Here's to a long life and a merry one.*
> *A quick death and an easy one.*
> *A pretty girl and an honest one.*
> *A cold pint—and another one."*

I put on my best Irish accent.

*"To live above with the Saints we love—*
*Ah, that is the purest glory.*
*To live below with the Saints we know—*
*Ah, that is another story."*

Mountjoy joins his hands in noiseless applause, tops off our drinks, raises his schooner and proclaims: "To April third, a day of reckoning!"

We drain our glasses.

# 26

Doomsday has arrived. Budgen drops me off at the train station and I purchase a first-class ticket to London and, perhaps, Hades. Go there in style.

On this trip Aloysius Magnus will drift into a majestic state of mind and devise a masterful strategy for the battle of Cockfosters Station. First, wash down five magic tablets with royal coffee, thereby banishing headaches from the realm.

Aha! Here's an empty car where the great one can doze off on his voyage south. But, alas, His Highness is a serial dreamer, and the most *outré* of nightmares come in the wake of lifting one jar too many. For a while it was those outlandish newspaper stories, but lately, it seems, the play's the thing . . .

ALOYSIUS

*Where am I? A brothel? What did you say... I mean, who did you say you were? Zoe? Life? You are life? Jesus. Life is a whore. Why are you smoking a Cuban cigar, and where's your twin sister, Thanatos? You don't know her? Your own sister, Death? Oh, Jesus, what are you doing? I must warn you. I won't pay. I never pay. Hey, you're giving me money. Yeah, that's okay. Who's that? Bella? She's the boss? Where'd she go? There you are. Elena, it's you, isn't it?*

BELLAELENA

*I am whoever you want me to be, but before you do anything else, I want you to look through this.*

(She points Aloysius toward a zoetrope, which he peers into.)

ALOYSIUS

*That's you Elena. Who's that slimy-looking character with you?*

BELLAELENA

*That's my husband, Dr. Delagracia. Let Zoe assist you while you watch. Zoe, throw that cigarillo away. Your mouth can be better engaged than with a cylinder of rank weed.*

(Zoe undoes Aloysius's belt, easing him down into a leather chair while kneeling in front of him—not, it seems, to pray. Dr. Delagracia takes out his black bag, opens Elena's blouse, and places his stethoscope on her left breast. He listens and nods, then has her lie supine while he lifts up her skirt. He takes a tiny brush out of his bag and strokes her red pubic hair with his left hand, while placing his stethoscope on her vaginal labia with his right hand. He listens intently, nods his head in approval, and proceeds to expose his black priapic member.)

ALOYSIUS

*What are you doing to me? I don't want to see this. Let me out of here.*

(Aloysius squirms to liberate himself but thickened leather straps project from the chair's arms and lock him in. Zoe gets up wiping her mouth, but Aloysius realizes it's not Zoe. It's Marthe Fleischmann.)

ALOYSIUS

*Marthe, what are you doing here?*

KITTY

*What's wrong with you, sir? Had a little too much to drink today? I'm not Marthe. I'm Kitty Higgins, and, good sir, may I ask, what in blazes are you doing here?*

ALOYSIUS

*Well...*

(Aloysius pushes her out of the way and sees a young woman in her early twenties pressing her face up against the window of the zoetrope.)

ALOYSIUS

*Deborah... is that you?*

DEBORAH

*It's me all right. Do you want proof?*

(She backs up and reveals a transparent rectangle in her abdomen. The window acts as a camera lens and zooms in on Deborah, who's now standing in front of a painting of a young boy in an Eton suit carrying a book called *Aloysius's Wake*.)

ALOYSIUS

*Who's that?*

DEBORAH

*That's your son. Or, I should say, that's what he'd look like today if you'd let me have him. Would you like to see what he really looks like today?*

ALOYSIUS

*No! Let me go.*

(Aloysius pulls in vain at the chair to release himself, only to realize his shoes have been nailed to the floor.)

DEBORAH
*Well, you will, whether you like it or not.*

(Aloysius tries to shut his eyes, but maggots have a restraining grip on his eyelids.)

(Deborah picks up a large jar with a male fetus immersed in formaldehyde. It's a dwarf's face, mauve and wrinkled.)

ALOYSIUS
*I was drinking heavily at the time.*

DEBORAH
*You always drink heavily. Tell your son that and see what he says.*

(She rushes toward him with the jar and pushes it up against the zoetrope's window. The image blurs, and the young woman and her jar disintegrate. The blurry face of a woman with anomalous eyes and auburn hair approaches Aloysius through the zoetrope.)

ALOYSIUS
*Ma?*

WOMAN
*Yes, Tabeel, it's your Mameleh. Don't listen to those who would bring you down with them. You are going to become a great man one day who helps others find themselves. Therein dwells your greatness. But to do this you must take control of your cup, your wallet, and your temperament. You must learn what the heart is and what it feels, and discover the power of the word known to all men... l-o-*

(She disappears without finishing the spelling.)

ALOYSIUS
*Mameleh!*

(A priest wearing a black cassock enters stage left. A large silver Celtic cross is hanging from his neck set against a blood-red circular woolen cloth. A Hasidic rabbi enters stage right, wearing a black *rekel* and a dark red *gartel* encircling his waist.)

PRIEST
*Why have you forsaken your son, my son?*

(He points to a Christlike figure on the cross, which metamorphoses into a fetus.)

RABBI
*And why have you forsaken the God of your forefathers—the God of Abraham and Isaac and Rosenbach?*

PRIEST
*Let us hear your sins. Your most grievous sins and your venial sins.*

ALOYSIUS
*Aren't sins their own punishment? Why am I going through this with you? I will not genuflect.*

(The priest becomes a wraith and vanishes. Aloysius stares at the rabbi.)

RABBI
*I will forgive you.*

(He traces the Star of David in the air with his index finger.)

RABBI

*Ego te absolvo a peccatis tuis in nomine Patris.*

(The rabbi vaporizes.)

"King's Cross Station. King's Cross Station." It's the conductor.

It's going to take all day to shake myself loose from that horror. Sleep's supposed to be a cure for what ails you. Sometimes it just magnifies the agony. The Greeks said the gods speak to you through your dreams. What are they trying to tell me?

Signal for a taxi.

"Russell Hotel, please." While climbing into the cab, I notice my redheaded, freckled-faced driver is wearing a sheepish grin. He points toward two dogs at the side of the station building. The male is on his haunches hammering away at the female, who looks like her thoughts are elsewhere. How life begins. The driver's license says Denis Florence MacCarthy. I tap on the divider and pose a question. "So, you're one of *them*, huh?"

"Probably. But which one of *them* are you referring to?"

"The Irish."

"Did you have to ask, with a name like mine?"

"I just wanted to confirm it. I'm Aloysius T. Gogarty. My people are from Kildare." I reach through the opening and get a wrestler's grip from him.

"I'm a Dub—a Dublin man—making a decent wage here and sending it home. You're an American, aren't you?"

"Yup."

"Are you on holiday, or is it business?"

This guy drives like Mountjoy. I glance out the window to see if I recognize any of the scenery, but we're moving so fast I can't identify anything. If I don't focus on the conversation, I'll have a stroke back here. "Well, both. I'm teaching up in Yorkshire and taking care of some American students."

"Like that mangy old mutt back there, taking care of that bitch, eh?"

"Well, not quite that way."

"You're not one of those quare schoolteachers who goes about buggering young lads, are you?"

"No sir. I get into enough trouble with the ladies as it is, thank you."

"Don't we all? You see this ring? I've had nine children by her already."

"Nine? Good for you. They should build you a monument."

"Good for me? This being a Catholic is killing me, and the missus will have nothing to do with that contraband or whatever the hell it is they call rubbers now. For Chrissake, I work me fuggin arse off day and night just trying to feed the fuggin tribe. It's a good thing I'm here. Otherwise, we'd have thirteen by now. Oh, she loves to go at it, but I'm the one who gets to pay the piper. The clan is back in Dublin, and I've got to send them almost every ha'penny I get a hold of. I keep just a few bob here and there to get a pint or two of the good, black, creamy stuff that makes you feel like a Catholic ought to feel."

I try to get a word in, but he'll have none of it. He's Irish all right.

"Should build a monument to me? They have. It's the round tower back in Glasnevin Cemetery, just north of Dublin. Most people think it's up there for Daniel O'Connell. But now, you and I both know that the good Lord put it up there for yours truly, not good old Danny O. Did you know his heart is buried in Rome and probably his balls too? The church has a grip on them whether you're dead or alive. Here we are. Russell Hotel."

I pay the fare while clutching a ten-pound note in the other hand. "Mr. MacCarthy, I've got something for you, but you'll only get it if you swear by the Blessed Virgin Mary you'll do exactly what I ask of you."

244

"If it's a murder, that's fine, but it has to be a Protestant. I don't kill Catholics."

I laugh out loud and answer, "I understand. But I still haven't heard a solemn oath coming from you."

"Begob. I swear on the sacred heart of Jesus, the Blessed Virgin Mary and Joseph. The lot!"

"Okay. Here it is. But there's a catch. You must spend it on Guinness and nothing else. Not your wife, not your children, not the church, no beggars, bakers or candlestick makers—just himself drinking the rich black brew."

"You drive a hard bargain, Gogarty, but you can count on Denis MacCarthy to do the right thing. And if I fail"—he crosses himself and raises his right hand—"may the devil break the hasp of me back!"

"Good day to you, Mr. MacCarthy."

"Thank you, Mr. Gogarty. You're a gentleman and a scholar."

Well, he's half right. Check in at the hotel and wait for Mountjoy's call.

Finally, the phone rings. "Hello, Your Lordship. . . . Ha! You're right. Why screw it up with plans at this stage? If I get there early and wander around outside Cockfosters, what sort of neighborhood will I be in?... It sounds decent enough. What about Waterloo?... That bad, huh? Sure boss, I know what you're talking about. We call it public housing. It's always a problem. What will you do if the locals try to mug you?... Ha! My money is on them. I'd better get going. Good luck at Waterloo. I'm on my way to Cockfosters. Bye."

Nothing unusual about the station, except its above ground. I like that. It's less nerve-wracking than that buried-alive feeling you get from the subway. There's a large clock I can see from the platform. Twenty after nine. Wait. Here's somebody. This could be de la Flora. Get close enough to be sure without letting him recognize you. Take off your beret and glasses and stroll casually in his direction.

It's not him. Uniform back on.

I pace up and down the platform endlessly and then check the time. The clock says ten twenty-five. No sign of Torquemada. Dammit. I wish something would happen this clock-watching is torture. What did Mountjoy say? Give it another half-hour and then fold up your tent. Finally, the clock strikes eleven. Well, I stood ready to serve, like Malachi wearing the collar of gold. Alas, to no avail.

Take the Tube back to the hotel and maybe get a good night's sleep this time. Mountjoy said we'd compare notes tomorrow. Probably didn't expect anything to happen. What's this? Oh yeah. I told them to leave an iced bottle of Dom Perignon in my room. There'll be no victory to celebrate tonight. So, what? They're all Pyrrhic victories, anyway. One thing's for sure: I can't waste this bottle of champagne. That *would* be criminal.

What's that noise? Where am I? Jesus, it's the chambermaid. I shout out I need a few minutes. It's eleven o'clock already? No nightmares. If I dress quickly, I can grab a cab and still catch an express train to Yorkshire.

There's a taxi right outside the hotel. "King's Cross Station, please." Mountjoy's going to ridicule me for wasting his time. I thought he'd call this morning, but he must have left at daybreak to get back to the university. Well, if Torquemada was nowhere to be seen, he's probably still breathing, and that's Elena's main concern. Maybe it *is* a victory. That is, unless Mountjoy encountered something. Jesus. I hope not. If anything happens to him, it's going to be me bearing the blame.

Here we are. Grab a stack of newspapers. I'm not sleepy and I don't have a headache. Maybe vintage champagne is the answer to my problem. At least it would be an elegant way to go.

"Sir, they just dropped off the latest edition of the *Daily Mail*. Would you like that one as well?"

"Yes. Please." I slip it under the pile and hustle to catch the train.

Boring. Boring. Bored. Let's see what the *Daily Mail* has to offer.

"Oh, my God!"

*BIZARRE INCIDENT AT WATERLOO STATION*

*Several travelers on the Bakerloo Line reported a most peculiar incident occurring at Waterloo Station between ten and eleven o'clock, on Wednesday night, as they exited from their carriages. While reports differ, there appears to be general agreement that four men were involved in a dispute that resulted in one of them discharging a firearm.*

Oh no.

*The incident took place at the opposite end of the station from which the travelers exited from their carriages. Witnesses at the scene all agreed they heard shouting in a foreign language from that direction, which one bystander identified as Italian, and the others as Spanish. Some pushing was observed among three of the gentlemen, two shots were fired in the air, and then something most extraordinary occurred. When the three men separated, a fourth man was seen stark naked in their midst, with both hands clasped over his head, slowly and methodically pirouetting.*

*Two of the men suddenly started running at a furious pace past the bystanders. One witness reportedly looked towards the end of the station and saw the naked man scamper to retrieve his discarded clothes and push the other man, an elderly gentleman, into the carriage of a newly arrived train. The naked man's momentum carried him and the older man into the carriage just as the doors were closing.*

*As the train passed by, several witnesses observed the naked man, thought to be in his thirties, dressing hastily, while the elderly gentleman sat bewildered. Witnesses agreed they saw only one person, a woman perhaps in her late fifties, in the car the two men entered. She is said to have been staring at the naked man with what appeared to be a smile on her face. The local constabulary was contacted, and the station was*

*shut down while police officials attempted to locate the bullets*
*allegedly discharged into the roof of the station.*
*Anyone who has information concerning what transpired at*
*Waterloo Station last night is asked to contact Scotland Yard.*

"This has to be Mountjoy. Nobody else is crazy enough to do something like that."

I can imagine the headlines in tomorrow's tabloids:

*MAYHEM IN THE BOWELS OF THE LONDINIUM METROPOLIS*

*PIROUETTING PEDANT'S PENIS PARRIES PERNICIOUS PLOT*

*DANGLING DINGUS DERAILS DESPICABLE DEED*

*WAYWARD WILLY WAGGER WOWS WATERLOO WATCHERS*

*FRISKY FRUMP FINDS FLASHER'S FLUTE FASCINATING*

## 27

"Good morning, Miss Popper. Would you, by any chance, happen to know where Mr. Mountjoy is?"

"And a good morning to you as well, Dr. Gogarty," she responds, more cheerfully than usual. "I'm afraid Mr. Mountjoy is in with the chairman at present."

"How is he?" I ask. That's awkward. Maybe I should've been more direct: Has Scotland Yard enquired about him? Any gunshot residue on his clothes? Was he wearing clothes? Is he still talking to me?

Miss Popper tilts her head to the left. "How *is* he? Fine, I suppose. No sign of any particular affliction or undue stress. I wonder if that's because he's been away from you for a while."

I look at her quizzically and see she's blushing. Miss Popper says, "I beg your pardon. That was a clumsy attempt on my part to be amusing. I do hope you're not offended by it."

"On the contrary, I take it as a sign of you being comfortable with me. Sort of like someone in the family taking a whack at you every once in a while." Oops! Now *she* is uncomfortable. "In other words, I take it as a compliment. There isn't anything you could possibly say or do which would offend me."

"Why, thank you. I think I do feel better now, Dr. Gogarty, but I'm never quite sure with you. Nevertheless, I'll address the question at hand. Mr. Mountjoy looks and sounds just tickety-boo. He and the chairman have been going over a list of new students and conferring on Mr. Mountjoy's itinerary for next year. I should think he's likely to emerge within the hour."

"When he does, could you kindly ask him not to leave before I see him? Oh, and could you give me a 'heads-up' ring over at my office?"

She smiles at the phrase and says, "By all means. Incidentally, your pigeonhole is at capacity once again. You might want to take a peek at it."

She's right. I'd better wade through all this correspondence in my office and deal with any pressing items one at a time.

Call Routledge first. "Hello, this is Dr. Gogarty from Yorkshire University; may I speak to Mr. Schiff?... Thank you.... Yes. I did receive your letter. It's most encouraging. I'm willing and eager to go ahead with you folks, but I need the actual contract, or at least a letter assuring me of a contract, and I need it soon.... Yes. I realize these things take time, but I must tell you there's *considerable* interest in my book at Oxford *and* Cambridge, and I'm fairly certain I could get a letter out of either one of them quickly if I asked. The question is— can *you*? I'd rather go with your people because *you* understand exactly what I'm doing in the book.... Yes; once I receive it, I'll send a response agreeing to enter into contract with Routledge and call to confirm it's on its way back to you.... Excellent! Goodbye."

The next item is... who else? Marthe Fleischmann. Well, she went ahead and married him. Let's see. The wedding was perfect. I'll bet it was, down to the exact number of pieces of shattered glass. She's working with Blum on an annotated translation of *Beowulf.* That should keep her busy. He'll be wearing dreadlocks by the time they get to the footnotes.

Here's another communiqué from my poison pen pal. It took a week to get here.

*March 24, 1968*

*Dear Professor Gogarty,*
*I hope that all continues to go well as far as our English center is concerned. If there's a way in which I can be of any*

*assistance to you, do not hesitate to inform me of it. I also hope you've given sufficient thought to assuming the position of resident director of our study-abroad program in Edinburgh, and I will hear from you soon concerning it. Considering the fact that you exceeded your authority in offering specific benefits to both the staff and the students at Edinburgh University (and I had to see to it that we could fulfill these obligations), I cannot imagine you will do anything other than accept the position.*

*As you may know, I sit in on the college Promotion and Tenure Committee in an ex officio capacity, and I wanted you to know they have begun preliminary deliberations on these matters. In that respect, and as dean of faculty, I feel obliged to remind you all documents relevant to tenure should be in their possession by next week. As I recall, you were completing a manuscript on Alexander the Great. It would be a critical factor in their considerations for you to provide proof your book has been accepted for publication by a reputable (i.e., scholarly) press. It will take a number of weeks before the committee makes recommendations to me, and then I, in turn, will offer my recommendations to the president regarding these issues. I urge you to be attentive to the paperwork involved and conscientious in ensuring that all material reaches the college on time.*

*There's another matter. You will of course need a replacement at your present post next year. With that in mind, and with the intention of the program's profiting from your own experiences over the past year, I am sending someone who may replace you in England next year. His name is Martin Secker. He's in the English department here, and his father's a prominent English businessman who's also very influential in English politics. I am directing him toward you, so you can provide him with an orientation in regard to the daily exercise of your duties. I'm also asking you to make your files*

251

*accessible to him so he can see how you've organized your operation there and ensure that there'll be a smooth transition during the 1968/69 academic year. He should be there in early April.*

*Sincerely yours,*

*Francis Irwin*

*Dean of Faculty*

*P.S. While writing this letter, I received a phone call from the president's office approving my request to give an extension to resident directors abroad for submitting their papers to the committee. It seems some of your colleagues have had difficulty in meeting the deadline. You now have until May 16 to submit your materials, but that deadline is hard and fast.*


That's good, but this guy Secker could be here any day now. He's probably another headache. My telephone rings.

"Hello? Yes, Amalia, thank you. Could you kindly tell him that I'll be right there?"

I knock meekly while poking my head into Mountjoy's office and enter crouched over in Iago fashion.

He pours some Macallan whiskey into the Australian schooners and gives me a stern look.

I drop my jaw and look at him through apologetic eyes. "It was that bad, huh?"

"Well, upon due reflection, I would've been better off loitering outside of Waterloo Station and getting mugged. At least I'd know what eventuated and why. I'm still foggy about the exact sequence of events, but of course the more I tell myself the story, the more cogent it becomes. Probably what I'm about to say bears only a vague resemblance to reality, but that's never stopped historians from telling others what it was like, has it?"

I'm at the edge of my seat with my mouth wide open, waiting to hear more.

Mountjoy continues. "I stood there on the platform at the station, becoming utterly bored, when an older man emerged from the stairwell and walked slowly down to the area where I was standing. To me, it appeared he was scrupulously following whatever instructions he'd received. The man bore an unmistakable resemblance to the Torquemada you described, and from that very moment I knew I was the chosen one.

"He scrutinized me and then shifted his attention to the stairwell. About a half hour elapsed before two Spanish-looking chaps appeared and began marching, in step, towards where we were standing. This, I must confess, is where I began to reflect on the wisdom of our *entente cordiale* and cursed myself for the boast I made about resolving the situation. Instead of remaining stationary, the elderly gentleman began to walk towards them. I followed cautiously.

"They all spoke Spanish in a subdued manner, at least at first. I gathered from what I could see and hear the older man knew one of the men, but no handshakes were exchanged. Torquemada seemed to be looking to authenticate the identity of the third party. Once that was accomplished"—Mountjoy speaks from the side of his mouth —"all hell broke loose.

"Your grand inquisitor began hurling Spanish obscenities at both of them. Not, by the way, the deep, richly crafted execrations of Arabic origin, but the more pedestrian vulgarities of the drunken sailor variety. The other two responded in kind, and as this operatic farce was reaching its crescendo, the third party began flourishing a revolver. His companion responded in kind, and at that point our stalwart inquisitor straightened his back, lifted his head as high as he could, and stood there, defying what looked to be his executioners."

"What were you thinking at that very moment?"

"I wasn't. If I were, I would have been halfway back to Yorkshire before any of them took their next breath."

"Oh Jesus."

"My thought, exactly."

I have to interrupt. "I'm especially interested in what happened next. I read a strange account of it in a London tabloid on the way up here, but they've probably got it all wrong. I still have it. Here, take a look."

He reads the article, and surprises me by saying, "This is closer to the truth than one would expect of the *Daily Mail*. You see, at one point there seemed to be little question that whatever plan Torquemada had concocted, it was destined to be his last. Suddenly, a resolution to the crisis flashed through my mind. As they continued to exchange insults and then shoves, I undressed as expeditiously as I ever have—except for one occasion at Charterhouse, when I was in the headmaster's quarters with his daughter's knickers down, and I sensed his return was imminent." He pauses momentarily to savor his memory of the episode.

"Well, where was I? Oh yes. Stark naked, I jumped in front of the two parties pointing their weapons at Torquemada and began, hands over head, rotating in pirouette fashion. They turned to each other, searching for a clue as to how to respond to such a disconcerting turn of events. They continued to stare at me incredulously and then looked at each other again. One man discharged his revolver twice in the air, hoping, I presume, to make me disappear. It didn't work. I kept pirouetting—with an engaging smile on my face by the way— and without warning, they turned and ran.

"There were some commuters at the far end of the station, and I knew if any of them had seen the gun or heard the shots, the police would soon appear on the scene. Just at that moment another train arrived, so I gathered up my clothes and proceeded to propel Torquemada into the nearest carriage."

"Stop! What in the world gave you the idea to intercede naked?"

"I'd learned what I needed to know through the observations of no less a luminary than Sir Reginald himself. In his notebooks relating to the criminal element, he observed that the only charge criminals found intolerable, and would do virtually anything to avoid, was homosexual intrigue of any sort. He speculated they would elect to chew their own legs off, like a bear caught in a trap, rather than be thought to have stooped to such ignominious behavior. That, my dear boy, inspired my intuitive leap. Obviously, it worked."

"Was anyone else in the car you and the old man barged into?"

"A woman. She must have been sixty or so, but quite an extraordinary woman. She never even blinked. Instead, she focused her stare on my genitalia with a broad smile as I attempted to dress myself in due haste. In fact, when I got out at the next station to walk back to Waterloo and retrieve my car, she waved an appreciative fare-thee-well to me."

"What about the old man?"

"He sat there dazed and just stared at me. I think he may have thought I was an apparition or, being Catholic, his guardian angel."

"So, are you a fugitive from the law now?"

"I rather doubt that. There was no bloodshed, no robbery, no assault; and even those who saw revolvers in play did so from a considerable distance. Their observations could very well be called into question. Therefore, the incident involved no crime other than possession of firearms and the discharge of one by a swarthy foreigner. I suppose one could claim indecent exposure as well, although the only spectator close enough for a glimpse at the crown jewels was demonstrably grateful for the opportunity. I seriously doubt that anyone recognized me. No one, save a few thousand women, has ever seen me disrobe, and none I recall is in the habit of riding the London Tube alone at that time of night."

I shake my head in disbelief. "I'll tell you one thing: I'm glad destiny chose you for this one. I wouldn't have had enough wits about me to dream of doing what you did, much less the balls to carry it out. This whole thing could have devolved into a bloodbath. *You* should get the V C for this."

"Quite right my dear boy, quite right. In fact, my testicular fortitude was tantamount to shagging old Butterworth, wasn't it? But the real question is: what will come of it, from your point of view?"

"There's no way of knowing until I hear from Elena. And, from the sound of things, her father's unlikely to offer Elena anything but an edited version of what actually happened."

"I very much doubt," Mountjoy says, "Torquemada will have a clear recollection of any of it. He seemed confounded by the whole affair, even before the fireworks began. If he had a plan, it had gone awry. He was perfectly composed up until the moment they confronted him, as if he expected things to develop quite differently. Then he looked the way we all do when a premise under which we've been operating with conviction collapses."

"Maybe he assumed that the third man was on his side, but he turned out to be a foe rather than a friend."

"Could very well be, but one thing is certain. By the time I jostled him into the train, I was afraid he might lapse into a catatonic state. He didn't, and in fact he gradually regained control of himself. He did stare at me as if I were a spectral vision of some sort. As I waited for the train doors to open"—Mountjoy distorts his mouth—"*to make my getaway*, I watched his reflection in the door window and observed him going through all that Catholic mumbo jumbo with his right hand."

"It's called blessing yourself."

"Yehhhhs. I think he was actually blessing me—or else engaged in an exorcism of some sort. I did turn to glance at him as the doors jerked open. He looked directly at me and mouthed, '*Gracias, San*' something or other."

"Well, you've done a remarkably noble thing here, and may have saved yourself several thousand years in purgatory."

Mountjoy slowly turns his head upward, carefully places his hand over his heart and breathes an insincere sigh of relief.

"Oh. I got a letter from Irwin, and some fellow under consideration to be my successor here at Yorkshire is supposed to be coming our way soon. He's an Englishman whose father is wealthy and a bigwig in English politics."

"Really? What's his name?"

"Let's see. Here it is. Martin Secker."

"Oh, good Lord."

"What's wrong?"

"His father is Cecil Secker, an indecently rich businessman and a political lobbyist. What's wrong? First of all, he's 'an Englishman' in the Somerset mold. At least his family had the decency not to usurp a distinguished English surname. Like your friend Somerset, their family emigrated here during the prewar years. They adapted, as chameleons are wont to do, and became what we call 'a champagne socialist.' He now has an ear at Ten Downing Street and is hawking proposals which, if acted upon, would socialize and bankrupt our country. Happily, most of them are shouted down by the more levelheaded MPs in Parliament. I've never met the chap, but knowledgeable people speak of him as a crypto-Communist looking to turn our country into a Soviet-style socialist state. And that, my dear boy, would be the death knell for England."

"Let's hope his son is of a different stripe. I know I've reached my quota when it comes to favors, but I'm going to have to ask you to tolerate this guy and help me do what has to be done. He's supposed to be showing up anytime now."

"There's nothing to ruffle your feathers about. We English are quite astute at being solicitous and patronizing simultaneously."

"So I've noticed."

"Beware of Secker. Americans are inclined to equate a polished English accent with some vague sense of nobility. In fact, the two rarely commingle. In all likelihood he's venal and reptilian, like dear old dad."

"Don't worry. I'll watch my step with him. He's an academic, and we know what *they're* like."

"Indeed, we do."

"The situation with Irwin is troubling me. I feel like I'm caught between Scylla and Charybdis."

"How so?"

"If I turn down the Edinburgh job, he'll drop the hammer on me when it comes to tenure."

"So, you feel compelled to take it."

"I should, but I don't. If I cower and succumb to that tumescent toad, I'll lose whatever respect I have left for myself, and probably Elena will as well. "

Mountjoy tilts his head and raises his index finger. "In regard to the latter, do remember what appears at a distance to be exquisite might resemble Scylla at close range. In other words, *caveat emptor*— beware of your ineffable Cuban."

"There are no roses without thorns, Your Lordship. I'm willing to take the risk. Australia looks attractive, but wherever I am, New York always beckons me home."

"You New Yorkers pretend to be cosmopolitan, but you're really quite provincial, aren't you? Always migrating back there like homing pigeons. It reminds me of Londoners."

"I was thinking about working for one of the tabloids in New York. Imagine getting paid for sitting around and dreaming up depraved headlines all day long. Then, in my spare time, doing what I've always wanted to do."

"Impale a white whale? Get trampled to death by like-minded morons in Pamplona?"

"No. I've mentioned this before. Write a novel."

"Oh yes. Now I recall. So now you want to become a novelist?"

"No. Writing novels is hard work. I'd like to follow in the footsteps of Harper Lee, Ralph Ellison, and J. D. Salinger and write one interesting book."

"Didn't they write other novels?"

"Nothing I know of as far as Lee and Ellison are concerned, and none by Salinger worth the paper they're printed on."

"So, will this be the great American novel?"

"Nope. Just a novel."

"What type of novel?"

"Nothing lurid, but a book out of the common groove. It has to have a scrim of irony and an unhappy ending. I love unhappy endings."

"Really? Why?"

"Because that's what ultimately happens in real life; so why not embrace it earlier on? Besides, there's a bittersweet quality to sad endings that's hard to let go of. You never forget them."

"Let me guess your favorite novel." He rests his finger on his chin momentarily, and then announces, "*The Metamorphosis*!"

I smile and nod. "Well, that's more a novella, but you're right, I love it. It's up there with *The Catcher in the Rye, The Ginger Man,* and my favorite, *Anna Karenina.*"

"It's odd that you mention *The Ginger Man.* Sebastian Dangerfield's always been my favorite character," Mountjoy muses.

"Somehow that doesn't surprise me, but let's get back to what happened in London. Richard, you were superb, absolutely superb! Sir Reginald would be beaming with pride if he were still among us."

"That, my dear boy, as your reprobate kith and kin might say, 'warms the cockles of me heart'."

# 28

Here it is at last, *the* letter from Elena. It'll have her version of Waterloo Station, the only version that counts. I open the envelope and inhale her subtle scent.

*April 16, 1968*

*Dear Aloysius,*

*I don't know what you did or how you did it, but you've done something very good and important, helping my father in a very frightening situation in London. He is a different man, a less angry man, a man who seems to be at peace with himself, a man who now accepts our situation as it is. He went so far as to say he was sorry I was worried about him traveling and reassured me that this was his last trip of any kind. From now on, Papá said, he will be staying here at home, helping me take care of Miguelito.*

*I must confess when he first got off the airplane, what he said to me was very disturbing. He kept talking about "the naked angel" who appeared out of nowhere and saved his life. He said some men were trying to rob him in a London subway station. I don't believe that part of his story. It must have had something to do with Cuba. I don't know what to make of the naked angel either, but my father has no doubts about it. It couldn't have been you because Papá knows you and never mentioned your name. But my instincts tell me somehow you* were there, making sure my father came back to me safe and sound. I presented you with a situation that was terribly confusing, and you were able to do the impossible and rescue padre mio from whomever those desperados were. That's what I believe, so please do not try to persuade me otherwise.

My father didn't return to New York right away, and that's why I waited until now to write to you. Immediately after the incident, he went back to his hotel and knelt down and prayed for an understanding of what he'd just been through. He asked to be enlightened as to who the angel was and why he was undressed. At first, he thought it might be the young man in the Gospel of Saint Mark who appeared in the garden of Gethsemane when Christ was betrayed. He was wrapped in linen and fled naked when they laid their hands on him. But Papá received no sign of confirmation of this. He continued to pray until his knees ached, but still received no sign. Then he got into bed and prayed himself to sleep.

It was in a dream the answer came to him. He dreamt he was at a beautiful seaside resort with my mother. At first, he thought it was Gibraltar, where my mother is from, but it wasn't. Then an angel appeared to him. He had a loincloth on. The angel was San Sebastiàn, the Roman soldier who was tied naked to a column and shot with arrows when he admitted he was a Christian. They left him for dead, but he was nursed back to life.

When my father woke up, he remembered after he and my mother were married in Gibraltar, they went to the city of San Sebastiàn for their honeymoon. It's a beautiful city on the Bay of Biscay in Basque country. On the first day they arrived there, they both went up to Mount Ulia, and my mother knelt and prayed to San Sebastiàn to become my father's guardian angel.

Papá was very much relieved by the dream. He was afraid his age was playing games with his mind, and the naked angel

261

*might have been an aparición. He's certain now my mother whispered a reminder to San Sebastiàn up in heaven, and that's why he came to the rescue.*

*When Papá called me from the hotel, he told me he was fine but had to go to Rome for a penitential visit before he returned home. It turns out he went there to pray for my mother and to offer his respects to San Sebastiàn at the Basilica Apostolorum. That's where his remains are entombed.*

*So, Aloysius, that's how this story ends. And it's a happy ending. My father now goes to Mass every morning at six o'clock and, as I already said, is at peace with himself. I could ask for no more than that. I'm very grateful to you for being there for us when there was no one else I could turn to. I want you to know I too will pray to San Sebastiàn, asking him to be there for you as he was for my father.*

*Yours,*

*Elena*

What's this crawling down my left cheek? It can't be. I never cry. Not even at my father's funeral. *Snap out of it, Gogarty.*

*De nada, mi amor.* As the fates would have it, I'm on a first-name basis with your father's guardian angel. We even have an occasional drink together. If you're looking for an intercessor, I'm your man. In fact, I'm on my way to have a chat with him right now.

I knock gently and enter solemnly, offering a slight bow.

"Greetings, San Sebastiàn."

Mountjoy peers up at me inquisitively and shrugs.

"Well, with you bearing the preposterous name Aloysius, and me being dubbed Sebastiàn, do I gather your peripathetic mind is mucking about in Evelyn Waugh's *Brideshead Revisited*?"

"Me the stuffed bear, and you the dissolute, effete aristocrat? Perfect casting, I'd say."

Mountjoy won't leave it at that. "Well, the subtitle of that book, to the best of my recollection, is *The Sacred and Profane Memories of*

*Captain Charles Ryder*, and I, for one, can't recall anything other than the profane in our relationship."

I respond reverently, "That was before my awakening and realization that all along I've been in the presence of something sacred, but, being spiritually blind, have been unable to let the scales fall from my eyes.

"What's *Brideshead* about? Ineluctable grace and its mysterious potency. If you were older, I'd equate you with Marchmain, but the younger version will do. The key to the book is in the words stolen from Chesterton: 'I caught him, with an unseen hook and an invisible line which is long enough to let him wander to the ends of the world, and still to bring him back with a twitch upon the thread.'"

Mountjoy responds, "The book seems to have made quite an impression on you. I thought it was rather good myself, and I must say I had great respect for old Marchmain until he went through that specious Catholic rigmarole at the end and spoiled the whole damn thing."

"Father forgive him for he knows not of what he speaketh. Personally, I was rooting for the old bastard to confess and for Charles Ryder to convert. That's what we Catholics do. Waugh doesn't tell you, but when Ryder kneels to pray, I think the hook is in him."

"How charming. Let's leave the metaphysical to you, shall we? You Irish seem to wallow in it. And, speaking of the Irish, you need a drink."

"Not quite yet, San Sebastiàn. I want you to be stone-cold sober when you peruse this epistle, remembering, as you read, the words of Burton in the *Anatomy of Melancholy*: 'Every man hath a good and a bad angel attending on him in particular all his life long.'

"What I'm about to pass on to you is what really took place at Waterloo Station. It bears an indelible— if imperceptible— *imprimatur* attesting to its authenticity. As you will come to see, you are one of us, even though you remain blissfully unaware of it. Rumors of angels abound in our devilry, and we, alas, remain oblivious to them."

He must think I've really lost my mind this time. Strike! I slowly remove Elena's letter from my inside jacket pocket, make the sign of the cross over it, and pass it to Mountjoy.

He starts reading with a dour look. The right corner of his upper lip begins to twitch. He's breaking into a full smile. Now he's chuckling. Finally, he jerks his head back, lets out a shriek, and explodes in a loud, phlegmy laughter.

"The naked angel. Of all the sobriquets bestowed on me at my best and worst moments in life, none, I daresay, will ever equal this! One thing is certain—this calls for a drink." He reaches for the Australian schooners, saying, "You Catholics have never really shaken yourselves free from your medieval moorings, have you?"

"Why should we? They work. The Catholic Church is a rich tapestry, inspiring awe and mystery. Can't you taste it and smell it— the odor of rosewood and wetted ashes?"

"That's atrophy you smell. It comes from pie-eyed priests fondling altar boys when they're not peering up the skirts of middle-aged women who've come to confess their impure thoughts."

"It's the arc of salvation, Richard. Not everyone in it, including men of the cloth, will grab the redemptive ring at the end."

There's a knock at the door.

Mountjoy says in a deep stentorian voice, "Just a moment, please." He pulls out the lower drawer in his desk, scoops up both glasses by their stems, and deposits them into his desk drawer without spilling a drop.

"Do come in."

"Gentlemen. Pardon my intrusion. I was told I could find Dr. Gogarty here. My name is Martin Secker."

I spring to my feet and extend my hand. Secker is English, all right. The accent, the suit, the college tie, everything about him broadcasts his background. Secker's much taller than I am, blond-headed, blue-eyed, wiry, and approaching forty.

"I'm Aloysius Gogarty, and this is Richard Mountjoy."

Mountjoy pulls over a third chair from the side of the room and gestures for Secker to join us.

"Well, I understand you'll be my successor here; is that right?"

"It's not set in stone. Dean Irwin hasn't made up his mind about me yet, and I'm not sure this is what I want to do. I had planned to come to England for a few days around now anyway to visit my family, and Irwin suggested I might stop by and find out how the program works here."

"Yes; of course. I'll help as much as I can, but I should tell you straightaway this man"—I point to Mountjoy—"has been the reason for whatever success I've enjoyed here." Mountjoy waves off the accolade.

Secker looks at Mountjoy and nods, prompting him to ask, "For how long shall we enjoy the pleasure of your company?"

"Just today, I'm afraid. I hope my intrusion will not upset your plans to any degree. I hate being a nuisance."

I reassure him, "No problem. You're most welcome. There's nothing pressing right now, although it can get frenzied around here. When it comes to students, one never knows. We're going into our third term, and, as I am sure you're aware, there's very little done in the way of instruction at that point. It's basically students preparing for their exams. You went to college here in England, didn't you?"

"Yes, I did."

Mountjoy interrupts and points to Secker's tie. "Sidney Sussex, I presume."

"Why yes: yes indeed."

Mountjoy sees my puzzled look and clarifies, "Cambridge."

"And you, Mr. Mountjoy?" He doesn't have his school tie on.

"Magdalen."

"Oxford?

Mountjoy nods.

"Oh, quite good."

They're rattling antlers, sizing each other up.

Secker turns to me again. "If this situation were to work out, we might be colleagues of sorts, what with you at Edinburgh and me here."

"Is that what Irwin said?"

"Yes. At least what he told me. Sorry. Did I misunderstand?"

"Not at all. That's probably how it will work out. Still, it's quite a few months down the road; and with Irwin, you never can be sure of where he'll wind up sending you. The program is burgeoning and always in a state of flux, as I'm sure you know."

"I'm beginning to learn that."

"What's your position at Municipal, if you don't mind my asking?"

"I don't mind at all. I'm an assistant professor in the English department, and I come up for tenure next year."

Irwin is working out a system here: get tenure-hungry assistant professors and sign up the poor bastards as indentured servants for his study-abroad program.

"What's your field?" I ask.

"Twentieth-century American culture. Dreiser, Odets and the like."

"The working class, eh?"

"Well, some of it, of course. Social movements, labor unions—that sort of thing. How about you gentlemen?"

I defer to Mountjoy.

"Nineteenth-century Northern England. Liverpool, of late."

Secker responds, "Quite a bit of social movement there. Very promising." He turns to me.

"I'm the antiquarian. Ancient and medieval. Right now, my focus is on Alexander the Great."

"Now there's the prototypical imperialist."

I start to react but take a cue from Mountjoy's slightly raised eyebrow and restrain myself. "You could certainly make that case." If you were a Marxist, that is.

He asks me, "You're coming up for tenure this year, aren't you?"

"I am."

"Well, good luck with that."

"Martin, I'm sure you have quite a few questions. Why don't we shoot over to my office and leave Mountjoy here to attend to his own work?"

Secker nods and we stroll over to my retreat, chatting about Municipal College, our careers there, and the study-abroad program.

When we arrive and sit, facing each other, I explain, "My office is somewhat removed from the hub of action, but it does have its advantages."

"Which are?"

"Well, for one thing, it's easier to get one's work done without constant interruptions." I look at my watch. "It's a good fifteen-minute walk from the campus center. Students, God bless their little souls, don't fancy going out of their way to get here, and faculty members wouldn't dream of making the effort."

I expect him to smile, but instead he looks at me curiously.

The look vanishes, and he asks, "You have how many students now?"

"Nine here and three at Berkshire."

"How are they getting on?"

"Quite well. I hear from them infrequently nowadays, and that's generally a good sign. I've asked their instructors to let me know if they're attending class and doing their work. They all seem to be performing well. Of course, we won't know how much they've learned until they take the exams. I've already arranged with the instructors here, and those at Berkshire, to give our students their exams at the beginning of June."

Secker looks at me pensively and says, "Do I understand correctly there was some trouble with one of ours here?"

"Yes, Franken—" I catch myself. "Frank Stein. A loose cannon of sorts I'm afraid, who became involved in a sordid scenario."

"How did you find out about it?"

"When I contacted the local constabulary and discovered they'd been monitoring his behavior."

"You mean you sought out the local police for something like this?" There's a look of astonishment, if not censure, on his face. He's about to say something but elects not to.

"Of course, I did. Do you think Stein was going to voluntarily tell me what he was up to?" This guy's starting to get on my nerves. Dissemble the anger. I lift a pencil out of my drawer and begin to roll it on the desk under my palm. Here's hoping this aggravates Secker like Irwin's little routine aggravated me.

"Oh no, of course not," he says, clearly retreating. "What sort of cooperation do you get from the administration here?"

"Well, the vice-chancellor is, of course, only to be seen on rare occasions, but Dr. Ogden, the registrar, is available when any important issue arises."

"So, you've seen the registrar how many times this year?"

"Exactly three. Once at a university-wide tea and twice when particular circumstances dictated I do so."

"Is he a cooperative sort?"

"Yes, if you cooperate with him."

Secker stares at the pencil I'm rolling. It's getting to him. Keep it up.

Then, out of nowhere, he asks, "What were the total expenses of the program... oh, let's say for the past month of March?"

"I don't have the figures at hand. In fact, I've got the books at home because I'm working out some projections for the remainder of the term."

If the truth be known, I don't have books of that sort anywhere. Well, they're in my head now, and, I'm afraid, destined to be lost on the way home.

"I see. Did you find yourself able to stay within the budgetary guidelines the program set for you?"

"Since this is the first group to go to England, there were no such guidelines in place, and I, of course, am the first resident director here. As Irwin's undoubtedly told you, we've had a rather bizarre concatenation of events occur, and, I suspect, under the circumstances there'll be a leveling of expenses next year. I'd have to consult the books to give you a more detailed picture."

He seems satisfied with that explanation, but quickly veers off in another direction. "How many meetings do you have with each of the students during a given term?"

"As many as are necessary. I follow an open-door policy for my students."

"Oh, that reminds me. How many classes do they have you teaching?"

"During the first term, I lectured in three classes. The second term, I had a lecture and a tutorial. In the third term, like everyone else, I'm not teaching at all."

"What role does Mr. Mountjoy serve in relation to the program?"

"He's officially the liaison, appointed as such by BEB—that is, Professor Bisgood, the department chairman."

"What does Mountjoy do?"

"He clarifies procedures, is invaluable in helping our students adjust to the English system and assists them in regard to the classes they schedule." I continue to roll the pencil, but more vigorously. He's getting distracted by it.

"How many meetings do you have with her—sorry, I mean him, let's say, during a given month?"

"When both of us are here, they're almost daily. However, Mountjoy represents the university on his recruitment trips and is frequently off campus."

"How about our students at Berkshire? I may or may not have the time to go there this trip, but I'm curious as to how the program works there."

"It works quite well," I say, smiling, opening my palms as if to ask why there should be a reason to elaborate on that.

"Oh yes, I see." He offers a perfunctory laugh.

The telephone intrudes. Thank God. I answer it, holding up my hand and smiling to let Secker know I have no secrets. His face relaxes. I quickly get back to the pencil, just to keep him on edge.

"Yes?... Oh, hello.... Sure, I understand. I'll pass it on."

I hang up and turn to Secker. "Mr. Mountjoy has been called into the chairman's office to discuss some departmental business; so, I'm afraid he won't be available until much later in the day."

"That's too bad."

Maybe for you, but not for him. I return to the pencil and start rolling it with zeal again. This is fun. I'm beginning to feel like Captain Queeg in *The Caine Mutiny*. "Well, we weren't forewarned you were coming today."

"Yes, of course. I beg your pardon. You're quite right. I've stolen a chunk of your day as well. Just another question or two, and I'll let you get back to the business at hand. Is that all right?"

"Sure. No problem. Shoot."

"Right. Well, there's something I hesitate to bring up. Our students at Berkshire—how are they adjusting to things?"

"Nicely, from what I can tell."

"When was the last time you were there?"

"About two weeks ago. Why?"

"May I say something that we can perhaps keep in confidence, since I'm unsure about the reliability of the story?"

"Certainly. Go right ahead." This can't be good.

"I don't know if you're aware of this, but my father occasionally gets involved in politics here."

"I am. He's also a businessman and a very successful one at that, I'm told."

"Yes, I suppose that's true. Well, anyway, my father, who in his position hears rumors of every sort, confided in me that a friend of the family's son, who's reading English literature at Berkshire, told his mother something that seemed rather odd, and which, if true, could conceivably have an impact on the program in some way."

"Really?" I hope this isn't what I think it is.

270

"It seems the boy's tutor has gone off and married one of the American students there."

Uh-oh, he knows. "There must be dozens of American students at Berkshire."

"Yes, but this one's name is Marthe Flesichmann, and I believe she's one of our students. You're familiar with her, aren't you?"

"Quite familiar with her. But rumors like this circulate on college campuses everywhere, and most of them prove to be just that—rumors."

"That may be so, but I gather you're totally unaware of the event in question." He stares at the pencil, which is now rotating at a rapid rate.

"You gather correctly. I'm sure Marthe—who by the way is our very best student—would've informed me of a situation of this sort. She's not only a brilliant young woman who someday will be a professor herself but has been working so diligently it seems highly unlikely she'd permit an *affaire de cœur* to distract her from her studies. Nevertheless, I very much appreciate the information and will make discreet inquiries to see if there's any validity to this tittle-tattle."

"Please don't get me wrong, Dr. Gogarty. The *last* thing in the world I want to do is interfere with any of this. I just wanted to let you know that prattle of this sort has been in circulation."

He's a weasel all right. "If I had to deal with all the hearsay directed at our students, they'd have carted me off to Bedlam by now. You may have heard that any serious problems we've had here were dealt with swiftly and decisively."

"I have. Dean Irwin himself apprised me of this. And, I understand, you did such a good job handling them you were commended by the registrar here and the American vice-consul himself."

"Yes, thank you. It worked out as well as it could have, thanks to the support of Mr. Mountjoy, the registrar, and... " I almost say the local police but catch myself, ". . . others here at the university."

"You did say '*problems*,' plural. May I ask, aside from Stein, what else occurred, and what other students were involved?"

Now he's gone too far. This calls for a counteroffensive. I take my hand off the pencil and watch the fluster disappear from Secker's face. I switch the pencil to my left hand and start rolling it again, this time slowly. His flustering rekindles.

"Well, since they all came to naught, in my opinion, I would be doing our students a disservice by sharing what supposedly happened with *any* third party. After all, there should be some degree of confidentiality here to protect *them*. Our students are generally of high moral caliber and go about their business in a responsible way. The last thing in the world I want to be guilty of is victimizing a student by passing on any idle talk that might prove to be nothing more than that. I should think that includes any gossip relating to Miss Fleischmann. Isn't that so?"

He feigns a cough, squirms in his seat, sits upright, and says, "Quite right. Yes, of course." Secker looks at his watch. "Oh my; time *is* fleeting, and I have to get back to London to see my father for a late dinner tonight." He stands erect, holds out his hand, and says, "I must say you've been most helpful, and I have a much better understanding of what this is all about. Thank you so much for your time and assistance." He glances at the pencil once more, turns and leaves.

I shout after him, "By all means. It's been a pleasure to meet and chat with you. Please pass on my very best wishes to Dean Irwin."

And, by the way, be sure to bring a subpoena with you on your next visit.

I lift up the pencil and give it a loud, wet kiss.

# 29

My God. It's mid-May already. *Tempus* is fugiting. I'd better saunter over to the department and look in on my counterpart.

"Hello, Miss Popper; is Mountjoy available?"

She checks her calendar.

"Not quite yet." Amalia waggles her thumb in the direction of BEB's office. "But I don't expect he'll emerge before half three. He's probably left his door ajar. I'm sure he'd have no objection to you letting yourself in."

Is that a sly smile on her face? What's this all about? I look at my watch. It's five of three. "Okay. Thanks."

Nothing in the mailbox? That's unusual for a Monday.

I walk into Mountjoy's office and see a pile of magazines, newspapers, and mail on his desk. The slip on top reads "Dr. Gogarty. Well done! Amalia Popper." These must all be from those interviews about my Alexander articles. What have we got here? *Der Spiegel.* "Alexander der Große—*ein Saüfer?*" A drunkard? *Jawohl, ich denke. Newsweek, Life,* the *International Herald-Tribune,* the *San Francisco Chronicle* and a dozen or so more. Irwin will choke on each and every one of them. Thank you, Dear Lord.

I hope they haven't turned what I've said inside out. How does this German piece read? Okay. *Newsweek.* Not bad. Wait a minute. Most of them seem to be reprints or rewrites of the *New York Times* article.

Not *Le Figaro*. This one's written by an Alexander expert. Let's see. He refers to "*son penchant pour l'alcool.*" *Vraiment, mon ami.* What's this? *Life* magazine? "On Immortality and Its Drawbacks." Hmm. Overreaction to my thesis is fascinating, he says. "The aggressive defensiveness of some is odd... as if Alexander's accomplishments, his place in history, and his very right to be considered immortal are all threatened by the possibility he was ill with one of history's most common diseases, a disease now epidemic in that hothouse of immortals: the United States Congress." Amen.

The *Australian Weekender* headline is, "Now it's Alexander the Grape!" What do *they* say? "Alexander the Great, conqueror of the world 350 years before Christ, was a sot." Not exactly how I'd phrase it. But I write history; they sell papers. What about *Punch*? No pretense here. This is hysterical. Who's the writer? The *editor* of the magazine? He's got Alexander pie-eyed from birth to death. I'll read this to Mountjoy – or should I say Sebastian now? - and brace myself for his mockery.

Where's the real mail? Here we are. *The* envelope from Routledge. Let this be the contract. Yup, it is. Quick read. Sign. Airmail a copy to New York. What's this? It looks like another study-abroad newsletter. I'll look at that later. I should get the contract out today, but I can't start treating Miss Popper like she's *my* secretary. I'd better go and ask her in person.

There she is, typing away. "Hi, it's me again. Thanks so much for your note and all that stuff. None of this would have happened without your help." The rosebud reappears. "After all you've done, I hesitate to ask, but do you think it would be possible to get a copy of this document off to New York today?"

"Yes; no problem," she says, removing her hands from the typewriter and giving me her full attention.

"Wonderful. Please send it to Dean Irwin. Here's a note to put on top of it. Any idea when it may get there?"

"In about a week, I should think."

"Good. Say, is Seb—uh... Mr. Mountjoy still . . . ?"

"Oh, he just left the chairman and I saw him behind you. He should be back in his own office by now."

"Good. Thanks."

I fling Mountjoy's door open, extend the palm of my right hand toward his desk, and say, "This, Sebastian, is what they call *kleos*. Or, to the Greekless—*like you*—*fama*, fame!"

He looks up from the paper he's reading, snarls, and says, "I must be unsparingly frank, Aloysius. I liked you better as a stuffed bear than I do in real life. I take it these are your press clippings."

"I didn't put them there. Amalia Popper did. Besides, I'm just following Your Lordship's instructions. I'm acting like an American by drawing attention to myself."

"Well, if the truth be known, there isn't a man in this department, including me, who wouldn't sacrifice his left testicle to have his research written up on the front page of *Thee Times*, as you did. Otherwise"—he glances at the mastheads, one at a time, carefully placing each in an appropriate place—"it's mostly trash. *Life Magazine*. The *San Francisco Chronicle*. What's that paper they publish in New York? The... eh... *Hobo News*? Have you made the *Hobo News* yet? Until you do—"

"How do you know about the *Hobo News*? Well, anyway, they don't publish it anymore. Otherwise, I'd be on their front page and proud of it!"

Mountjoy nods in snide agreement and continues to rummage through the pile. "Hang on there, old boy. There are actually some respectable—at least up until now—magazines and newspapers here."

"I'm afraid you're wasting your time except for *Der Spiegel*, *Le Figaro*, and *L'Europeo*. The rest of those articles simply parrot the *New York Times*. Note that, with a choice between the two, they *do not* follow *Thee Times*."

He grimaces.

I add, "That should tell you something."

"Yes, something Spenglerian. How about the *Further and Indefeasible Decline of the West*?"

"'Indefeasible'? Now, there's a sign of decline if there ever was one. Wait, though." I reach for the Australian paper and hold it up in front of my face so that Mountjoy can read the headline.

He smiles expansively. "Yehhhhs."

I add, "I love those Australians. Oh, here's something else for you." I show him the cover of *Punch*.

"Well, well, well. What have we here?"

"There's an article in here *written by the editor himself* parodying my articles."

"Really? He and I were school chums."

"Is there anyone of importance you weren't a school chum with? Well, he's written a very funny piece. He tells us Alexander's drunken father left his son eighteen thousand empties as his inheritance. Upon becoming king, young Alexander marches into Thrace, where he finds the pubs closed because of licensing hours, and proceeds to vent his fury on the local tribes. Alexander decides to conquer the Persian Empire when he hears the first two drinks are on the house there. He fights elephants all right, but they're pink elephants."

Mountjoy roars.

"Let me take a peek at it. That chap always was quite amusing. Hmm. Well, he does give you credit and, by the way, cites *Thee Times*, not that pretentious rag in New York. Do you mind if I read this?"

"Go right ahead. I need to catch up on the earthshaking news coming out of the study-abroad office."

It looks like they're minutes from the staff meeting of May seventh. That's . . . let's see . . . a week ago. What? "Mountjoy! Listen to this. 'Dr. Secker's Report.'"

Mountjoy drops what he's reading and wrinkles his eyebrows in concern.

I start reading aloud.

> *"'Dr. Martin Secker, who's being considered for a resident director's position with the program, visited our centers at*

*Yorkshire and Berkshire universities and voluntarily submitted a report of that visit to Dean Irwin. In it, Dr. Secker noted a lack of institutional control in the operation of the program. This was characterized by irregular and infrequent meetings with the students at both centers. Reports to New York were filed on an ad hoc basis or simply in response to a direct request from the dean's office. Contact with lecturers and tutors who were working with our students was sporadic, thereby posing problems as far as the evaluation of our students' work was concerned. Budgetary considerations were treated in cavalier fashion, and no discernible effort was being made to create clear guidelines for these matters for the future."*

I take a deep breath and continue.

*"'Despite this, it was quite evident that key officers in the administration of both universities were quite pleased with the efforts of Dr. Gogarty and remained receptive toward the program continuing there because of his successful handling of troublesome issues that came to their attention'."*

"One day a peacock," I point to the stack of magazines, "the next a feather duster." I raise the newsletter over my head.

"Is this a disaster?"

"What do *you* think?"

"I think academia is a warren of weasel rats. That's what I think."

"Well, in my opinion," Mountjoy says, "you're allowing yourself to be unduly rattled by this. Do you want an unjaundiced point of view?" He reaches for the Glenfiddich and fills two fresh glasses. "There's not a damned thing they can do to you as far as"—he makes quotation marks with his fingers—"'the program' is concerned. You've done what you were supposed to do, in that both universities will continue to accept your students, at least for another year."

"How could I get a good report from Berkshire? I've never even met their vice-chancellor or registrar. In fact, I don't know anyone there except our students and the ill-fated Lionel Blum."

"You're not Cecil Secker's son. The perfidious Secker evidently made it a point to drop in on the Berkshire people during his visit here. Their indulgent remarks don't surprise me one bit. As I see it, there are several possibilities. One is Ogden passed on his own sentiments about you to the registrar there and the registrar passed them on to their vice-chancellor. A second is your students have blended in with the landscape, and there's no reason for any concern on their part. Or, maybe they've become aware of the Blum/Fleischmann *amourette* and are resorting to that old chestnut: 'things are just splendid.' It's quite English, you know."

"I'm beginning to learn that. You warned me about Secker. I should have listened to you and been more prudent in what I told him."

"He's a swine. I knew that by his name, background and college. The motto of Sidney Sussex, by the way, is *Dieu me Gard de Calomnie.* God protect me from calumny. Note there's nothing in their motto about protecting others from *their* calumny. Nevertheless, what you said to him wouldn't have made the slightest difference."

"Why not?"

"He would have plucked whatever words you employed and used them as grist for his self-serving mill."

"Won't this discredit *him*? If I were Irwin, I'd be uneasy with a Judas like him in my midst. He could just as well turn around and deliver the *bacio della morte* to Irwin. Ambitious as he is, Secker might be looking to take over the whole damn operation."

"I doubt if Irwin has anything to fear from Secker. It's a marriage of convenience. Secker doesn't want to take on all of the responsibilities of your piteous program. It would discredit him in this country, and he damn well knows it. Becoming the director of an American study-abroad program? I mean, really!

"My guess is Secker may be maneuvering to get back here while being paid twice the salary he'd get at our universities. That is, if any of them were desperate enough to take him on. He may very well want to return to England to plant seeds for a lobbying career of his own. In addition, by using the younger Secker as a pawn, your dean will have access to his father, a political celebrity here. From what you've told me about Irwin, he's probably daydreaming about being introduced to the prime minister, if not the queen herself!"

I point to the memorandum. "Okay, but let's get back to this. What about the way I come off in it?"

I glance at Mountjoy, who crosses his eyes and tilts his head sideways to dramatize what he's about to say. Speaking like one of Dickens's coistrels, he spits out, "We must think of our reputation, sir, mustn't we?"

I can only manage a half smile.

Mountjoy takes a deep breath and says, "For whatever it's worth —and I say this advisedly—your *reputation* will likely remain intact. After all, Irwin needs *you* if he wants to be certain of Edinburgh for next year."

"That's the problem."

Mountjoy says, "Let's step back for a moment. What type of resolution are you seeking?"

"Well, the optimal outcome would be I go back to New York with tenure, court the fair lady Elena, marry her, and live happily ever after. If I'm out at Municipal, I'm off to Australia; hopefully, with the ineffable one."

"Have you heard from Australia?"

"Oh yeah, sorry. I haven't had a chance to tell you. Macquarie University offered me a job as lecturer, which, with a book contract, would become senior lecturer."

"I thought that chap would come through."

"Thanks. I doubt if I would have gotten it without your connection."

"Probably not. But that's neither here nor there." Mountjoy looks down at his desk calendar and announces, "May fifteenth, my dear boy. Soon things will draw to a close." He uses his pinky to wipe an imaginary tear from beneath his eye.

"They must be into discussions about my tenure now."

"Shouldn't all of this have been dealt with already? If they reject anyone at this time of the year, the poor chap has precious little time to seek employment elsewhere."

"You're right. Ordinarily, the whole process is over by now. But Irwin invented a new timeline for those who serve abroad. Now there's a delay in considering us, supposedly because it's difficult to collect the necessary materials from people overseas. In reality, it allows him to continue toying with his resident directors until their work in the program is complete. He never takes chances, just hostages."

"There must be a *terminus ad quem*, even for you 'hostages.'"

"There is. He has to let us know by June tenth. There's another ambivalent date. That's when James Joyce first laid eyes on Nora Barnacle, the love of his life, but also the day on which Alexander died."

"Could you stick to the point?"

"Students enjoy my digressions."

"They have no choice."

"Sorry, boss. What I really need to know is what tack I should take about the Edinburgh position. I'm cooked if I refuse. On the other hand, if I agree and do an about-face, Irwin's recriminations will have long-term consequences for me."

"Silence is often our best weapon. If he prevails upon you for an answer, tell him you're going to accept the position. Then contract a mysterious illness forcing you to decline for medical reasons."

"Now that you mention it, there was a professor from Berkeley who was originally supposed to be here this year. I'd bet my bottom shekel he came down with his 'illness' after he read the applications. In fact, Secker mentioned on our way over to my office that he saw the man in question in London and he looked perfectly healthy. But I doubt if I could get away with this 'mysterious affliction' business. It would take someone sinister to pull off something like that. You'd be good at it."

"Yehhhs."

"We're in entirely different circumstances. You've got family, and I mean family in an English sense. You've also got money, or at least will have it, providing your mother is kind enough to expire before you do."

"Any alternative is unthinkable. Now then, I have to meet with BEB to discuss more department gibberish. Let's see each other again *before* you act in rash fashion, shall we?"

"Good idea. I've got paperwork to do, and I think I'll take it home. I'm figuring out a marking system for my American students. I have to translate the grades they get from instructors here into what goes on their records back home."

"Isn't it advisable to wait until they've been assigned grades by our people?"

"I will. But your grades are far more severe than ours, and if we transfer them onto our students' records as is, yet another disaster would present itself. Word would get out about the negative impact on a student's grade-point average for participating in the program, and nobody would apply.

"What I'm going to do is look at each student's grading pattern at Municipal and make sure their grades conform to it. In fact, at this stage in a student's academic career, his grade-point average ordinarily goes up quite a bit, and I have to factor that in as well."

"So, the grades we submit to you are, for all practical purposes, superfluous."

"Just between us, yes."

"There's a delectable irony in what you say. You see, several of my colleagues are relishing the opportunity to humble some of your more garrulous students with unspeakable grades. Thus, while we conspire to degrade them, you simply ignore our assessments and accommodate your, ehh, *customers.*"

"That's what it comes down to."

"So, tell me, what sort of grades will a student like Marthe Fleischmann be able to boast of, if and when she returns to New York?"

"Straight A's. Without question."

"Why doesn't that surprise me? Incidentally, I never did ask what she had in store for you in Berkshire when she needed you to be at her disposal for an entire day."

"All I can tell you is that it was either humiliating or hilarious, depending on your point of view. Someday I'll give you a candid account of what occurred. Maybe I'll include it in that novel of mine. I'm not brave enough to own up to it yet."

"So, is Fleischmann still holding a revolver to your head?"

"Yup."

"Well, she's married now and apparently blissful in the relationship, isn't that so?"

"Yes... and?"

"Well, it means that *she* now has something to lose."

"Huh?"

"Well, should Fleischmann attempt to blackmail you again, you can checkmate her by threatening to tell Blum *your version* of what happened between you two."

"Eureka! Why didn't I think of that?"

"Must you ask?"

# 30

---

I glance at my desk calendar. Jesus. It's almost June. I'll be gone soon. Better check in with His Lordship.

"Good morning. Miss Popper."

She responds with a sour expression and turns her back on me. Well, it appears Miss Amalia Popper is out of plumb today. I'd better let her be and see how Mountjoy's faring.

"Mawwwwning, Sebastian."

A barely audible, "Yehhs."

"Uh-oh. What's wrong?"

"Unable to play the *poseur* today, old boy—lost forever in Stygian gloom." He reaches for the malt scotch and pours generously into each of two schooners.

"Miriam, one of the undersecretaries—the scatterbrained Miriam —opened up not just one, but both envelopes from Georgina, despite the fact that each was clearly labeled *personal* and *confidential*. She *finally* noticed the caveats, and promptly passed the materials on to Amalia."

"Did she read them?"

"Who?"

"Miriam."

"I think not. She was distraught over her error and on the verge of tears so she poured the lot onto Amalia's desk."

"Miss Popper read them though, didn't she?"

"How do you know?"

"The bloodstains on my collar. They're from the daggers hurled in my direction a moment ago."

"Amalia knows, all right. She stormed into my office yesterday afternoon, threw Georgina's correspondence at me, and announced, scornfully, 'Miss Miriam Huffington opened this letter in error. She apologizes for her indiscretion.' Amalia then added, tears welling up in her eyes, 'Sometimes apologies just aren't enough, are they?' Then she flew out of the office and hasn't exchanged one word with me since."

"What did the letter say?"

"The usual, 'I long for the day we can at last be together, etcetera, etcetera'."

"Isn't Miss Popper aware of your situation with Her Ladyship? Wouldn't she understand your seeking comfort and companionship elsewhere?"

"The problem is Amalia interpreted my failure to respond to *her* as something noble in me. In her eyes; I've been the stalwart husband, ever faithful to his whining, frigid, frumpy bitch of a wife. Now I'm reduced to the status of a garden-variety adulterer. Of course, if I'd taken up with her, Amalia would have looked upon our relationship as having been ordained in heaven."

"But Amalia's no dope; surely she realizes both of you would have endangered your positions here if you got involved."

"I daresay she would have been willing to risk it. I do know one thing, however. Offering her the explanation, as I might you, that carrying on, with a woman several hundred miles away is wiser than keeping company with someone you work with, would've been anything but comforting to her."

What can I say to console him?

"Surely you remember Oscar Wilde's telling question: 'How can a man expect a woman to be happy if he treats her as if she were a rational creature?'"

"Precisely. We're dealing with elements beyond our ken here."

"Will this information go past Miss Popper?"

"Not likely. But it can still cripple me without her delivering the actual death blow. Amalia is—was—my *espionne*, my *attaché* to BEB, the source of my strength in the department. Now all I can expect is icy *politesse*. With her at odds with me, I, my dear fellow, am undone."

"This isn't how she *wants* to think of you. You need to give her a reason to prop you back up on your white horse."

"How in the world would I ever accomplish that?"

"First of all, when did these letters from Georgina begin arriving?"

"In early October, as I recall."

"Perfect."

"Why?"

"You need a scapegoat, a villain, and it must be a credible one— someone who's been undermining your high-minded instincts." I point at myself with a pumpkin-like smile on my face.

Mountjoy stares at me curiously.

Elaboration is called for. "Women usually look at us as if we're children, and whether they're wives, mistresses, spinsters, or even nuns, they all have a maternal streak in them. Mothers are perpetually blaming their worthless son's misconduct on the company he keeps. What makes you think Miss Popper wouldn't want to do precisely the same thing?"

"You really think so?"

"I do. Anyway, it's worth a shot."

"How would I go about it?"

"Take her out to dinner."

"She would scoff at the idea."

"Plead tearfully, if necessary, that you simply *must* explain *everything* to her if it's the very last thing you do on earth. Curiosity will get her; it always does. Besides, she'd like nothing better than to believe you were merely satisfying bestial instincts, and there's nothing of substance in the relationship. I wouldn't even call it a relationship. I'd refer to it as an arrangement or, better yet, a rash mistake. Tell her you've come to your senses and you're putting an end to it here and now!"

"And when letters continue to arrive?"

"They won't. That'll come to an abrupt halt. Surely England has post-office boxes you can rent?"

"We do."

"There's your answer."

"You then, my dear boy, loom as the culprit in all this."

"A man is judged by the company he keeps. You have just begun to realize you've been drinking far too much since I arrived and fear a severe blow has been dealt to your once-steadfast moral system."

"Ehhh... what moral system?"

"The one she thought you had."

His eyebrows rise. "So I'm a victim of circumstance, am I?"

"Your all too frequent exposure to Mephistopheles eroded your sense of dignity and self-respect. I, of course, would have to pull a disappearing act."

"That's neither practical nor necessary. Amalia knows I'm supposed to be your liaison and I'm obliged to meet with you. I can't afford to avoid you completely."

"True. But we can forgo any conspicuous extracurricular activities; at least by leaving the building separately and at different times. That would provide tangible proof you're earnestly striving to mend your ways. Anyway, this Saturday is June first, and I'll be gone in two and a half weeks. You can undergo a miraculous recovery, a spiritual resurrection, once the air has been cleansed by my departure."

"That does hold promise, and lacking an alternative, I may give it a go. Of course, Oxford would have to be out of the question now."

"Yup—that is, at least as far as your official itineraries are concerned. But if your present scheduling pattern is any indication"—I point to his pin-laden map—"you have the imagination and willpower to create a master plan allowing you to tack on a few extra yards to each trip south."

"True. However, if this plan proves to be serviceable, you can expect a look of steely disdain on Amalia's face whenever you approach her, along with frosty excuses for not being able to do whatever it is you ask of her."

"If that's the price that need be paid, it will be well worth it."

"What about your own plight? What's the latest chapter in your ongoing fiasco?"

I lightly tap the right side of my head several times.

"I forgot to tell you. I've sent a letter to Elena asking if I may court her upon my return. What did Lope de Vega say? *'Que amor non es más que porfía: No son piedras las mujeres'.*"

"Gogarty, yours is a nation of linguistic cripples and your obscene pronunciation screams for a cogent translation, which is, ehh, something like, 'The suitor must persist, for no woman has a heart of stone.' Obviously, de Vega never met my mother. What do you think your Dulcinea's response will be to such an overture?"

Aha! So, Somerset did pilfer "linguistic cripples" from Mountjoy. "I don't know how Elena will react. She does feel indebted to me. What's more important is how Torquemada feels about it."

Mountjoy raises his voice, pounds on the desk, and shouts, "If all else fails, we'll arrange for an epiphany." He bolts out from behind his desk, positioning himself between me and the office door, and starts flicking his thumbs across his suit jacket.

"I'll disrobe stealthily, slip into the old sod's bedroom when he's sound asleep, station myself at the foot of the bed, and begin singing *'Tantum Ergo.'* Softly at first but rising to a crescendo until I've fully awakened him. Then, in my best Bela Lugosi tone, I'll begin chanting: 'Release your daughter from bondage, turn her over to Aloysius Gogarty... release her... let your daughter go... or'"—he deepens his voice—"'be excommunicated!'"

Mountjoy's been pedaling backwards during his performance. He now puts his right hand behind his back, opens the office door, and slowly backs out into the corridor.

When he reenters, Mountjoy finds me in the midst of a coughing fit. I gasp for breath and am finally able to say, "That should do it, all right. Is that the voice you used in London?"

"I remained silent at Waterloo, afraid I'd bollocks it up by laughing. I never did read the manual on epiphanies and was uncertain whether one made solemn pronouncements. It thus seemed advisable to appear ethereal and leave it at that. It turned out to be a good choice."

"Well, that should work. That is, unless Torquemada dies of a coronary there and then. By the way, I finally made up my mind about Edinburgh."

"And?"

"I'm going to tell Irwin I won't accept the position."

Mountjoy leans back on his chair with a startled look on his face. He sighs, purses his lips, and nods his head in a way that leaves me unsure if he's signaling stoic resignation or begrudging admiration.

"What repercussions do you expect?" he asks.

"I can't be sure, but my guess is he'll sabotage my tenure."

"So, after all you've been through, you won't be able to grab the brass ring. Failure is galling. Are you sure this is the wisest course of action? You might recall a warning from one of our poets: 'Some rise by sin, and some fall by virtue'."

"Shakespeare, how *à propos*. Well, anyway, I'm tired of playing both ends against the middle. Maybe Aristotle was right when he said internal victories are all that counts. It's about time I simply did the right thing. I'm sending a letter to that effect today."

Mountjoy says, "Fine. Just bear in mind there's usually a price to pay for lapsing into integrity. What will you do if he forces you out?"

"Well, I have the Macquarie job. They've given me three weeks to decide. One whelm at a time. Good luck with Miss Popper. I'll be seeing you, but only occasionally from here on in."

# 31

Irwin must have the letter by now. Why isn't he putting the screws to me? Maybe he's keeping it to himself, or just can't believe I mean it.

My phone rings.

"Hello.... Oh, Mountjoy; what's up?... You're kidding. *Elena*? When?... And?... She'll call back in fifteen minutes? How did she sound to you?... Human? Ha! I'll be right there."

I'm out of my office like a shot off a shovel and still gasping for air when I arrive at Mountjoy's office. When I'm finally able to talk I say, "Well, Your Lordship, speaking of women, Miss Popper just glared at me like a coiled snake about to strike. When she spoke, it was like my kindergarten teacher after she discovered my wall painting in the cloak closet. Should I take it to mean that our plan is working?"

"It seems so. At dinner, I described my plight as you suggested, and I think it went rather well. I wouldn't expect her to be exchanging pleasantries with you in the near future, if ever. Amalia's suggested I place you—a rotter, by her description—in quarantine and see you only when absolutely obliged to. She also reassured me this too shall pass with your departure, like, in her words, an outbreak of cholera."

"Cholera? That's not bad. I would have settled for leprosy. I guess my theory about maternal instincts has validity."

"Not in all cases. M'mah's biggest fear was that I'd corrupt my playmates and alienate the more distinguished women in her little coterie."

"Now there's an alert woman with a sense of priority."

"Yehhhs."

Mountjoy's phone rings.

He stares at me momentarily and says, "Why don't *you* get it?" He waves me into his chair.

"Yes, Dr. Gogarty speaking. I'll hold.... Hello? Elena. Thank you so much for calling. I know this isn't easy for you.... What? That's all right. I'd rather hear the unvarnished truth.... That's okay. It's what I asked for, and it helps a lot to know where I stand. Thank you ever so much.... Goodbye, Elena."

Mountjoy says, "That didn't sound very promising."

"Elena overheard the dean talking to the chairman of the tenure committee the other day, and Irwin was in effect damning me with faint praise."

"Did she mention the name of that chairman? Do you know anything about him?"

"His name is Ettore Schmitz. He knows me, and we get along quite well. In fact, he was one of the few people I let read the prologue to my Alexander book. It's so unconventional I was afraid of how other colleagues might react. Schmitz understood exactly what I was doing. He loved the concept and urged me to see it through. Later on, I let him look at a few chapters, and he was very impressed with what he read. "

"Would Schmitz be willing to act against Irwin's wishes on your behalf?"

"I don't know. He's an associate professor, which is one rank below full professor. Irwin makes sure full professors don't get chairmanships. That would mean less leverage for him since they wouldn't need that last promotion. If Schmitz goes against the grain, he may never become a full professor there. Irwin's not exactly a subtle adversary. It looks to me like all the chickens are coming home to roost. Australia, here I come."

"Well, in my anything but humble opinion, you might want to give this just a tad more time. Rarely, but every now and then, an unanticipated boon appears from out of nowhere and works in one's favor."

"So now we wait for a miracle. Is that the game plan?"

"When all else fails, seek divine intervention. It worked for *Señor* Torquemada."

"If it means your stripping naked again, no thanks; I'll take my chances with Irwin."

He smiles, and the phone rings. I hand it back to Mountjoy.

He listens, then says, "Why yes, of course. He's still here; hang on, please." Mountjoy passes the phone back to me and mouths, "Elena."

"Hi . . . They just spoke again? Did you hear what Schmitz said to Irwin?... Good for him. How did Irwin respond?... That figures. Exactly what did he say?... Thank you so much for going out of your way for me.... As of now, it looks like I'll be back by the middle of the month. Let me check the calendar. I'll touch down in New York on June fourteenth. Maybe we can celebrate Bloomsday together on the sixteenth and share a gorgonzola cheese sandwich and a glass of burgundy?... I'll explain what that means when I see you.... You'll do what? That would be great. You really are something special. Thanks." I hang up.

"Well?" Mountjoy asks.

"Elena did some eavesdropping on another conversation between Schmitz and Irwin. Schmitz raved about my book; agreed Irwin knew more about what's best for the college than he did; but said he'd still have to think the whole matter over. I don't know if he'll stand up for me against Irwin; I'm not even sure I would do the same for him."

"Maybe *he's* a *bona fide* man of principle. What's the timeline here?"

"The dean sees the president for a consultation on Friday, June seventh. On Monday it goes to a vote in the committee. That's when my fate is determined."

"You should have asked your Cuban to call you after the committee's meeting and let you know the outcome."

"I didn't have to. Elena said she'll call as soon as she knows what's happened. I'm going back to my office to write an acceptance letter for the Macquarie job."

"And send it?"

"No. Not yet. I didn't have a chance to tell you that with all the publicity and word of my Alexander book getting around, a couple of other colleges in the States have approached me. I'm waiting on a possibility at Stanford. Cornell is interested as well. I sent my *curriculum vitae* to both places and made it clear I'd only come with tenure and as an associate professor. Strike while the iron's hot."

"Did you send them your manuscript?"

"Not all of it. Just some sample chapters, the footnotes, and the bibliography. I did tell them I signed a contract with Routledge, though. That should help."

"The *bibliography*?"

"Yup. It's fifty-three pages long, and Somerset said it's 'the most complete bibliography ever assembled on Alexander scholarship.' That's a lot coming from him. I passed his comment on to both universities. His praise should help. 'Alexander' seems to be the key. Oh, I've also inquired at Harvard for Somerset, and they're definitely interested."

"That will please the ignominious imp and delight BEB. I know Harvard, and I've heard of Stanford, but where on earth is Cornell?"

"New York. But not in the city; it's in Ithaca, which is upstate."

"So, if you accepted a position there, you would set sail for Ithaca after your sojourn in Albion."

I nod and say, "I think I'll write a general letter of acceptance for all three places, just in case. From now on, though, the less I'm here, the better for you."

"That's regrettably so."

I walk to my office with the intention of sorting out priorities, but no sooner do I set step into the room than the telephone rings.

"Yes?... Oh, hello Miss Popper.... Another telegram? Should I come over and pick it up?... All right. Thanks a lot."

I hurry back to the department and am met by Miss Popper's scornful stare.

"Hi. Thanks very much for letting me know this is here."

She slides the telegram across the desk without saying a word, gets up from her chair, and marches toward the ladies' room. She's probably going to disinfect herself.

Who's the telegram from? I think I'll sit down in the foyer and read it here. I hope it's not Irwin. Jumping Jesus, it's from Elkin Mathews, Municipal's president. He's probably the one that fires people. What the—?

NEW YORK. JUNE 7 1968. THE PRESIDENT OF MUNICIPAL COLLEGE AWARDS AN ANNUAL MEDALLION TO A MEMBER OF THE YOUNGER FACULTY WHO SHOWS OUTSTANDING PROMISE PARTICULARLY AS A TEACHER BUT ALSO IN SERVICE SCHOLARSHIP AND OTHER AREAS STOP THIS YEAR THAT AWARD GOES TO DR ALOYSIUS T GOGARTY ASSISTANT PROFESSOR OF HISTORY STOP PROFESSOR GOGARTY IS PRESENTLY IN ENGLAND WHERE HE IS RESIDENT DIRECTOR OF OUR STUDY ABROAD CENTERS AT YORKSHIRE AND BERKSHIRE STOP HE HAS BEEN TEACHING AT THE COLLEGE ONLY SINCE SEPTEMBER 1 1965 BUT IN THE THREE YEARS DR GOGARTY HAS BEEN WITH US HE HAS WON THE RESPECT AND ESTEEM OF BOTH STUDENTS AND FACULTY MEMBERS FOR HIS STIMULATING TEACHING INCISIVE SCHOLARSHIP AND OUTSTANDING SERVICE TO THE COLLEGE STOP

PROFESSOR GOGARTY HAS WON WORLDWIDE RECOGNITION FOR HIS SCHOLARLY ACHIEVEMENTS IN

ANCIENT HISTORY STOP PARTICULARLY HIS ORIGINAL AND EXCITING WORK ON ALEXANDER THE GREAT STOP HE HAS ALREADY PUBLISHED SEVERAL ARTICLES ON ALEXANDER AND PROFESSOR GOGARTYS BIOGRAPHY OF THE MACEDONIAN CONQUEROR IS SCHEDULED FOR PUBLICATION BY A HIGHLY RESPECTED ENGLISH PUBLISHING HOUSE STOP

BUT IT IS IN THE AREA OF TEACHING PROFESSOR GOGARTY HAS GAINED HIS UNIQUE DISTINCTION HERE AT MUNICIPAL STOP ON CAMPUS HE IS KNOWN AS A PROFESSOR WHO GIVES EVERYTHING OF HIMSELF IN THE CLASSROOM AND CONSISTENTLY PROVIDES STUDENTS WITH AN EXPERIENCE THAT ENHANCES THEIR KNOWLEDGE AND STIMULATES THEIR INTEREST STOP AS ONE STUDENT COMMENTED TO ME QUOTE PROFESSOR GOGARTYS HUMOR, CHARISMA, SENSE OF DISCOVERY AND ENTHUSIASM FOR HIS SUBJECT MAKE SITTING IN HIS CLASSROOM AN ELECTRIFYING ADVENTURE QUOTE STOP

IT IS THEREFORE MY PRIVILEGE AND HONOR TO PRESENT THIS AWARD TO PROFESSOR ALOYSIUS T GOGARTY AND IN DOING SO TO RECOGNIZE WITH PROFOUND RESPECT THE IMMEASURABLE IMPACT A TEACHER CAN MAKE UPON STUDENTS STOP

TO BE AWARDED TO PROFESSOR ALOYSIUS T GOGARTY AT THE THIRTY-FIRST COMMENCEMENT EXERCISES OF THE MUNICIPAL COLLEGE OF NEW YORK STOP

PERSONAL NOTE STOP YOU WILL BE PRESENTED WITH A PARCHMENT SCROLL OF THIS AWARD SUITABLE FOR FRAMING AS WELL AS A GOLD MEDALLION FOR EXCELLENCE IN TEACHING WHEN YOU RETURN TO THE CAMPUS STOP CONGRATULATIONS STOP ELKIN MATHEWS STOP

Don't STOP! I want to hear more. This is it. The unforeseen event Mountjoy spoke of. Irwin can't torpedo me now. He must be beside himself. It makes sense. This is the only matter other than fund-raising President Mathews handles himself. Not even Irwin knows who's getting the teaching awards until Mathews makes his announcement.

Wait until Mountjoy sees this. Uh-oh. Miss Popper's back. I can't just waltz down to his office anymore. How should I handle this?

"Miss Popper." She looks up and stares right through me. "May I ask you something?"

She answers with a Medusa-like stare.

"I recently had a conversation with Mr. Mountjoy and got the distinct impression I've done something grievously wrong. He's distant and unresponsive to me. Is it something I said? I would be devastated if I've offended him in any way."

Miss Popper's upper lip begins to draw back in an instinctual smile, but it's suppressed. She looks at me and says sternly, "It is neither my place nor my inclination, *Dr. Gogarty*, to comment upon or offer counsel in regard to questions of that nature. I am here to provide secretarial services to the staff and confine myself to executing my duties, unlike, I'm afraid, *some people* around here."

No death-row pardon from *this* governor. Back to my outpost to arrange a clandestine rendezvous with His Lordship.

"Yes, Mountjoy, it's me. Guess what? I've got some good news for a change.... You too? What's yours?... Wait. Let me get this straight. Miss Popper came into your office with a pot of tea and biscuits? What did she say?... So, basically, she's proud of you, because you did what you had to do once you saw the situation with moral clarity.

"A 'my kinda guy' moment, huh? You see that?... We Catholics had it right all along. Redemption *is* available to everyone, even the likes of you.... Me? I told her my concern over your changed attitude toward me, and she advised me, basically, to start acting like an adult. In other words, to leave you be....

"My news? Are you sitting down? I have in hand a two-page telegram from the president of Municipal College informing me that at our commencement exercises this year—next week in fact—I'm being presented —*in absentia* of course—with the annual teaching award given to an outstanding younger faculty member at the college....

"What does it mean? It means I get tenure. It means Irwin will be apoplectic. It means I don't have to start all over again at a new place. It means I can go home to Elena. It means we can celebrate big-time tonight. How does that sound to you?...

"You'll come to my office, and we'll leave from here? Good idea. What time?... Perfect! The pubs will be opening up just as we get there.

"Oh, won't we have a merry time... drinking whiskey, beer and wine . . ."

# 32

Mountjoy arrives with his head rotating as he looks in vain for anything other than a desk, two chairs and a wastepaper basket in my office. He settles into the empty chair with a "we get what we deserve in this world" expression on his face. It changes, though, as he looks up at me. "This, my dear boy," he says in a sincerely regretful tone, "appears to be our swan song."

"Why?"

"Amalia knows me all too well to believe I'd readily forsake the joy of communing with the prince of darkness. She's bound to keep track of my meanderings to make sure she's not being played for a fool."

"O she of little faith! Okay. From here on in, you act as if I'm a leper."

"Act?"

"Well, I'm practically gone. So, let's treat it like *Götterdämmerung*, the twilight of the gods. How about risking a farewell tour of the local pubs? Let's see if we can breathe some life into Dickensville."

"First of all, my dear fellow, I not only know what *Götterdämmerung* means, I know how to say it, unlike *some* people. With your fortunes on the rise and my equanimity restored for the moment, I agree festivities are called for. I'm constrained, however, to be moderate in my consumption. The coppers are running amok with that blasted breathalyzer."

"There's no need to worry. Budgen is at our disposal and on his way here as we speak. I've informed him we shall be carousing with gay abandon tonight."

"So, off on the razzle, are we?"

"You took the words right out of my mouth. We'll have a glorious drunk to astonish the druidy druids. This is our last hurrah, and it may be the last one of all for me. I've been wrestling with the idea of doing something about my drinking. If I'm going to do justice to Elena, now is the time to grapple with it."

"Now?"

"Not *right* now. I mean when I return to New York. As far as our 'razzle' is concerned, what say you choose some pubs with engaging names, and my job will be to tell you something about those names?"

"And I, in turn, shall apprise you of how misbegotten your observations are? Behold: an inflated windbag, waiting to be uncorked."

"It's more akin to Aeolus, the lord of winds and the patron saint of professors everywhere. As to the credibility of my comments, that remains to be seen, does it not?"

"Granted. I'm simply positing a likelihood."

"All right, Your Lordship, I'll set some ground rules. I don't want to hear 'The Half Moon Inn' or 'Hogshead' or 'The Red Lion' or any *dreck* like that. I need something I can work with."

He snaps back, "You're unlikely to hear drivel, if that's what you're referring to. You see, I have honored every square inch of this pathetic excuse for a city with my presence. So, in the spirit of your own impoverished argot, you, my dear boy, 'are on'."

As we settle into Budgen's car, I ask Mountjoy, "How do we keep score on this?'

"I'll be the scorekeeper," Mountjoy proclaims, "the judge, jury, and executioner. You are on trial. As for the scorecard, this"—he extends his thumb parallel to the floor, thrusts it up, and then jerks it down—"is it."

"So, we're keeping it simple, eh? Imperiously simple. Do you know what a stacked deck is?"

"Yehhhs. The only deck I ever play with."

"Not in this house, old sport. Budgen, how would you like to be the judge?"

He absentmindedly brushes the cigarette ash from his gray lapel, shrugs his shoulders, and says, "Don't mind if I do, sir."

"This, Budgen," I explain, "is going to be a peripatetic symposium."

He raises an eyebrow. "What does that mean, sir?"

Mountjoy brightens and rolls out, "Puhhhrfect."

"What's perfect?" I ask.

"Your Budgen here as judge. He's totally unencumbered by esoteric disconcertions."

Budgen looks at me in the mirror and asks, "Is that good, sir?"

"*You're the judge*, Budgen. Let me explain. We," I point to myself and Mountjoy, "are the sort of people encumbered by esoteric disconcertions. Kindly tell us the truth Budgen, would you like to be one of us?"

"With all due respect, gents, not on me worst day."

Mountjoy grins. "Do you see what I mean? Puhhhrfect."

"I do. However, I have to lay down some guidelines. Here's the *agon*—that is, contest, Budgen. Mr. Mountjoy is going to choose the pub. You'll take us there; we'll have a few libations, and I'll offer commentary on the name of the pub. If my remarks are deemed by you to be informative and entertaining, you'll give me a thumbs-up." I lean forward and reach out so Budgen can see me jerk my right thumb up and out in umpire fashion. "If they're off target, shallow, or bland, you turn your judicial thumb down." I lower my thumb toward the floor. "Get it? Good. Carry on, Mountjoy."

"Do you know where the Felon and Firkin is?" Mountjoy asks Budgen.

"Over on George Street, sir. I know where every pub in and around this town is."

"We're off then, and the game is afoot. Pray tell, Aloysius, what are we drinking? If we consume pints of bitter, we'll be bloated in no time. But if we drink large measures of malt whiskey, we'll be bevied before having accomplished anything of value."

"Why don't we wet our whistle with a few glasses of lager and work our way up to more muscular beverages as the night progresses? We don't have that much time, what with these medieval licensing hours. Let's string the bow and see how many axe handles we can accurately shoot our way through."

"You're taking this notion of odyssey seriously, aren't you?"

"*Homo ludens*, Your Lordship. As you well know, without play, we're nothing."

Budgen steers us to the Felon and Ferkin, and we decide to sit at the bar.

"Two cold lagers, please."

We drain them, and I call for a refill.

Mountjoy says, "Well?" and braces himself for my commentary.

"I'll take Firkin first, if I may." I look toward Budgen, and he shrugs indifferently.

"A firkin is a quarter of a keg of ale or wine or a lesser liquid that contains nine imperial gallons. Two firkins make one kilderkin. Two kilderkins make one barrel."

Budgen looks unimpressed.

Mountjoy sighs. "Everyone knows that."

"Okay. Let's see if I can acquit myself better with Felon. I quote, 'They sent a check to the felon that sprang from an Irish bog'."

Mountjoy objects. "Nothing autobiographical, *please*."

"And no interruptions, *please*—at least not yet." I clear my throat and start over again:

> *"They sent a check to the felon that sprang from an Irish bog.*
> *They healed the spavined cab-horse; they housed the homeless dog.*

*And they sent (you may call me a liar) when rebel and beast were paid*
*A check for enough to live on to the last of the Light Brigade."*

Mountjoy protests, "That's not Tennyson, you fraud."

I respond, "Of course not, you Magdalen mooncalf. It's Kipling. *Rudyard* Kipling?"

Budgen nods and jerks his thumb upward.

Mountjoy grimaces. "You concur, Budgen?"

Budgen responds without hesitation, "'*The Last of the Light Brigade.*' Of course, I'm familiar with that poem, but there's something you two may not know."

"Yehhhhs?" asks Mountjoy, furrowing his brow.

"The very last surviving officer of the Light Brigade's charge was Sir George Wombwell, who died at Newbury Priory right here in Yorkshire."

Mountjoy and I look at each other, turn to Budgen, and in unison present him with a thumbs-up.

Budgen displays one of his rare smiles. His teeth are as yellow as his smoking fingers.

I say, "The score is 1–0, in my favor. Whither goeth we?"

"Gents," Budgen suggests, "in the spirit of 'the charge,' you might consider Lord Cardigan's next. After all—"

"Just a minute, Budgen," I scold him. "Let's not confuse our roles here. It's Lord Mountjoy who's choosing our destinations."

"Pardon me, sir, and you, Your Lordship. Lord Cardigan's Pub is quite a way's out on Hough Lane anyway."

Mountjoy regains control. "What say we follow a course with some semblance of logic, at least in terms of distance. We could, I'm tempted to say, wend our way over to the Nag's Head, but I would doubtlessly have to endure untoward remarks about Her Ladyship. Or we could forge ahead to the Faversham, although there I'd probably be subject to an unbearable misinterpretation of *Four Feathers*."

"*Four Feathers*? The movie? I love it." This calls for a drink. "Let's stay where we are for now." I signal the bartender for another round.

I start in. "Balaclava. There I was at the head of the old Sixty-Eighth, riding straight into the teeth of the Russian guns as they blazed away at us. I turned around... and there was Faversham... and *there* was Faversham... and *there* was Faversham... "

Mountjoy sighs with exasperation. "Enough butchering of that marvelous closing scene. Now, *there's* a film."

"Yes. And it took a true Brit to make it, didn't it. What was his name again? Oh yeah, Zoltan Korda. Now there's a good old British name. Right up there with the Courtenays, Pelhams, Stanleys, and Talbots, *wot*?"

Mountjoy sighs again. "Not yet. But at the rate we're regressing, that day will come. All I can do for now is hope and pray when that's so, I will have shuffled off this mortal coil."

"So, it took a Hungarian Jew to celebrate blithe spirits and stiff upper lips, eh?"

"Granted. He did a damn good job but, of course, inevitably gave himself away."

"How?"

"When the British officers are at a ball at a private estate, they're shown wearing red uniforms. Any Brit worth his salt knows their uniforms should have been blue in that setting. You see Jewishness, *Gogarty*, reveals itself in spite of outer trappings."

I turn to Budgen and ask, "You're not Jewish by any chance, are you?"

"Please, sir; I've got enough problems of me own as it is."

Mountjoy laughs boisterously, clears his throat, and then continues to hold forth. "Let's carry on here. We've dispensed with *Four Feathers* without even setting foot on the premises. I hate to think of your sense of bereavement without having said adieu to that oasis of wog gentility you frequent—the Prince of Wales."

"Hear, hear. Good call. Budgen: *excelsior*—onward and upward."

Budgen replies, "More like onward and downward, gents, when it comes to that pub."

"Easy does it, Budgen. Don't get carried away with your moment of glory. Just get us to the next pub."

Budgen grumbles and follows directions.

As soon as we arrive, I settle onto a bar stool, as does Mountjoy. Budgen stands. This place has a beery smell to it, but no trace of urine. It's noisy and crowded, but always feels comfortable. I suggest, "How about a half-pint of bitter for nostalgia's sake? Then we'll mix it up a bit. What say ye, Your Lordship?"

"It's fine by me. I do, however, challenge you to hold forth reliably on *any* Prince of Wales."

I snap back, "Child's play, Your Grace. Here we're only a stone's throw away from where the Black Prince himself sits on his horse in stately fashion and overlooks the city square. He prevailed at the battles of Crécy and Poitiers and helped found the Order of the Garter. Would you like me to expound on either one of those battles, or the Order of the Garter? I could give you at least an hour on each."

Mountjoy grunts as if he's in pain and says, "I'd prefer to spare myself the torture. Budgen, can you tell us anything we don't know about the statue?"

Budgen nods. "I can. It was Lord Mayor Harding himself who they say paid for it, but there were a lot of unhappy townsfolk when they discovered he took the money out of the city treasury. The Black Prince's mother was a darkie, but he didn't give a two-penny damn about the common people. Not a democratic bone in his body, that bugger."

"Down the hatch, Mountjoy. We've only just begun. How about some stout?"

Mountjoy agrees reluctantly.

We both empty our glasses and I announce, "I'm getting thirsty!"

Mountjoy replies, "Well then. Let's try Lord Nelson's Inn and see what you can do to sully his legacy."

We arrive in less than ten minutes. It's time to get serious. "We," I tell the bartender while pointing to Mountjoy and myself, "will have large shot glasses of Smirnoff vodka, Beefeater gin, and Hudson's Bay 120-proof rum, along with some tonic water and Coke to wash them down."

The bartender looks at me skeptically until I shuffle several ten-pound notes in his direction.

Mountjoy looks at me incredulously and asks, "Are we celebrating or self-immolating?"

I respond, "Both. Now, Lord Nelson's case would be interesting even if he hadn't been a one-handed adulterer and a cyclops. For me, it's dying at Trafalgar at just the right moment that made him a happy man. Alexander would have given his eye teeth to have had such a heroic exit. What else do I like about Horatio? His mistress Lady Hamilton, the daughter of a blacksmith, who became a muse for that English painter... uh... I can't remember his—"

Mountjoy smirks and says, "Romney, George Romney. You're drifting away from the subject."

"Thank you for reminding me, kind sir. Have you seen Romney's painting of her as Circe? She was also his Ariadne and his... uh... hmm... "

Mountjoy closes his eyes and says, "Cleopatra."

"Why was good old Horatio lucky to die at Trafalgar? Not just because of whatever it is I've already said, but because his ravishing paramour later turned into an obese lush who wound up in debtors' prison and died of liver disease. *Tyche*, the goddess of fortune, smiled upon Horatio. He was spared her gruesome disintegration at the hands of demon rum." I reach for my Hudson's Bay and down it in one gulp while gesturing for another round.

Budgen calls attention to himself with a few dry coughs and announces his decision with an emphatic thumbs-down.

"*Et tu*, Budgen? Pray tell, what've I done to deserve that?"

"No mention of Trafalgar Square and Nelson's Column in the middle of the square. Poor form, I'd say."

Mountjoy chips in, "My dear fellow, I'm amazed Dr. Gogarty here hasn't driven *you* to drink. Let's get on with it. Off to the Wellington."

Budgen asks, "Low Road or Wetherby?"

Mountjoy answers, "Wetherby."

He turns to me. "Now, my dear Aloysius, before you start dithering on about Waterloo and mutilating Wellington's strategy and tactics there, let me plead with you to tell us something we're *unlikely* to know about this imposing figure."

"Fair enough. But first, let's wet our whistles."

Mountjoy protests. "That last mélange of vile decoctions would leave the most accomplished of topers—among whom I count myself —scrooched. I therefore propose that we restrict our intake to liquids of quality."

"Okay, boss. What do you suggest?"

He summons the barkeep and says, "Say, old chap, do you have some malt whiskey with a pedigree to it?" The bartender disappears between two curtains leading to the back, then surfaces with a bottle he wipes clean with a terry cloth. Gently but firmly he stations it on the bar with the label pointed toward us.

"If I open this one up, guv, it's going to cost you."

"My dear fellow, I'm drinking with an American; money is of no concern to me."

The barkeep looks at me, and I nod approvingly.

"A twenty-five-year-old Ardberg, eh?" Mountjoy says appreciatively. "Twill do. May we have large glasses with some water chasers, my good man?"

The bartender issues a warning, "Gents, you'll have to drink up at least thirty quid worth of this for me to open her up."

Mountjoy and I nod our heads in unison, and Budgen indicates he's abstaining from the revelry.

Mountjoy and I taste the whiskey. "This *is* good, Dickie boy," I tell him. "It should help restore equilibrium. I was getting a little wobbly myself with that last sequence. Now, instead of re-creating the Battle of Waterloo with flawless precision, which I am, of course, capable of. I will offer you the *Daily Mail*'s version of what's worth discussing. But first, I'll provide a digression at no extra charge. Did you know the Iron Duke had more in common with Alexander the Great than he did with Lord Nelson?"

Mountjoy looks at me blankly.

"I didn't think so. Let me enlighten you.

> *"Asia and Europe, saved by thee, proclaim:*
> *invincible in war thy deathless name,*
> *Now round thy brow the civic oak we twine,*
> *That every earthly glory may be thine."*

A distant looks on both their faces. "Elementary, boys. The inscription on the Wellington Testimonial in Phoenix Park, Dublin. Wellington *was* a Dubliner, you know."

Mountjoy asks, "Are you finished, or do you intend to keep prattling away?"

"No and yes. That was the prologue." I shout Budgen's name to get his attention. "Both Wellington and Alexander had reputations of invincibility, but neither of them really was. Both were insomniacs. Both loved to drink. The duke drank a full bottle of the best wine available at every dinner. Alexander was willing to guzzle anything available as long as it had a jolt to it. They both, by the way, contracted severe cases of diarrhea that damned near killed them."

Mountjoy beckons the barkeep for a refill and then turns to me. "So, this is what you talk about in class, eh, Dr. Gogarty? Dipsomania, insomnia and diarrhea. No wonder our students enjoy your classes."

"Have any of them complained about me?"

"No; you strike them as quirky, refreshingly quirky. I'm astonished and alarmed to report they speak highly of you. Just another example of American pestilence spreading high and low across the land."

"Anything is an improvement over English food."

306

Mountjoy declares, "Well, I am willing to go to one more pub, and that, my dear boy, is it for me. Since you are the patron, I'll give you a choice between the Nobody Inn, the One-Eyed Rat, and Rose Bud."

"*Hmm.* The first two are either too Homeric or too close to home so let's go with Rose Bud."

As we arrive Mountjoy pleads, "I beg you, no more elaborate homilies."

I summon the bartender. "Your very best malt whiskey, please. A couple of tall ones."

The barkeep answers, "The guvnah has a bottle locked up in the back, and he says to me, he says, 'Only open this bottle if some berk is willing to cough up ninety-three quid.' That's me orders."

Mountjoy volunteers, "Not to worry. We have some such berk in our midst."

I frown and complain, "Now wait a minute, Mountjoy, I resent being called a Burke. That's a derisive term for an Irishman, isn't it? That's what your customs thugs called me at Heathrow."

Mountjoy sighs. "Yet again. A common language dividing two peoples. How do *you* spell what *you* are thinking of, Dr. Gogarty?"

"B-U-R-K-E!"

"Well, my dear boy, the term in question is spelled B-E-R-K, which means a—how can I put this tactfully—jackass! You need not be Irish to earn that epithet, but it certainly affords an advantage."

I declare, "Well, how do you like that? You learn something every day, don't you?"

The barman returns, bottle in hand.

Mountjoy's eyebrows peak, and he says, "Let's take a closer look before we do anything rash here." The bartender wipes off the dust-laden bottle with a damp rag, points the label at us, and says, "Here we are."

Mountjoy and I look at each other in disbelief. Then His Lordship unfurls his panoramic smile, and I burst into uncontrollable laughter, falling to the barroom floor and drawing the attention of everyone within earshot. Budgen backs away from both of us.

Mountjoy, unfazed, glances down and extends his right hand to help me up. The label reads "Saint Magdalene." I lift it up, hold it in my left hand at arm's length, scrutinize its contents, and mumble, "Maudlin... irrrrrrh-eeehh-ahhhh"—*cough, cough,* clear throat —"sssplendid. Crack it open, my dear fellow."

"Sorry, sir, but I need full payment up front with this here bottle. If I don't get me ninety-three quid, the guvnah will be fit to be tied. You do understand, gentlemen, don't you?"

"Of course, we do." I reach for my roll of ten-pound notes and toss ten of them onto the bar. The bartender takes the money and deposits a fiver and two singles in front of us.

Mountjoy takes the first sip. "Aloysius, old boy, you've finally spent your—that is, *their*—money wisely, instead of squandering it about as is your wont. I can't recall ever tasting whiskey as good as this."

"I knew you'd like it," I say smugly, while slipping the bartender the change and asking him if we can have larger glasses and help ourselves to the bottle. He shrugs his shoulders impassively, and I pour a couple of hefty ones for us.

Budgen looks bored.

I ask, "How am I doing so far, Frank?"

"You're losing ground, sir."

"Well, they're not going to get me this inning. This is revelatory, and audience participation is required. Have either of you seen the movie *Citizen Kane?*" Budgen shakes his head, and Mountjoy stares straight ahead without responding. I nudge him to finish his drink, and he complies. Then he stares vacantly and says, "Spare me."

"Okay. I give up. Let me do what I do best: drink. Wait a second," I say angrily, "who's been drinking out of our bottle? Christ! It's two-thirds gone. We'd better pour ourselves a stiff one before these leeches polish it off behind our backs. Where's Budgen?"

I tap a man of his build on the shoulder, and he turns around.

"Budgen, what's happened to you? You look thirty years younger." I grab him by the shoulders and shake him. Suddenly, I feel a fist in my stomach.

"Keep your fookin' hands off me, you fookin' maniac." He shakes his head and shouts, "These fookin Americans!"

A tap on my shoulder. I clench my fists ready to fend off another assault. "Budgen... What the... ? You look like yourself again."

He grabs me by my jacket collar with his left hand and turns me around, while gesturing menacingly to the guy who's just punched me. "You joined the wrong party, sir."

"Where's Mountjoy?" I ask.

"He's at the loo and looks the worse for wear. I'd better take you both home before you get yourselves into a right sprattle here."

"Oh my God, I get it. You're not Budgen. You're Eumaeus. I'm going home... finally."

Budgen says, "Here's your mate, sir."

Mountjoy wanders toward us in a trance. I pat him on the back to get his attention. "Good old Dickie; I hate to tell you this, but you look like death warmed over. We'd better pack it in. I want to go home. That's all I ever wanted, was to go home. *Nostos.* You get it? *Nostos.*"

Mountjoy snaps out of it, looks at Budgen, and explains, "Greek; it's Greek. Just ignore him." He sways perilously and starts to fall backwards. Budgen wraps himself around Mountjoy's waist and sets him back on his feet. I shout out as loud as I can, "Great catch, Budgen. Drinks on the house for one and all!" A roar goes up and I throw a fistful of tenners at the bartender. Mountjoy regains his balance, smiles, and pats Budgen on the back.

Budgen says, "We'd better be off, sir," in an urgent tone.

"We're off already, Budgen, way off, but we can't waste this bottle. Don't you know there are children in China who are dying for a drink?"

"Well, I don't know about that, sir, but I do know it's a good idea to make our way out of this pub while everyone's still grateful for the drinks you bought."

"I understand. Make a getaway at your peak. You're right. Alexander did it. I'm going to do it, too. Let's just finish this last drink, and the journey home begins."

Mountjoy raises his glass and, to everyone's astonishment, bellows at the top of his lungs: "Here's to Aloysius the Great, who endured one ordeal after the other, but always came out smelling like a *rosé*!" He stares at the floor, glass in hand, and begins to sway again. I grab the glass, and Budgen catches Mountjoy. We're on our way.

"Where are we?" I ask, and answer my own question, "It's the palace gate!"

Budgen clarifies, "It's 77 Ecclesiastical Street, luv."

"Hey, that's where I live. Take me right up to the front door, Okay, Budgen?"

"I'd have to drive straight through the gate to do that, sir, and ruin your beautiful lawn. Are you sure you want me to do that?"

"Why... uh... no . . . of course not. Oh, Mountjoy is crashing at my place. He's too drunk to go home and face Her Ladyship."

"I'll help you both up, sir."

"No thanks, Budgen. I'll handle it." I stuff some ten-quid notes into Budgen's vest pocket. He takes them out and slips them back into my pants pocket.

Budgen sighs and leaves, shaking his head. I turn to Mountjoy. "Lean on me, Your Lordship. There's only a hundred yards to go for the touchdown." I buck him up in orthodox Samaritan fashion.

"I'm afraid, dear boy... I must relieve myself."

"Hang on. We're almost there."

Mountjoy insists. "Now!" He stops and proceeds to do just that.

I join him, asking, "Is that as far as you can pee? No wonder the empire's falling apart."

Mountjoy grunts again and his expression magnifies as he projects a longer stream.

"So, you think you've won, huh? Can you do this?" I whirl my member back and forth in the air, forming a bow.

"Of course, I can, but, alas, I'm running out of ammunition."

I mechanically reach into my back pocket for my latchkey, but it's not there. "We're a keyless couple, old buddy." I gesture for him to follow me to the side of the building where there's a dwarf wall and, down below it, another entrance to the house. "Mountjoy, sit here for a minute."

"What on earth are you doing?"

"I'm going to jump down and get in through the pantry. There's another key down there."

He gets up, lurches over to the wall, and peers down blinking. "That's about three meters. You could break your neck."

"I'm an athlete. That's nothing. I'll show you." I jump down and hit the pavement with a thud. I look up and raise both my thumbs in triumph, then limp toward the pantry door. Aha! The key's there under the mat. I point for Mountjoy to go back around to the front door as I let myself into the pantry. Mr. Kgnao welcomes me with hungry green eyes. Hobbling upstairs, I bow to Mountjoy at the front door. "Welcome to my humble abode, Your Grace."

Mountjoy stumbles downstairs after me.

Brought back to consciousness by my aeronautical feat, he sits in a chair at the kitchen table. I get a plate of food for Mr. Kgnao and reach into the refrigerator for a bottle of milk. I heat the milk in a saucepan and pour it into two large cups with cocoa mix in them.

"What on earth are you poisoning me with?"

"It's cocoa, the staff of life. Drink it. It's good for you."

"This is revolting."

"You need an incentive." I rummage through the cupboard and come up with a bottle of Napoleon brandy.

"Here." I splash some of it into our cups and make the sign of the cross over them. We sit there, silently sipping away.

Mountjoy jumps up pointing and screeching, "Good heavens. Something's on fire. It's a sheet of paper on the stove."

"Don't worry, everything's under control. I'm a fireman's son." I grab a towel and smother the flame, but the towel catches fire.

Mountjoy reaches for the brandy and pours it over the towel. The flames coruscate, and I dash into the adjacent bedroom to grab a comforter. Somehow, I manage to smother the flames, smiling at Mountjoy triumphantly. He looks at me through glazed eyes and says, "I don't know how you do it, old boy, but I've had enough. I just saw a miniature black panther with flashing green eyes. I need sleep."

"Me too. We've got seven bedrooms here. You can take whichever one you want. Just go up those stairs." I point. "Can you manage?"

Mountjoy nods.

"Good. Look to the right at the top of the stairs and you'll see the master bedroom. I'll sleep down here in the servants' quarters; they're more comfortable."

"You need not explain, my dear boy. Of course, you're more comfortable there. Good night."

It should be one hell of a dream tonight. San Sebastiàn, *I implore you*—no nightmares. Something celestial for a change, please.

# 33

---

*Torquemada is dressed in formal cardinal's attire with a white rochet and scarlet vestments: the cassock, mozzetta, zucchetto, and biretta. God looks about seventy, has gray stubble on his face, and wears a small black beret tilted slightly to the right. He's dressed in soiled jeans, high-top sneakers, and a gray tattered sweatshirt with the letter G emblazoned in black print at its center.*

GOD
*What am I doing here?*

TORQUEMADA
*You're supposed to be everywhere. Have you forgotten? I summoned you.*

GOD
*Really? I'm not as young as I used to be, and my memory fails me occasionally.*

TORQUEMADA
*I need to know certain things.*

GOD
*There are some things you're not supposed to know. Only I'm privy to them.*

**TORQUEMADA**

*You'll tell me what I want to know—or else!*

**GOD**

*Or else what? Are you going to kill me—again?*

**TORQUEMADA**

*You'll tell me what I want to know because I'm the Grand Inquisitor and you're only . . . well... God.*

**GOD**

*No. I'll tell you what you want to know because I want to get this over with. You conjured me up when I was right in the middle of picking a date for Armageddon.*

**TORQUEMADA**

*The end-of-the-world threat again, eh? That's not going to work around here. Let me get right to the point.*

**GOD**
*Please do.*

**TORQUEMADA**

*There are some missing pieces to my inquisition into a certain Aloysius Tabeel Gogarty.*

**GOD**

*I like that middle name. Catchy, don't you think?*

**TORQUEMADA**

*I don't need editorial comments, just information. I'm well aware of your tendency to embroider stories, and that won't be permitted here. I'm simply looking to confirm that we're speaking about the same individual when I refer to Mr. Gogarty.*

GOD

*He's the only one I know with such a cockamamie name. It's Dr. Gogarty, by the way. Okay. He's not a real doctor. He's what my people call a fakakta doktor.*

TORQUEMADA

*Your people? And what does that unintelligible term mean?*

GOD

*My people. You come across quite a few of them in your line of work. What does fakakta doktor mean? A doctor who doesn't do you any good. Like... uh... ah... uh. . . a professor.*

TORQUEMADA

*Good. We're on the same page. That's the man.*

GOD

*You want me to tell you about him? Well, one day he walks into a bar with this capuchin monkey on his shoulder . . .*

TORQUEMADA

*Stop. That's enough.*

GOD

*You gotta be kidding me. Most people spend their entire lives waiting to hear from me, and you're cutting me off?*

TORQUEMADA

*I'm busy. Just answer the questions. I don't need to know about your problems. I've got enough of my own. What about Gogarty's friends? His colleagues? Who's his closest friend at Municipal College?*

GOD

*It's Abe Rosenbach, another landsman of mine. They fight like cats and dogs, but they have a lot in common. They both drink a lot. They're both bad Jews. Well, at least Rosenbach. Gogarty? I'm not sure what he is. They're both smart and they both like reading some Irish author even I can't understand. They're an odd couple.*

TORQUEMADA

*Well, is Gogarty a Jew or not? This is important.*

GOD

*Uhh... maybe... it's better if you think of him as a Christian, and a Catholic one at that.*

TORQUEMADA

*How well did Gogarty handle his assignment in England?*

GOD

*Basically, he couldn't have done better. Everyone in England of any importance loved him, except for some secretary. He finagled his way through some lollapaloozas I threw at him. He may be a shikker, but I like him. His boss in New York doesn't like him because he won't kiss that gedlan's tuches. Who can blame the professor?*

TORQUEMADA

*Gedlan? Tuches?*

GOD

*A presumptuous putz. You of all people should know what a putz is. Tuches? That's you too.*

TORQUEMADA (waving his index finger)

*Watch yourself.*

GOD

*I don't have to watch myself. It's your type that needs watching.*

TORQUEMADA

*How did Gogarty treat his students in England?*

GOD

*The Americans? Fine. Most of them he ignored, and they were happy about that. Some he got a little too close to.*

TORQUEMADA

*What do you mean by that? Are you talking about fema*le students? Were there any improprieties? Any sinful activities?

GOD

*Not students, student. Sinful? It depends on how you look at it.*

TORQUEMADA (with quill in hand)
*Who is it? What's her name?*

GOD

*Fleischmann, double N, Marthe, with an E at the end.*

TORQUEMADA

*Exactly what transpired?*

GOD

*I don't know about transpired.*

TORQUEMADA

*Happened. Explain it in simple terms. Preferably in Latin.*

GOD

*My Latin's kinda rusty. I don't know why you're always talking to me in that language; I have trouble understanding what you're saying. Hey. Don't spread that around. I'd never be able to get anything done if everybody talked to me in Yiddish.*

TORQUEMADA

*You're digressing again. What did he do that was iniquitous with this* (he looks down at his parchment) *Marthe Fleischmann?*

GOD

*It's what she tried to do with him. She had a master plan to bring one of my prodigal sons—I have a lot of them—back into the fold and needed a tune-up with the professor before she brought her Delilah act to him.*

TORQUEMADA

*Exactly what happened?*

GOD

*None of your business. You're looking for a victim. If you push me on any of this, I'll pull my disappearing act. Watch out. I'm good at it.*

TORQUEMADA

*Was her plan diabolical? Did she use witchcraft to endanger his immortal soul?*

GOD

*Where do you get these ideas? She just wants this Blum fellow to be a good Jew, and she's using the gifts I gave her to accomplish that. She's going to make him happy by making him unhappy. That's what all Jewish women do, and that's what all Jewish men want, no matter what they tell you.*

TORQUEMADA

*So, they'll have a happy life, and the professor helped them to accomplish it?*

GOD

*Now you're getting it. Don't get caught up in the details. You know who hides out there.*

TORQUEMADA

*All right. Were there any other students who presented problems? What effect did Gogarty have on them?*

GOD

*His biggest headache was another one of my chosen people: Frank Stein. He's always looking for me, and here I am standing right in front of him. What a schmendrick. He got involved with all sorts of drugs, and Gogarty had to lie, cheat, take my name in vain, whatever, in order to save the pisher's tuches. He made a nice job of it.*

TORQUEMADA

*What about "Thou shalt not lie"?*

GOD

*Don't take everything so literally. You ever hear of casuistry?*

TORQUEMADA

*No.*

GOD

*Well, look it up, and don't do it. That's a commandment, you schmeckle!*

TORQUEMADA

*What?*

GOD

*Let's say nincompoop. You know nincompoop?*

TORQUEMADA

*What happened to this Stein boy? Did Gogarty do him any good?*

GOD

*Not really; at least for now. Stein went back to New York, dropped out of school, used and sold drugs, and continued to write poetry nobody can make head or tail of. He's on the brink of disaster at this point, and everybody except Mameleh Stein has given up on him.*

TORQUEMADA

*So Gogarty did him no good whatsoever? Therefore, the boy's doomed?*

GOD

*Not really. In fact, he liked the professor and never forgot what he said to him and did for him. He's going to survive and do well later on in life. But I can't tell you about the distant future. That's all you're going to hear from me on this.*

TORQUEMADA

*Did Gogarty follow canon law in everything he did?*

GOD

*Legal, schmegal. He gave the kid a break. Is that a mortal sin?*

TORQUEMADA (ignoring the question)

*What about his associate at the English university—this Mountjoy person? I've never heard any praiseworthy things about him. It seems he's in trouble even at his own university.*

GOD

*So, it's guilt by association again, is it? I should pay more attention. I thought you people had come a long way since Adam. Mountjoy's not in any trouble at the university. He's got a problem with his wife. So, what's new? We all do. He's got a secretary at work who was on the warpath against him the last I looked. It's a personal problem. It'll pass. She's crazy about him. Don't get so puritanical. You Catholics can't afford to be.*

TORQUEMADA

*Gogarty had dealings with another colleague at that English university—a Professor Somerset. Did he offer Christian love and understanding to this man?*

GOD

*Somerset? Understanding? He's harder to figure out than that Irish knocker Gogarty's always torturing himself with. Don't worry about Somerset. Gogarty's getting him set up at Harvard. They deserve him. He'll live unhappily ever after there.*

TORQUEMADA

*I also have information about a student named O'Brien who may have been involved in illegal activities while under the supervision of Professor Gogarty. What do you know about that?*

GOD

*Everything. Didn't anyone in that church of yours ever tell you that I'm omniscient? You know omniscient? The only question concerning O'Brien was what he did in Ireland. Was he involved in some IRA shenanigans? The answer is no. In fact, he spent a whole week retracing the steps of this Leopold Bloom, a fictional nobody, through the streets of Dublin. Talk about meshuganosis!*

TORQUEMADA
*Explain what that means.*

GOD
*You'd never be able to grasp it. Let's get on with this already. I've got things to do, dates to set, people kvetching.*

TORQUEMADA
*Just a few more questions about Gogarty. Is he secure in his job?*

GOD
*At his college? Yes. His boss had no choice but to support his... what is it they call that? Tenure? By the way, I never created that. It's the handiwork of that other guy—you know, the one from down south.*

(He chuckles)

TORQUEMADA (with a grim and menacing look)
*You say he had no choice. Does that mean the professor may pay for it later on? Does it mean he'll have trouble getting promoted in the future? Did the professor do anything I don't know about to aggravate his boss?*

GOD
*No. All I can tell you is the dean... what's his name? Oiwin?—has set his sights on a pretty fancy university, and his days at the college are numbered. He'll soon be out of Gogarty's hair.*

TORQUEMADA
*The following two are the last and most important questions I must ask you. First of all, what are his intentions toward Elena Delagracia?*

GOD

*Well, I suppose you could say they're both honorable and dishonorable. Does he love her? He thinks he does. Does he want to shtup her? Sure, he does, but that doesn't mean he doesn't love her. What do you think was going on with Adam in the Garden of Eden after I dropped the Eve bomb on him? He had mixed emotions about her too.*

TORQUEMADA

*Here's the most important question of all: Will he treat her decently and make her happy?*

GOD (wagging his index finger)

*Aha. There you go again poaching on the future. All I can tell you is he's got the best of intentions. We'll have to see how it plays out. If he can do something about his drinking, they've got a good chance. I may have to give him a hand with that. His heart's in the right place. In other words, if I were you I wouldn't worry so much about my daughter. Even I have no control over them. Take Eve. Please, take her.*

TORQUEMADA

*They could never be married. Elena already has a husband. He's a scoundrel, all right, but her husband, nevertheless.*

GOD

*I got news for you. Hot off the press. That husband of hers got himself another wife, some hot tamale in Cuba.*

TORQUEMADA

*What? He can't remarry, and neither can Elena.*

GOD

*He did. That gonif doesn't know religion from borscht. Her? Even in your church she can remarry if he dies, and I've got more news for you. I can tell you about this because by the time Gogarty gets back to America, it's going to be true. That hot tamale is a carrier of some mysterious disease, and the conniving doctor will be dead within a week.*

TORQUEMADA

*That's wonderful!*

GOD

*I knew you'd react like a true Christian to that.*

TORQUEMADA

*Elena has a son. How will Gogarty treat her son?*

GOD

*He'll be a great father. He'll treat the boy as if he were his own. Well, maybe not quite . . . uh...*

TORQUEMADA

*Go on.*

GOD

*That's enough. I have to go, but I'll leave you with a smidgen of wisdom free of charge: Afh yenems tuches is gut sepatchen.*

TORQUEMADA

*What?*

GOD

*It's always easy to whack the other guy's ass.*

TORQUEMADA

*You can't talk like that.*

GOD

*If I can't, who can? I do it all the time. My wife complains about it too.*

TORQUEMADA

*Your what? How dare you?*

GOD

*You really are a boobnick, aren't you? I should have stopped this whole farce with the Greeks. You remember what Xenophanes said? "If a horse could paint and painted God, God would look like a horse." I'm different from you. You just don't get it. Spinoza? He got it.*

TORQUEMADA

*Who?*

GOD

*Never mind. If you knew about Spinoza, you'd persecute him, too.*

TORQUEMADA

*If you aren't like us, why do you look the way you look now?*

GOD

*I don't. This is just to get your attention. I could've put on white robes and my long gray beard, but that's no fun. I thought I'd be an old New York Jew. I like the way they talk. You can't beat an alteh kocker. I know. I've tried them all.*

TORQUEMADA

*One more question. Why does Gogarty wear those dark glasses?*

GOD

*He says he's got this eye disease. It's his shtick. Don't worry. Your daughter will make him put them away. You know what they're like. I've gotta go.*

TORQUEMADA

*Don't you dare, or I will anathema—*

(God disappears.)

TORQUEMADA

**?**

# 34

---

"Well, hello there, Professor."

I look up as I'm boarding the airplane, and it's none other than Gerty, the stewardess who was on my flight when I came here in September. "Hey, Gerty, you've done your hair differently. I like it. Is that a frosting?"

"Why, yes. How do you know about such things? Oh, of course you do; you're a professor."

"So now you're a strawberry blonde, huh?"

"Promise me you're not going to sing that dreadful song about Casey waltzing with the strawberry blonde."

"If I did, that husband of yours would probably come waltzing out of the cockpit and toss me into the Atlantic."

"You're safe on this trip. He's flying to Casablanca."

"You mean—" I get bumped by someone trying to get by me.

"Professor, could you please step over here for a moment and let the other passengers pass?"

"Oops. Sorry."

Gerty asks her colleague to continue greeting those boarding the plane and slips into the first row of seats, gesturing for me to sit beside her.

"You can call me Aloysius."

"Aloysius? Is that your real name?" She stifles a laugh. "What's your middle name? Maybe I'll call you that."

"Believe it or not, it's worse. Even as is we'd make quite a couple. Gertrude and Aloysius. I can see it now." I look up and wave my hand. "Antony and Cleopatra, Lancelot and Guinevere, Paolo and Francesca, Gertrude and Aloysius... uhhh... maybe not."

She laughs.

"You can call me Gogarty."

"All right, Gogarty."

"So, you and your husband are on different flights."

"The trip you came over on was an exception; we're rarely on the same flight. Besides, that's the way we like it. It gives us space, and we don't have to worry about the other one paying too much attention to what we're up to."

"Aren't you concerned that Ingrid Bergman might be waiting for him back in Casablanca?"

"He should be so lucky. But who cares? I've got Humphrey Bogart on my flight. That's what I'll call you: Bogie. Nonetheless, I'd better get back to earning my salary. Where are you sitting, Bogie?"

"Twenty-six A, Miss Bacall."

She smiles. "Would you like me to upgrade you to first class?"

"Why, are you working there this trip?"

She shakes her head.

"Okay. I'll stay put so I can keep an eye on you and make sure you're not flirting with anyone else."

She winks at me and says coyly, "Don't count on it."

I'm beat. These six a.m. flights are murder. Budgen drove me all the way to London. My Sancho Panza. He's even taking Mr. Kgnao home. God bless his soul. I'll miss Mountjoy most of all. My second self. Maybe I'll import him. No; my Gatsby days are over.

It's only been nine months, but it feels like decades. Here I am, the ancient mariner, with tales of dwarfs and cyclops and sirens and mothers and cannibals and cannabis and connivers and ghosts and wives and brothers-in-love. What have I learned of them? Of me? Well, one thing's for certain. The theater of the mind can match Homer's Mediterranean, or even Joyce's Dublin.

Gerty approaches, concealing miniature bottles of gin in her hand; she must remember slipping me the extra booze on the way over. I'm tempted, but I wave her off. She looks surprised but smiles and tucks the bottles into her apron pocket. I'd better get some sleep before I change my mind. When we land, I'll wash up, go to the college and present myself to Elena. I'm exhausted. To sleep, perchance to dream. Ay—there's the rub...

*It's me on the telephone. I'm at Kennedy Airport. Elena no longer works there? Gone where? No. No. She wouldn't do that. Gertrude, get me out of this. Where is she? No one in the aisle. No one else is on the airplane? We're losing altitude and plummeting into the sea and O that awful deep down torrent pushing up against the sides of the plane . . . GERTRUDE... GERTRUDE... GERTRU—*

"Bogie, Bogie, Bogie. We're landing. In a deep sleep, huh?"

"Sorry. I had a bad dream. Thanks for waking me up."

She whispers, "Maybe we can make reality more appealing than your world of dreams. I'm free tonight. Perhaps we could meet for a cocktail."

I hear her song. *Bind yourself to the mast. Stuff wax in your ears.* "Sounds great. Let me clear my head and think about what I have to do today."

"No problem."

"Thanks."

A smooth landing.

Gerty announces, "You may unfasten your seat belts," and sidles up to me.

"So, Bogie, what's the verdict?"

"Gerty, it's very tempting—*very*—but I have to catch up with so many things it's just not going to work."

"Not to worry. Perhaps our paths will cross again; if not in person, up there on the silver screen."

"Thanks for understanding."

Gerty scurries off. What's that? There's a hitch in her gait. Is she lame? Poor girl. Elena's likely to have a limp as well, although it may come in a different guise. I have one—that's for sure.

Which reminds me—where's my brother's number?

I locate an airport pay phone and dial him.

"Tommy, you're home. Good. I just got back. Is it okay if I bunk with you until I find an apartment?... Thanks. Oh, those meetings you go to—the ones about booze. Do you mind if I tag along on one of them?... Oh, some Scottish bartender planted the thought in my head. . . . You want to go *tonight*? Uhh . . . well . . . Okay. You're on.... No thanks, I'll grab a taxi. I have to stop off at the college. See you later."

That's strange. As soon as I agreed to go with him, a feeling of relief came over me. Could drinking be the key? I thought it was Alexander—or Irwin—or Elena.

Speaking of Elena, I'll give a call and tell her I'm on my way to Municipal. The extension is . . . oh yeah . . . 1922. "Yes, I'm looking for Mrs. Delagracia. She's not? Will she be in later? No?" Why isn't she at the office? I told her I was coming back today. Maybe I shouldn't have.

I look through the airport's glass doors. Holy Mary, Mother of God, there she is, as radiant as the eye of heaven. There's a rose in her hair. As Elena walks toward me, sunlight flickers across her eyes and there's a change in color. My mouth feels dry. I can scarcely talk.

"Is that you?"

Elena stops in front of me, stands on the tips of her toes, removes my glasses, and drops them into an open bag at her side. Interlocking her hands behind my neck, she pulls me down to where I inhale the scent rising from her perfumed breasts. Her mouth opens wide and my parched tongue is drawn into her soothing moisture and a faint hint of *pastelito*.

My Calypso. My Penelope.

And on this summer day I am folded into the world's mysterious embrace.

## ABOUT THE AUTHOR

John Maxwell O'Brien is an emeritus professor of history (Queens College, CUNY) who has written numerous articles on ancient history, medieval history, and the history of alcoholism. His best-selling biography, *Alexander the Great: The Invisible Enemy* (Routledge), has been translated into Greek and Italian, and he authored the article on alcoholism in the *Oxford Classical Dictionary*. Professor O'Brien's second life has been devoted to his first love, creative writing. Professor O'Brien has published a variety of poems and short stories in literary journals. *Aloysius the Great* is his debut novel and was inspired by James Joyce's *Ulysses*.

For memorable fiction, non-fiction, poetry, and prose,
Please visit Propertius Press on the web
www.propertiuspress.com

Made in the USA
Coppell, TX
11 January 2022